THE SPRITES OF KERNOSY CASTLE

The Other Voice in Early Modern Europe:
The Toronto Series, 105

FOUNDING EDITORS
Margaret L. King
Albert Rabil, Jr.

SENIOR EDITOR
Margaret L. King

SERIES EDITORS
Vanda Anastácio
Jaime Goodrich
Elizabeth H. Hageman
Sarah E. Owens
Deanna Shemek
Colette H. Winn

EDITORIAL BOARD
Anne Cruz
Margaret Ezell
Anne Larsen
Elissa Weaver

HENRIETTE-JULIE DE CASTELNAU,
COUNTESS DE MURAT

The Sprites of Kernosy Castle

Edited and translated by

PERRY GETHNER *and* ALLISON STEDMAN

Iter Press
NEW YORK | TORONTO

2024

© 2024 Perry Gethner and Allison Stedman

The copyright owner grants Iter Press an exclusive license for publication and distribution. For information and permissions, contact Iter Press: 347 Fifth Avenue, Suite 1402-332, New York, NY 10016, USA; IterPress.org.

Printed in the United States of America

978-1-64959-106-7 (paper)
978-1-64959-107-4 (pdf)
978-1-64959-108-1 (epub)

Library of Congress Cataloging-in-Publication Data

Names: Murat, Henriette-Julie de Castelnau, comtesse de, 1668-1716, author. | Gethner, Perry, editor. | Stedman, Allison, 1974- editor.

Title: The sprites of Kernosy castle / Henriette-Julie Castelnau, countess de Murat ; edited and translated by Perry Gethner and Allison Stedman.

Other titles: Lutins du château de Kernosy. English

Description: New York : Iter Press, 2024. | Series: The other voice in early modern Europe: the Toronto series ; 105 | Includes bibliographical references and index. | Summary: "A subversive novel from 1710 that questioned political and aesthetic ideologies in eighteenth-century France. This novel reflects a shift in French values at the turn of the eighteenth century, which saw increased interest in the private lives of the aristocracy and the pre-Enlightenment questioning of political and religious orthodoxies. Novels of fiction and leisure gained popularity, and it was during this time that Henriette-Julie de Castelnau, the Countess de Murat, published her second leisure novel, The Sprites of Kernosy Castle. Combining humor, social satire, and a proto-feminist outlook, Murat crafts a well-constructed plot where the supernatural is debunked. Murat's career was cut short when a series of "misdemeanors" related to the countess's homosexual tendencies led to her arrest in 1702. Sprites, which was released during a partial reprieve from prison, is the final published work of this independent-minded early feminist author. "-- Provided by publisher.

Identifiers: LCCN 2024010338 (print) | LCCN 2024010339 (ebook) | ISBN 9781649591067 (paperback) | ISBN 9781649591074 (pdf) | ISBN 9781649591081 (epub)

Subjects: BISAC: FICTION / Literary | LITERARY COLLECTIONS / Women Authors | LCGFT: Novels.

Classification: LCC PQ1875.M8 L8813 2024 (print) | LCC PQ1875.M8 (ebook) | DDC 843/.4--dc23/eng/20240313

LC record available at https://lccn.loc.gov/2024010338

LC ebook record available at https://lccn.loc.gov/2024010339

Cover Illustration

"Portrait of Henriette-Julie de Castelnau, Countess de Murat," signed engraving by Jacques Harrewyn (1660–1727), ca. 1698. Bibliothèque Nationale de France, N2 MURAT, 55A7037.

Cover Design

Maureen Morin, Library Communications, University of Toronto Libraries.

Contents

Acknowledgments	vii
Illustrations	ix
Introduction	1
The Other Voice	1
Early Life and Works	2
Murat and the Development of the Literary Fairy Tale	6
Scandal and Exile	13
Murat and the Art of the Leisure Novel	14
A Female Quixote	20
Theatrical Life in 1700	24
Reception and Revision	26
Conclusion	30
A Note on the Translation	30
The Sprites of Kernosy Castle (1710), by Henriette-Julie de Castelnau, Countess de Murat	
Part One	33
The Story of Madame de Briance	59
The Story of Zariades	75
Part Two	81
Continuation of the Story of Madame de Briance	81
The Story of the Count de Tourmeil	99
Bearskin, by Marie-Madeleine de Lubert (addition to the 1753 edition of *Sprites*)	125
Etoilette, by Marie-Madeleine de Lubert (addition to the 1753 edition of *Sprites*)	143
Bibliography	171
Index	179

Acknowledgments

The purchase of reproductions of the original 1710 edition of Murat's novel, as well as the 1753 edition of the novel with Lubert's additional fairy tales, was made possible by a grant from the Gladys Brooks Foundation on behalf of the Bucknell University Library. Images and other digital reproductions were paid for by the Department of Languages and Culture Studies at UNC Charlotte. UNC Charlotte undergraduate Kellie Giordano assisted with the cross-comparison of the texts of the Murat and Lubert editions of the novel. We would also like to thank the anonymous reader, Margaret King, and William Bowen for believing in the project and for the many helpful edits and suggestions offered by the former two, which greatly improved the final result.

Perry Jeffrey Gethner passed away on November 14, 2023 at the age of 76. Words cannot express the debt of gratitude that I owe him for suggesting that we undertake this project in the fall of 2016, and for his generosity and collegiality throughout its many phases. Perry, your friendship over the last 20 years has been without peer and you will be deeply missed.

Illustrations

Cover. "Portrait of Henriette-Julie de Castelnau, Countess de Murat," signed engraving by Jacques Harrewyn (1660–1727), ca. 1698. Bibliothèque Nationale de France, N2 MURAT, 55A7037.

Figure 1. "La Maison-Fort (XIV siècle)," engraving by Edmond Bussière (1807?–1842), representing the Chateau de la Maison-Fort in Bitry, France, near Saint-Amand. [Joseph-Napoléon] Morellet, [Jean-Claude] Barat, and E. [Edmond] Bussière, *Le Nivernois, album historique et pittoresque*, vol. 2, ed. E. [Edmond] Bussière (Nevers, France: E. Bussière, 1840), p. 71.   32

Figure 2. "Noble-Thorn and the Fairy Azerole," engraving by Clément-Pierre Marillier (1740–1808). Clément-Pierre Marillier, [*Recueil. Oeuvre de Marillier: Illustrations pour les* Voyages imaginaires]. [Paris: 1786], p. 68. Bibliothèque Nationale de France, Réserve EF-79-4.   126

Introduction

The Other Voice

Henriette-Julie de Castelnau, Countess de Murat, was in her day an esteemed writer of poetry and fiction whose works represent a willingness to experiment with both form and content. A noted participant in the late seventeenth century's salon circles, from which emerged a large of number of important literary figures, she was one of the young female authors whose initial encouragement to take up the pen came from this milieu. The salons, semiprivate intellectual gatherings hosted by cultivated aristocratic women, allowed male writers the chance to read and discuss their works in progress with a sympathetic audience while enabling women to participate directly in the cultural life of the time and to add their own perspectives. Murat was not the only noted female author of the era to get a start in the salons; others included the poets Henriette de La Suze and Antoinette Deshoulières, the playwright Françoise Pascal, and the novelists Marie-Catherine de Villedieu and Marie-Catherine d'Aulnoy.

Like others in this milieu, Murat frequently used her writing to highlight matters of importance to women. She was opposed to forced marriages and to the prevailing view, especially in aristocratic circles, that women were little more than socioeconomic pawns. She also emphasized the value of female solidarity and female friendship, the very possibility of which was typically denied by male authors. Likewise, at a time when "learned ladies" were viewed with suspicion by many religious and social conservatives, Murat was outspoken in her belief that women should be allowed a good education and unfettered access to cultural life. She also shared the position of the salon participants that the chivalric code derived from the Middle Ages, in which men were required to practice self-control, display good manners, and treat all women with respect, retained both aesthetic value and moral relevance as an ideal for a refined modern society.

When we examine Murat's engagement in the early stages of her career with the newly introduced genre of the literary fairy tale, her feminist outlook comes to the fore. Like other female practitioners of the form, she shows a preference for heroines who are energetic and capable of filling traditional male roles with distinction. She displays skepticism about the "happily ever after" convention, sometimes choosing to have her protagonists end up sad and disillusioned, having learned that love and desire do not always last. In addition, her participation in polemical discussions about the origins of and target audiences for fairy tales indicates her recognition of the need to find a "modern" art form bound neither by the legacy of the Greeks and the Romans nor by the literary rules promulgated by male-dominated academies and appropriated by the king and court.

When in 1699 Murat turned from the fairy tale to the leisure novel, a highly popular subgenre at that time, the more realistic setting did not prevent her from retaining elements of her feminist agenda. In her novels, heroines who have already been pushed into forced marriages or are currently threatened with them are ultimately given the chance to pick their spouse based on affection and compatibility. Salon-like gatherings are formed in which the female participants are properly valued and allowed to exercise their talents, and all the sympathetic male figures fully embrace the chivalric code. Female solidarity and friendship are given a key role in the development of the plot, and female characters who refuse to model such behavior are ridiculed and sometimes excluded. Murat presents aristocratic leisure, liberated from social and religious constraints, as a positive value for men and women alike, both as a means to achieve a happy and fulfilled life and as a carefully veiled protest against the rigid conformity demanded by Louis XIV's absolutist regime.

Murat's feminism was also evidenced in her own life, when she defied prevailing norms and expectations by engaging in a series of lesbian relationships, and she suffered the painful consequences of flouting aristocratic conventions on multiple levels: she was disowned by her family and sent into a multiyear exile by the king. Throughout this ordeal, she maintained a defiant attitude, as indicated in her diary of 1708–1709, which was not intended for publication, and in her final novel, where she combines the concepts of exile and freedom through leisure in an original way.

The current volume presents the first-ever English translation of that final novel, *Les Lutins du château de Kernosy* (*The Sprites of Kernosy Castle*), first published in 1710 and reprinted at least three more times over the course of the eighteenth century, though not since. The novel is generally considered to be the best short-form leisure novel of the French tradition, and many critics call it her masterpiece. It constitutes the last public statement of freethinking from a writer willing to suffer for her refusal to bend to the established rules.

Early Life and Works

It should come as no surprise that one of the finest practitioners of the leisure novel was herself a product of the aristocratic society that she depicted. Henriette-Julie de Castelnau, Countess de Murat (1668–1716),[1] who would become one of the most popular and influential authors of her generation, had a highly respectable

---

1. Although Murat's early biographers often give the birthdate of 1670 (actually the birthdate of Murat's sister), Frédéric Lemeunier's research in the archives of La Buzardière establishes that she was in fact born in 1668. Her death date can be established by an announcement in the October 1716 issue of the Parisian periodical, the *Nouveau Mercure Galant*, which states that Murat died of dropsy on September 29 in her chateau La Buzardière, located in the Maine region of France. Her death certificate states that she was buried there on October 1. See further, Geneviève Clermidy-Patard,

background: both of her grandfathers had been marshals of France and members of the high aristocracy, and her father had been the governor of Brest until his death in 1672.[2] Although her nineteenth-century biographers maintained that Murat's family was originally from Brittany and that Henriette-Julie remained there until she was presented to Queen Maria Theresa, the wife of Louis XIV, in 1686,[3] historians have since confirmed that Murat's family did not have Breton origins, and testimonies from Paris's elevated literary circles (among them the famous letters of the Marquise de Sévigné) attest that Murat spent the majority of her childhood in Paris in the company of her mother and sister.[4] Accounts of her adolescence paint the picture of a young noblewoman who understood her role in society and who accepted this role at least publicly, attending social functions with her mother and eventually marrying, in 1691, Nicolas de Murat, Count de Gilbertez, a well-respected colonel of an infantry regiment, who had previously been married to Marie de la Tour d'Auvergne, one of Henriette-Julie's cousins.[5] The union was the talk of the social papers of the time, as it served to unite a number of the most ancient and illustrious French noble families, including the Castelnaus, the Caumonts, the La Tour d'Auvergnes, the Foucaults, the Daugnons, the Dampierres, and the Murats. The following year, Murat gave birth to a son, César, who was the couple's only child and who did not survive into adulthood.[6]

During the early years of her marriage, Murat made a name for herself in Parisian high society on account of her ability to entertain her salon contemporaries with poems and with short stories in verse. Salons were informal gatherings where writers, artists, intellectuals, and members of the social elite had the opportunity to meet, socialize, and share their literary creations with one another, usually on a regular basis and at the home of a female intellectual. Although the majority of Murat's poetry from this period has been lost,[7] her renown in this

---

Madame de Murat et la "défense des dames": Un discours au féminin à la fin du règne de Louis XIV (Paris: Classiques Garnier, 2012), 14.

2. He died on December 2, 1672, as a result of wounds suffered near Utrecht during the Franco-Dutch War (1672–1678).

3. These rumors were debunked in the mid-1970s thanks to the work of A. P. Ségalen, who pointed out, among other errors, that in 1686 Queen Maria Theresa of Austria had been dead for three years. See further, "Madame de Murat et le Limousin," *Le Limousin au XVIIe siècle* (Limoges, "Trames," 1976), 77–94.

4. See, for example, the letters dated May 16, 1672; January 5, 1674; August 12, 1675; and January 10, 1689 (Patard, *Madame de Murat et la "défense des dames,"* 15–16).

5. Marie de La Tour d'Auvergne had recently died in childbirth.

6. César de Murat, seigneur de Vareillettes, is listed in the Geneanet-Pierfit online database as being born in 1692: https://gw.geneanet.org/pierfit?lang=fr&p=nicolas&n=de+murat. For a reprint of his death certificate, see Sylvie Cromer's *Edition du Journal pour Mademoiselle de Menou*, np.

7. A sonnet by Murat appeared in the *Recueil de pièces curieuses et nouvelles* (A collection of new and interesting pieces), published in Amsterdam in 1695, and several other poems appeared after her

medium is attested to in the *Oeuvres meslées* (Mixed works, 1695) of her fellow salon contemporary Marie-Jeanne Lhéritier de Villandon. Lhéritier's collection contains three letters to Murat, along with letters to two other well-known female poets of the time: Marie de Razilly, famous for her alexandrines on heroic subjects, and Charlotte de Melsons Le Camus, whose poetry would eventually earn her induction into the prestigious *Accademia dei Ricovrati* (Academy of the Sheltered) in Padua on the same day as Murat.[8] In her first letter to Murat, Lhéritier expresses admiration for some short tales in verse that the former had recently penned and tries to convince her to branch out into prose writing.[9] In the second two letters, Lhéritier discusses the literary merits of bouts-rimés (rhymed ends), a type of poetry that was popular in late-seventeenth-century salons in which one person creates a list of words that rhyme with one another and gives these rhymes to a second person, who must compose a sonnet using those words as the rhymes. In addressing these letters to Murat, Lhéritier clearly intended to encourage her friend to participate in a salon game that had recently resulted, for Lhéritier, in the composition of a bouts-rimés that had won the Floral Games Prize from the Lanternists Society of Toulouse earlier that year.[10] According to a journal that Murat composed between April 1708 and June 1709, the *Journal pour Mademoiselle de Menou*, Murat would be awarded the same prestigious poetry prize for one of her eclogues, likely either in late 1700 or early 1701.[11] In addition to describing the author's daily activities, Murat's journal contains a substantial number of both new

---

death. For eighteenth- and nineteenth-century publications, see the bibliography.

8. The Academy of the Sheltered was one of the few literary societies to accept women at that time. Charlotte de Melsons Le Camus (also referred to as "de Melson Le Camus" or "Le Camus de Melsons") was inducted on the same day as Murat (February 9, 1699). See further, Geneviève Clermidy-Patard, ed., *Madame de Murat: Journal pour Mademoiselle de Menou* (Paris: Classiques Garnier, 2016), 88n2. Other members of Murat's literary circle who were accepted into this society include Marie-Catherine d'Aulnoy, Catherine Bernard, Charlotte-Rose Caumont de La Force, and Lhéritier herself; see Lewis C. Seifert and Domna C. Stanton, *Enchanted Eloquence: Fairy Tales by Seventeenth-Century French Women Writers* (Toronto: Iter and the Centre for Reformation and Renaissance Studies, 2010), 231. On the other members of the Academy, see Fabio Blasutto, David de la Croix, and Mara Vitale, "Scholars and Literati at the Academy of the Ricovrati (1599–1800)," *Repertorium Eruditorum Totius Europae* – RETE (2021) 3:51–63. https://doi.org/10.14428/rete.v3i0/Ricoverati. On Razilly, Le Camus, and the other members of Lhéritier's literary circle who are mentioned in the *Oeuvres meslées*, see Allison Stedman, "Le rôle de la poésie dans la société mondaine de la fin du XVIIe siècle," in *Le poète et le joueur de quilles: Enquête sur la construction de la poésie (XIVe–XXIe siècles)*, ed. Olivier Gallet, Adeline Lionetto, Stéphane Loubère, Laure Michel, and Thierry Roger (Mont-Saint-Aignan, France: Presses Universitaires de Rouen et du Havre [PURH], 2023), 169–178.

9. Marie-Jeanne Lhéritier de Villandon, *Oeuvres meslées* (Paris: Jean Guignard, 1695), 229, 297–298.

10. Lhéritier, *Oeuvres meslées*, 399.

11. *Madame de Murat: Journal pour Mademoiselle de Menou*, ed. Geneviève Clérmidy-Patard, 86–88.

and previously composed poems (including a number of bouts-rimés), three fairy tales, two short stories, and a variety of other short works in prose and in verse.[12]

Although during the early years of her marriage, Murat may have appeared content to compose poetry and to frequent respectable salon gatherings, such as those of the Marquise de Lambert,[13] she nonetheless had a subversive streak that would manifest both in her actions and in her fiction in the years that followed. Rumors circulated as early as 1694 that she was involved in a libel against the king's morganatic second wife, Madame de Maintenon,[14] and by 1697, she was already taking on some of the most prominent male authors of her time, establishing herself as a feminist social theorist avant la lettre with the publication of a two-volume collection of pseudo-memoirs, titled *Mémoires de Madame la Comtesse de M**** (Memoirs of the Countess of M***, 1697). Murat published this novel as a response to the *Mémoires de la vie du comte D*** avant sa retraite* (Memoirs of the life of Count D*** before his retirement, 1696), a work that was publicly attributed to the exiled essayist Charles de Saint-Évremond (although authored by the moralist critic Abbé Pierre de Villiers)[15] and that portrayed women as being fickle and incapable of virtue. In her pseudo-memoirs, Murat responds to Villiers with an explicit defense of women and of the female sex in general, arguing that women's failings are more often the result of misfortune than of moral weakness and that it is thus the responsibility of women to protect and to defend one another's reputations. Noting that the majority of female tribulations occur because of a "pitiful lack of solidarity among women,"[16] Murat exhorts her female readers to consider the consequences to the female sex as a whole before initiating rumors about other women and before perpetuating behaviors that have the potential to set women against one another.

The importance of female solidarity would go on to become a dominant theme in almost all of Murat's subsequent literary production and would take on particular significance in the context of her leisure novels, which provided

---

12. Murat, *Journal pour Mademoiselle de Menou*, 12. It is not clear if Murat and Lhéritier were still on good terms at the time of the composition of the *Lutins* (any mention of Lhéritier is conspicuously absent from the *Journal*). However, Murat appears to pay a kind of homage to her former salon contemporary in volume II of *Les Lutins* when the characters who compose bouts-rimés recycle the same rhymes that had previously appeared in Lhéritier's *Oeuvres meslées*, using them to create new poems. See Lhéritier, *Oeuvres meslées*, 394–396. See further, translated text, note 73.

13. Anne-Thérèse de Lambert (1647–1733). See Roger Marchal, *Madame de Lambert et son milieu* (Oxford: Voltaire Foundation, 1991), 226–227. See also Seifert and Stanton, *Enchanted Eloquence*, 232.

14. According to Geneviève Clermidy-Patard, these rumors were later determined to be unfounded.

15. The Villiers attribution is corroborated by the editor Barbier (quoted in the BNF database). See further, Seifert and Stanton, *Enchanted Eloquence*, 320. Madame de Murat, *Mémoires de Madame la Comtesse de M**** (Paris: Claude Barbin, 1697), 2:395–396.

16. Murat, *Mémoires de Madame la Comtesse de M****, 2:395–396. Translations of the French quotations are our own.

models for how supportive female relationships could result in positive outcomes for women in situations that mirrored those of Murat's contemporary reality. While in *A Trip to the Country*, for example, the happy resolution to the novel's love plot takes place largely because the friendship between the female narrator (Mademoiselle de Busansai) and Madame d'Arcire is shown to be impervious to outside manipulation, in *The Sprites of Kernosy Castle*, the solidarity between the three main female characters—the Kernosy sisters and their close friend the Marquise de Briance—is shown to play a key role in the ability of all three women to achieve their amorous objectives at the novel's conclusion. By the same token, women who resist involving other women in networks of mutual support find themselves both outwitted and excluded from the central group in the context of these novels. Such is the case for Mademoiselle de Busansai's rival Madame de Talemonte in *A Trip to the Country* and for the viscountess in *The Sprites*.

Murat and the Development of the Literary Fairy Tale

In 1695, when Lhéritier first encouraged Murat to try her hand at prose fiction, she did not have in mind the collection of pseudo-memoirs that ended up constituting the latter's official literary debut. Rather, she had hoped that Murat would assist her in the creation and proliferation of an emerging literary genre, the *conte des fées* (fairy tale).[17] The literary fairy tale was a genre that first came to prominence in France in the 1690s, having begun as a salon entertainment.[18] It was cultivated mostly by female authors, who found it amenable for many reasons, including increasing dissatisfaction with stories from classical mythology, which could be linked to absolutist propaganda, and the fascination with imaginary worlds where female figures like fairies wielded power, usually in a benevolent way. The genre also became a useful vehicle for making indirect criticism of the reigning social and political institutions. Between 1690 and 1710, 112 literary fairy tales were

---

17. Lhéritier, *Oeuvres meslées*, 297–298. Marie-Catherine d'Aulnoy is credited with inventing the term (*Contes des fées*, [Tales of the fairies]) for her first collection of fairy tales, published in 1697. Murat would use a similar title for her first collection of fairy tales (*Contes de fées*, [Tales about fairies]) in 1698. See further, Allison Stedman, "Henriette-Julie de Murat, *Histoires sublimes et allégoriques*," in *Marvelous Transformations: An Anthology of Fairy Tales and Contemporary Critical Perspectives*, ed. Christine A. Jones and Jennifer Schacker (Toronto: Broadview, 2013), 201. Murat had a lot of admiration for d'Aulnoy and made frequent intertextual references to her works. See further, Rori Bloom, *Making the Marvelous: Marie-Catherine d'Aulnoy, Henriette-Julie de Murat, and the Literary Representation of the Decorative Arts* (Lincoln: University of Nebraska Press, 2022).

18. See, for example, Sévigné's letter dated August 6, 1677, where she describes listening to Madame de Coulanges tell a fairy tale that lasted over an hour; see Allison Stedman, *Rococo Fiction in France, 1600–1715: Seditious Frivolity* (Lewisburg, PA: Bucknell University Press, 2013), 130–131.

published in France, sixty-eight of which were authored by women and forty-one by men; three remain anonymous.[19]

At the time that Lhéritier reached out to Murat, however—dedicating the fairy tale "L'Adroite Princesse" ("The discreet princess") to her and urging Murat to compose a fairy tale of her own in the context of her *Oeuvres meslées*—the genre was still in a state of initiation and theorization. Following Marie-Catherine d'Aulnoy's publication of the first literary fairy tale of the French tradition, "The Island of Happiness," which was written in a descriptive and digressive style similar to that of its framing novel,[20] Charles Perrault, a member of the French Academy and relative of Lhéritier's,[21] took it upon himself to steer the nascent genre in a different direction, composing a series of short moralistic tales in verse and in prose. In 1695, the same year as the publication of the *Oeuvres meslées*, he appended a preface to the fourth edition of his 1691 tale *La Marquise de Salusses, ou la patience de Griselidis* (*Patient Griselda*), in which he made a case for the fairy tale as the "modern" (and superior) iteration of the kinds of moralistic fables and short tales that the "wisest and most learned" authors of antiquity had relied upon to educate their children.[22] However, in contrast to the model advanced by d'Aulnoy, who had envisioned the fairy tale as an extension of the novel, Perrault maintained that fairy tales were a pedagogical genre, suitable for children and originating from the folktales of wet nurses and peasants. As a result, not only should such tales strive to replicate the simplicity and concision of the original oral stories, but also they should eliminate any plot details that might distract the reader from the central moral truth that the story proposed.

---

19. Nathalie Rizzoni and Julie Boch, eds., *L'âge d'or du conte de fées: De la comédie à la critique (1690–1709)*, Bibliothèque des Génies et des Fées, vol. 5 (Paris: Honoré Champion, 2007), 613–616. For a list of individual fairy tales by female writers, see Seifert and Stanton, *Enchanted Eloquence*, 311–313. For a bibliography of works containing fairy tales, see Raymonde Robert, *Le Conte de fées en France de la fin du XVIIe à la fin du XVIIIe siècle*, ed. Nadine Jasmin (Paris: Honoré Champion, 2002), 493–506.

20. "L'île de la félicité" (The Island of Happiness) appeared as an interpolated story in d'Aulnoy's novel *Histoire d'Hypolite, comte de Duglas* (Paris: Louis Sylvestre, 1690), 2:143–181. The majority of French fairy tales appeared as interpolations within novels or in mixed collections that contained a variety of genres. On this publication strategy, see Stedman, *Rococo Fiction in France*, 3–4.

21. Lhéritier's mother's maiden name was Françoise Le Clerc, and Perrault's mother was also a Le Clerc, but the exact relation between the two is unclear. See further, Lewis Seifert, "Marie-Jeanne Lhéritier de Villandon (1664–1734), *The Teller's Tale: Lives of the Classic Fairy Tale Writers*, ed. Sophie Raynard, 75. We are grateful to Volker Schröder for this clarification. Perrault is often referred to as Lhéritier's uncle.

22. Charles Perrault, "Préface," *La Marquise de Salusses, ou la patience de Griseldis* (Paris: J.B. Coignard, 1695). See further, "Perrault's Preface to *Griselda* and Murat's 'To Modern Fairies,'" ed. and trans. Holly Tucker and Melanie R. Siemens, *Marvels and Tales: Journal of Fairy-Tale Studies* 19, no. 1 (2005): 125–128. In his original version of the tale, Perrault alternated between the forms Griselde and Griselidis; in the later version, he standardized the name to Griselidis.

This was not the vision for the genre that the original, salon women writers had intended, and Lhéritier's argument for enlisting Murat's help in its development accordingly included the following three reasonings. First, in an effort to support d'Aulnoy's conception of the fairy tale as a form of worldly literature, Lhéritier retheorized the genre's "modern" origins, claiming that fairy tales were descended not from the common folktales of peasants and wet nurses but rather from the poetry of the medieval troubadours. As such, Lhéritier maintained, the reading and composition of such stories was as suitable a pastime for upper-class aristocrats as the novels and other salon-generated literary forms that had evolved from the courtly literary traditions of the medieval French feudal nobility.[23] Second, although Lhéritier agreed with Perrault that modern fairy tales could achieve the same moral objectives as the fables of antiquity, she took issue with his claim that the goals of such tales were uniquely pedagogical and destined for an audience of children. Instead, Lhéritier asserted that the fairy tale, as an extension of the novel, was highly suitable both for metaphorical social commentary and for the entertainment of adults. Third, Lhéritier maintained that fairy tales provided an ideal way for modern writers (like Murat) to attract the attention of "the finest minds in France" because of the genre's ability to accommodate a degree of innovation and creativity that was not possible in most other literary contexts due to the mandates of verisimilitude and propriety that governed the majority of contemporary literary production. As Lhéritier assured Murat, although fairy tales certainly deserved their current reputation for pleasing children and adults alike, "these fables would be pleasing to the greatest minds, / If you would wish, beautiful Countess, / To adorn such narratives with your happy talents."[24]

If Lhéritier's plea to Murat did not sufficiently convince the latter to try her hand at the genre in 1695, then it appears that a shift in Murat's personal circumstances, combined with the publication of Perrault's *Histoires ou contes du temps passé* (*Tales of Times Past*, 1697), achieved the desired result. Perrault's collection, also known as the *Contes de ma mère l'oye* (*Mother Goose Tales*), was introduced by a preface that insisted to an even greater degree than his introduction to *Grisélidis* that the fairy tale was a form of children's literature whose origins could be traced to the tales of common people—even going so far as to announce that the present collection was in fact composed by a child (Perrault's youngest son, Pierre Perrault Darmancour) as a gift to another young person of his son's generation (Élisabeth-Charlotte d'Orléans, niece of Louis XIV).[25] Following the publication

23. On the broader implications of this argument, see Allison Stedman, "Proleptic Nostalgia: Longing for the Middle Ages in the Late Seventeenth-Century French Fairy Tale," *Romanic Review* 99, no. 3–4 (May–November 2008): 363–380.
24. Lhéritier, *Oeuvres meslées*, 297–298.
25. Pierre Perrault Darmancour (1678–1700), Perrault's youngest son, would have been nineteen at the time of the publication of the *Contes*, while Élisabeth-Charlotte d'Orléans would have been fifteen

of this preface, the Abbé de Villiers, the moralist critic whom Murat had previously debated in the context of her pseudo-memoirs, published *Entretiens sur les contes de fées* (Inquiries on fairy tales, 1699), a multi-volume treatise that gave a scathing critique of the kind of lengthy, digressive, and descriptive fairy tales penned by the majority of the female authors, concluding with a brief defense of Perrault's model of fairy-tale composition. For Villiers, the lengthier novelistic tales composed by women in recent decades had resulted in what his Parisian narrator describes as "piles of fairy tales that have been annoying us to death for a year or two." He adds, "If we didn't have any of those ignoramuses who stubbornly desire to write books, we would never have seen so much nonsense published."[26] In contrast to these works, which constitute some of "the worst merchandise in the world,"[27] according to the Parisian, the recently published tales by Perrault prove that it is still possible to effectively apply the rules of eloquence, even to the most trivial or amusing subject matter, provided that the author has a sufficient command of the French language and is thoroughly instructed in its terms. As Villiers's Provincial narrator sums it up, although most of the recently published fairy tales fall short, one still needs to acknowledge "that the best tales we have are those that best imitate the style and simplicity of nurses. For this reason alone, I am quite pleased with the tales attributed to the son of a celebrated member of the French Academy."[28] While both the Provincial and the Parisian narrators concede that nurses may be ignorant, they agree that their folktales can still be transformed into meritorious stories, provided that the author of these stories is "clever enough to imitate the simplicity of their ignorance deftly,"[29] as Perrault has recently done in the work that he publicly attributed to his son.

Both in anticipation of and in retaliation against points of view resembling Villiers', Murat published three collections of fairy tales between 1698 and 1699: *Contes de fées* (Fairy tales, 1698), *Nouveaux contes de fées* (New fairy tales, 1698), and *Histoires sublimes et allégoriques* (Sublime and allegorical stories, 1699), all of which were written in the digressive and descriptive novelistic style decried by Villiers. Although the first collection makes no direct reference to the ongoing

---

or sixteen. The *Contes* were circulating in manuscript form by 1695. The degree to which Perrault's son was involved in the creation and publication of the tales is unclear. On the varying accounts of his involvement, see Christine A. Jones, *Mother Goose Refigured: A Critical Translation of Charles Perrault's Fairy Tales* (Detroit, MI: Wayne State University Press, 2016) 24–27; and Natalie Froloff, "Preface," *Contes de Perrault* (Paris: Gallimard, 1999), 7–10.

26. Pierre de Villiers, "Conversations on Fairy Tales and Other Contemporary Works, to Protect against Bad Taste (1699), from the *Second Conversation*," in *Enchanted Eloquence: Fairy Tales by Seventeenth-Century French Women Writers*, ed. and trans. Lewis C. Seifert and Domna C. Stanton (Toronto: Iter and the Centre for Reformation and Renaissance Studies, 2010), 294.

27. de Villiers, "Conversations on Fairy Tales and Other Contemporary Works," 295.

28. de Villiers, "Conversations on Fairy Tales and Other Contemporary Works," 309.

29. Lhéritier, *Oeuvres meslées*, 297–298.

debate, in the latter two collections Murat prefaced her tales with dedicatory poems and epistles that clearly indicated her ideological position both as a composer of fairy tales and as a female writer who wished to advocate for the other authors of her sex. In the dedicatory preface to the *Nouveaux contes de fées*, Murat takes on the idea that fairy tales are a pedagogical genre destined for children by offering her collection to Louis XIV's adult daughter Marie-Anne de Bourbon, Princess de Conti (1666–1739), a wealthy and financially independent patroness of the arts whose beauty and eloquence rivals those of the fairies, according to Murat's dedicatory poem.[30] In offering these tales as a gift to Conti, Murat affirms both the fairy tale's aristocratic origins and its suitability for an adult audience, making it clear that salon-style fairy tales are worthy of being read even by some of the most admired and high-ranking members of Louis XIV's court.

It is in the preface to the final collection of fairy tales that Murat takes her most dramatic stand, however, engaging with both Perrault and Villiers directly and even distinguishing herself and her own tales from those of her fellow *conteuses*. Instead of dedicating this preface to a potential reader or patron, Murat dedicates the collection to her fellow female fairy-tale *authors*, whom Murat refers to as "Modern Fairies" (*fées modernes*), metaphorically eliding the identities of these authors with those of the fairies who appear in their tales. In contrast to the "ancient fairies," whose tales served as the inspiration for Perrault's collection and who are content to "sweep the house well, put the pot on the fire, do the wash, rock the children to sleep, milk cows, churn butter, and a thousand other low things of this nature," modern fairies "concern [themselves] with only great things," using their charms and (literary) talents to animate royal courts and magic palaces alike.[31] While the ancient fairies who inspired Perrault "were almost always old, ugly, poorly dressed and poorly housed," the modern fairies who compose in the style of d'Aulnoy are "beautiful, young, well formed, gallantly and richly dressed and housed."[32] While the magic of ancient fairies consisted of "danc[ing] by the light of the moon" and transforming themselves into "Crones, Cats, Monkeys and Phantoms in order to scare children and weak spirits," modern fairies have taken a different route, "giving spirit to those who have none, beauty to the ugly, eloquence to the ignorant, riches to the poor and clarity to the most obscure things."[33] According to Murat's description, one can easily see that modern fairies are the winners of this reappropriated quarrel between the "ancients" and the "moderns," as the modern fairies are clearly wealthier, more cultivated,

---

30. Murat, "Pour son altesse serenissime Madame la Princesse Douairière de Conty," in *Nouveaux Contes de fées* (Paris: Claude Barbin, 1698), ii. The Princess de Conti had been widowed thirteen years earlier at the age of twenty.

31. Murat, *Histoires sublimes et allégoriques* (Paris: F. et P. Delaulne, 1699), ii–iii.

32. Murat, *Histoires sublimes*, iii–iv.

33. Murat, *Histoires sublimes*, iii–iv.

and intelligent than the ancient fairies.[34] However, the greatest testament to the superiority of the modern writers according to Murat is the fact that the quantity of the stories that the modern fairies have recently published far outpaces that of the ancients, a number that Murat proposes to augment with "several tales of [her] own." The "piles of fairy tales" by modern fairies may be annoying to Villiers, but for Murat the fact that their model has resulted in a veritable literary explosion, whereas Perrault's model has not inspired any imitators, provides sufficient proof that whatever Villiers might think about Perrault's literary appropriation of works by the ancient fairies, public taste has clearly ruled in favor of the style of the "moderns."[35]

In the "Notice" that follows the dedicatory preface, Murat weighs in one final time on the debate surrounding the literary origins and merits of the fairy tale. However, here she addresses what appears to be an allegation that modern fairies plagiarize one another while also resisting the earlier assertion by Lhéritier that the tales by Murat and her fellow female authors originated in medieval France in the courtly literary traditions of the feudal nobility. According to Murat, the fact that the plots of some tales by modern fairies resemble one another is not a result of collective composition. Rather, it is a result of the fact that "modern fairies" have taken their inspiration from a common source, namely the Renaissance Italian novellas of Giovanni Francesco Straparola,[36] first published in Italian in 1551. As Murat describes that phenomenon:

> I am pleased to indicate two things to the Reader. The first is that I took the ideas for some of these Tales from an earlier [*ancien*] Author entitled, *Les facétieuses nuits du Seigneur Straparole*, printed for the sixteenth time in 1615. These tales were apparently very fashionable

---

34. Perrault was one of the most outspoken "moderns" in the literary controversy known as the Quarrel of the Ancients and the Moderns (1687–1715), which sought to establish whether the classical literature of ancient Greece and Rome offered models of literary excellence that were superior to modern literary models. In describing Perrault's fairies as "ancient," and in asserting that her modern fairies are superior to Perrault's, Murat thus seeks to reconfigure the stakes of the debate, effectively "out-moderning" Perrault. See further the "Translators' Introduction" to Tucker and Siemens, "Perrault's Preface to *Griselda* and Murat's 'To Modern Fairies,'" 125–126.

35. As Anne E. Duggan has shown, Perrault's argument in favor of the "moderns" in the context of this debate is paradoxically even more misogynistic than the arguments made by the "ancients"; see Duggan, *Salonnières, Furies, and Fairies: The Politics of Gender and Cultural Change in Absolutist France*, 2nd ed. (Newark: University of Delaware Press, 2021), 114–126. See also Gabrielle Verdier, "Figures de la conteuse dans les contes de fées féminins," *Dix-septième siècle* 180 (July–September 1993): 481–499.

36. Murat, *Histoires sublimes et allégoriques*, i–vi. Straparola's two-volume collection, *Le piacevoli notti* (Facetious nights, 1551 and 1553) contained various types of short stories, including fables and fairy tales. His treatments of fairy tales are considered to be the earliest to appear anywhere in print.

during the last century as there has been so much discussed about this book. The Ladies who have written up until now in this genre have drawn from the same source, at least for the most part. The second thing that I have to say is that my Tales were written since last April, and that if there are similarities with one of these Ladies in discussing some of my Subjects, I did not use any model other than the original, which will be easy to prove by the different paths that we have taken. However mediocre the Works that we give to the Public, we always feel for them a fatherly love [*amour de père*] that obligates us to justify their birth, and we would be upset to see them appear with any defect.[37]

As Holly Tucker and Melanie R. Siemens have described, the fact that Murat chooses the phrase "fatherly love" to describe her affection toward her own tales continues her preface's broader theme of authorial reappropriation—a reappropriation that is directed in large part toward Perrault and toward the moralist critics like Villiers who disparaged the modern fairies' literary talents and artistic contributions.[38]

Although Murat would subsequently move on to other types of fiction, she never fully abandoned the fairy tale, as evidenced by the fact that she included one (though without direct mention of fairies) in her first leisure novel, *A Trip to the Country*,[39] and included another three in the *Journal pour Mademoiselle de Menou* composed between April 1708 and June 1709, which remained unpublished at the time of her death.[40] Her decision to turn to leisure novels nonetheless constituted a deliberate break from the fairy-tale vogue that had propelled her to fame, as the frame narratives of these works call into question both the conventions of the fairy tale and the role of the supernatural as a novelistic element in general. As Rori Bloom has pointed out, Murat's demystification of the supernatural in her first leisure novel encompasses a similar impulse to that of d'Aulnoy in her 1691 *Voyage d'Espagne* (*Travels into Spain*), which featured characters who were similarly skeptical of the legends they encountered while touring the Spanish countryside.[41] Unlike in d'Aulnoy's *Travels*, however, in *A Trip to the Country*, the demystification of the supernatural occurs at the home of a fictional nobleman, whose country estate is located a little more than a day's drive from Paris. In the latter work,

---

37. Murat, *Histoires sublimes*, vii–viii. Translated by Tucker and Siemens, "Perrault's Preface to *Griselda* and Murat's 'To Modern Fairies,'" 129–130.

38. Tucker and Siemens, "Perrault's Preface to *Griselda* and Murat's 'To Modern Fairies,'" 126.

39. Madame de Murat, *Voyage de campagne par Madame la Comtesse de M**** (Paris: Veuve de Claude Barbin, 1699).

40. *Journal pour Mademoiselle de Menou*, Paris: Bibliothèque de l'Arsenal. Ms. 3471. The journal would not be published until more than two hundred years later.

41. See further, chapters 4 and 5 in Bloom, *Making the Marvelous*, 131–176.

there is only a minimal central plot, and the bulk of the novel consists of stories told by the participants to the assembled company, mostly for the purpose of entertainment. Those stories are mainly autobiographical (characters discuss their love lives, or, in the case of the widows, their marriages) or supernatural (multiple ghost stories and one fairy tale). Although not technically a leisure novel, the *Journal pour Mademoiselle de Menou* bears many similar elements to *A Trip to the Country*, in that the poems, fairy tales, and short stories are interspersed with information about Murat's health, daily life, and leisure activities.

Scandal and Exile

In December 1699, one month after the publication of *A Trip to the Country*, Murat's literary career came to an abrupt hiatus when scandalous rumors about the nature of the nightly gatherings she was accustomed to hosting at her Paris apartment led to a yearlong formal investigation and ultimately to severe punishment. According to the records of the Parisian chief of police René d'Argenson, Murat's home had been on law enforcement radar since at least 1698 on account of the excessive gambling reported to be taking place there. Murat had received an order from the king to reform her behavior on September 29, 1698.[42] However, the gambling continued, as did the complaints from Murat's neighbors, who over the course of the year that followed would report her not only for fostering gambling but also for "a number of [other] shocking practices and beliefs." These included a range of domestic improprieties, such as presiding over a "debauched environment," in which "appalling swearing," "dishonorable dinner conversations," "dissolute songs being sung at all hours of the night," and "the insolence of people pissing out the window after long nights of eating and drinking" were regular occurrences.[43] However, they also included a more serious allegation: tribadism (the early modern term for lesbianism).[44] While one neighbor reported witnessing one of Murat's lovers violently destroying a portrait with a knife when Murat abandoned her for another woman, others describe Murat as being in "a continual state of adoration" with respect to her new lover, Madame de Nantiat, who had moved in with Murat some months prior.[45] Estranged from her husband and disinherited by her mother, Murat agreed to be exiled from Paris if the king would pay for her moving expenses and if other arrangements could be made for her seven-year-old son.[46] But the inability of law enforcement to prevent her from

---

42. René d'Argenson, *Rapports inédits du lieutenant de police René d'Argenson (1697–1715) publiés d'après les manuscrits conservés à la Bibliothèque Nationale*, ed. Paul Cottin (Paris: Plon, 1891), 3.

43. Argenson, *Rapports inédits du lieutenant de police René d'Argenson*, 11.

44. See Seifert and Stanton, *Enchanted Eloquence*, 8.

45. Argenson, *Rapports inédits du lieutenant de police René d'Argenson*, 11.

46. Argenson, *Rapports inédits du lieutenant de police René d'Argenson*, 17–18.

returning to the capital, and from continuing her relationship with Nantiat both there and in the provinces, ultimately led to Murat's being placed under house arrest in early 1702 at the royal prison at Loches.[47] She remained there until the summer of 1709, at which point she managed to obtain a partial liberty through the intercession of the Countess d'Argenton, for whom she had composed some flattering poems.[48] Upon her release, she returned to the Limousin region and to the home of her aunt, Mademoiselle Dampierre, following an exile of nearly ten years. It was there that she wrote what eighteenth-century bibliographers would consider to be her finest novel, *The Sprites of Kernosy Castle*.[49] This work would also mark the end of her literary career, however, as her health suffered a serious decline in the years that followed. She died in 1716, not long after having been officially rehabilitated by the regent.

Murat and the Art of the Leisure Novel

The eighteenth century was a period when the novel achieved unprecedented popularity, in large part because the form offered readers an opportunity to peer into the private lives of others, especially members of the upper class. While some of the new subgenres focused on the bedroom, others—most notably leisure novels like Marie-Catherine d'Aulnoy's *Don Gabriel Ponce de Leon* (1697) and her *Nouveau gentilhomme bourgeois* (The new bourgeois nobleman, 1698), Murat's own *Voyage de campagne* (*A Trip to the Country*, 1699), and Catherine Durand Bédacier's *Les Petits soupers de l'été de l'année 1699* (The light suppers of the summer of 1699, 1702)—presented a more in-depth portrayal of the lives of the idle rich. These latter works, which were part of the subgenre's peak in popularity around the turn of the eighteenth century, today comprise some of the best-known examples of a literary trend that had slowly risen to prominence over the course of the 1600s, culminating in the final decades of the seventeenth century due to an increasing fascination with the members of the nobility who resisted life at court in the wake of Louis XIV's centralization of aristocratic society at Versailles.

---

47. Argenson, *Rapports inédits du lieutenant de police René d'Argenson*, 87–88. Murat was imprisoned in the chateau de Loches, in the Touraine region, on April 19, 1702. However, she attempted to escape on multiple occasions, resulting in her being transferred to the chateau de Saumur in 1706, and eventually to the chateau d'Angers in 1707, before returning to Loches to finish out her sentence. She documented the final years of her exile in a diary she dedicated to her cousin Mademoiselle de Menou. See further, Clermidy-Patard, ed., *Madame de Murat*, 20–21.

48. The Countess d'Argenton was the mistress of the Duke d'Orléans. Murat was pardoned on May 15, 1709, but was not allowed to return to court until after Louis XIV's death, in 1715.

49. The work received an *approbation* (preliminary official approval) on September 1, 1709, and obtained a royal privilege a few months later on November 20. It was published in 1710.

Like more traditional examples of the genre, leisure novels generally featured an overarching framework with a love plot. However, in the majority of texts, these love affairs fade into the background of the rhythm of the characters' daily lives, allowing the reader to take part in the entertainments that the characters themselves enjoy in "real time," such as telling stories, composing poems, singing songs, performing skits, or going to concerts or plays. The single greatest impetus for the rise of the leisure novel during the final decades of the seventeenth century was the increasingly obvious public appetite for glimpses into the lives of "real" people, as already noted. This interest in exploring people's private lives manifested itself in several new fictional genres. In addition to the leisure novel, the epistolary novel, with its ability to reveal characters' intimate feelings and actions, was first introduced in France during the latter part of the seventeenth century.[50] While this trend helped fuel the popularity of monthly periodicals like Jean Donneau de Visé's *Mercure galant*—where a compilation of literature, news, entertainment, and gossip was interpolated into fictional letters from a Parisian gentleman to his lady friend in the provinces—it also encouraged novelists to reimagine how fiction could reflect ordinary life. In the case of Murat, the "ordinary life" she wished to portray corresponded to the world she knew best: that of wealthy and cultivated aristocrats who valued their independence, kept their distance from the political sphere, and enjoyed lively conversation and the arts. As concepts of "leisure literature" evolved from simply providing an outlet for leisure (as in reading for pleasure) to actually memorializing the wide range of leisure activities enjoyed by real or invented groups, a number of novelistic works appeared that deemphasized plot and characterization in order to focus instead on conversation and entertainments.[51] This change of focus resulted in the novel's undergoing significant formal and stylistic changes. Most notably, novelists began to turn from long works featuring lengthy and complex central plots, often involving embedded tales and sometimes even stories within stories, to shorter works of a hybrid nature, in which the hierarchy between primary and secondary narratives came to be called into question.[52]

50. Prominent examples of the epistolary genre from this period include Gabriel-Joseph de Guilleragues's *Lettres portugaises* (*Letters of a Portuguese Nun*, 1669), Marie-Catherine de Villedieu's *Le Portefeuille* (The briefcase, 1674), and Edme Boursault's *Lettres de Babet* (Letters of Babet, 1683).

51. On this transition, see Henri Coulet, *Le Roman jusqu'à la Révolution* (Paris: Armand Colin, 1967), 288. On literature as an outlet for leisure, see Marc Fumaroli, Philippe-Joseph Salazar, and Emmanuel Bury, eds., *Le loisir lettré à l'âge classique* (Geneva: Droz, 1996). On literature as a way of memorializing leisure activities, see Juliette Cherbuliez, *The Place of Exile: Leisure Literature and the Limits of Absolutism* (Lewisburg, PA: Bucknell University Press, 2005), and Stedman, *Rococo Fiction in France*. See also Perry Gethner, "Murat, Durand and the Novel of Leisure," *Creation, Re-creation and Entertainment: Early Modernity and Postmodernity*, ed. Benjamin Balak and Charlotte Trinquet du Lys (Tübingen: Gunter Narr, 2019), 25–36.

52. Indeed, the most popular novels from the period 1620 to 1660 were gigantic works, published in as many as twelve volumes, that provided not just convoluted plots and thrilling adventures but

Murat herself had utilized this hybrid plot structure in her previous novel, *A Trip to the Country*. However, in *The Sprites of Kernosy Castle*, Murat tried a somewhat different approach. Although the latter novel remains within the generic category of a hybrid leisure novel, there is a greater focus on the main plot, consisting of four interconnected love stories, one of which is humorous. The stories about supernatural phenomena are reduced to one, and only three of the main characters (the Count de Livry, the Marquise de Briance, and the Count de Tourmeil) relate their adventures. Even there, Murat treats the convention differently. The autobiographical stories are told not to the whole company but rather to a smaller audience consisting of between one and four people. Most importantly, however, the information contained in these interpolated narratives is directly relevant to the main plot, something that had not been the case with earlier novels of this type, like Charles Sorel's *La Maison des jeux* (The house of games, 1642), the anonymous L.C.'s *La Promenade de Livry* (An outing in Livry, 1678), or Catherine Durand's *Les Petits soupers de l'été de l'année 1699*. The Count de Livry's story gives background information about the love relation between the two brothers and the two sisters. The story of the Marquise de Briance tells of her love relation with the Count de Tourmeil and his heroic defense of her brother, information that will become essential for the reader to understand the main plot's eventual resolution. Tourmeil's story, though not as closely integrated into the main plot as the others, nonetheless displays important thematic connections to it by showing that a man of the present day can still further his social and political ambitions by behaving like a knight in chivalric romances. Murat's success in striking a balance between hybridity of form and synergy of content, evident in the way that the novel's conclusion resolves the plots of the frame narrative and the interpolated stories simultaneously, likely contributed to *The Sprites*' being hailed as Murat's best work at its time of publication, a reputation that it continued to enjoy through the end of the century.

The Sprites diverges from previous leisure novels not only because of its innovative novelistic structure, however. It also testifies to the emergence of an exciting new intellectual climate. The decades just preceding and following 1700 saw a radical shift in French thinking, away from absolutist ideology and toward an all-questioning rationalism that would come to be known as the Enlightenment. As one might expect, the fiction of that period manifested the new spirit in a variety of ways, and Murat's final novel is to a considerable degree a clever and lighthearted reflection of this. As the title indicates, the work is set in a dilapidated medieval castle that is largely cut off from society and believed to be haunted,

---

also models of refined behavior and speech aimed at the upper classes. Many of the leading practitioners of this type of fiction were themselves members of the aristocracy, notably, Marin Le Roy de Gomberville, Gautier de La Calprenède, Georges de Scudéry, Madeleine de Scudéry, and Honoré d'Urfé. While these novels continued to be widely read in the following generation, writers gradually gravitated toward shorter forms of fiction.

symbolizing the benighted elements in France's past. The castle's transformation into a place of gladness and robust cultural activity, combined with the debunking of the supernatural, since the sprites are in fact amorous young men in disguise, can be viewed as an extension of the new and more progressive order that was currently emerging in other areas of society in contrast to the court. While critiques of the reigning social and political institutions remain discreet, probably because of Murat's disgrace and banishment from court, the work is nonetheless undergirded by a carefully constructed feminist agenda: women should be allowed intellectual freedom, including unfettered access to cultural life; the practice of arranged marriages, especially those predicated on financial gain, should cease; and men should recognize the need to treat women with proper respect, preferably by resurrecting the medieval code of chivalry and reintegrating it into present-day social interactions, something also featured in fairy tales. Perhaps most importantly, however, the novel offers an implicit critique of society by breaking down the boundaries between life and art, granting refined and honorable aristocrats the chance to craft new identities for themselves and to isolate themselves from the increasingly conformist and joyless world of the court. It is significant that none of the young male characters take any interest in political matters; they show no interest in Louis XIV or Versailles and, when called to serve in the king's wars, they perform capably but with no enthusiasm. That being said, Murat's feminism in this novel is less overt than in her pseudo-memoirs and some of her fairy tales. The female character who displays the greatest amount of agency (not surprisingly, a widow) is a comic figure, while the younger heroines, however spirited and resilient, are largely powerless and must rely on resourceful male suitors to rescue them. The decision to make the young men the most active characters, even with respect to the novel's title, presumably reflected the author's recent experiences with exile.

In eliminating the supernatural from a novel that explicitly announces itself to be about "sprites," Murat continued the process of distancing herself from the fairy-tale tradition that she and a number of other Parisian salon women had established during the 1690s, a process that Murat had begun shortly before her exile in 1699 with the publication of *A Trip to the Country*. In the earlier novel, not only does the ghost story replace the fairy tale as the most popular entertainment genre among the aristocratic storytellers, but also the novel's narrator, who tells the only interpolated fairy tale in order to stave off boredom while hosting a group of inopportune guests, expressly embellishes it by *eliminating* fairies, a choice that she justifies to the other characters as follows: "The supernatural elements that are seen in other tales of this type are not present here. . . . I wanted to eliminate the fairies to see whether I could make my lovers happy without the aid of those good women, who correspond to gods coming out of machines, so condemned by the ancients."[53] Moreover, even the ghost stories in that novel

---

53. Madame de Murat, *A Trip to the Country*, ed. and trans. Perry Gethner and Allison Stedman (Detroit: Wayne State University Press, 2011), 63.

reflect the Enlightenment perspective: although in some cases the apparitions are presumably real, in others they are shown to be hoaxes, and the frame characters openly debate about whether it is possible for ghosts to exist.

In *The Sprites*, Murat takes the strategy of replacing fairy magic much further, however. She uses the supernatural for humorous purposes and places it completely within the realm of human innovation and manipulation, as the "interventions" take place almost exclusively within the main plot: the well-intentioned young men impersonate sprites in order to gain access to the supposedly haunted castle and to terrorize the characters who present obstacles to their plans.[54] The sprites are amusing figures, and even though they abandon their disguises well before the midpoint of the novel, their initial masquerade establishes a lighthearted tone that prevails throughout the majority of the book. Perhaps not surprisingly, given the early Enlightenment context, Murat's choice to eliminate the "genuine" supernatural and to use belief in sprites for comic effect did not keep her novel from appealing to the same public that had devoured fairy tales during the previous decade.

Leaving aside the diversions directly executed by the sprites in disguise, the majority of the leisure activities that the characters enjoy over the course of the novel are cultural in nature, thus emphasizing their refined taste and their genuine appreciation of France's cultural riches. Like the characters of the more "traditional" leisure novels mentioned earlier, those of *The Sprites* view their choice of entertainment as gallant. It should be noted that in this period the terms "galant" and "galanterie" had acquired a specialized meaning in regard to the French aristocracy. Basically, this had developed into a code of conduct, both ethical and aesthetic, involving all aspects of social interaction, and it included the adoption of courtly love practices derived from medieval chivalry, to which people at least paid lip service.[55] Cultivated aristocrats were increasingly expected to be able to converse eloquently and wittily, have a basic competency in matters of culture, display good taste in their appreciation of all the principal art forms (literature, painting, music, dance), and be proficient in at least some of them. Of course, males were also expected to be well trained in standard male pursuits, such as swordsmanship and hunting. As will be noted later, a lack of proper training in these areas was a marker of lower social status and could serve to make social

---

54. The only intercalated story that does not advance the plot and functions as an entertainment for the whole company (since the "lottery" assigns to Saint-Urbain the task of reciting a tale) has an element of the supernatural in that the two protagonists fall in love through seeing the other person in magically induced dreams. But even in this case, Murat is careful to distance herself from the fairy-tale tradition: as Saint-Urbain openly acknowledges, the story she tells is not drawn from folk tradition but rather adapted from a Greek author, Athenaeus, recently translated into French.

55. The topic of "galanterie" has recently gained a more sympathetic response from literary historians. See, for example, Alain Viala, *La France galante* (Paris: PUF, 2008); Delphine Denis, *Le Parnasse galant: Institution d'une catégorie littéraire au XVIIe siècle* (Paris: Champion, 2001).

climbers look ridiculous. Not surprisingly, the gallant entertainments featured in this novel include dancing, attendance at concerts and plays, masquerades, improvised storytelling and poetry composition, and the organization of elaborate fêtes to celebrate a friend or beloved. Some of these are executed by professionals: the young men import a troupe of actors and musicians to put on daily performances, consisting of tragedies, comedies, operatic selections, and the premiere of a new mini-opera. The other entertainments are executed by the castle residents and visitors, such as reciting or improvising poems, singing, dancing, conversing, gambling, and playing games. In some cases, non-salon events are programmed, such as a hunting party and an excursion to a nearby estate. For the most part, the organizers get to choose their audiences, although there are a few unwelcome and rather uncouth intruders. Usually, the activities are only mentioned, as opposed to being transcribed in "real time," which was a feature of some of the other leisure novels of the period, as well.

However, Murat again innovates on the leisure-literature tradition in that, in this work, the entertainment almost always functions on both superficial and serious levels. Entertainments that might appear to the uninitiated as simple diversions, and that would have constituted nothing more according to the traditional leisure-literature model, here have the additional function of furthering the personal agendas of those in the know and/or of providing a mode of clandestine communication among those same characters. Many of the plays, especially the comedies, are presumably selected for performance not just for their value as entertainment but also because of their ability to communicate sensitive information to the intended parties via metaphor and symbolism. Thus, through the plot of Hauteroche's *L'Esprit follet* (The mischievous spirit), where the heroine and her maid pretend to be sprites in order to advance their amorous interests, the Kernosy sisters (the two principal heroines who live in the castle) get a clue regarding the identities of the entertainment's organizers. Molière's *Monsieur de Pourceaugnac*, which features a pompous but silly nobleman from the provinces whose lack of refinement and sense results in his being tormented and expelled, similarly foreshadows the fate of the inopportune Monsieur de Fatville, whose lack of cultivation is also exposed and mocked by the performance of Molière's *Le Bourgeois gentilhomme* (*The Bourgeois Gentleman*), in which a wealthy but inept commoner attempts unsuccessfully to turn himself into an aristocrat. Champmeslé's *La Coupe enchantée* (The enchanted cup) echoes the novel's protagonists' strategy of devaluing the supernatural when it links marital happiness to the men's refusal to avail themselves of a (presumably real) magic cup that reveals whether or not wives are faithful; while the same author's *Le Florentin* (The man from Florence) shows young lovers outsmarting a tyrannical guardian, which mirrors the hopes of the Kernosy sisters. The tragedies performed for the protagonists also present parallels to their individual situations, though to a lesser degree than the comedies. Two of the tragedies, for example, share ties with the stories of the Kernosy sisters and of Madame de Briance: Racine's *Mithridate* (1673), which features a tyrannical father who tries to separate true lovers; and Genest's *Pénélope* (1684), which celebrates female fidelity despite great obstacles. The allegorical dimension is most explicit in the mini-opera that comes near the conclusion of the novel. This idyllic pastoral piece, for which the text is included in the novel, features two faithful lovers who are quickly reconciled after a temporary misunderstanding. This opera represents both the sincere love of Tourmeil, the librettist, for the marquise, and the feigned love of Tadillac, the producer, for the elderly viscountess, whom in reality he intends to marry for her money.

A Female Quixote

One of the key elements of the novel's plot is the desire on the part of the viscountess to make her real-life experiences correspond to the ideal world of chivalric romances. Her fantasy is buttressed by the fact that the medieval world is not totally removed from her: she lives in an old castle, and there is an ongoing war, allowing her to associate current-day military officers with knights of yore. However, her desire to literally become the heroine of a courtly love story makes her a figure of ridicule, since she has trouble grasping the distinction between fantasy and reality; moreover, she fails to realize how far she is from the standard fictional heroine, given that she is middle-aged, unattractive, and ill-tempered. At the same time, it is significant that the chivalric tradition that inspires her is so well-known that a cultivated young nobleman like Tadillac can undertake to play the role of the ideal lover and do so perfectly enough to sweep her off her feet and induce her to marry him. It is also significant that some of the young suitors, especially Tourmeil, fully live up to the chivalric ideal in real life.

The theme of self-delusion induced by reading fiction was far from unknown at the turn of the eighteenth century. It first achieved prominence with *Don Quixote*, the enormously influential novel by Miguel de Cervantes (part 1, 1604; part 2, 1614). Quickly translated into French, it inspired multiple dramatic adaptations over many generations, several of them during Murat's lifetime. The title character, viewed by the French as a purely comic figure combining the traits of a lunatic with those of a braggart soldier, became emblematic of those who try to re-create in real life the impossible exploits of fictional superheroes. The fascination with Don Quixote stems in large part from the contradiction between his reasonable side (he derives moral inspiration and a sense of self-worth from the chivalric code) and his unreasonable side (he imagines that superhero knights and supernatural beings really existed; he thinks that the world of chivalry can be brought back; and he constantly projects the people and places he encounters onto episodes from fiction and treats them accordingly, with disastrous results). For Don Quixote, however, reality ultimately wins out: the protagonist is brought home by family and friends and finally comes to his senses.

Although Don Quixote, being an aristocratic male, has the option to go out into the world and attempt to re-create the sorts of adventures he has found in works of fiction, a delusional female reader generally required a separate type of model. Murat found such a model in Molière's one-act comedy *Les Précieuses ridicules* (*The Pretentious Young Ladies*, 1659). In this play, two young women from the provinces who have recently moved to Paris are revealed to be social snobs eager to gain admission into the branch of high society associated with by the salons. At the same time, however, they have convinced themselves that they can re-create in their own lives the world of contemporary salon-inspired novels, especially Madeleine de Scudéry's *Le Grand Cyrus* (1649–1653) and *Clélie* (1654–1660).[56] Opposed to arranged marriages, and even to marriage in general, Cathos and Magdelon think they deserve to have access to the same glamor and excitement as their fictional role models. They adopt elegant names derived from classical antiquity, and they expect their suitors to follow the same formalities of gallant tenderness as those found in the novels, including prolonged and extreme acts of submission. They even hope for such plot complications as jealous rivals, kidnappings, and the discovery of one's true (and noble) parentage. Molière presents them as both deranged and inept, displaying a lack of good taste as well as a lack of good sense. The plot is organized around a trick that the rejected suitors play on their fiancées: they have their valets impersonate aristocratic salon poets, and the young women are deceived even though the impostors' performance verges on the grotesque. When the suitors return, they beat the valets and strip them of their finery before announcing that they will have nothing more to do with the young women. Humiliated and powerless, Cathos and Magdelon will presumably be kept locked up at home in the future, but they are not cured of their obsession with fiction.

Murat, who was clearly influenced by Molière and who refers to him multiple times in her novel, reworks the plot of *Les Précieuses* in several crucial ways. For one thing, her delusional reader is much older, financially independent, and living in the provinces, all of which means that she can indulge her fantasies with little or no social censure to contend with. Second, the viscountess is more passive than her predecessors: she can simply wait for the ideal man to show up and does not need to try to re-create situations derived from salon fiction. Third, she is not cured of her illusions at the end; indeed, since the people around her are willing to assist in the apparent fulfillment of her dreams, she can expect to spend the rest of her days in a state of deluded contentment. In this regard, Murat may have taken a

56. Adrien de Subligny's novel *La Fausse Clélie* (1670) plays on the same theme, as the heroine comes to believe that she is the new incarnation of the title character of Scudéry's novel *Clélie*. She is a more sympathetic character than the others discussed here; she is not totally delusional, and she finds happiness and sanity at the end. Although Murat was likely aware of this work, she did not imitate it or even refer to it in her own text. Apart from novelistically induced delusions, the viscountess and Subligny's protagonist have virtually nothing in common.

cue from several of Molière's later comedies, especially *Le Bourgeois gentilhomme* (*The Bourgeois Gentleman*, 1670), which is explicitly referenced in the novel, and *Le Malade imaginaire* (*The Imaginary Invalid*, 1673). In both of these plays, the deranged protagonists are allowed to remain permanently in their fantasy worlds, as their friends and family decide that there is no point in disillusioning them. Once their domestic authority has effectively been neutralized, their fantasies are seen as harmless; the marriages of the young lovers are allowed to take place, and the hypocrites who are exploiting the protagonists are expelled.

In playing off of the plots of Molière's plays, Murat employs a similar strategy to that used by d'Aulnoy in her leisure novel *Le Nouveau gentilhomme bourgeois* (1698). In this text, d'Aulnoy reworks Molière's satire of wealthy members of the bourgeoisie who aim to enter the aristocracy with the creation of the character Monsieur de La Dandinardière. La Dandinardière, like Molière's Monsieur Jourdain, is a wealthy merchant who retires from business to live a life of elegant leisure. However, La Dandinardière goes further in that he assumes a bogus (French) title of nobility, imagines that he is genuinely a descendant of medieval knights, buys a chateau in the provinces for his permanent residence, and rides around wearing rusty armor. Although semi-delusional, he retains certain traits of bourgeois sense: he expects a bride to bring substantial wealth into the marriage, and he recognizes, though he will not openly admit it, that he is a coward. He gains a small measure of sympathy because he genuinely falls in love with the older daughter of a local nobleman and also because he appreciates fairy tales and would even like to be able to write such works himself, though, of course, he has no talent. Significantly, the happy ending goes further than in Molière's comedy. In d'Aulnoy's version, the protagonist finds a bride who is likewise immersed in fantasy and fairy tales and who is perfectly willing to share her husband's delusions. Thus, when the reasonable characters decide to play along instead of attempting to disillusion the hero, it is not just because they find him amusing but also because doing so is to their advantage (the heroine's father, who is a real baron, is impoverished and needs a wealthy son-in-law to keep his own estate afloat). While Murat does not incorporate all the elements of her friend's satirical novel, there is a partial parallel between its ending and the marriage between the viscountess and Tadillac. Certain traits of La Dandinardière are also apparent in Murat's character, Monsieur de Fatville. Although Fatville does not go so far as to impersonate medieval knights in order to legitimate a (presumed) noble status acquired only recently,[57] he nonetheless becomes an object of ridicule by overdoing, or imitating badly, the aristocratic conventions of the previous century. These include dressing in exaggerated court fashions

---

57. In addition to occupying a ministerial position, which was often a path for members of the bourgeoisie to gain access to noble status, Fatville has clearly not received the same aristocratic education and cultural foundation as the other characters and thus is unable to effectively participate in their pastimes without becoming an object of ridicule.

regardless of the occasion and demanding to be seated on the stage during theatrical performances.

Murat also appears to have found an alternative model for the delusional female reader in d'Aulnoy's leisure novel *Don Gabriel Ponce de Leon* (1697). In this text, Don Estève, one of the young suitors in pursuit of a pair of sisters resembling the Kernosy sisters, actually compares himself and his cousin Don Gabriel to Amadis and to Don Quixote, both because of the improbable nature of their adventures and because they are successfully adopting a false identity in pursuit of a romantic goal.[58] However, the narrator does not extend that comparison to Juana, the precursor to the viscountess, in that Juana, although she does enjoy reading romances, does not attempt to replicate such adventures in real life. It is thus unexpected when Juana falls madly in love with Don Estève, whom she believes to be an injured pilgrim. While in Murat's novel the delusional character is a widow who wants to remarry and is in search of a chivalric hero, in d'Aulnoy's novel the elderly aunt who wishes to keep her nieces shut away in order to preserve their virtue has never married or fallen in love, placing religious duties above all else; her passion is involuntary, and the young men have no interest in humoring her. Needless to say, the novel's ending is radically different from Murat's: Juana remains single, and she is so resolutely opposed to the desires of her nieces that the young people have to outmaneuver her in order for their marriages to ultimately take place.[59]

As for the chivalric works that the viscountess has been reading,[60] the principal one, Garci Rodriguez de Montalvo's *Amadis of Gaul* (1508), had been translated into French by Herberay des Essarts in 1540; it would remain an international bestseller for several hundred years and furnish the most widely accepted model for the ideal knight who is both superhero and super-refined lover. Since French readers assumed that "Gaul" referred to their own country, they viewed Amadis as a prototype of ideal Frenchness. It is thus not surprising that King Louis XIV himself chose this novel as the subject for a new opera and that the treatment of the title character reflected the king's project of image-making. *Amadis* (1684), with libretto by Philippe Quinault and music by Jean-Baptiste Lully,

---

58. Madame d'Aulnoy, *Contes des Fées*, ed. Nadine Jasmin (Paris: Honoré Champion, 2008), 408–409.

59. See further, Bloom, *Making the Marvelous*, 209n1.

60. It is likely, although this is not stated explicitly, that the viscountess has also been reading works of recent French novelists such as Scudéry and Villedieu, in which the well-known exploits of famous men from antiquity and the Middle Ages are intertwined with imagined love plots and in which the relations between the sexes frequently conform to the chivalric model. The continued popularity of the *Amadis* in the seventeenth century is attested, most notably, by the theologian Jacques Du Bosc in his treatise *L'Honnête femme* (*The Respectable Woman in Society*), trans. Sharon Diane Nell and Aurora Wolfgang, first published 1632–1636: "There are more women who learn by heart the tales of Amadis than the maxims of *The Holy Court* [a collection of edifying Christian stories]" (Toronto: Iter and the Centre for Reformation and Renaissance Studies, 2014), 57.

was the first of the French tragic operas to abandon classical mythology and feature a medieval setting, though it should be noted that the chivalric model, where the male protagonist displays all the qualities of the ideal knight, predominated in many of the earlier operas as well. *Amadis* was also the last of the Quinault-Lully operas to have a happy ending in which love and glory are fully compatible, with no personal sacrifice required.

While the reference to Amadis's brother Galaor, who does not appear in the opera, suggests that the viscountess has some familiarity with the novel, it is primarily the opera that influences her thinking. Significantly, the opera, unlike the novel, makes only a few passing references to Amadis's superhuman exploits. Instead of showing him win victories in combat, Quinault has him display only his moral virtues, such as courage, loyalty, and altruistic dedication to the service of others, plus a steadfast loyalty in love; indeed, the opera focuses exclusively on his love life. In a world where supernatural elements abound, Amadis manages to overcome all obstacles thanks to his sterling character and to the aid of a powerful enchantress who is committed to protecting virtuous knights and ladies.[61] The influence of the operatic *Amadis* is most apparent in the Shining House episode near the end of the novel, which includes Tourmeil's mini-opera; here the borrowings are intended to be recognized and appreciated by the spectators. The Shining House serves a further ideological function by reappropriating, for private and nonpolitical use, some of the key signifiers of Versailles, especially in regard to the types of entertainments offered, such as court masquerade, comedy-ballet, and opera.[62]

Theatrical Life in 1700

The Sprites is one of a very small number of documents capable of shedding light on the composition and repertoire of theatrical companies based in provincial cities at the turn of the eighteenth century. Since it is likely that Murat's fictional

---

61. See further, Buford Norman, *Touched by the Graces: The Libretti of Philippe Quinault in the Context of French Classicism* (Birmingham, AL: Summa, 2001).

62. The huge success of the operatic *Amadis* not only led to a renewed interest in the original novel. It also inspired multiple dramatic parodies and a lighthearted exchange of poems, published in the *Mercure galant*, which frequently included short literary texts. Antoinette Deshoulières, one of the most esteemed salon poets from the second half of the century and an author highly valued by Murat, composed a *ballade* beginning "A caution tous amants sont sujet" (All male lovers should be viewed with suspicion). In this poem, she laments the loss of chivalric attitudes toward love on the part of the younger generation, with the refrain "People no longer love as they loved in days of yore," and she specifically references Amadis as the model lover. The first of the poetic responders, the minister Saint-Aignan, used as his refrain: "I still love as they loved in days of yore." The point of this exchange was to signal that chivalric literature still remained popular and that many readers cherished the ideals presented in those works, especially those regarding courtly love, even if those ideals did not prevail in real life.

troupe was inspired by the real-life troupes she may have encountered during her lifetime, including the portion of her childhood spent in Brest, we can draw multiple inferences. First of all, since this company has a home base, it is likely that it has a permanent theater with an extensive costume shop; the latter also functions in the novel as a source for costumes needed for nontheatrical purposes (sprites, maskers, personnel in the Shining House). The troupe probably has over a dozen actors, since for the tragedies mentioned in the novel, they would need at least ten performers, with a minimum of four women, and an even larger cast for the comedies. Second, the fictional Rennes troupe has adopted the practice of following the main play, whether a tragedy or a full-length comedy, with a comic afterpiece in one or three acts, which had become typical of Parisian troupes starting around 1660. Third, given the development of the comedy-ballet subgenre by Molière and the increased use of songs in comedies by his successors, the Rennes troupe must have recruited a certain number of actors with good singing voices. That would also explain how they are able to perform the mini-opera, which requires three soloists and constitutes the centerpiece of the novel's climactic fête.

Although the choice of plays is probably dictated in large part by the young lovers, in order to suggest parallels with their own situation, as already noted, it can hardly be a coincidence that the plays also reflect the canonization that was underway during the final quarter of the seventeenth century. Five of the six tragedies named in the novel are by the two authors who had emerged as the supreme French practitioners of that genre: Pierre Corneille and Jean Racine. One may surmise that by 1700, few if any other tragedies written prior to 1670 remained in the repertoire of provincial companies. There is also evidence of canonization happening with comedy. Of the six comedies named, two are by Molière and the others are by some of the leading playwrights from the generation that succeeded him. It is probably not a coincidence that the troupe avoids the more cynical and risqué comedies from that period by playwrights like Dancourt, Regnard, and Dufresny, many of which achieved great success in Paris. The one work by Dancourt that they perform remains within the bounds of decorum for the type of audience found in Kernosy Castle.

In addition to shedding light on theatrical activity at the turn of the eighteenth century, the text also showcases the new directions in which opera was heading at that time. For example, although the mini-opera commissioned by the baron may startle modern opera lovers by its extreme brevity and simplicity, the work fits within the conventions of a type of court entertainment that had been prominent since at least the 1680s, although it has been relatively forgotten today. Often given the name *idylle*, these were short, fully sung works that were commissioned for special occasions involving the royal family or the top ranks of the nobility, such as victories, births, marriages, recovery after illness, or return after a voyage. They were set either in the palace where the performance took place or in an Arcadia-like fantasy world. The characters were typically gods, pastoral figures (shepherds and shepherdesses, nymphs, fauns, and satyrs), and allegorical figures. Most of the text revolved around the glorification of the patron, plus a celebration of the standard pastoral values: peace, harmony, happy and faithful love. Only a minority of *idylles* had even a rudimentary plot, and when one was featured, it simply involved relationships between shepherds and shepherdesses, such as getting a reluctant person to accept love or foiling the plans of jealous rivals. Often the entertainments included episodes of dance, although this is not always indicated in the printed libretti. Some of these works were staged, meaning that there was a set and that the singers and dancers wore costumes. In such cases, people referred to them as operas, as happened with *L'Idylle sur la paix* (Idyll in Celebration of Peace, 1685, text by Racine, music by Lully). Only in rare instances did the form expand into what we would recognize as genuine one-act opera, as with *Diane et Endymion* (1711, text by Louise-Geneviève de Sainctonge, music by Henry Desmarest). The mini-opera in Murat's novel clearly fits within these parameters: it is intended for a one-time private performance, requires a small cast, uses a pastoral setting, and explicitly flatters the dedicatees.

At around the same time that the *idylle* was developing as a court entertainment, full-length pastoral opera was experiencing a revival of interest and starting to compete with the tragic-chivalric operas that had dominated since the 1670s. The term *pastorale héroïque* came to be used for operas using a pastoral locale throughout but featuring heroes and/or gods as protagonists, alongside the usual shepherds and shepherdesses. These works were usually in three acts, though some were in five acts. They most often had a happy ending, and they were not royal commissions, though the majority of them retained the convention of starting with a prologue glorifying the king or a member of the royal family. The considerable success of two of these works, *Acis et Galathée* (1686, text by Jean Galbert de Campistron, music by Lully) and *Issé* (1697, text by Antoine Houdar de La Motte, music by André Cardinal Destouches), probably influenced Murat's decision to give the mini-opera in her novel an exclusively pastoral setting, although she obviously did not include gods and heroes. Moreover, the appeal of pastoral opera for Murat was not limited to its popularity. It clearly had an ideological appeal for a writer whose relations with the king were very strained: the pastoral world, far removed from royal courts and authority, is a place where individuals can express their feelings freely and reject all external constraints.

Reception and Revision

While Murat's novels were not reprinted during her lifetime, they were by no means forgotten in the decades following her death. In 1735, for example, the French scholar, historian, and literary biographer Nicolas Lenglet Du Fresnoy had this to say of her final work:

> This little novel [*The Sprites*] ... has been written with a lot of ingenuity, embellishment and good taste. Its appeal lies in the amusing diversity of the events and the originality of the characters. It is typical of the Countess de Murat, who was so well-known in the intermingled, gallant society of the past.[63]

Another reason for the lasting appeal of Murat's novel was the fact that it had originated during a period of literary experimentation when all genres were opened up to accommodate new themes and techniques. It was precisely the openness of that literary aesthetic that made *The Sprites of Kernosy Castle* an easy target for expansion and interpolation by a new generation of novelists. This happened at a time when Murat's works seem to have enjoyed a resurgence in popularity, thanks to a second vogue of French fairy-tale publication that occurred between 1730 and 1758.[64] As Lewis C. Seifert and Domna C. Stanton have noted, although the few late seventeenth-century critics who had bothered to comment on the genre were convinced that by 1702 the vogue would be "banished forever" (in the words of Abbé Jean-Baptiste Morvan de Bellegarde), public interest in fairy tales did not fade away. Instead, new tales published in the novelistic style pioneered by d'Aulnoy would continue to be produced for another half century, a corpus that would be reprinted multiple times in the decades leading up to the French Revolution.[65]

Toward the end of the second vogue of French fairy-tale production, Marie-Madeleine de Lubert (1702–1785), a *conteuse* who published more than a dozen novels and fairy tales between 1737 and 1758 and who was known for her devotion to the form and style of the tales pioneered by d'Aulnoy from the original vogue, decided to revise two novels that had originally been penned by female writers of the first vogue period: Louise de Bossigny, Countess d'Auneuil's *La Tyrannie des fées détruite* (The Fairies' Tyranny Destroyed, 1702)[66] and *The Sprites*.

---

63. Nicolas Lenglet Du Fresnoy, *De l'usage des romans, où l'on fait voir leur utilité et leurs différents caractères* (Amsterdam: Vve Poilras, 1734), 2:101.

64. Robert, *Le Conte de fées littéraire en France*, 321.

65. Seifert and Stanton, *Enchanted Eloquence*, 34–36. A notable exception to the novelistic-style fairy tales published during the majority of the eighteenth century are those of Jeanne-Marie Leprince de Beaumont (1711–1780), whose tales follow Perrault's model. Leprince de Beaumont is best known for her "now-classic" version of "Beauty and the Beast" (Seifert and Stanton, *Enchanted Eloquence*, 36).

66. The new version of d'Auneuil's novel appeared in Paris in 1756 under the title *La Tyrannie des fées détruite, ou l'Origine de la machine de Marli* with the publisher Hochereau (not to be confused with the 1752 edition of the novel, which is faithful to the original). See further Blandine Gonssollin's review of *Contes*, by Mademoiselle de Lubert, ed. Aurélie Zygel-Basso, *Féeries: Études sur le conte merveilleux, XVIIe–XIVe siècle* 4 (2007), 258, https://doi.org/10.4000/feeries.473. On Lubert's literary career, see Mademoiselle de Lubert, *Contes*, ed. Aurélie Zygel-Basso, Bibliothèque des Génies et des Fées, vol. 14 (Paris: Honoré Champion, 2005), 7–66.

When she worked on Murat's novel, in addition to doing substantial rewriting of the novel proper (mostly minor changes of stylistic nature), she added to it two fairy tales of her own composition: "Peau d'ours" ("Bearskin"; in volume 1) and "Etoilette" ("Little Star"; in volume 2). She published this "new and improved" edition in 1753, announcing on the title page that the original novel had been "revised, corrected and augmented with two [fairy] tales." Her version was so successful that a number of other editions appeared both in France and abroad in the years that followed, including a pirated edition bearing the title *Le Séjour des Amans ou les Lutins du Château de Kernosy* (The lovers' sojourn or the sprites of Kernosy Castle), which was published anonymously in Leiden in 1773.

Lubert, in reversing Murat's decision to eliminate fairy tales from her final work of fiction, presumably wished to re-problematize the role of the marvelous supernatural in a comparatively realistic type of novel and perhaps also wished to pay homage to another important work from the first wave of fairy tales, d'Aulnoy's *Don Gabriel Ponce de Leon*.[67] Lubert not only assigns the telling of the fairy tales to the novel's most refined characters but also provides discussions where people praise the genre and do not bother to inquire whether the supernatural elements are real. Her goal was to show that it was possible to successfully resurrect a popular salon pastime from half a century earlier with its original intentions intact: to separate the nobility from the bourgeoisie and to reinforce essentialist notions of aristocratic identity. In other words, in the tales by women writers from the first vogue, the happy endings always legitimated noble status, whereas in Perrault's tales and in eighteenth-century fairy tales, it was common to see social mobility in that bourgeois characters, particularly women, were rewarded for good behavior by being permitted to marry into the nobility. These were principles that Murat appears to have questioned starting in 1699, when her fairy-less fairy tale in *A Trip to the Country* linked nobility to merit, rather than to birthright—an authorial move that anticipated the more powerful and direct critiques of social institutions that would take place during the French Enlightenment.

The Lubert reworking maintained its popularity right up to the eve of the French Revolution. In 1788, her version of *The Sprites* was included in volume 35 of the well-known literary anthology *Voyages Imaginaires, Songes, Visions et Romans Cabalistiques* (Imaginary voyages, dreams, visions and cabalistic novels). Clearly, the novel's portrayal of a cultivated and charming aristocracy, later combined with supernatural tales, still resonated with a large percentage of the

---

67. In attributing to the viscountess a passion for fairy tales, which is not found in Murat's original version, Lubert was presumably inspired by Juana, the character who corresponds to the viscountess in d'Aulnoy's *Don Gabriel Ponce de Leon*. Juana not only enjoys reading fairy tales and hearing others recite them, but is also capable of reciting them, herself. Juana praises the fairy-tale genre at great length, insisting on its literary merit and appeal to people of good taste, as well as to its value as entertainment. In Lubert's edition, the viscountess echoes Juana when she delivers a brief praise of the genre following the recitation of the second fairy tale, "Etoilette."

reading public nearly eighty years after its first edition. As the 1788 editors describe the novel when advertising it to the public:

> This little novel is very agreeable and well-written; the scenes presented in it are amusing, cheerful, varied and embellished with delightful episodes, the most interesting of which is the story concerning Madame de Briance. The two fairy tales that have been added by Mademoiselle de Lubert are also well embellished. We will say nothing of these two ladies, famous for their fairy tales which can be found in the *Cabinet des Fées*;[68] of note, those of Madame de Murat are in the first volume and those of Mademoiselle de Lubert are in volume 33 of the collection: we refer our readers to it.[69]

Although the editors evidently saw the addition of Lubert's fairy tales as a selling point for their new edition, they also took pains to make sure their readers would understand that the supernatural is treated with skepticism in the context of the novel itself, clarifying for anyone who might misinterpret the novel's content on account of its title: "[In this work] it only appears that the events are supernatural; there is nothing but fake magic; or to better explain ourselves, in *The Sprites of Kernosy Castle* one only comes across false enchantments, imposter magicians and wizards whose sorcery is nothing more than a clever ruse to achieve their desired ends."[70] While the combination of frivolity and skepticism apparent in *The Sprites* and in other leisure novels of the period clearly held enduring appeal, it is likely that the same features that made the subgenre so attractive to eighteenth-century readers ultimately contributed to the obscurity in which these types of works, including Murat's, have languished ever since. *The Sprites* has not been reissued since 1788.

Although Murat's novels have not generated much scholarly interest until now, it should be noted that her fairy tales have finally been accorded the recognition they deserve. A complete edition of her tales in French appears in volume 3 of the *Bibliothèque des Génies et des Fées*, and some of her tales have been translated into English and included in anthologies of French or worldwide fairy tales, including, more recently, Christine A. Jones and Jennifer Schacker's *Marvelous Transformations*, Seifert and Stanton's *Enchanted Eloquence*, and Nora Martin Peterson's *Miracles of Love*. A modern English translation of *A Trip to the Country* appeared in 2011 with Wayne State University Press, and a modern French version of the same novel appeared in 2014 with the Presses Universitaires de

---

68. *Le Cabinet des fées* (The fairies' private study) is a forty-one-volume collection of seventeenth- and eighteenth-century French fairy tales and exotic tales, published by Charles-Joseph Mayer in 1785–86.
69. Preface (Avertissement) for Madame de Murat, "Les Lutins du château de Kernosy," in *Voyages imaginaires, songes, visions et romans cabalistiques*, vol. 35 (Amsterdam, Paris: Garnier Frères, 1788), xi–xii.
70. Preface (Avertissement), *Voyages imaginaires, songes, visions et romans cabalistiques*, x–xii.

Rennes. A modern edition of her *Journal for Mademoiselle de Menou* appeared in 2016 with Classiques Garnier. Recent critical attention to Murat's novels includes the role of these works in contributing to the seventeenth-century phenomenon of "rococo fiction" (Stedman) and their contributions to literary representations of the decorative arts at the turn of the eighteenth century (Bloom). In short, Murat has emerged from obscurity to take her place as one of the more thoughtful figures from a pivotal generation in French cultural history.

Conclusion

Murat was a writer who challenged established conventions both in life and in art. She was not afraid to experiment, particularly when it came to the innovation of new genres like the literary fairy tale, the literary ghost story, and the short-form leisure novel. Even more significantly, however, Murat was also not afraid to undo her own innovations, as she did in *A Trip to the Country* and in *The Sprites of Kernosy Castle*, when she progressively eliminated the marvelous supernatural associated with the fairy tale, for reasons both aesthetic (desire to use only realistic means to resolve a novelistic plot) and ideological (pre-Enlightenment skepticism about all forms of the supernatural).

In *The Sprites*, Murat undertakes what appears to be her final and her most significant gesture of literary innovation and reversal. After showing her ability to master the short-form, hybrid leisure novel with *A Trip to the Country*, she abandons the loose structure of this subgenre by weaving *The Sprites'* four primary interpolated narratives back into the main plot, resolving both main and subplots simultaneously in the final, unanticipated conclusion. The novel demonstrates the virtuosity of one of the late seventeenth century's most popular female writers while foreshadowing one of the dominant trends of the French Enlightenment novel, in which hybridity would be abandoned in favor of more unified, linear plots. As such, the original edition of the novel provides important documentation about a little understood moment of literary and artistic transition.

A Note on the Translation

We have decided to translate the original 1710 version of the novel as written by Murat, the text of which has never been reissued. As we have argued, it has genuine artistic merit as well as great importance for the history of the French novel and for the development of pre-Enlightenment thought. At the same time, however, we felt it desirable to append the two fairy tales later added to the novel by Lubert, since they are enjoyable to read and testify to changes in taste and ideology in the mid-eighteenth century. We are pleased to make these delightful and thought-provoking works available for the first time to the English-speaking reader in the Appendices.

The Sprites of Kernosy Castle *(1710)*

by Henriette-Julie de Castelnau, Countess de Murat

La Maison-Fort. (XIV siècle.)

Figure 1. "La Maison-Fort (XIV siècle)," engraving by Edmond Bussière (1807?–1842), representing the Chateau de la Maison-Fort in Bitry, France, near Saint-Amand. [Joseph-Napoléon] Morellet, [Jean-Claude] Barat, and E. [Edmond] Bussière, *Le Nivernois, album historique et pittoresque*, vol. 2, ed. E. [Edmond] Bussière (Nevers, France: E. Bussière, 1840), p. 71.

The Sprites of Kernosy Castle[1]
Historical Novel

Part One

The Viscountess de Kernosy used to spend almost the entire year in her castle, which she esteemed to be the most charming residence in all of Brittany. It is a noble fiefdom, of which her ancestors successively bore the name, where she herself had been raised since her most tender youth and whose advantageous location offered from every side something unique and very agreeable to the eyes. Her two nieces, both of them very pleasant and young, lived in this place with her and found it quite unfortunate to spend their finest days in an abode so solitary and so far from worldly society, being ten leagues from the closest city and a quarter league from the village.[2]

This castle is an antiquated building, which nonetheless conserves an air of grandeur. The first thing to be seen there are iron doors, enormous towers, deep moats, drawbridges half in ruin; followed by large galleries, totally unadorned, spacious halls and rooms whose windows are so narrow that the daylight can scarcely enter through them; in the summertime, grass grows on the terraces as high as in the middle of a field. In sum, this castle is precisely of the same model as those to which it is said that spirits return. This was also the common opinion of those who lived in that area; for more than a hundred years, they had told extraordinary tales about it. The young Kernosy ladies had known all the stories of the castle's sprites since their childhood, their governesses had told them the tales about them a thousand times, but although they had lived in that place for most of their lives, they had never seen or heard anything that could persuade them that there was any truth to this popular belief.

One evening when the old viscountess had gone to bed at a very early hour, the young Kernosy ladies retired to their bedchamber. They sat down beside the fire, not wishing to go to bed so early.

"What fine weather to be in the countryside," said Mademoiselle de Kernosy, listening to the wind that was whistling about the windows. "In truth, I can no longer prevent myself from dying of the boredom my aunt causes us."

---

1. Murat may have drawn her inspiration for the name of this fictional castle from the medieval Kernisy manor, which is also located in Brittany near Quimper along the Roman road to Douarnenez. According to the Archeological Society of Finistère, during the seventeenth century, the manor belonged to the Le Baud family and was renovated with the addition of numerous dormers and a pediment over the front door in the classical style of Louis XIV.

2. At the end of the seventeenth century, a French league or "lieue de Paris" equaled 12,000 feet, or roughly 2.4 miles.

"You are right, dear sister," replied Mademoiselle de Saint-Urbain (which was the younger sister's name). "I am in a state of despair over being here, and my despair increases," she added with a smile, "when I imagine that in Paris at this very hour people are running from one ball to the next, while we remain in this wretched castle, besieged by snow and with nothing to amuse us."

This charming girl was about to elaborate on all the advantages of Paris during carnival season[3] when all of a sudden Mademoiselle de Kernosy jumped from her chair, uttering a loud cry. "What is the matter, sister?" [Saint-Urbain] asked, shocked by her actions. "Look, look!" Kernosy replied, all in a fright. Saint-Urbain looked and saw a letter attached to a small silver chain that was descending down the chimney, being held up high enough to prevent the paper from catching fire. "What?" said Saint-Urbain. "You have gotten so scared on account of a note? I thought you had seen some terrifying apparition. Let's see," she continued, taking the fire tongs to retrieve the note without burning herself, "let's see right away what this is about." "How can you consider taking that piece of paper?" exclaimed Kernosy, trying to stop her. "You can't be serious! Leave it alone, dear sister, I beg you, and let's call someone." "Then let's call my aunt," replied Saint-Urbain. "She will scare off the ghost." "Don't laugh!" replied Kernosy. "I am terribly afraid." "But of what?" replied Saint-Urbain. "You can very well see that the ghost is not in here because he is taking pains to write to us." Having finished these words, she took the paper with the fire tongs and opened it that very moment, in spite of Kernosy, who was dying of fright. "The spirit's handwriting is very legible," said Saint-Urbain, examining the note. "Let's have a look at what he wants to tell us." She read it and found these words.

Both of you are too charming to spend all of your time alone in such a solitary place as this. Anyone who has seen you would find it impossible for his heart to remain insensitive both to your beauty and your troubles. Entrust us with the task of attending to your pleasures, and we will do all that we can to delight you; we will succeed without a doubt if it would seem to you that tender and faithful hearts are worthy of your attention.

THE CASTLE SPRITES

"What's all of this?" said Mademoiselle de Kernosy, who had had time to reassure herself a little. "I don't know," responded Saint-Urbain. "But we are being

---

3. The Paris carnival season began with the Feast of the Epiphany on January 6 and lasted several months until the beginning of Lent, the date of which could vary by up to thirty-five days. During this time, Parisians celebrated by attending operas, balls, and theater productions, many of which were written specifically to celebrate this period in the liturgical year, as theatrical activity was banned during Lent. We will later learn that the girls had attended Carnival the previous year.

promised pleasures and faithful lovers. I am of the opinion that we accept this offer."

Kernosy did not dare take a single step in her bedroom, and Saint-Urbain, having looked into the chimney, no longer saw the small chain. She told that to her sister. "It has disappeared!" Kernosy cried out. "Let's call our servants!" At that moment, a spark fell from the candle that was beside the paper, which was already very dry from having been suspended for some time in the chimney; the paper easily caught fire and was consumed by it swiftly enough.

This very natural accident almost made Kernosy faint, and even Saint-Urbain lost all assurance. She summoned their chambermaids, who were sleeping in a tower quite nearby and who came running. Saint-Urbain told them, all in a fright, that her sister had just taken ill. They attributed her fright to this fainting spell. They immediately threw water on Mademoiselle Kernosy's face and put her to bed, and a little while later she felt much better, but she ordered her maidservants to remain in her room; Saint-Urbain went to sleep beside her in order for them to feel more secure, if they should again hear something.

"You were right not to tell our maidservants about the fright we had," Kernosy whispered to her sister. "Tomorrow it would have been spread all over, and as we no longer have the note, people would have accused us of seeing things." Saint-Urbain agreed that they should not talk about their adventure; finally, having been reassured by the arrival of daylight, they fell asleep.

Neither the one nor the other was awakened until noon, by the noise of a carriage and horses, which could be heard in the courtyard of the castle. "What can this noise be?" Kernosy asked. "Maybe it's the pleasures that the sprite is sending us," responded Saint-Urbain. "Oh, dear sister!" replied Kernosy. "I have still not completely recovered from my fright; if it's possible, let's forget the sprite." At that moment, one of the viscountess's maidservants entered and informed them that a theater troupe had just arrived, that they had brought with them a letter for the viscountess, that she had read it, and that after that she had told the actors to remain in the castle.

"How can this be!" they exclaimed as they got up. "Our aunt would like them to stay? There absolutely must be some supernatural power intervening." They had barely finished these words when they heard more noise in the courtyard. They sent for word to find out what it was, and someone came to tell them that a troupe of violinists and musicians had just arrived.[4] Then Saint-Urbain said to her sister, locking arms with her, "Let's go see what these people look like." They went to the bedchamber of the viscountess, who, as soon as they had entered, spoke to them with an air of joy that they had never seen before on her: "Well, my young

---

4. Professional theater troupes employed musicians to play selections of their choice before the play began and between acts. These small orchestras generally consisted of only a group of violinists, but for more elaborate plays the troupes often added wind instruments (oboes and sometimes bassoons). In the novel, the orchestra will also provide music for balls and for purely musical entertainment.

ladies, you will no longer have cause to complain about your boredom in this area. Now it seems that you have quite enough entertainment arriving. But what can be the matter with you?" she asked, seeing the frightened Kernosy. "There you are, in a disagreeable mood at precisely the wrong moment." "I had a fainting spell last night," Kernosy replied, "but I'm sure that nothing will come of it." "Ah, dear aunt," interrupted Saint-Urbain, "from what country are so many pleasures arriving for us?" "You are too curious," responded the viscountess with a chilly demeanor. "Leave me alone, I have things to do. Go and see the preparations that are being made for this evening." "My aunt is most assuredly the sprites' confidante," Saint-Urbain whispered to her sister. "You see that she is keeping their secret." They walked into a large hall, where they found workmen busy erecting a theater and arranging decorations, which seemed to them to be quite beautiful and in good taste. From there, they went to the chapel of the castle to perform their devotions,[5] and some time afterward the servants came to call them for dinner.[6] As soon as they left the table, they returned to their bedchamber to change out of their morning attire and to get dressed in honor of the troupe. Saint-Urbain found a note in her pocket. She read it to Kernosy. Here is what it contained:

You see that we have kept our word to you; we seek to entertain you, and we have found the secret to softening the bad temper of your insufferable aunt. Mademoiselle de Kernosy's fainting spell has given us much worry; be not afraid, love should never be frightening when one is young and beautiful.

"These sprites are quite gallant," she said, as she finished reading the note. "But this note does not scare me at all; it did not arrive on its own as the other one did, and someone could easily have put it in my pocket while I was watching the painter who was touching up one of the decorations. Let's see what all this will amount to; but let's be careful that this note does not catch fire as did the first one, which scared us so much. We should lock it away in a safe place; maybe one day we will recognize the handwriting on it." The two sisters spent the rest of the day at their dressing table; and their beauty, with this little assistance, was so astonishing that it was esteemed that they could have gone on to dazzle at any of the most splendid parties in the world.

Mademoiselle de Kernosy was blonde. Her complexion was of a brilliant whiteness, the shape of her face was agreeable, and she had large blue eyes that could penetrate to the depths of the soul; her gracious smile revealed beautiful teeth and even increased the radiance of her mouth, whose lips were of a color as

---

5. The sisters likely attended the Sexts, or "Sixth Hour" services, which take place at noon as part of the daily cycle of services held in accordance with the canonical hours. During the Sexts, people meditated on the theme of Christ's crucifixion, which was believed to have happened at this hour, according to the Roman Catholic tradition.

6. The midday meal, usually the main meal of the day.

bright as coral. Her bosom and her hands further enhanced all these advantages from nature, and so many beautiful qualities could doubtlessly cause a person to fall in love; but her tall stature, accompanied by a noble air, were imposing to such a degree that a person was able to look upon her only with feelings of respect. And her serenity of spirit made people notice in all her words an accuracy that can be acquired only by worldly experience and by a perfect knowledge of fine literature.

The young Saint-Urbain had a round face, a light complexion, although a little bit darker than that of her sister; her hair was black, and her eyes of the same color were almond-shaped and of surprising intensity; her mouth, small and gracious, contained beautiful teeth, white as ivory and perfectly straight. An air of ease, which emanated from her entire being, did not prevent a person from noticing that she had as a majestic a bearing when she danced as when she walked; and although she was not as tall as Kernosy, her figure was so admirably proportioned that one would have had difficulty making up one's mind to choose one over the other of these two sisters. Her inviting manners, cheerful by nature, inspired joy in people's hearts the moment that she appeared among them. She had quick repartees full of cleverness. Indeed, quite often she found the way to animate a languishing conversation by abruptly uttering something bold. At first, one might have said that she did this without thinking, but she supported her remarks with a reasoning that was so solid that never was there anything that escaped from her mouth that did not show good sense, that did not edify, and that was not worthy of her high birth.

These two charming sisters had not yet left their bedchamber when someone came to tell them that a man on horseback had just announced to the viscountess that on this very day three ladies from the neighboring area were expected to arrive at her castle. "So much the better!" Saint-Urbain said. "I will find the play more agreeable if there are a lot of people in the audience. Do give us the names of these ladies." "It is the Marquise de Briance, the Countess de Salgue, and the Baroness de Sugarde," one of their maidservants replied. "This is very good company indeed," said Mademoiselle de Kernosy, "but it seems to me that it would be even better if the brothers of the Marquise de Briance were in the region. They will not be returning so soon; when one is in Paris, surrounded by pleasures, one rarely remembers the ladies one has left behind in the provinces." "That depends," laughed Saint-Urbain. "Do you think that in that city the Count and the Chevalier[7] de Livry can find very many ladies more amiable than we are? I clearly recall that we did not find such a great number when we were there six months ago."

---

7. "Chevalier" is the official designation for the younger son of a titled nobleman who is not in the regular line of succession to the title. There is no equivalent title in English, but men of similar rank could be referred to as "Sir." The literal translation of "chevalier" is "knight."

At that moment, the marquise's entourage entered the courtyard, obliging the two sisters to go downstairs to greet them. The Viscountess de Kernosy had been the first to rush out, dolled up like a young person; her evening dress, which she insisted was amaranth brown, was in fact made of velvet the color of a blazing fire. The ladies went up to her apartment and seemed amazed to see a theater, which had just been erected in the great hall. "A troupe of actors arrived here this morning," the viscountess told them, "and I asked them to stay in order to amuse my nieces during this carnival season." She was praised for her obligingness, and the entire company made their way into her bedchamber.[8]

The viscountess was almost sixty years old; she wanted to be beautiful, even though she had not been so even in her youth. Never has there been a more ill-humored woman. She was very rich, widowed five years earlier, and her plan to remarry had not yet been executed because she had not yet found anyone, or so she said, "who knew how to love well enough." She would have wanted a hero like Amadis, for Galaor seemed too fickle to her;[9] Alexander did not love tenderly enough, and Caesar had far too many mistresses.[10] In short, she was looking for an Amadis, and not having found one in Brittany, she had taken a trip to Paris, where not having found one there either, she returned to her castle to wait for fortune to send her a knight worthy of being her lover.

As she was rich, of high social status, and as she owned the most beautiful lands in the province, a number of lords from this region hastened around her, but it is easy to see how a person who absolutely insisted on a hero could find these provincials hardly gallant, for the first thing they spoke about was marriage.[11]

The younger Kernosy ladies were at the mercy of this capricious person. They had lost their mother as children, and their father, upon his death, had

---

8. During this period, it was not uncommon for aristocratic women to entertain guests in their bedchambers, as rooms were multipurpose and beds could be moved out of the way when entertaining guests. The practice was standard in Parisian salons and was particularly common during the winter, as bedchambers were usually warmer than other rooms in the house.

9. Amadis was the hero of one of the most popular chivalric romances, *Amadís de Gaula* (*Amadis of Gaul*), written by the Spanish author Garci Rodríguez de Montalvo. Published posthumously in 1508, the work was translated by Nicolas Herberay des Essarts and met with great success in France, thanks in part to the belief that the protagonist was of Gallic origin. Galaor, the younger brother of Amadis and an eminent knight in his own right, is often the companion in arms of his older brother. However, unlike Amadis, he is not a model of fidelity of love; he has multiple brief liaisons and even fathers a son with one of his paramours before settling down and marrying a beautiful queen.

10. Alexander the Great was known for having several wives at the same time, and Julius Caesar, who was married several times, was known for abandoning one of his wives merely because he suspected her of infidelity. These are thus not models of gallantry.

11. The viscountess shares the exaggerated ideas of the heroines of Molière's comedy *Les Précieuses ridicules* (*The Pretentious Young Ladies*, 1659); like her, these heroines are unable to separate the adventures of gallant novels from reality and as such are unable to find a realistic marriage partner.

obliged them in his will to remain under the tutelage of his sister-in-law, the Viscountess de Kernosy, and so these agreeable girls had been living with her for the past four years.[12]

The viscountess was in no hurry to marry them off. She had refused the offers of all of the potential suitors who had presented themselves, even though there had been some prospects that were highly advantageous; one was not worthy enough, another was unattractive, another was not of a suitable age;[13] in short, no one could be found to suit her whims. In the meantime, she was peacefully enjoying the inheritance of her two nieces, which was quite a considerable sum of money.

This capricious person loved to play the role of the great lady of the house on her turf; the manner in which she received the company showed clearly enough that large expenditures did not intimidate her. While people were conversing, she commanded that a light meal be prepared where all of the most exquisite seasonal foods in the castle were served. Her orders were executed in such a punctual manner that everything was found to be ready for the play at the very moment that each person arose from the table.

All of the ladies made their way into the hall. There, they found a small and well-lit theater. The stage was decorated to represent a magnificent bedchamber. At last, all of the high-ranking people of the same sex took their seats.[14] The servants of the viscountess, together with all the people who lived in the area, and who had rushed over upon hearing about the party, made up the standing-room section and were easy to please.[15] Eight violins and four oboes played the overture, and the actors began the play, which was called *The Mischievous Spirit*.[16] The subject of this play is a lady with whom a knight falls in love without knowing her identity. He happens to be a friend of the lady's brother, he stays with the brother, and the lady makes use of a door hidden behind the tapestry of his bedchamber

---

12. If the viscountess was raised in this castle, she is presumably a relative of the heroines' father. The fact that she, as a widow, bears the title of Viscountess de Kernosy indicates that she had been married to the heroines' father's next of kin, who inherited the title of Viscount after their father died.

13. Most men during the early modern period did not become financially independent until the age of thirty.

14. It was not common practice to separate men and women in a theater audience, except in the case of the parterre (standing room area), which was reserved for men. It is likely that the three noblewomen who came to visit, and who were not accompanied by a husband or another member of their families, decided to sit together and that the members of the Kernosy family sat with them.

15. It would not have been customary for members of the aristocracy to open their private homes to the public. However, this was occasionally done for court spectacles, particularly in conjunction with a special occasion (in this case, carnival season).

16. The play being performed is *La Dame invisible* (The invisible lady), a five-act comedy, also known under the title *L'Esprit follet* (The mischievous spirit) by Noël Le Breton, whose stage name and pen name was Hauteroche (1685).

to bring him letters and presents and tries to persuade him that it is a spirit who is in love with him. The valet of the lover, who is easy to scare, is quite persuaded of the spirit's power, and his fright is naturally and agreeably expressed.

This play was rather well performed, and since it had a lot of connections to the adventure that had happened to the two sisters the night before, they looked at each other several times but were unable to say anything to one another; the Marquise de Briance and the Countess de Salgue were seated in between them. At the end of the play, the orchestra played some excellent pieces from *The Triumph of Love*.[17]

The company moved into the adjoining room, where they were served a magnificent supper; the viscountess had designed the menu, and it was the only thing that she knew how to do perfectly. The conversation was lively; the baroness and Saint-Urbain were saying that a ball was lacking from the pleasures of that day. They were still supporting their argument with enthusiasm when a man-servant appeared who came to speak to the viscountess. "Let us go, my ladies," she said to them a moment after the meal was finished. "If you will, please make your way with me to the small gallery." The company was pleasantly surprised to see illuminated chandeliers, violins, oboes, and several groups of people wearing masks.[18] There were some who were very good-looking, and whom the ladies did not believe they had seen among the actors who had performed *The Mischievous Spirit*.

One of them, dressed as a Greek, came to take the hand of the viscountess, who began the ball with a courante. As she finished, she assured everyone that she would have better success at the minuet and at other less difficult dances.[19]

Kernosy and Saint-Urbain performed wonders; never had anyone seen such agility and precision; their dances were accompanied by every sort of charm that a Breton woman knows how to project. The masked man who was dressed as a Greek almost never left the viscountess's side, to the great astonishment of her nieces. In the meantime, a handsome masked man came up to Mademoiselle de Kernosy; his frock coat was made of black velvet in the Spanish style; he had feathers the color of fire in his hat; he had a handsome figure; he had just finished dancing, and the subtle gracefulness of his footwork, accompanied by his astonishing agility, had charmed everyone.

"The castle sprites are quite unfortunate to have terrified you," he said to Kernosy. "But tonight you look so beautiful that they can flatter themselves that your health is perfect." Kernosy wanted to make a hurried departure upon hearing talk of the sprites again. "Wait a moment, I beg you," said the Spaniard, trying

17. *Le Triomphe de l'amour* (The triumph of love), an elaborate ballet created for the court of Louis XIV in 1681, was among the great successes of Jean-Baptiste Lully, one of the most important figures in the creation of French opera.

18. Masquerade balls were a feature of the carnival season.

19. The minuet did not require the same rapid footwork as the courante (at least in some versions).

to stop her. "I will explain last night's adventures." He removed his mask, and Kernosy, upon recognizing him as the Count de Livry, brother of the Marquise de Briance, was almost as surprised as if she had seen the very sprite whose apparition had made her faint.

However, this sudden shock brought on an emotion that was quite different from that of fear. She no longer thought of trying to escape. "Why, it's you, Count!" she said to him. "And what reasons can you have for appearing in this disguise in a place where you are just as welcome as your sister?" "I have too many answers to the questions you ask to dare to give them here," replied the count, "and yet I am dying of impatience to enlighten you; I beg you, upon leaving here, do me the favor of coming to my sister's bedchamber. Will you go there, Mademoiselle?" he continued, seeing that Kernosy was lost in a daydream. "Can I flatter myself with being able to see you for fifteen minutes without suspicious onlookers? How many things I have to tell you!" "The marquise is too close of a friend," replied Kernosy, blushing, "for me to refuse to go and be enlightened in her presence about all that is transpiring here."

At that moment, the viscountess came to take the Spaniard away to dance, interrupting the conversation. Kernosy wanted very much to tell Saint-Urbain about her adventure, but she had little doubt that her sister had already been informed of it when she saw kneeling beside her a short, masked man dressed like Scaramouche[20] who was performing wonderfully on his guitar. His figure was thin and perfectly handsome; a large quantity of beautiful and naturally curly black hair made it easy for Kernosy to recognize him as the Chevalier de Livry. She left to him the task of explaining to Saint-Urbain the identity of the castle's sprites.

The ball did not end until after midnight. Madame de Kernosy immediately took the countess to her apartment. Saint-Urbain accompanied the baroness back to hers, and Kernosy, who had been a friend of the marquise for a long time, accompanied her to her bedchamber. Saint-Urbain was too impatient to find much enjoyment from the baroness's company; she wanted to meet up with the others, who as she knew were to be in the marquise's room. She paid a few respects and went straightaway to join them. She had scarcely entered the room when the Count and the Chevalier de Livry arrived, having quickly changed clothes.

At first the conversation was tumultuous. People asked a thousand questions without giving one another time to respond. But finally, Kernosy, having begged the count to give her a full account of the plan that had caused them to come incognito to a place where everyone was among their friends, [and] as there was no one in the room who could be suspected of disloyalty, each of them took a place beside the fire and the count began his story as follows:

---

20. A stock character of the Italian commedia dell'arte who was made popular in France by Tiberio Fiorilli during the second half of the seventeenth century. Originally a jester, this character type became more refined over time, and he often appeared playing the guitar.

"It has been about a year since we had the honor of seeing you for the first time," he said, addressing his words to Mademoiselle de Kernosy. "One remembers a sight that charming for a long time: you came to my sister's home with your aunt; we were just returning from the army, my brother and I, and at that time we had no other desire than to go to Paris and to spend all the time that we could there, while on leave from our regiments.[21] The pleasure of seeing you made us change our plans; we could think about nothing else than remaining in a region where we hardly believed, upon arriving, that we would be able to spend eight days before dying of boredom. I took the liberty of declaring what I was thinking to Mademoiselle de Kernosy, and I do not doubt that the chevalier also explained himself to Mademoiselle de Saint-Urbain."

"That is not your story to tell, Count," interrupted Saint-Urbain, smiling. "You should leave the chevalier something to tell, in case it also strikes his fancy to recount his adventures." The marquise laughed at Saint-Urbain's idea; and after Kernosy begged the count to continue, he took up his speech in this way:

"Therefore, I will no longer talk about Mademoiselle de Saint-Urbain, because she has forbidden me to do so. Mademoiselle de Kernosy received the tokens of my respectful attachment with a chilliness that would have caused any other heart but mine to freeze over. I continued to show her gestures of tenderness and respect, but she seemed only faintly moved by them.

"If Mademoiselle de Saint-Urbain permitted me," he continued laughing, "I would say that the chevalier was either luckier or less in love than I; for it is certain that he seemed happier." "You judge based on flimsy appearances," interrupted Saint-Urbain. "You are only too happy that I can take a joke." "I plan to tell my story as well," interjected the chevalier, "and we shall see whether I am unable to make such reflections when my turn comes."

"Be quiet, chevalier!" said the marquise. "There are a thousand things that I do not already know that I wish to learn from this narrative." "We were summoned to the court for some obligatory business," continued the count. "We were constrained to go, and never had I felt such sorrow. The Kernosy ladies had returned to their home; their aunt had taken them there the same day that I received the cruel letter that forced me to leave this region. I flattered myself that I would at least have the satisfaction of saying farewell to Mademoiselle de Kernosy; but my sister informed me that the viscountess did not allow her charming nieces to receive visits from people our age.

"The marquise may well remember the eagerness with which I begged her to bring me to Madame de Kernosy's home, but she had a lingering fever and was as unmoved by my pleas as if she had been seriously ill." "It is true that I behaved

---

21. Since the story is apparently set at roughly the same time as the novel's composition, the war in question is likely the War of the Spanish Succession (1701–1714). Royal officers typically had permission to return to France during the winter if a ceasefire occurred during that season.

that way," replied the marquise, "and I would like to tell you the reason why: I was afraid that if you saw such charming people again you would be slow to do your duty on account of your love."

"Therefore we left, the chevalier and I," said the count, picking up where he had left off, "and we barely said four words to each other along the way. I wrote to Mademoiselle de Kernosy on my way off, and I left a manservant behind to make sure that the letter would be delivered to her. The chevalier also entrusted him with a letter from him to Mademoiselle de Saint-Urbain; we impatiently awaited his return to Paris. Finally, he arrived and assured us that he had delivered our letters, and that the Kernosy ladies had refused to respond to them.

"A few days later, this manservant disappeared and took one of our horses with him. This action made us doubt that he had faithfully delivered our letters; we were thinking about going back to find out for ourselves when all the colonels received an order to return to their regiments. We were obligated to obey; this region was too far away for us to be able to pass by it on our way off and we no longer had time to spare. We left, overcome with grief, and I carried away in my heart the beautiful image that Mademoiselle de Kernosy had imprinted upon it.

"I wrote to my sister to beg her to find out, if at all possible, what had become of our letters. She sent word that she was unable to obtain any information for me because Madame de Kernosy had gone to Paris, and she had taken her two charming nieces with her. This mishap of leaving Paris, precisely when these charming ladies were about to arrive, increased my suffering.

"Upon arriving at our regiment, we came across Tadillac, who is a close relative of mine, a gallant man with pleasing features and a very cheerful disposition; we saw each other often, we told him of our sorrows by acquainting him with the viscountess's personality; he wanted to come up with a way to approach this castle without scaring her; and after having used quite a bit of imagination, he settled on a plan to make her fall in love with him.

"He is not rich, [and] the hope of gaining access to Madame de Kernosy's wealth appealed to him; he begged me in all seriousness to help him to succeed in this enterprise, and said that in exchange, he would facilitate my happiness. I told him that the viscountess had been unable to bring herself to remarry because she had not yet found a knight in shining armor, nor a heart capable of loving with refinement.

"'Leave it to me,' replied the Baron de Tadillac, 'I will appear before her as a hero out of a novel, and I will have even more refinement than she can imagine. There will be no great harm,' he added, 'in pushing things to the point where they become ridiculous, for this would only be even more in accordance with our love story.'

"This plan amused us during the entire campaign; the baron was delighted with it, but as for me, I was truly worried because I was truly in love. The troops were quartered for the winter, and at last we set off to return to this region in an incredible state of joy. We arrived at my sister's home ten days ago; it was night. We forbade her servants to speak of our arrival; I asked the marquise for news about you with an eagerness that caused her to surmise that absence had not diminished my love.

"We concerted with the baron to see how we could gain free access to this castle; he went to Rennes to find some actors and some musicians; he brought them to my sister's home by stagecoach; and during that time, having won over one of your servants, it was easy for me upon the baron's return to carry out this mischievous prank that so scared Mademoiselle de Kernosy.

"We made a small hole in the floorboards of the room above in order to lower the note and the little chain. The baron wrote the note because no one was familiar with his handwriting; he executed this enterprise quite well, and I was in a state of despair when I realized, on account of the noise that we heard, that Mademoiselle de Kernosy had fallen ill. I would have gone at that very moment to beg her pardon a thousand times for our silliness if I had not been afraid of revealing myself to her servants, whom we heard in her room and who did not leave.

"We went to rejoin our men in a village that is about two leagues from here; we sent our actors from that place this morning; one among them delivered a letter from the baron to Madame de Kernosy. This is what it contained:

To the Beautiful Viscountess de Kernosy, from an Unknown Lover
I first saw you in Paris six months ago, madam. Such a view! My heart is unable to forget it. I followed you to all the performances, but as I am as respectful a lover as I am a tender and faithful one, I did not dare to declare my love to you. My duty called me back to the army; it was with pleasure that I pursued glory because I know that you esteem it. Love has called me to return to you; therefore I come, madam, to attempt to make myself worthy of pleasing you through my attentions and my affection. Love wishes to be surrounded by enjoyment and entertainment; please allow this theater troupe to amuse you; I will go myself this evening to be in your presence.

"Madame de Kernosy was charmed by this letter," the count continued. "She had the theater troupe remain in the castle; we arrived in disguise along with the musicians. An hour later, the baron adeptly placed a letter in Mademoiselle de Saint-Urbain's pocket while she was watching the theater being completed.

"Now you have the explanation of the adventure that has given you some small cause for concern; my sister graciously favored us with her presence and with that of the other two women she brought with her, even though they are not aware of our plans. The baron, dressed as a Greek, has wooed the viscountess this evening, exactly as he intended; he told me upon leaving the ball, with his usual gaiety: 'I was correct that in Brittany I could pass myself off as a hero.' He would not explain himself further, but he is expected to appear here to apprise us of the success of his love affair.

"It seems to me that all would be favorable to our intentions if Mademoiselle de Kernosy and her charming sister would allow us to hope that they will not be against us, if we are able to convince the Viscountess de Kernosy to accord us the honor of her alliance."

Mademoiselle de Kernosy, who had always conserved a tender impression of the count in her memory, responded to him very graciously; Saint-Urbain responded equally politely to the chevalier, who was speaking softly to her, and she informed him that she and her sister had never received their letters.[22]

That matter was beginning to be brought to light when the baron entered the room, still dressed as a Greek. He was handsome; he was only nineteen years old. His face was very agreeable and he had a beautiful blond head of hair. "How now?" the count said to him, upon seeing that he was still wearing his masked disguise. "Have you been running from one ball to the next?" "No," replied the baron, "but soon I'll have my run of the fields; two more conversations like the one I just had and the deal will be sealed; but in compensation, if I'm losing my mind, my heart's desire is benefitting from it quite a bit, for I have conjured up the finest feelings in the world. Madame de Kernosy has assured me that she has never read of any so delicate and so tender."[23]

"But why are you still dressed like a fool?" asked the chevalier. "Surely a good overcoat would be better than this old brocade, given the weather." "Not at all, if you please," replied the baron. "A lover dressed as a Greek is even more charming in the eyes of the viscountess than a lover dressed simply as a Frenchman. She even began by comparing me to Alcibiades."[24]

"You truly are half mad, baron," said the marquise, "but let's get to the point. How far have you gotten?" "I am in the hopeful stage," replied the baron, "and I'm being encouraged to have a lot of it, so I will remain here to make myself worthy of this honor. As such," continued the baron, looking at the count and the chevalier, "it will be necessary for these gentlemen to arrive here as if they were coming from the home of the Marquise de Briance, and, having not found her at home, it will be very plausible that they will come looking for her in a place so full of good company."

Everyone approved of the baron's opinion, and since it was already very late at night, the count and the chevalier thought it best to take their leave and spend

---

22. This is likely due to the infidelity of the manservant tasked with delivering them. However, it would not have been uncommon for letters to get lost, especially during wartime.

23. Another reference to the heroes of the chivalric romances that the viscountess is accustomed to reading.

24. Alcibiades (or Alkibiades) was an Athenian military general, statesman, and disciple of Socrates who was renowned for his physical beauty and amorous exploits (450–404 BC).

a few hours in the closest village, so that they might return to the castle before the midday meal. The two charming sisters, after having said good night to the marquise, retired to their apartment. They did not fall asleep for a long time; the joy of finding that two very agreeable men were still faithful to them gave them plenty of things to talk about. Finally sleep reigned peacefully throughout the castle, except in the bedchamber of Madame de Kernosy. She would have found it against the rules [of romance and gallantry] to sleep, even if she had had a great desire to do so, after a conversation like the one she had just had with her hero.

The ladies did not arise until noon. The viscountess, on the other hand, had arisen quite early, and she had made two or three attempts at the composition of tender letters, before occupying herself with caring for her appearance. Her two charming nieces awakened with the kind of joy that is strongly felt when one hopes to spend the day with one's beloved. Each lady had a different preoccupation. The Countess de Salgue had not been able to resist the charms of the young Baron de Tadillac, and the Marquise de Briance was sighing in secret for a young lover who was absent from the company. In the end, love had decided to declare victory in this old castle and to leave no heart unperturbed.

At noon or around that time, the count and the chevalier arrived in a chaise;[25] at once they requested to see the Marquise de Briance. She presented them to the viscountess and told her all that had been concerted between them. The aunt, followed by her two nieces, received them with joy and invited them to stay, "in order to take part in all the entertainments that fortune has sent us," she said, smiling inelegantly.

The baron, who had also had orders from the viscountess to act as though he had just arrived, arrived almost at the same moment, dressed in a large country frock coat and riding on a horse that he had left a few steps away from the castle. He had his arrival announced. The viscountess assured the company that he was an old friend of hers. Kernosy and Saint-Urbain had a lot of trouble preventing themselves from laughing. It was already late; the viscountess's compliments had considerably prolonged the conversation. Saint-Urbain interrupted her to remind her aunt that it was time for the midday meal; the sight of the baron had made her forget about everything.

Everyone sat down at the table; they remained there for some time. The conversation was very lively, everyone sought to be appealing, and the love that sparkled among them took on many different forms. The old viscountess was charmed by the young baron; he was telling her in all seriousness things that would have been capable of amusing the most melancholy people in the world, and she was in a perpetual state of wonderment. The Countess de Salgue looked tenderly at Tadillac; the attentiveness that he was demonstrating toward the old viscountess gave her a thousand causes for worry. Since she was not aware of his plans, she

---

25. *Chaise de poste*: A small two- or four-wheeled carriage designed to transport only one or two people at a time. The carriage had been invented in 1664, during Colbert's ministry, by La Gruyère.

feared that he might be in love with either Kernosy or Saint-Urbain and that he was seeking to dazzle the viscountess in order to better conceal his passion.

Madame de Salgue was young and beautiful, and her wit was charming. She had married an old lord from the region, whose business affairs kept him in Paris for almost the entire year, without his ever granting his wife permission to accompany him on this trip. He was persuaded that in the provinces no gentleman would dare show him such a lack of respect as to speak to his wife about love. This liberty had already been taken, however; but the countess's heart, which had remained untouched until that point, had finally reached its fatal hour.

The baron noticed that she did not find him displeasing; he did not dare to speak to her in front of the old viscountess, but his glances made her understand what she was beginning to inspire in him. The count was even more touched by the beautiful Kernosy than he had been before, and she seemed satisfied to see these feelings in him.

Saint-Urbain and the chevalier were charmed by each other. The baroness, who found the chevalier infinitely pleasing, soon noticed that the two of them had an understanding, but she had a good enough opinion of herself to flatter herself that she was capable of making him unfaithful. She was a bit of a flirt, and the chevalier would doubtlessly have responded to all the gracious things she said to him if his heart at that moment had not been occupied by a very serious passion.

With respect to the Marquise de Briance, the only thing keeping her in this place was her brothers' interests. Sometimes a tender memory would plunge her into a profound reverie, but her gentle disposition and the quickness of her wit prevented people from noticing what was causing her pain. Her conversation was so agreeable that people eagerly sought her company, and they were never bored, no matter how long they were around her. Her facial features were very harmonious, her forehead, her eyes, her mouth, her teeth were worthy of admiration, and this whole combination formed a perfect beauty. She was very rich, a widow for three years; and all of the most important lords that could be found in that province had sought to please her without having been able to succeed.

Such was the fine company that Cupid had taken pains to gather at Kernosy Castle. People had just finished eating when they heard the arrival of a carriage. Everyone was cross about it, since they did not wish for any more company. Someone came to announce Monsieur de Fatville, councilor at the Parliament of Rennes. "What a man!" said Mademoiselle de Kernosy. "Now he will make us sorry that we did not dare to spread the word around the countryside that we are not at home!" "Oh well," said Saint-Urbain, "he will not bore us quite so much. In truth, he's a pompous fool;[26] it is necessary to have at least one to serve as the butt of our jokes."

---

26. The humorous name Fatville is derived from the French word "fat," which had as one of its principal meanings, "pompous fool."

The viscountess, who wanted to flaunt her good sense while the baron was watching, gave a strong reprimand to Saint-Urbain for this joke. It would have gone on for a long time, if the councilman had not entered. He had on a red frock coat adorned with silver tassels, a large sword hung from a wide leather belt that was placed on top of his justaucorps,[27] a hat with gold edges and an old yellow feather, and a blond wig that was very long and so full of powder that it scattered all over his frock coat and the area around him.

Upon entering, he bowed ten or twelve times without stopping, each one as deep as the next; then approaching the viscountess, he said to her with a disconcerted air: "The company at your home is too good, madam, for you not to wish to increase it." The viscountess responded with the standard compliment, saying that he gave her too much honor. "I have made my carriage, with all of its strong springs, hurry to arrive here as soon as possible," said Monsieur de Fatville, "for I have been in a state of extreme impatience to see the incomparable Mademoiselle de Saint-Urbain." He approached her and prepared himself to kiss her hand.

"I am very obliged to you," said Saint-Urbain, promptly retracting her hand, "for having sacrificed the springs of your carriage on my account." "Oh, they have not been spoiled yet," replied Fatville, "my lackeys have assured me of that. I cannot prevent myself from expressing to you the joy that I have to be dressed in this gallant manner," he continued while looking at himself in a large mirror. "I only wear my black frock coat in the morning." "My word, that is quite prudent of you," said the baron, "for the one you have on suits you perfectly." Fatville thanked the baron with three deep bows, and fortunately for the company, to whom he was causing immense boredom, someone came to inform them that the theater performance would begin as soon as it would please the ladies to command it. "You have a theater here?" said Fatville. "As far as I'm concerned, I have been to the theater four times in Paris, but I don't like it unless I'm placed on the stage."[28] "Long live people with good taste!" replied Saint-Urbain. "You will most assuredly be on the stage, Monsieur de Fatville. You could not be in a better place, both for you and for us."

The company moved into the hall, where they found the chandeliers lit and the violins playing the overture. The baron and the chevalier set Fatville up on the stage; they even had the guile not to have him given a seat, and he had the stupidity not to ask for one, because they told him that people of fashion never sit during performances.

---

27. Justaucorps: A long, knee-length coat popular in France from the second half of the seventeenth century to the eve of the French Revolution.

28. During this period, it was customary for male aristocrats to sit on benches placed directly on the stage. The custom originated in the 1630s, following the tremendous success of Corneille's play *Le Cid*, and persisted to the middle of the eighteenth century. Those who chose to sit on the benches were often noisy and constituted a spectacle in and of themselves. Fatville, who only knows about this custom through hearsay, does not know that he has the right to ask for a proper seat.

They performed *Andromache* and *Monsieur de Pourceaugnac*.[29] The performance of these two plays and the demeanor of Monsieur de Fatville were equally amusing to the company. People could see that he was already tired from his travels and taking great pains to keep himself upright. Even the viscountess made a joke on his account, because she saw that the baron had a liking for it. Fatville stared almost constantly at Mademoiselle de Saint-Urbain with gestures that were as unbearable as they were ridiculous.

A large supper followed the performances. People spent a long time around the table, and after having drunk to everyone's health, a custom that people rarely fail to observe in the provinces, they also drank to people's loved ones. Mademoiselle de Saint-Urbain began, raising a glass very gracefully. She informed all of the gentlemen that that they would not be allowed to drink from theirs until after each one had composed a couplet to the melody of a song to toast the health of such lovely ladies. "With pleasure," said the chevalier, "I will provide the example." He asked for a drink and sang the couplet, which he improvised on a well-known air.[30]

Everyone found this couplet very pretty, and the old viscountess, turning toward the baron with what she believed to be a very tender air, asked him if he didn't have a love interest worthy of being sung about in such good company. "The Chevalier de Livry creates verses so easily that people should not be shocked if he has gotten ahead of me," responded the baron. "I will amend my fault." The viscountess herself poured him some sweet wine. A moment later, he sang while turning his head in her direction, and she was charmed to be able to flatter herself that these verses were for her; but upon finishing the couplet, he looked tenderly at the countess, who understood what he was thinking. "It is thus my turn to create some verses too," said the count while laughing. "As I am the last, and consequently I have had more time than the others, I have created two couplets." "So much the better," said Mademoiselle de Kernosy. "We will have even more pleasure to hear you." The count, who had a beautiful voice, sang these two couplets:

> The love that sparkles in your eyes
> > Forces all things to surrender.
> It's so sweet, so dangerous, no one dares
> > Against it to be a defender.

> It's not a sign of weakness if
> > For your charms divine I'm burning.

29. *Andromaque* (*Andromache*) is a tragedy by Jean Racine (1667) and *Monsieur de Pourceaugnac* is a three-act comedy-ballet by Molière (1670). The custom of staging a small play in one or three acts after a longer, five-act play dated from the middle of the seventeenth century.

30. This practice of composing new words to existing melodies was a popular social game during the late seventeenth and early eighteenth centuries. It was also sometimes used as a strategy for critiquing the monarchy, as when words in praise of the king were set to the melody of a drinking song.

> Even reason itself would not dare to
> Condemn my tender yearning.

Saint-Urbain and the chevalier maintained that these words were too serious to be sung at table. The count responded to them that his heart had dictated them to him, and that he could not trifle with something as serious as his love. The viscountess approved of this opinion. "But," said Saint-Urbain, who feared that her aunt was about to throw herself into a conversation about feelings, "Monsieur de Fatville loves me, and he hasn't even written me a single verse." "I was only ever taught to write them in Latin," replied Fatville. "I won first place for such poems two times at school." "Well then, do a drinking song for us in Latin," said Saint-Urbain, "and you can explain to me what it means in French." Fatville said that he was not familiar with the air that the others had just sung. "Then how about a madrigal,"[31] she replied, presenting him with writing tablets.

Fatville thought that he would be dishonored if he did not compose some verses. He did not try to compose them in Latin, because he knew only a few words from that language; he took the tablets, and went to shut himself in a small private study so as not to be interrupted.

Meanwhile the whole company moved into another room, to which the oboists had been summoned. People listened to them for a while, then danced all of the usual short dances. After two hours, Fatville arrived, the tablets in hand. Everyone had believed he had gone to bed, but he told them that he had used all of this time to compose some verses. "It will no doubt be an elegy,"[32] said Saint-Urbain. "Let's see what is in question." She took the tablets, which were scrawled upon from one end to the other, and so marked up that she could not make out a single word. "Read them yourself," she said to Fatville, handing him back the tablets. "We cannot understand anything here." "It's a draft," responded the councilman, "and if I had had more space to write, I would have worked wonders, because I was just beginning to get going, but I will finish tomorrow." "Read us the beginning," said the viscountess. "I am terribly fond of tender verses." Fatville obeyed immediately, and read, while seated next to a pedestal table with a lit candle, the two verses he had just composed.

> Iris,[33] more beautiful than day,
> Could she in her turn feel love's sway?

---

31. Madrigal: a short gallant poem written on the subject of love, which contains verses of varying syllables. (A musical form by the same name, which had been very popular during the sixteenth century, had fallen out of fashion several decades earlier.)

32. Elegy: a sad poem that usually presents a serious reflection on either love or death.

33. Iris: a stock name for a shepherdess, typical of the gallant poetry of the time period.

He reread these same two lines four or five times. "How now," the count said to him, "is there any more finished besides that?" "No," said the councilman. "Isn't this quite enough for the time that I spent on it? And what's more, I made plans for the continuation of this madrigal." "Truly," said Saint-Urbain, "these two verses are worth more than an entire madrigal." "Mademoiselle de Saint-Urbain is an expert in everything," replied Fatville while laughing with an air of self-satisfaction. "And Sir chevalier, who is also a poet, what has he to say?" "I find this beginning to be so beautiful," answered the chevalier, "that I feel like finishing it. Lend me the tablets for a moment." "There you will see the rest of the plans," replied Fatville proudly. "Use them if you wish." The chevalier drew away from the company, which was amusing itself by watching our councilman dancing as badly as he wrote verses; some time later, the chevalier returned. "Let's see, Monsieur de Fatville, if I have indeed followed your plans; here is the completed madrigal." Everyone gathered around him and he read the following verses:

> Iris, more beautiful than day,
> Could she in her turn feel love's sway?
> Will the most ardent fire, the tenderest sighs,
> Touch her heart by making her realize?
> I asked that of the god who sports a bow.
> "I fashioned her to be pleasing," Cupid replied.
> "But loving is a different matter quite.
> Wit, sweetness, grace—all that I can bestow—
> I agree to shower her with each day anew;
> No person could hold out against her blow."
> With that, he leaves me, fleeing swiftly from my view.
> "Do you think, little god, you're telling me something new?"
> I cried out. "All that, better than you I know."

This madrigal got a lot of applause, and Saint-Urbain was very grateful to the chevalier for having taken advantage of Fatville's stupidity in order to perform this act of gallantry for her, which the viscountess did not find inappropriate because she only took it to be evidence of the chevalier's cleverness. "You see," said Fatville, who was hearing the praises being given to this madrigal, "I was right that the plan for the end would be amusing." People laughed at the councilman's impertinence; and as it was late, everyone went to bed. The apartment that Fatville had been given was close to that of the baron. This proximity gave him yet another occasion to play the role of a sprite, in order that Fatville would not dare leave his room, and so he would not notice that every night people gathered in the marquise's bedchamber after the viscountess had gone to bed.

The next day, the baron went to pay court to the viscountess before the ladies had left their apartment; he spoke to her of his love while striding back and forth, almost without looking at her. The good lady was charmed by all that he was doing, and she even assured him that he had the most graceful stride in the world. As soon as he had left, all the ladies came to the viscountess's bedchamber to pay her a visit, and they did not leave until two o'clock for the midday meal. After that, people played games; some played chess, some played ombre,[34] some played backgammon. Fatville lost sixty louis,[35] and although he seemed upset about it, the baron, who had won, said, rather humorously, that if this continued, he could finally make a friend of him. At six o'clock, people moved into the room with the theater, where *Horatius* and *The Doctor in Spite of Himself* were quite well performed.[36] Fatville, preoccupied by his losses, forgot to place himself on the stage.

After supper, they summoned an actor and an actress who had charming voices, along with one of the musicians who played the bass viol[37] well. Mademoiselle de Kernosy had servants bring all the operas by Lully that she had in her room; people sang the finest pieces from *Proserpina*,[38] and she accompanied on the harpsichord. Saint-Urbain sang with the count, who had a sonorous vocal quality, and these two charming people were perfectly in tune with one another. They began with the Elysian Fields scene. The baron sang in the choruses, so as not to appear an unnecessary participant to the viscountess. At one hour past midnight, everyone retired to their apartments, and the two charming sisters went to the marquise's bedchamber, where they found the count and the chevalier, who were waiting for them. They talked about the viscountess's passion for the Baron de Tadillac; Kernosy doubted that it would produce the effects that they had hoped for, and Saint-Urbain, more prone to believing whatever she found pleasing, was persuaded that their plans would have a happy outcome. The Count and the Chevalier de Livry were also hoping, and the Marquise de Briance was continuing to give them advice.

They were all speaking with great diligence when Tadillac entered, dressed in a strange outfit, red and black, which resembled those that are used at the

---

34. Ombre is a fast-paced card game for three to four players that originated in Spain and was known for its difficult rules and complicated point score. These kinds of parlor games were very much in vogue during Louis XIV's reign and were often played with monetary stakes, which contributed to the impoverishment of the nobility at the court of Versailles.

35. A gold coin with the king's portrait on it, worth approximately eleven pounds.

36. *Horace* (*Horatius*) is a tragedy by Pierre Corneille (1641). The French text follows the custom of referring to it in the plural (*Les Horaces* [*The Horatii*]) even though the brothers of the eponymous hero do not appear in the play. *Le Médecin malgré lui* (*The Doctor in Spite of Himself*) is a three-act comedy by Molière (1666).

37. A stringed instrument with a fretted fingerboard, six strings, and a flat back. It was played upright with a curved bow, similar to the modern cello.

38. *Proserpine* (*Proserpina*): an opera by Philippe Quinault, with music by Lully, created in 1680. The fourth act takes place in the Elysian Fields, where the title character, after having been abducted by the god Pluto, finds herself warmly welcomed by the Blessed Spirits.

opera to represent devils.[39] He had on a frightening hat, from which serpent-like creatures were hanging; and if he had had his mask on, he would have terrified the company without a doubt, for they were not expecting it; however, they were aware of his plans to frighten Fatville. "Here you are, as imprudent as ever," the count said to him. "So, let's find out what you intend to do." "Mademoiselle de Saint-Urbain must put on an outfit that will be brought to her," said the baron, "and then you only have to follow my lead." "I am almost afraid of those clothes," said Saint-Urbain. "However, in order to get rid of Fatville, there is nothing I could not undertake."

The baron's manservant appeared at that moment, dressed in an outfit that was even more frightening than that of his master; he had brought with him another outfit made to look almost like his, for the actors had brought along a great number of these in every fashion. Saint-Urbain put it on over her clothes and picked out an extremely ugly red mask. Lambert, the manservant, led the group to his master's apartment without encountering a single servant. Everyone in the castle had been asleep for more than two hours. Tadillac had discovered a door that led to Fatville's bedroom. He saw this at once as a favorable opportunity to execute the scheme he had been planning. This door had been sealed off for some time, and one would enter from a different part of the councilman's apartment, which was adjacent to that of the Baron de Tadillac. The apartment of the marquise and that of the Livry gentlemen were neighboring, and all of these together formed a wing where people could make a lot of noise without being heard in the rest of the castle, because it was necessary to cross a fairly long, open gallery in order to reenter the other wing, which created a kind of symmetry with the former.

When these people had arrived at the baron's apartment, they entered very quietly, and Lambert, who wanted to prove that he was worthy of the confidence that he had been honored with by his master, begged the group to wait a moment. He went up alone into the large unoccupied bedchambers that were above the apartments of the wing, and with a machine that he had invented, he made a loud noise that was not a bad imitation of thunder. Fatville woke up and went to open the window. Lambert, who heard this, set fire in several different places to some of the gunpowder he had purposefully brought with him. The night was very dark, and the light from this fire surprised Fatville; he closed his window even more quickly than he had opened it, very astonished to see lightning and to hear thunder in the middle of winter. He turned around to try to find his bed; he was still looking for it when Lambert came to open the connecting door that he had taken care to unseal; he entered the councilman's bedchamber, holding a small torch

---

39. Although the underworld figured in only a very small percentage of early modern French operas (most notably, Lully's *Alceste* [*Alcestis*], *Psyché* [*Psyche*], and *Proserpina*), many others had scenes that featured furies and other malevolent allegorical characters (Envy, Hatred, etc.) singing and dancing and accompanied by their followers. There are also several scenes in which sinister magicians conjure up demons.

that was illuminated. This light, suddenly followed by darkness, blinded Fatville to the point that at first he was not able to make out the face of the person who was carrying it; he caught sight of his bed, he threw himself into it and hid himself under his covers. Lambert did not let him remain long in this situation; he pulled the covers off of him and bowed to him three times with great respect, then he lit four large candles, which he had brought with him, and placed them in various parts of the room.

Summoning all his courage, Fatville cried out in a tone of voice that was quite shaken by fear: "Baron, help me!" "Alas," responded the baron, who was watching with the ladies through the partition, "there is no way for me to get out; some sprites have just entered here!" Meanwhile Lambert, after having lit the candles, approached the bed, and Fatville hid his head beneath the headboard more than ever before. Lambert took advantage of this moment to let in the baron and Saint-Urbain; once the connecting door was closed, all three of them approached the bed, preventing Fatville from hiding his head, and bowed deeply to him. Lambert took a small violin from his pocket, played a minuet, to which the merry sprites danced very lightly, and fear persuaded Fatville that they were rising all the way up to the ceiling. When this nocturnal ball was finished, the sprites put out the candles and left without his being able to learn how they got out; as such he thought that it had been some spirits who had vanished. Everyone was careful not to make noise in the adjoining room. Lambert played the violin and the baron cried out: "Monsieur de Fatville, I'm dead! The sprites in here are dancing like the damned." Fatville did not dare reply, but everyone having heard him stir, they judged that he had not fainted; however, he came close to doing so. The sprites made their way back to their bedchamber so as not to be caught doing the job of spirits. The baron called for servants as soon as he was undressed, and he told the story of the sprites, the way he wanted it to be believed. Fatville, who had not had the confidence to get up, finally resolved to go and open his door when he heard a good number of people talking near him. The paleness of his face and his fright, which were so artlessly apparent, made the spirits' apparition even more persuasive to the viscountess's servants; there was not a single one of them who was not convinced they had heard noises. Others claimed to have seen something black, which was walking along the gallery;[40] in the end, fear produced all the effects it usually produces on the minds of the common people and valets.

The viscountess, who was prone to fright, had no doubt that a cat who happened to have been shut in her bedchamber that evening, and who had broken a piece of porcelain while jumping, was in fact a sprite who had taken on this form.[41]

---

40. The long open gallery that connected the two wings of the castle, alluded to earlier.
41. Possibly an allusion to the story about the poetess Antoinette Deshoulières, which appeared in Murat's earlier novel *Voyage de campagne* (*A Trip to the Country*, 1699), in which Deshoulières proves that a ghost who is said to haunt one of the bedchambers of a friend's house is actually no more than

To confirm her thinking, the marquise recounted that she had heard a large dog walking around all night; the count affirmed that he had heard something like a galloping horse; and the chevalier said that he had seen three fat Indian chickens; the Kernosy ladies simply said that they had heard frightening noises. The Countess de Salgue and the Baroness de Sugarde, who had neither seen nor heard anything, were no less frightened by this.

When it was daylight, everyone went back to bed; no one dared to be alone in his or her room. The sprites, tired from their nightly task, got up very late. During the entire day, people spoke about nothing but ghosts. The servants related the story about them to the actors, who more or less suspected what this could have been since their costumes had been borrowed; but they had been paid by the baron and by the Livry gentlemen not to say anything; they were not even expected to have heard the castle sprites because they were being lodged in the courtyard, where there was a small, fairly accommodating building.

Fatville ate almost nothing at the midday meal; he could not recover from his fright; the manner in which he spoke of the agility of the spirits who had danced made even the most frightened people laugh; there was not a single agile movement that he did not believe to have seen them do, so greatly does fear overpower the eyes. "But how could you have seen all of that," the viscountess asked him, "since you were without light?" "Ah, madam!" replied Fatville, "they lit large candles around my room, and then everything disappeared in an instant." "Did they dance without accompaniment?" asked the baron, taking on a serious air. "Oh, certainly not!" responded Fatville. "They had instruments, and there may even have been trumpets." "I don't know anything about that either," replied the baron, "although I saw them dancing just as you did." "Truly," said the Countess de Salgue, "I think you both have gone a little mad."

This dialogue did not prevent everyone from believing in the appearance of ghosts. Some people even affirmed that in books there were a thousand examples of similar things. People recounted a variety of stories on this subject, which increased the fright of the viscountess and her servants. Finally, people got up from the table, and to distract from the distress that the sprites had caused, the Marquise de Briance asked whether they would have a play performed or not. "There should be one every day," said the baron, who was beginning to act like the man of the house. "I will get an update on it."

He returned a moment later to tell the ladies that the actors were ready to begin. People moved into the great hall, where they saw *Mithridates* and *The Enchanted Cup*.[42] Fatville fell asleep, tired from the bad night he had had. People

---

a dog who is able to enter the room each night because the lock on the exterior door is broken. (This apparently true story also appears in Madame Deshoulières's first published biography.)

42. *Mithridate* (*Mithridates*) is a tragedy by Racine (1673), and *La Coupe enchantée* (The enchanted cup) is a comedy by Charles Chevillet de Champmeslé, adapted from a tale by La Fontaine and

began playing games after leaving the theater, and after supper they were not slow to retire for the evening, each one to his or her own apartment. But no one went anywhere alone in this house anymore: the slightest draft caused dreadful startles.

Fatville could not bring himself to return to the bedchamber where he had suffered so much. He was given a different one; he had his two lackeys sleep near him. The countess and the baroness slept together, and the Baron de Tadillac ordered Lambert, in front of everyone, to come and sleep in his room.

The viscountess had two of her maidservants sleep on either side of her bed. She had a manservant and two lackeys placed a little farther off and her coachman near the door. Monsieur Pierre, her chaplain, was ordered to move his bed near the chimney, for the good woman feared that the spirit might make his entrance by way of that place.

The chaplain, who was extremely old and very inconvenienced, pointed out in vain to the viscountess that the strong winds that rushed down this immense chimney were going to end up making the rheumatism from which he had been suffering for ten years incurable; nothing could bend her will. "Truly," he said, while looking sadly at his bed, "I have always recognized that my lady has no consideration for her foster brother."[43] What words! The viscountess had heard them, even though Monsieur Pierre had said them in a rather low voice. At that moment, she did not want to bring up that foolish remark, but after the company had retired to bed, Monsieur Pierre received a terrible reproach, and rage took such good hold of the viscountess's mind that fear found almost no more room there.

The Baron de Tadillac waited until everyone had gone to bed, and without losing time, he went, accompanied by Lambert, to make a good bit of noise in the large, unused attics that extended above all of the apartments in the castle. This confirmed people's belief in ghosts, and the following day they each accounted for what they had heard with such a variety of explanations that the baron understood that it was sufficient to intimidate people by making noise and to leave to fear the task of diversifying the nature of the ghostly apparitions.

He had plenty of other activities besides that of playing a sprite. He had to persuade the viscountess that he was in love with her, and his heart was leading him to make Madame de Salgue fall in love with him. For several days the look in his eyes had provided sufficient confirmation of the passion he felt for her. Finally, weary of this mute language, he wrote her a note, and having returned to the viscountess's apartment, he found her still at her dressing table, and he

---

sometimes erroneously attributed to this poet (published in 1710, first performed in 1688).

43. The French term is *Frère de lait*, meaning that the chaplain and the viscountess were nursed by the same woman. If the mother of the chaplain had served as the wet-nurse of the viscountess, this would mean that Monsieur Pierre and Madame de Kernosy are the same age. Since Madame de Kernosy is so anxious to appear young, she does not appreciate being reminded of this inconvenient fact.

complimented her on her beauty. Just as he was beginning to put pressure on her to declare herself in his favor, the Marquise de Briance, the Countess de Salgue, the Baroness de Sugarde, and the two charming sisters entered. The Livry gentlemen arrived shortly thereafter, and Fatville appeared at the moment the group was sitting down at the table to dine. His fear and the noise that the sprites had made were the subject of the conversation for almost the entire meal. Afterward, people played a few more rounds of ombre, and at six o'clock it was time for the usual entertainment. *Cinna* and *The Scolder*[44] were very well performed.

The Count de Livry gave his hand to the viscountess to move into the great hall: the baron had asked him to do so. It was because of this auspicious occasion that he approached the Countess de Salgue, and having offered her his hand, he said to her in a low voice, "Please learn, madam, please learn of the one thing in the world that is the most essential to my good fortune. This note will enlighten you." He passed it to her surreptitiously and left her side as soon as people entered. The viscountess was already looking around to see what he was doing while apart from her.

The Countess de Salgue put the note in her pocket, and Tadillac had the pleasure of seeing that her eagerness to read it did not allow her to wait until people had left after the play. Having gotten up during an intermission to say a word to Mademoiselle de Saint-Urbain, instead of returning to her seat, she approached a pedestal table where there was a candelabra. She opened the baron's note and read it with an attentiveness that made him very happy.

"Madam," said Saint-Urbain, "how come you are taking time away from the play to read your letters?" "It was among those that I received this morning from my house," said the countess, "and I had forgotten to open it." The actors interrupted this conversation, and the baron, taking advantage of the fact that the viscountess had fortunately dozed off for a moment, did not take his eyes off Madame de Salgue. She noticed this, and the confusion that he saw on her face caused him not to lose hope for his happiness.

People did not play games for long after supper. Everyone went to bed fairly early: each needed rest and wanted to make up for the two poor nights' sleep that the sprites had caused them. The baron did not fail to make noise, so that people would not be so quickly cured of their fear; the commotion was short: the sprite was as weary as the others.

The following day the weather was very beautiful, the sun came up with radiance, people went to amuse themselves in the garden, and the viscountess, having important letters to write, spent the afternoon in her private study. Tadillac took advantage of this time to talk with Madame de Salgue. "Have you thought

---

44. *Cinna ou la Clémence d'Auguste* (*Cinna or the Clemency of Augustus*) is a tragedy by Pierre Corneille (1643) and *Le Grondeur* (The scolder) is a three-act comedy by David-Augustin Brueys and Jean de Palaprat (1691).

of me at all," he said to her in a low voice, "since I dared to write to you about the feelings you inspire in me?" "How can you claim that I should think of favoring you?" Madame de Salgue replied to him, while looking at him with tenderness. "You have come here with a plan about which I have still not been enlightened; I only know that I had no part in it; love could have brought you to this castle; the Kernosy ladies are charming and pretty, it even seems to me that Mademoiselle de Saint-Urbain is the one whom you prefer."

"What a mistake!" said the baron. "Madam, you must believe a heart that has never burned for anyone but you. Love played no part in my plans until I had the honor of laying eyes on you. I will explain whenever it pleases you . . ." He was going to continue, when the old viscountess, opening the door to her private study, made it necessary for them to separate and to draw nearer to the rest of the group, who were taking pleasure in watching the marquise, Kernosy, and the baroness play a game of ombre as prudently as possible. The viscountess was only in the bedchamber for a moment; she asked for a candle and returned to seal her letters.

The baron moved closer to Madame de Salgue. She had noticed the swiftness with which he had just left her side. "How is that?" she said to him, while moving a little farther away from the rest of the group, "so it is the viscountess you love? I would never have suspected it." "You plainly see, madam," replied the baron, "that one should not judge by appearances. You play too much of a role in my plan's outcome for me to wait any longer to enlighten you about it." He told her about his plan to secure his fortune, and about the commitment he was pursuing from the viscountess. Madame de Salgue thought that her lover was right. She wished almost as much as the baron did that he could secure a situation that would keep him in the same region where she was forced to reside.

People came to alert the ladies that the actors were ready. "Go on, Baron," Madame de Salgue said to him with a smile. "Go along to alert the viscountess yourself; I maintain that she should be obliged to me for reminding you of your duty."

As she finished these words, the viscountess emerged from her private study; the baron gave her his hand all the way to the room with the theater, where Fatville was already seated; and the entire group had remarked that, fearful of remaining alone in the viscountess's bedchamber, he had left before all the ladies, not even thinking to offer them his hand.

Berenice and *The Fair at Bezons*[45] were performed. After the play, people played little salon games where wit did not fail to shine; people told several stories that were made up on the spot. Saint-Urbain, who was beginning to grow bored, had the idea, upon finishing her own narrative, to let Fatville finish the novel that

---

45. *Bérénice* (*Berenice*) is a tragedy by Racine (1671), and *La Foire de Bezons* (The fair at Bezons) is a one-act comedy by Florent Dancourt (1695).

she had begun. This led people to become joyful again; never has a man given so many poor excuses to avoid having to speak. Finally, supper got Fatville out of his bind, and the viscountess was unable to forgive Saint-Urbain for not continuing with her novel, because she had resolved that when it came her turn to tell a story, she would lay out before the baron the most beautiful sentiments in the world.

People again went to bed early; the sprites left all of the castle's inhabitants in peace. Fatville was engaged in a conversation with the Countess de Salgue, who had come into his bedchamber, no longer being afraid after she had learned from Tadillac the game with the sprites. The count and the chevalier remained for a little while with Kernosy and Saint-Urbain in the marquise's bedchamber.

After they had left, these two charming sisters begged Madame de Briance to make good on the promise she had made to them to give an orderly account of her adventures, which they had discussed only in bits and pieces, assuring her that none of her friends could take more part in all that concerned her. The marquise, while sighing, made it known that telling this story would renew her suffering. [However,] she did not fail to satisfy their curiosity and began her story as follows.

The Story of Madame de Briance

"You know, ladies, that I am the daughter of the late Marquis de Livry, whose house is one of the oldest and most reputable in this region. I lost my mother a few months after my birth; my father was extremely affected by this loss; he had always loved her tenderly. She was only twenty-four years old at the time. She was beautiful, and those who have wished to flatter me have told me that I resembled her. You both said as much when you did me the honor of coming to my home last year, where you saw her portrait. My father, who was only twenty-nine, affected by true suffering, firmly refused all of the proposals that people made to him for remarriage. He loved us, my brothers and me, with a tenderness that cannot be expressed. There were only the three of us children, the count, the chevalier, and myself; the oldest was only four at the time, the youngest was three, and I was only six months old. We were, all three of us, brought up with infinite care.

"As soon as we were of a competent age to begin learning things, my father left the chateau where he had made his primary residence since the death of my mother. He took us to Rennes, where he had a fine house. He had a skilled private tutor brought from Paris to instruct my brothers, and I can say that this was also done for me, since my father wanted me to learn Latin,[46] geography, classical literature, and history along with my brothers. He did not think that ignorance

---

46. In their discussions on the education of women, most writers felt that Latin, which was a central component of the education of boys, was not appropriate for girls. Some theologians, like Fénelon, even discouraged girls from learning mythology. M. de Livry is thus exceptional in adopting the same educational system for his sons and his daughter. That being said, Marie-Jeanne Lhéritier de Villandon

needed to be part of a woman's lot in life; and he had found, through the example of my mother, that a cultivated mind, in which knowledge is absorbed without affectation and without banishing its natural agreeable qualities, has charms that are always new, more sustainable than beauty, and even more pleasant in the daily business of life.

"My brothers succeeded perfectly well in their studies, and I took delight in learning, which came to me very easily. We were the talk of the whole city; we were invited to the most prestigious social gatherings, and people had an admiration for us that must have greatly contributed to our being spoiled. My father was making great expenditures; he was rich, and my mother was the sole heiress to a wealthy household, distinguished by the nobility of her family; to sum up, we had cause to be content with our fortune.

"I was fourteen when the Marquis de Briance arrived in Rennes; he was a lord who, being tired of his obligations in war and at court, had come in search of rest to our region, where he had a large quantity of land that brought in substantial revenue.

"He stopped in Rennes, he paid visits to all the important people in the city, and he came to my father's house, where he found preparations being made for a gathering that was to take place there that evening.

"Monsieur de Briance said very gracious things to us, with the politeness of a perfect courtier. My father begged him to stay and assured him that the invited guests would be honored by his presence; he accepted this offer with joy.

"The conversation was lively; from one moment to the next, young people dressed up for the ball were arriving. The Marquis de Briance was studying all of the young ladies carefully and was always finding qualities in me that were even more remarkable, which he was complimenting. My father, who loved me passionately, was thrilled to hear the constant praises that he was according me.

"Although Monsieur de Briance was not of an age to be desired as a lover, most of the beautiful women at the gathering were jealous of his attentions toward me; the approval of a man who had spent his whole life at court seemed to them to hold more weight than that of the people from the region.

"Monsieur de Briance was still quite good-looking, even though he was almost sixty; he was well built, extremely rich, and of a distinguished rank. As he was unmarried, there was not a single young lady who did not wish to see him attached to her. As for me, I did not pay one moment of attention to all the flattering praises he was giving me. I only interpreted them as gestures of politeness.

"One hour before supper, Monsieur de Briance's squire came to ask for him; he returned after having spoken to him in the antechamber. 'Mademoiselle,' he said, addressing himself to me, 'I am going to present to you one of the most

---

and a number of women in Murat's circle also knew Latin and Greek, and Lhéritier was making her living off of her translations of ancient texts into French at the time that Murat was writing this book.

handsome gentlemen in France, provided that the Marquis de Livry grants me permission.'

"'These kinds of permissions,' replied my father while smiling, 'are sometimes dangerous to grant. You are the master, sir, and you may bring in here whomever you wish.' 'The person about whom I have just spoken to Mademoiselle de Livry,' replied Monsieur de Briance, 'is the Count de Tourmeil; he is only seventeen. Never has anyone ever had more potential for success. I will say nothing of his wit, nor of his appearance, you will be the judge of that yourself. As for valor, which is always the most important quality to be desired in a man of the nobility, I can assure you that I have been surprised by the marks of courage and even leadership that he showed during the last three military campaigns he took part in. He absolutely insisted on following me into the army when he was only fourteen; I consented to that, and I have had reason to be satisfied with my decision. I love him as if he were my own son.'

"'Does he have the honor of being a relative of yours, sir?' I said to him with a burst of curiosity that had been inspired in me by the portrait of Tourmeil he had just made. 'No, mademoiselle,' Monsieur de Briance replied to me, 'Tourmeil is not my relative, but his father and I were good friends; he was wounded on an occasion when I was in command, and a few days later he died from his wound. Never has anyone been as affected as I was by the death of a friend; while dying, he commended to me his son, whom he loved tenderly; I promised to give him my every attention and my friendship; and I have kept my word to him exactly.'

"At that moment, people came to say that supper was served. Everyone moved into the great hall and sat down at the table. I will confess to you that I did not hear the door to the room open during the entire meal without feeling a strong emotion that I had never felt before. I kept thinking it was the Count de Tourmeil, and I felt some sadness, despite the preparations for the ball, of which I was very fond, when I saw that people were getting up from the table, without my having seen the arrival of the person who was already causing me some uneasiness.

"The place that had been set aside for the ball was a large gallery; there were a great number of chandeliers and candelabras, whose light was reflecting off of large mirrors inserted into the wall paneling, which made the illumination of the room even more brilliant, and made the lights appear more numerous.[47] This gallery was painted white, with monograms and other ornamental decorations in gold; the furniture was made of velvet the color of fire and ornamented with tassels. Several people who were known for their good taste paid compliments to my father on the magnificence of this room.

---

47. The Manufacture Royale de Glaces, better known by the town where it was located, Saint-Gobain, was established in 1665 with the primary goal of furnishing mirrors for the king. This increased the general availability of mirrors in France. However, at the time of the novel's publication, mirrors would still have been considered a luxury item. Rooms lined with mirrors, of which the Hall of Mirrors at Versailles is the best-known example, were often featured in palaces in fairy tales.

"There were twelve of us young ladies and as many young men, the most high-ranking in the city, who were supposed to dance; the rest of the company sat down on seats in the second row. Monsieur de Briance, who was accustomed to being invited to the most illustrious gatherings, did not fail to assure us that he had never seen one so agreeable. My brother the Count de Livry began the ball with a young lady who was extremely beautiful and the daughter of the principal magistrate of Rennes; all the guests admired both the one and the other. Next, she was going to take the hand of my brother, the chevalier, who as you know is a little scatterbrained; without considering his obligation, as the host of the ball, to do these kinds of honors, he came instead to ask me to dance as soon as he had finished his courante. I danced with him, and we received a thousand rounds of applause; my father was charmed as he listened to them.

"It was my turn to choose someone from among the guests; I was afraid of making the wrong choice; I asked my father; he told me to take Monsieur de Briance: I went to curtsy before him, he begged me to excuse him on account of his age, and said, while introducing me to the Count de Tourmeil, who had just arrived: 'Here is a young man who will better acquit himself than I can of the honor you wished to do me.' My father ordered me to take his hand; he danced with a distinctive grace that is unique to him, and I think I danced less well than I had the first time, for I could not take my eyes off of him.[48]

"His lean body was more well-formed than that of most people at age fifteen,[49] he had a noble demeanor, and his beauty was beyond all words. He had a large quantity of black, naturally curly hair, which came down to his magnificent scarf, which he was wearing over a blue velvet frock coat, lined with gold brocade. Monsieur de Briance had sent him word that he should come to my father's home, that there was going to be a ball there, that illustrious people were in attendance, and that he should not fail to dress elegantly.

"Tourmeil seemed so different from all of the young men from our region, even though some among them were quite handsome, that everyone hastened to lay eyes on him. Monsieur de Briance was delighted with all of the applause [Tourmeil] was receiving. How my heart was in agreement! The confused feelings I had felt while watching him dance got quite a bit stronger when I realized that everyone was admiring him.[50] Whatever pain this confusion caused me, I found it pleasant, and I did not yet know where it was coming from.

---

48. As in Marie-Madeleine de Lafayette's famous novel *La Princesse de Clèves* (*The Princess of Cleves*, 1678), the first encounter between the heroine and the man she falls in love with takes place during a ball, where the couple dances together before having been formally introduced.

49. Since the Marquis de Briance said that he was seventeen, this must be an error on Murat's part.

50. By making Tourmeil so objectified in this scene, Murat carries out a gender reversal of the situation in *The Princess of Cleves*, where the beautiful stranger is the heroine.

"At the beginning of the ball we had been lined up with all the women on one side and all the men on the other. Tourmeil, in a fit of impatience for which I was very grateful, was the first to disrupt this arrangement; he crossed through those who were dancing with a charming grace and came to kneel before me. Monsieur de Briance was quite pleased by this act of gallantry, and he pointed it out to my father, who was nearby. Tourmeil's action caused all of the young men in attendance to follow suit; each imitated his example. My brother the count believed himself obligated to remain with the same partner he had had at the beginning of the ball, and the chevalier began a conversation with a fairly pretty girl who was next to me.

"Tourmeil, pleased with what he had just done, looked tenderly at me, and his words were as touching as they were witty. We danced together the whole night; he was committed to dancing with no one but me. Once, when Monsieur de Briance asked him to dance with the young lady with whom my brother had been dancing, Tourmeil replied, smiling graciously: 'I cannot obey you, sir, because my heart is ordering me to do the opposite.' After these words, he came and bowed to me. This response infinitely pleased Monsieur de Briance, but my father found it too strong for a man of his age.

"The ball finished rather late; however, I found that it was ending too early. Tourmeil made me aware of how sorrowful he was to leave me; he expressed this sentiment so naturally that my heart was moved to tenderness. He asked permission to come see me the following day; I was in a state of confusion that did not allow me to respond very precisely. Finally, people separated; my brothers, who had been charmed by Tourmeil, begged him as they said goodbye to have the honor of counting him among their friends; he responded like a man who was familiar with high society. I went to bed, and the tranquility of slumber, which up until that day had never left me, was suddenly interrupted. Thoughts of Tourmeil were constantly entering my mind; sometimes I was admiring his appearance, a little while later I was worried that I had not been witty enough in the conversation we had had together; a number of thoughts crowded all at once into my imagination and increased my worries. Finally, I fell asleep, but I believe that love was in communication with my dreams, which consisted of nothing but Tourmeil and his advantageous qualities.

"I woke up late; my brother the chevalier told me that after the midday meal he was supposed to bring the Count de Tourmeil to the homes of the prettiest ladies in the city and that afterward he would accompany him to our home. Love had resolved not to lose a single opportunity to enlist my heart so forcefully that it would never to be possible for me to break its chains.

"I encountered Tourmeil and my brothers at the home of a lady who was a friend of my aunt's, whom we had gone to visit. They were getting ready to leave, but as soon as I entered, Tourmeil turned to my brother the chevalier. 'Now you will no longer reproach me,' he said, 'for the worry I felt in all of the other places we have been. I beg you, find a pretext for us to remain here.' The chevalier told me of Tourmeil's plan and then told the rest of the guests that he would not leave because he was hoping that Mademoiselle de . . . , the daughter of the lady whom we were visiting, would play the harpsichord if I asked her to, for he had not had the courage to ask her for this favor.

"Her mother ordered her to play the harpsichord; we listened to her with pleasure; after she had played for a while, I asked her to play a piece I am quite fond of; it is a saraband;[51] its ancientness had done nothing to diminish its beauty. 'I wish there were new lyrics for this saraband,' I said to Mademoiselle de . . . , 'for it is my favorite song in the world.' 'The Count de Tourmeil will be able to satisfy that request,' my brother said to me: 'Monsieur de Briance showed us some of his verses today after the midday meal, and they are in very good taste.'

"Everyone put pressure on Tourmeil to create verses for this saraband; he protested politely. But finally, I spoke up and said: 'As for me, sir, will I also be refused?' 'No, mademoiselle,' Tourmeil replied to me. 'I will even obey you before you ask me to.' He took the writing tablets that I offered him; he distanced himself a little, and a few moments later he handed them back to me. We found the following words:

> Between the gods who can my verse inspire,[52]
> Divine Iris, make no mistake, beware.
> When I tell you that I love your beauty rare,
> The charming god who now lends me his lyre
> Is not the one who makes me express my fire.

"Tourmeil sang this couplet himself, and Mademoiselle de . . . accompanied him on the harpsichord. All the guests admitted with sincerity that no one could play the harpsichord better nor sing with better precision. I returned to my father's house with my aunt; Tourmeil begged my brothers not to pay any more calls. He arrived at the same time that I did and gave me his hand as I got out of the carriage. We found Monsieur de Briance playing chess with my father; he told Tourmeil that he was delighted to see him among such good company.

"My father's house was always filled with all of the most distinguished people in the city: people stayed for supper fairly often, and before or after supper people played games or chatted; in that respect, they each did whatever they enjoyed the most. There were a lot of people present that evening; I watched them play games for a little while, and Tourmeil's attentions were entirely on me; he spoke to me from time to time but in a respectful tone that pleased me a great deal.

51. A slow dance of Spanish origin, very popular among the nobility.
52. The deity in question is Apollo, god of music whose instrument was the lyre, while the god who inspires love in the narrator is Cupid.

"Monsieur de Briance caught sight of us; he spoke to my father in a low voice, then he called Tourmeil over. 'Count,' he said to him, 'I will have supper here; but we would take undue advantage of Monsieur de Livry's hospitality if we both stayed.' My father begged Tourmeil to stay, but Monsieur de Briance signaled that he should do the opposite.

"Never has anyone been struck so strongly by the most terrifying words than Tourmeil seemed to be upon receiving this order; as he approached me, his demeanor was as upset as if he had bid me farewell for a long time. 'I have been ordered to take leave of you, mademoiselle,' he said to me. 'The misfortune of having to obey Monsieur de Briance's orders a second time is too painful for me.'[53] He left as he finished these words, and I was extremely affected by his absence.

"As we got up from the table, I saw my brother the chevalier reading a letter that had just been delivered to him: he waited until my father had returned to his bedchamber and signaled to me that I should stay. 'Here,' he said to me, 'is a note that I beg you to read.' I opened it and found the following words:

"*What have I done to attract this misfortune? Of the great number of people who were at your home this evening, I am the only one who was not permitted to stay. Nothing can come close to my despair; one would have to have the same feelings that you inspire in me to truly understand the torment that your absence makes me suffer.*

"This note was not signed, but I could easily see that it was from Tourmeil. I blushed as I read it, and as I handed it back to my brother, I asked him: 'How is it that you have been entrusted with this commission?' 'A reason that is even stronger than that of my friendship has obliged me to show you his note and the letter that he wrote me,' the chevalier replied to me. Tourmeil was begging him not to view his obedience to Monsieur de Briance as a lack of courage; he was protesting that after this last gesture of respect he would never obey him again in his life, and he indicated specifically that he would be waiting for him [Briance] in his bedchamber in order to make him aware of the grief he had caused him. My brother could well see my astonishment as I read this letter. 'Tourmeil,' he said to me, 'is going to do something rash that will cost him his fortune. Monsieur de Briance loves him as if he were his son; even yesterday he told us about the considerable sums of money he had given him. It would be quite cruel for a thing of so little consequence to bring true misfortune upon him.' 'I would be in a state of despair if that happened,' I replied to him, very moved by Tourmeil's alleged misfortune.

---

53. Tourmeil is upset at receiving another disagreeable order, but in fact he previously disobeyed his mentor at the ball.

"My brother the count came to see what we were doing. We informed him of our concerns. 'There is not a moment to lose. Go, my brother,' he said to the chevalier, 'prevent Tourmeil from having a falling out with Monsieur de Briance. In order for this to be easier for you to accomplish, it is necessary for my sister to write him a note.' I expressed some reservations, but we did not have time to deliberate, and advice from two people aged fifteen and sixteen was not likely to result in a very prudent course of action. The chevalier gave me his writing tablets, saying that he would bring them back, and that in this way my letter would not remain in the hands of Tourmeil; I wrote him these words:

"How can you consider having a falling out with Monsieur de Briance? I dare to beg you to continue to pay to him all of the respect that you owe him for the friendship he has shown you. Is not seeing me for one evening such a great misfortune? And if you find that it is one, after having told me so, must you continue to complain of it?

"The chevalier took the writing tablets and ran to Tourmeil's home. I went back into my father's bedchamber; he was finishing a game of chess with Monsieur de Briance. I, however, was daydreaming about Tourmeil. It seemed to me that a man who was ready to give up his fortune in order to see me for a few more hours had to be truly in love. How dangerous these reflections were! I knew well that I had to defend my heart against love, but I thought I could allow it to be given over to gratitude.

"People finished the game, and Monsieur de Briance, upon approaching me, continued to praise me as he had the day before. I responded so badly that I have no doubt he must have had a poor opinion of my cleverness; I let him leave the house without worrying about what he could have thought of it. I was waiting impatiently for the chevalier to return; he did not return to my father's bedchamber; I found him waiting for me in his.

"'Well then,' I said to him, with a strong emotion that I could not conceal. 'Will Tourmeil be sensible? Have you persuaded him?' 'No,' the chevalier replied to me, 'all of my efforts were in vain; but as soon as he saw what you had written on my writing tablets, he seemed as submissive to your orders as he had been unmoved by my advice. He kissed your handwriting a hundred times, and never has anyone ever seen a man so in love.'

"My brother's all too faithful account moved me deeply; I was preoccupied with it for the rest of the night. Tourmeil was charming and his birth was equal to my own. 'Who can forbid me from hoping that I will be happy one day on account of my fondness for Tourmeil?' I said to myself. 'My father is looking for a more advantageous match for me than those who have presented themselves so far; he will certainly take note of Tourmeil's merits.'

"These reflections occupied my thoughts for the entire night; and my heart, flattering itself, gave itself over to all the dangers of a passion in its early stages: I did not fall asleep until daybreak. The first thought that struck me when I woke up was that of Tourmeil. I got up and got ready with more care for my appearance than I had ever taken before; this desire to look appealing to him showed me more than anything else the degree to which he was occupying my mind. He came early to my father's house; he encountered a lot of ladies there; he had nothing but polite formalities for them, and I applauded myself a thousand times for being the only one to have touched his heart.

"It was proposed that we go to see the actors who had come to Rennes for the carnival; my father consented to let me go along with the other ladies. My brothers were among that group, and Tourmeil, who was only looking for pretexts in order not to leave my side, came along as well. We found them to be the worst actors that had ever appeared in the region. The play, although poorly acted, did not seem to have lasted for very long: Tourmeil was seated next to me; I could not be bored.

"As bad as the play was that we were watching, it did not fail to attract a lot of people. When everything had finished, everyone was in a hurry to leave. My brother the chevalier gave his hand to a lady from our group, and as he tried to pass through the door, a man from the province who had the same idea pushed him brusquely aside; my brother extended his arm, for fear that the woman he was leading would be squeezed. This action, which prevented the provincial man from leaving, sent him into a rage; he made some vicious remark to my brother, who responded by slapping him in the face. We were nearby; we saw this action. Tourmeil and the count approached quickly, certain that the chevalier and the man were going to come to blows. My brother had drawn his sword, but we were quite surprised to see the provincial man, without continuing the quarrel, disengage himself from the crowd and coldly continue on his way as if nothing had happened to him.

"We returned home; we remained there; Monsieur de Briance came to call and told us that the incident at the theater was already the talk of the entire town. We had already informed my father about it, so that he would not learn of it from elsewhere. He gave the chevalier a reprimand for having reacted too quickly, but he did so as a gallant man, for he treated my brothers more as his friends than as his children. He was not so indulgent with me, even though he loved me dearly: he would say that girls were obligated to obey more exactly than men were.

"A little while after supper, my brother the chevalier, who wanted to visit a lady with whom he was in love, left my father's room; I noticed it. The quarrel that he had gotten into that afternoon worried me; I found it very imprudent of him to go out alone into the streets at night, to expose himself to the resentment of the offended man, who as we had learned was a person from the regional nobility who had arrived in Rennes only a few days earlier.

"I followed the chevalier and I told him that I would warn my father that he wanted to go out unless he consented to being accompanied by five or six of our manservants. 'That would make quite a fine team,' he said to me while laughing, 'to go off on an amorous adventure.' He wanted to escape from me; but finally, seeing that I was ready to warn my father, he said to me: 'Well then, because you absolutely do not want me to go out alone, tell Tourmeil to come with me, and we will take along an escort.' I went back into my father's room, I begged Tourmeil to go with the chevalier; he generously offered to be of service. I really wanted to double the number of escorts I had proposed to the chevalier when I saw that Tourmeil was among them.

"The count was occupied in a game with my father and Monsieur de Briance; for this reason I did not dare speak to him. My brother and Tourmeil departed alone; they were not a hundred steps from the door when they found themselves ambushed by six well-armed men. They were shot at, [but] the darkness of the night saved them; only one shot hit Tourmeil and pierced the sleeve of his doublet. He and my brother drew their swords; they defended themselves without being able to see what they were doing; the moon came up, and in this pale light the chevalier recognized the provincial man, who, standing a little farther off, was encouraging his men in this fine endeavor.

"My brother wanted to take him on, but he was against the outer wall with three men in front of him. Tourmeil had two others before him; he eliminated one; this blow intimidated the second and made him withdraw quite far off. Tourmeil, seizing the moment, ran like a lion to take down the provincial man, who after having defended himself for a while received a blow from a blade that penetrated his entire body, and fell on the cobblestones. Tourmeil went quickly to rescue my brother, who had only a minor wound in his arm, but his sword had just broken. He saved his [my brother's] life by warding off his three enemies.

"One of the three was not moving, having been gravely wounded; the other two made no signs of resistance, seeing the provincial man unconscious and bathed in his own blood. 'He is dead,' said one of the assassins. 'Let's escape.' But before taking flight, he stabbed Tourmeil in the back with his sword. Two of the chevalier's friends, who were returning from a night out having fun, recognized him on their way home. They told the lackey who was holding their torch to turn off toward my father's home, where they brought our two wounded men. People were still playing games; I was worried, and I had a feeling that something bad had happened. I ran as soon as I heard noise in the courtyard; my brother and Tourmeil, both covered in blood, were already there. Upon seeing this, I let out a frightful scream. My father heard it, he jumped up, all the guests followed him; and the chevalier, seeing how upset he was, said to him: 'This is nothing, father. I am not dangerously wounded. But I beg you to turn your attention to having someone help Tourmeil, for he has just saved my life.'

"Tourmeil was losing a lot of blood; people laid him down on a daybed that was in the antechamber; Monsieur de Briance and my father were equally upset by this horrible spectacle. I was inconsolable over it, and I wept with all the pain that friendship and love can inspire. 'How happy a person could be,' Tourmeil said to me at that moment in a languishing voice, 'to give all of his blood in order to merit such precious tears!'

"I responded only by crying twice as hard: my father and Monsieur de Briance did not hear what he was saying to me; they were speaking to the surgeon who had just arrived. The surgeon had found my brother's wound to be minor, but he seemed uncertain about Tourmeil's; he even assured us that if we were to try to move him, we could make his injury considerably worse.

"My father, who was touched by Tourmeil's fine qualities and by his generosity, begged Monsieur de Briance to let him remain in our home until he was fully cured. The servants, whom he had sent out to the place where the fight had taken place, returned to tell him that the man from the provinces had been removed and that they had brought along one of the wounded men who remained there. My father ordered that the man be bandaged and that they should take care of him. This unfortunate man was so surprised to be well treated in the home of a man whose son he had just tried to assassinate that the very next day he requested to make a deposition about what had happened. His deposition was then used to resolve the incident in favor of Tourmeil and the chevalier. It stated that the incident had involved four horsemen from the entourage of the provincial man's brother, along with one of his friends whose name he did not know; that the provincial man was still alive; and that his two companions, seeing no one left, had returned and had taken him away; that they had also promised to return for him [the man making the deposition] and that he had consequently been quite shocked to see that he was being carried off by servants other than his own.

"How I suffered during the night! The fact that Tourmeil was on the verge of death for having defended our interests was constantly on my mind. I was sorry for having urged him to go out with my brother. 'He has saved his life,' I was saying to myself, 'but he has sacrificed his own, and I am the one who has caused it all.' These thoughts, followed by many others, kept me in a perpetual state of unrest.

"Finally, daylight appeared; I went to my brother's bedchamber. I was told that he was resting. He hardly stayed confined to bed; and he managed to emerge from the incident unscathed, apart from having his arm in a sling for a while. I sent for news of Tourmeil, and I learned that he was running a slight fever. I did not dare ask for news about the state he was in; I was still afraid that I would learn of something fatal, and this apprehension did not cease until eight days after he had been wounded. His fever left him; the surgeons assured us that he was out of danger and brought me some degree of peace of mind.

"Although my father's attention was constantly occupied with curing Tourmeil and the chevalier, he did not fail to inform the authorities. There was more than enough proof to convict the provincial man of murder. Criminal charges against him were pursued; he did not dare to remain in the city. One of his relatives had him brought, as wounded as he was, to his country home, where he remained in hiding while the preliminary investigation was underway.

"During that time, I was in a fairly pleasant position: Tourmeil was feeling better, I saw him almost every day, my brothers led me to his bedchamber and sometimes even compelled me to remain there. Both were deeply touched by the service he had done us and spared no effort to show him a perfect gratitude. They kept telling me that my father could not choose a husband for me who would be more charming or from a better family than Tourmeil. They even promised him to speak to my father about it together once he had recovered his health. This is what he was most ardently wishing for, and the hope that he had of being able to marry me played no small part in his recovery.

"It seems to me, ladies, that it is too late to continue telling you of my adventures; I promise to finish the story tomorrow, if that which I have told you already makes you curious to know the rest."

Kernosy and Saint-Urbain let the marquise know how much they were interested in everything she had just told them and that they would take great joy in learning the rest. After having spent a few moments discussing what they had just heard, they took leave of the marquise and retired to their apartment.

The story that the Marquise de Briance had just recounted renewed the memory of when a budding passion had become deeply rooted in her heart; time had not erased the idea of Tourmeil, which love had sharply imprinted there. The efforts that she made during part of the night to dissipate this sad memory were useless. Finally sleep interrupted her sorrows.

The next day the weather was as beautiful as it can be in winter; the sun, over the course of the past few days, had dispelled some of the cold of this harsh season. The Livry gentlemen and the Baron de Tadillac went hunting in the morning and returned to the castle at the time of the midday meal with a large quantity of game. For the ladies, the beauty of the day gave rise to the desire to take a short walk in the woods that surrounded the garden. The Baron de Tadillac wanted to entertain them by taking them hunting; the Livry gentlemen were also ready to oblige. To this effect, they begged the viscountess to have brought from the castle two female hounds, who had been of service to them that morning.

"It was a singular pleasure for the ladies to watch these gentlemen, all three of whom were marvelous shots and never missed their target. The viscountess admired the baron's dexterity and was constantly singing his praises. Saint-Urbain, still determined to persecute Fatville, asked him why he was not shooting; she told him that he had the appearance of being adept at this exercise. The councilman, made proud by this speech, took the gun of a gamekeeper and prepared to shoot; he aimed so badly that, in missing the game he was intending to hit by a long shot, he wounded a fine black cow who had been peacefully walking by a few steps away from them.

"The viscountess flew into a genuine rage against Fatville; the black cow was her favorite, she would partake of her milk, and she had named her Isis,[54] in order to better underscore her worth. This accident unsettled him; and angered in turn by some biting words she had said to him, he began to become sick of being in the company of nobles, for which up until that point he had felt a strong inclination, and he set off for the castle in a rage. The group followed him, and upon their arrival they found everything ready for the performance of *Penelope* and *The Man from Florence*.[55] This short comedy filled everyone's hearts with so much joy that no one wanted to continue playing games after supper, as they had on the previous evenings. People wanted to find a pastime that required less concentration, and it did not take a long time to come up with one. The baron proposed to organize a kind of lottery, with the promise that each person would execute whatever the content of the ticket they drew required of them.[56] He created seven tickets, wrote on them, folded them, and the Marquise de Briance drew them. The first one was for the viscountess, it contained: *You will tell a secret to someone in the group.*

"My secret is all ready," she said, glancing at the baron with a delicate air.

The second ticket was for Mademoiselle de Kernosy. On it, she read: *You will recite a madrigal.*

"I will get off cheap for that," said Kernosy. "All this takes is to have a little memory."

The marquise gave the third ticket to Saint-Urbain; on it, there was: *You will tell a story.*

"What a ticket!" said Saint-Urbain. "Truly, madam, you would have done well not to give it to me; I would have preferred any other to this one."

"We are never happy with what we get," responded the marquise, "but let's see the baron's ticket." *You will give a party for the ladies in three days' time.*

After having read it, he cried out like a terrified man: "Oh, how afraid I am of not obeying properly!"

---

54. A mythological reference. Io, a nymph who had been seduced by Jupiter, was subsequently transformed into a cow and cruelly tormented by Jupiter's wife, Juno. After Jupiter was able to obtain a pardon for the nymph, she regained her human form and was transformed into the Egyptian goddess, Isis.

55. *Pénélope* (Penelope) is a tragedy by the abbé Claude Genest (1684), and *Le Florentin* (The man from Florence) is a one-act comedy by Champmeslé (1702, first performed in 1685), often falsely attributed to La Fontaine.

56. This type of lottery, in which participants (usually, all the participants) must improvise a poem or a tune, was a popular salon game. There were also "gallant lotteries," which served as a pretext for distributing presents to each of the participants. (Traditional lotteries also existed during the time period.)

Next the marquise gave a ticket to the Count de Livry; he found on it: *You will criticize the story that the person tells.*

"Here I am, inspector of Mademoiselle de Saint-Urbain," said the count. "I warn her that in this role, I will be very rigorous with her."

The chevalier opened his ticket, and he read the following: *You will fill out some bouts-rimés.*[57]

The Countess de Salgue found on her ticket: *You will listen to the others.*

"So much the better!" she said. "Here you have me quite content to be the audience."

Next the baroness read the ticket that had been drawn for her; it read: *You will provide the bouts-rimés.*

"Let's see then," said the marquise, "what fortune has reserved for me"; she opened her ticket and read: *You will recite a song.*

"That will not be hard," she said. "But Monsieur de Fatville's ticket is still here. Take it, sir," she said to him, holding it out to him, "read what your lot will be." He found written there: *You will go to find out how Isis is doing.*

Everyone laughed at this foolishness, which brought back the memory of [Fatville's] hunting prowess; he well suspected that this ticket had come to him on purpose. Indeed, the marquise had set it aside, in concert with the baron, and she had drawn the others at random.

"Let's get started," said the baron, sitting down. "We must execute everything that is written on the tickets; it is my job to give the orders, since I am directing the game. The viscountess will be so kind as to start us off." She arose gaily and told him secretly, with a mysterious air, that she found him worthy of her esteem. The baron responded very little, so as to appear to be a faithful recipient of the secret that had just been confided to him.

Mademoiselle de Kernosy received the applause of the entire group for her madrigal, which she recited from [memory]. And Mademoiselle de Saint-Urbain put off telling her story until after supper, following the order that the baron prescribed to her at the moment that she was about to begin her narration: "In order," he said to her, "for the group to have something agreeable to amuse them for the entire evening and for the count to be more at leisure to criticize it." After that it was the baron's turn to acquit himself of what his ticket was requiring. He set a date for the party that he had been commanded to throw, choosing a reasonable time frame, in order to better succeed at it, and he continued in this way to give his orders. "Let's get on with it, Chevalier, presently it is a question of your bouts-rimés." "I cannot finish them," replied the chevalier. "The baroness has not given them to me; you know that her ticket commands it." She asked for help to invent

---

57. Bouts-rimés, literally "rhymed ends," was a poetic game popular in the salons in which one person creates a list of words that rhyme with one another and gives these rhymes to a second person who will have to compose a sonnet using those words as the rhymes.

them. The chevalier took up the pen, each one provided a word, and here are the bouts-rimés just as he received them.

Ambrosia
Whirlwind
Chimes
Thoughts
Madness
Bright red
Butterflies
Asia

Thread
Cast aside
Light

Destiny
First
Sprite[58]

"This will not be easy to finish," said the chevalier while rereading them. "Mademoiselle de Saint-Urbain would have done well not to include the word 'sprite' on that list; I can well see that he is destined to torment even the poets of this castle." People joked about this idea. The countess did not take up the subject. Rather, she told the group: "As for me, I am fulfilling my duty by listening to the others." The Marquise de Briance did not let the topic of the sprite be dropped. She went on and on about this spirit's guile, and about the courage of Fatville, who had faced a number of them with incredible intrepidity, without having had a single unpleasant accident befall him. And a moment later, she sang the following words to a popular melody, in order to acquit herself of the duty that had been prescribed for her on her ticket.

> Unwelcome reason, stop causing my heart's strife
> With fears and suspicions that you bring with you.
> My shepherd promises me to be ever true.
> Let me surrender to that flattering hope;
>   It makes the happiness of my life.

---

58. In the French, of course, the words rhyme: Ambroisie / Tourbillon / Carillon / Fantaisie. Frénésie / Vermillon / Papillon / Asie. Cordon / Abandon / Lumière. Destin / Première / Lutin.

People found this song infinitely pleasing. They repeated it so many times that the whole group learned the tune as well as the words. Only Fatville was not singing, because he did not know anything about music; as a child, he had been made to understand that music was not necessary for those who sought to obtain a substantial fortune.[59] The baron asked him for news of Isis. "If we had been in Rennes," he answered, "I would have only good news to report to you; I would have had her bandaged by a fine surgeon, and the viscountess would no longer be angry." Everyone was very grateful to him for this joke.

The chevalier said that he had completed the bouts-rimés that he had been given. The curiosity to hear them immediately seized the group. He read the following:

Bouts-rimés Sonnet

The most charming of the gods who on ambrosia live
Brings to my heart, through you, a whirlwind full of flames.
The troublesome sound of chimes from jealous men and rivals,
By loving you, unceasingly disturbs my thoughts.

I feel, when I'm near you, that my gentle state of madness
Fills me with fear, makes me turn pale, then turn bright red;
I undergo the fate of butterflies through your eyes;
They could well have subdued the conqueror of Asia.

The three Fates will soon cut the thread of my existence;
With pleasure I cast aside concern for my life's web.
If I'm without you, love makes me scorn the light of day.

This god awaited you to fix my destiny.
Elsewhere I merely trifled; you're the very first
To make me feel the power exerted by this sprite.

This sonnet did not fail to be well received, even though the words had come in an impromptu manner and the composition had been executed in the same way. "For this campaign, the only thing we are involved in criticizing is Mademoiselle de Saint-Urbain's story," said the count. "Even so, it is required only because there was an explicit order from the lottery ticket." When it was Saint-Urbain's turn to tell a story, she said that because she did not want anyone to be startled by fabulous adventures, people would be more pleased to hear a story that

---

59. This trope would be reversed during the Enlightenment in works like Voltaire's *Jeannot et Colin* (1764), in which aristocrats who receive a worldly education, as opposed to a practical one, are the subjects of ridicule.

had been written by Athenaeus,[60] a Greek author, whose work has been translated into French. Immediately after this prologue of sorts, she began her story.

The Story of Zariades

"Hystaspes, who was the ruler of Media, had two sons[61] whom the people referred to as the children of Venus and Adonis because they appeared to be gods; they were flawless in appearance, and their beauty attracted the gaze of everyone who laid eyes upon them.

"The oldest, who was named Zariades, had gone off, in his early youth, to be ruler of the entire region that extends from the Caspian Sea to the banks of the Tanais river.[62] This prince, having become tired while hunting one day, lay down under a cluster of trees that were growing near a fountain, the agreeable sounds of which sent him into a deep sleep, providing him with a rest that was peaceful in appearance but that brought plenty of agitation into his heart. In a dream, he saw a young woman lying on a bed of grass in the middle of a lovely garden, magnificently dressed, who was holding in her hands a small portrait, which the god [Morpheus], crowned with poppies, had just presented to her. 'How handsome he is!' she cried, gazing at the portrait with rapt attention (it was a portrait of Zariades). He thought that he heard her speak, and the sound of the young woman's words, charming on account of the radiance of her beauty, made such an impression on his mind that nothing could ever erase the idea that he had formed of it. 'What a goddess Cupid has just shown me!' he said upon awakening. 'Is it possible that this was nothing more than a trick? No, without a doubt: that god created this image in order to triumph over all hearts.'

"Zariades could think of nothing else but this dream; his heart had been penetrated by it, and he was being driven to despair over his inability to find out whether this magnificent beauty was no more than a beautiful illusion of which there was no original in the universe. He knew how to paint better than any man

---

60. Athenaeus of Naucratis was a Greek rhetorician and grammarian who flourished at the end of the second and the beginning of the third centuries CE. Around 200, he composed *The Deipnosophistae* (*The Philosopher's Dinner*), which features a lengthy series of conversations on a number of diverse subjects. The story chosen by Saint-Urbain is adapted from an anecdote that appears in book 13, section 35. In Athenaeus's version, the narrator claims to have taken the anecdote from a story about Alexander the Great, written by Chares of Mytilene, who was a court official under Alexander and author of a ten-book series dealing with the king's private life. In her adaptation, Saint-Urbain adds a number of additional episodes and details to the original, rather short, Greek text.

61. In Athenaeus's version, Zariadres is not Hystaspes's son but rather his younger brother, and the two brothers are rulers of neighboring countries. Since Hystaspes was a historical figure, we have retained this spelling, rather than that of Murat, who calls him Histape.

62. The Tanais river, now called the Don, is currently located in Russia, as is part of the block of land in question. Media, now located in the northwest of Iran, was in ancient times a strategically important area. It was sometimes an independent kingdom and at others a province of the Persian Empire.

of his time; and being unable to live apart from such a divine creature, he painted the portrait of this charming person whose features had been deeply engraved in his memory by Cupid; he put it in his private study, and those whom he allowed in admired it as a masterpiece of nature and of art. This prince, believing that this might assuage his anxieties, recounted his adventure to his confidants and to the important people at his court whom he cherished the most. They sympathized with his heartache, but that was a weak remedy.

"A foreign prince, having arrived at the court, asked permission to pay him his respects. Zariades received him in his private study. After exchanging the usual formalities associated with such occasions, the conversation turned to the great number of rare and priceless objects that had been collected in this luxurious place. Surprised to see the portrait that Zariades had placed in the center of a number of paintings by the most famous painters in antiquity, the foreign prince paused to look at it for a long time, and while in the state of astonishment that the piece had placed him in, he blurted out: 'Never has anyone ever seen a more perfect resemblance.' These words at once aroused Zariades's attention. Love, joy, and curiosity shook him all at the same time; but having recovered a little from his initial emotions, which were causing him unexpected pleasure, he asked what realm was fortunate enough to have witnessed the birth of this heavenly person.

"'Her name is Otadis,' replied the foreign prince. 'I have seen her a thousand times at her father's court; his name is Omartes, he rules over the provinces on the other side of the Tanais river.' 'What!' cried Zariades. 'It is the princess Otadis whom I have heard spoken of as the most beautiful person in all of Asia! My destiny is too favorable.'

"The foreigner who had given him such pleasant news was lavished with honors and presents. [Zariades] told him confidentially about the dream and the passion that it had given rise to for the beautiful Otadis; this foreigner accepted the proposition that was made to him to accompany the ambassadors that Zariades wanted to send to Omartes's court, and he left hastily along with them in order to get to that court as soon as possible. Upon arriving, they asked for Otadis's hand in marriage on behalf of their prince.

"Omartes knew how powerful Zariades was; he had heard talk of his good looks, but he did not want to want to send the princess, his daughter, far away from him. She was the heiress to his kingdoms, and since he did not have any male children, his intention was to have her marry a prince of his own race.

"Otadis had not been able to bring herself to make a choice that ran so contrary to the feelings she had locked away in her heart; Cupid had wounded her with the same arrow that he had used to enflame the heart of the handsome Zariades: Morpheus,[63] the god of dreams, had given her a vision of this amiable prince whose charms seduced all hearts; and the princess, faithful to this pleasant illusion,

---

63. In the original French edition, Morpheus is erroneously confused with Momus, the god of satire.

disdained all of those who presented themselves as potential husbands. Nothing was comparable to this lovely person who filled her imagination; she was unable to love another. This man was not a work of nature; the gods had created him.

"Meanwhile the foreign prince whom Zariades had charged with visiting Otadis on his behalf, requested an audience with her, which was given to him. Prostrating himself before the princess, he told her that Zariades, the son of Hystaspes, ruler of Media and handsomest of all men, assured her of his deepest respects; he said that this prince had sent him to tell her of his ardent desire to make her his own; ever since the gods had given him a vision of her divine beauty in a dream, she was the only woman capable of making him the happiest of all men. The similarity of their fates led Otadis to become interested in Zariades; but how great was her shock when the foreigner, presenting her with a portrait of the prince, made her realize that he was in fact the same one that the gods of love and slumber had so clearly revealed to her, an image that they had so often renewed in her mind. At that moment, she felt a good deal of sorrow over the fact that her father wanted to send the ambassadors home without granting the request they had made, and her passion compelled her to confide her sentiments to this generous foreigner, who seemed so zealous for Zariades.

"A short time later, the ambassadors from Zariades, whom he had accompanied, had their farewell audience; he returned with them to give their master the sad news of Omartes's refusal, and he calmed the rage that the prince was about to fly into by giving him a faithful account, in private, of all that the divine Otadis had said in his favor and of the true feelings of her heart, the secret of which she had revealed to him.

"Zariades, transported by love, raised some troops and hastily led them to the banks of the Tanais, hoping that through his valor he would be able to force Omartes to give him his daughter the princess, or to make himself possessor of her, whatever the price. He had several boat bridges built over that river, so that his army could cross more easily. Meanwhile he sent the foreign prince back to Omartes's court, where he was to see Otadis in secret and instruct her about everything that was being prepared in order for the initiative to be successful.

"This tireless prince was constantly going to the banks of the Tanais to encourage the workers. One day, while he was busy maintaining good order among them, in order to stave off the confusion that could prevent their works from being quickly finished, he saw arriving in a small boat a man with a pleasant expression whom he recognized at first sight; it was the foreign prince, his closest friend. 'Well then,' he said to him, embracing him. 'Has the divine Otadis approved the plan that my love has devised for her?' 'Yes, my lord,' responded the foreigner. 'The adorable Otadis would be yours if her heart were in charge of her destiny; but it can no longer be concealed from you that her wedding will be celebrated in three days, and after that it would be no use even if you conquered all of Asia.

Omartes is all-powerful, Otadis will not dare to go against his orders. After a sumptuous banquet, she will receive a golden cup from her father's hand, it is the tradition in this country, and she will present it to the happy mortal who will be chosen to be her husband.'[64] 'Then let us go at once to receive it, this precious cup,' cried the handsome Zariades, completely transported by rage and by love. 'Let us disrupt this cruel wedding, or die at Otadis's feet.'

"From that moment on, he consulted no one but his own despair. Suddenly abandoning his army, he left in secret, followed only by the foreign prince and a small number of his men. After having crossed the Tanais on one of the boat bridges that had just been completed, he threw himself into a small carriage pulled by eight horses, at a speed so tremendous that in three days they arrived at the court of Omartes, where he put on an outfit that was similar to those worn by people in that country, for fear of being recognized. Having entered the palace, he went all the way into the banquet hall, where he saw Otadis, who was holding in her hand the golden cup that Omartes had just given her. The grief she felt over being so close to the moment that was going to decide her destiny caused her to shed a few tears, which only increased her beauty; she left the banquet hall accompanied only by her maidservants, to go and say her prayers in a nearby room, as was the custom.

"Zariades followed her step-by-step; he entered this room stealthily and approaching the princess, he said to her, 'Here I am, ready to deliver you from tyranny.' Otadis would have taken him for a god who had rushed to her aid if, in the features of his face, she had not recognized those of the prince whose image the god of sleep had engraved upon her heart. She presented him with the golden cup that was to decide her choice of husband, and consenting that he take her away with him, they both escaped through a staircase where few people could encounter them, and from there, crossing the palace gardens, they reached the gate where the carriage of the lucky Zariades was waiting for them along with his escort and with the foreigner, his closest friend.[65] As soon as they climbed in, everyone made such tremendous haste that they found themselves on the banks of the Tanais before Omartes, distressed by the abduction of his daughter the princess, could learn the identity of the person who had undertaken such an audacious action.

"They crossed the river on one of the boat bridges that we have already mentioned. Zariades, without wasting a moment, led the princess to his camp, where

---

64. Here Murat makes a significant deviation from the ancient Greek text. In Athenaeus's version, Omartes demands that his daughter marry, but he allows her to choose her own husband and it is the princess who sends a message to her lover to beg him to be present at the ceremony. The French version contains a more direct critique of the custom of arranged marriages.

65. In Murat's version, the lovers' escape seems to take place as if by magic. In Athenaeus, the ladies in waiting, along with the other palace servants who are aware of the princess's passion, assist with the escape, and then tell the king they are not sure in which direction she went.

their wedding was celebrated with as much splendor as possible. The whole army was filled with joy; the generals, the officers, and even the soldiers showed their dedication to Zariades by their eagerness to lay eyes on the divine Otadis, who had just given very generous gifts to the troops. Their constant cheers revealed the joy that each of them felt on account of this union, which would make their leader's happiness complete, as he now possessed the most virtuous and most charming princess in the world. The god Mars took a break from his thunderbolts so that Cupid could host the party in peace and so that the two spouses could send ambassadors to Omartes in total security, to inform him of the pleasing success of their wedding."[66]

This is how Mademoiselle de Saint-Urbain finished her story. The Count de Livry, far from criticizing it, as his ticket had ordered, lavished praise on it. The Marquise de Briance and the Chevalier de Livry said that the story had been abundantly enhanced with embellishments that had been very appropriately added to it; that the ancient author's account, which they had read, told the story too succinctly; that it was more pleasant to enliven the telling of such an implausible story with a few embellishments than to recount it simply and meticulously and to make it languish with too faithful an account. The viscountess quibbled, criticizing Otadis for the fact that she had allowed herself to be carried off by her lover and that she had married him without her father's permission. Mademoiselle de Saint-Urbain responded that it was not permitted to change key facts of such importance and that in those days people forgave anything to do with love, but that now people were more sensible.[67] Finally, each went to bed, pleased with what they had just heard.

The two charming sisters led the Marquise de Briance to her apartment and stayed with her, as they usually did. The Count and the Chevalier de Livry came to call. The Baron de Tadillac came there soon after. Saint-Urbain asked him if he had seen Madame de Salgue; he played the part of the discreet lover and said that he only spoke to her in public, that his greatest passion was to see the viscountess soon entirely declaring in his favor, that she had been promising him her undying affection, but that he was not in the mood to wait for years on end pining away and feeling sorry for himself. Madame de Briance said that the

---

66. Subsequent editions of the text modify the denouement to make it more in accordance with propriety, if not more verisimilar. In these editions, the newlyweds send their ambassadors with a message to Omartes that seeks his pardon, and Omartes, recognizing the merits of Zariades, eventually consents to the union and reconciles with his daughter. (There is no reconciliation in Athenaeus's version.)

67. In later editions, at this point in the novel, the viscountess expresses her preference for fairy tales, and the Count de Livry proposes to indulge her by recounting one. The other ladies are thrilled, but Fatville again shows his ignorance by asking if fairy tales are true stories. When he learns that the stories are fiction, he goes to bed. The interpolated story, titled "Peau d'ours" ["Bearskin"] is by Marie-Madeleine de Lubert. We include it in an appendix.

viscountess wanted to engage in protracted courtly love and to go no further; that it was necessary that they each think seriously about their own concerns; and that they would meet up again the following day in the evening to give their opinions and to find a solution capable of assuring them a favorable outcome. The Livry brothers had no other designs. The baron also only cared about a happy ending. All three of them approved of this idea, and Madame de Briance sent them off. Kernosy and Saint-Urbain, being the only ones remaining, begged her insistently to inform them of the rest of her adventures. The marquise had already committed to doing so, and since she was unable to honorably excuse herself, she obligingly continued her story as follows.

End of Part One.

Part Two
Continuation of the Story of Madame de Briance

"You remember, of course, ladies, that my brother was cured of his wound, and that Tourmeil was beginning to feel better; his greatest suffering then was the apprehension that the return of his health would soon put him in a position to leave my father's house and deprive him of the happiness of seeing me every day. He had not yet managed to get out of bed when Monsieur de Briance received letters informing him that his presence was necessary in Paris, for the judging of a very important trial, [and] that the people on the other side were heatedly pressing ahead during his absence with the design of taking advantage of the situation. Monsieur de Briance, recognizing what their intention was, made all the preparations for his departure, and came to Tourmeil to give him the news. From there, he made his way to my father's apartment; they remained shut up in there together for a long time and did not leave until the arrival of my brothers gave them a reason to do so. He approached them, taking leave of them, and he begged them to continue their care of the sick man whom he was leaving in their house; his wound, which kept getting better every day, gave hope for a speedy recovery.

"The next day my father, while in his private study with my brother the chevalier, received a letter from Monsieur de Briance. A servant came to seek him, and he left abruptly after having put that letter inside a desk that he had not locked; my brother brought it to me at once, and we hurried together to Tourmeil's room, not doubting that it would reveal to us the subject of their conversation, which we all were very eager to learn. Here is what it contained:

"*I am departing with a genuine sorrow to be leaving you, sir, but I hope to rejoin you in a month or two; I will wait impatiently for that time, since, in accordance with the promise that you gave me the honor of making to me, I can count on completing the matter that we have agreed upon and that I ardently wish for. You will speak of it to Mademoiselle de Livry when you deem it appropriate; I believe that she will not find it disadvantageous. Continue, I beg you, sir, all the kindness you show for Tourmeil.*

The Marquis de Briance.

"How great was our joy upon reading this letter! It seemed to us that my father and Monsieur de Briance had agreed to arrange our happiness. I gave my heart over to the fondness that I felt for Tourmeil, who experienced joyous raptures that cannot be expressed. I looked on him as a husband, chosen by my father and by my inclination. My brothers were delighted by this alliance that they had so greatly wished for, and they went at once to put the letter back in my father's desk, so that he would not notice this little theft.

"Tourmeil, once he was finally restored to perfect health, went to thank him and then he withdrew into the home of Monsieur de Briance. We were very surprised by this fatal separation, for we were not expecting this sudden blow. On the contrary, we were hoping that this occasion would bring my father to make a declaration in our favor; and what confirmed the suspicion we were feeling, namely, that he had not changed his resolution, was a letter from Monsieur de Briance that Tourmeil had just received, in which he indicated to him that he should go at once to Paris to be with him, because his business matters obliged him to spend the winter there.

"Tourmeil, far from obeying, spent the carnival season quite pleasantly in the city of Rennes, where his good qualities had earned him the affection of well-bred people. No one organized a party without inviting him to it, and he was received there in such a manner as to make him understand that if he offered his love to someone, he would be favorably received. But since he found himself only at gatherings where I was present, he was always faithful to me, and more disposed to lose his fortune than to renounce the happiness of possessing me. He pretended that he had not received the letter from Monsieur de Briance, in order not to be obliged to answer it. Finally, since he could no longer delay without writing to him, he sent him word, in order to have a pretext to remain near me, that his wound was not yet perfectly healed. When his business obliged him to spend a whole day without seeing me, he would write me letters, in which he would send me verses of his own composition, full of wit and fire. That did not seem surprising to me, for I clearly felt that love was dictating them to him.

My father found himself obliged, out of courtesy, to permit me to go and spend two days in the home of a lady in his circle of friends, who had a beautiful home close to Rennes. Although this absence was of rather short duration, I felt it keenly, and Tourmeil was inconsolable over it. I had expressly forbidden him to come there: I feared my father, who might have become angry to see him introduce himself into a company where he had not been invited. The day following our arrival, as I was crossing the main hall, I encountered a young peasant, who presented me with a basket filled with very beautiful flowers of the season; it was Tourmeil's personal valet. I did not have the time to communicate to him the joy that his master's continual attentions caused me; the lady whose home we were in entered unexpectedly; he noticed that and withdrew speedily, for he had orders not to make himself known; I made a quick decision, not doubting that his entry had been seen. 'I believe, madam,' I told her, 'that I must thank you for the gallant presents that I am receiving in your home. Here is what one of your servants has just given me.' 'I don't have any servant,' she replied to me, 'who is capable of having made such a lovely thing, but I wish I had had the cleverness to arrange for it.' She looked at the basket attentively, and upon lifting up a bouquet that was in the middle, she found a note. I remained a bit disconcerted, but when I saw it was only a poem, which was not even in Tourmeil's handwriting, I felt reassured. Here is the poem:

> The gloomiest haunts of the most savage climes
> Would lose, on seeing you, their hideous air.
> To enchant each place you set foot on betimes
> Is the least effect of your eyes' powerful stare.
>   The fields, on seeing you come here,
> Must have taken on again their springtime hue.
>   The queen of flowers,[68] though brilliant too,
> Has less right than you to cause them to appear.
>
>   The gods living in this rustic spot,
> Content, in the deep woods, with the felicity
>   Of an eternal liberty,
> Will, 'gainst the god who mastery over gods has got[69]
>   No longer have security;
>   They'll encounter you likely as not.

"The lady of the house recounted this story to the whole company. I kept on pretending to believe that the poem and the flowers that I had received were from her; my father also believed it because I had made no secret of it.

"The following day, as we were at table, we heard playing by the best oboists there were in Rennes; when they were asked who had sent them, they replied that a man had come to fetch them on behalf of the lady in whose house we were staying, and that he had even paid them very handsomely in order to make them set out with greater haste. I recognized Tourmeil by this gallant present, which was again attributed to my father's lady friend, for the oboists kept on maintaining that it was on her behalf that they had been sent for. In fact, they themselves had been deceived. 'Never,' she said, laughing, 'has it cost me so little to do the honors in my own house.'

"Finally, we returned to Rennes; we arrived there late, and I was about to go to bed when I heard violins and oboes under my windows. The orchestra was composed of the best musicians available in the city; they played various selections from operas, plus 'The Follies of Spain,'[70] a piece that I am very fond of. Shortly afterward, a very beautiful voice sang a song in several stanzas set to that

---

68. Flora, the Roman goddess of flowers and gardens.
69. Since this is a love poem, the god in question is Cupid.
70. A tune of Italian origin that had become internationally popular by the end of the seventeenth century. Several variations of the tune existed.

same air with a theorbo accompaniment. Here are the first two stanzas, which I still remember:

> The lovely Sylvia[71] once again I'll see.
> Her sweet charms will add beauty to this place.
> She alone creates life's happiness for me.
> Can I again find that bliss in her face?
>
> The sparkle of youth in her complexion's hue
> Makes everyone her heavenly traits admire,
> And the god who wounds us and bewitches too
> Has given her his power, arrows and fire.

"The orchestra[72] played solos between each stanza, and I have never heard anything so attractive. What charms could better bewitch my heart? My brothers easily understood who was the author of this gallant present, and my father resolved as of that moment to inform me of his plans and to declare them to everyone, in order to remove those people who might have any romantic interest in me.

"The day after our return to Rennes, Tourmeil came to the house at the earliest hour that decorum allowed; he saw me again with a satisfaction that people know only when they are in love. I asked him with what pursuits he had occupied himself during the two days he had spent away from me. His response was that he had left his rooms only once, not having been able to get out of going one evening to a house, where I was not to suspect that he would have had the intention of being entertained, since ordinarily the only people one met there were lower-ranking officers, who, despite their insipid and irrelevant comments, were listened to in preference to men of intelligence who would have had worthwhile things to say; and this depraved taste had moved him to write a poem using preexisting rhymes that had become famous through the honor of their having served for the most charming princess in the world.[73] I took the paper on which he had written them. It contained the following.

---

71. This was another of the conventional names of shepherdesses in pastoral literature; those names were used in love poems as a way to associate the real-life lady with an idealized world of blissful pleasure.

72. The term "orchestra" (alternately spelled *simphonie* or *symphonie* in Murat's version) referred to a solo for instruments either before or during a vocal composition. The large-scale "orchestra" known today originated in the latter half of the nineteenth century.

73. In French, the preexisting rhymes are as follows: "Buste / Glaçons / Moissons / Robuste / Auguste / Leçons / Chansons / Juste / Accueil / Digue / Ressors / Prodigue / Transports." In 1695, Murat's friend Lhéritier had used the same rhymes to pay homage to the Princess de Conty (Lhéritier, *Oeuvres meslées*, 395). Conty, born Marie-Anne de Bourbon (1666–1739), was a legitimized daughter of Louis XIV and a patroness of writers in the *galant* style, including several women. She was also the dedicatee

Bouts-rimés[74]

Here no wit is to be found in any torso;
Ice crystals fill the least cold conversations,
And people make such rough harvests of boredom
That in one day they could kill the hardiest man.

In vain does reason, through its august presence,
Try to lay out the lessons of common sense;
Whatever it would say would pass for rubbish;
They make it a law to not speak fittingly.

One sees twenty nymphs, filled with insipid pride,
Give a favorable reception to tall soldiers
And offer no resistance to their sweet talk.

Plumed helmets there stir up every heart-spring.
In short, I see that Cupid is too lavish:
He inspires raptures for fools, just as for us.

[Postscript to the sonnet]

Here all unpleasant things appear by turns;
They all cause in me bad humor, lassitude.
But once I see my loved one here,
I will even prefer this spot
To the place where the gods reside.

"My brothers and I recognized in these verses the personalities of all the people about whom this poem had been written; Tourmeil had the habit of amusing himself by talking to us about them, but our joy was too great to last for long. A nobleman from our region, among the most esteemed for his high rank and for his great wealth, had asked my father to give my hand to his eldest son, who was

---

of Murat's 1698 collection of fairy tales and of her previous leisure novel, *A Trip to the Country*, 1699. In addition to using these rhymes to pay homage to the Princess de Conty, Lhéritier had also used them to glorify the king's military exploits (*Oeuvres meslées*, 394) and to honor her patron the Duchess d'Epernon (*Oeuvres meslées*, 396). The *Oeuvres meslées* also included several poems dedicated to Murat, one of them a bouts-rimés (382–385).

74. Once again, we have provided a fairly literal translation, since it would be impossible to use the rhyming words and rhyme scheme of the original without composing a radically new poem.

a tall youth of nineteen, neither handsome nor ugly, and who, never having had experience of the world, would fall into inconceivably childish behavior.

"This new suitor caused Tourmeil anxiety; he was sure of my heart, but I was not mistress of myself; finally, he made up his mind to make my father declare his position. My brothers were in total support of him and openly disapproved the marriage that was being proposed with the youth from the provinces; they treated him with extreme coldness, and I would say disagreeable things to him, but this young man with no education did not grasp them; nothing would make him cross.

"One evening when my father was not having supper at home, my brothers invited Tourmeil to stay. Our youth from the provinces, who was not asked to stay, did so anyway. After being angry for some time, we made up our minds to make fun of him; Tourmeil spent the whole meal making him drunk with praise. Finally, we were alerted that my father would come back soon; we did not want him to find Tourmeil in the house; I asked him to go away, and my new suitor said, upon seeing him depart, 'I am sorry that Monsieur de Tourmeil is going away; that youth amuses me greatly; if he wants to come to my home to spend four or five months, we will entertain each other pleasantly.' 'That being the case,' the chevalier told me, 'I do not advise you to oppose your marriage to him.' I was unable to reply to that silly remark, for my father came in and we beset him to such a degree that it was not possible for the youth from the provinces to speak except to take his leave from the company.

"The frequent requests that were made to my father to conclude my marriage with the youth from the provinces finally caused my brothers and me to take the resolution to speak to him of Tourmeil's intention to form an alliance with us. The Count de Livry, my oldest brother, undertook this business. He chose his moment well, such that he had the necessary time to converse with my father in private and to explain to him that, besides all the advantages to be found in that alliance, he believed that we had an indispensable obligation to do something in favor of Tourmeil and that such a consent would constitute only a small token of gratitude for the great service that he had just rendered to our family. 'It has already been some time,' my father replied, 'that I have noticed the intention that you are declaring to me on Tourmeil's behalf. I have infinite esteem for him, but he is not rich enough; it is necessary for him to rebuild his family fortune. Monsieur de Briance wants to have him wed a young woman whose wealth is so sizable that he will restore his finances; I believe it is useless to tell you how advantageous that is for him; you see it as well as I; and it is no less advantageous for your sister to wed Monsieur de Briance, who is coming back very shortly in order to conclude this business. She would have trouble finding a better match; I hope that she will obey me willingly, for my word has been given, and I declare to you that I will hold to it.'

"This short speech, pronounced with a tone of fatherly firmness, disconcerted my brother and threw him into a consternation so great that he could not inform me of the sad news without my being able to notice the sadness with which he was filled. Tourmeil was in a state of despair, and I was inordinately upset. Our passion grew even stronger because of this obstacle to our happiness. However, I had to conceal my tears; my brothers upheld my interests to the point of drawing my father's anger upon themselves.

"Tourmeil did not dare appear any longer; however, I saw him occasionally; my brothers themselves would admit him in secret. But our entire conversations were spent shedding tears. Finally, my father informed me what his resolution was on this matter; I did everything I could think of to make him yield; it was in vain, and I fell into such a state of depression that I fell prey to a fever and was at death's door for eight days. Some time later my brothers, finding me slightly improved, devised the plan to bring some relief to my illness by introducing Tourmeil into my room one evening. Indeed, the pleasure that I took in seeing him made no small contribution to the restoration of my health, and the welcome that I gave him consoled him in his misfortune.

"It seemed surprising to me that my father, who loved his children so tenderly, could resolve to make me unhappy. But I must do justice to his memory here: he believed that I would easily forget Tourmeil once I would no longer see him, and he wanted to give me a social status above the other ladies of the region by having me wed Monsieur de Briance. It was a matter settled between them. And the letter that we had intercepted [and which we had interpreted] in accordance with our wishes had no other aim but this marriage; my father declared it right at the moment when the contract was signed; he received compliments over it from everyone. Each person considered me very fortunate, because the public was not informed of the agitation within our family, which undoubtedly would have revealed the pain that I was feeling. And one can say, to Tourmeil's credit, that in spite of his despair he never breathed a single word that could indicate his passion. The profound respect that he had always had for me sealed his lips. Satisfied with my tenderness, he accused no one but his own bad fortune for his misery.

"Finally, Monsieur de Briance came to see me; I will remember for my whole life that day, which was so cruel to my peace of mind; I had summoned up my courage in order to obey graciously, but Cupid did not wish it: I made minimal replies to everything that Monsieur de Briance, acting as a man of refinement, said to me; I was in low spirits due to my illness, and even more due to my grief, and, unfortunately for me, I appeared so beautiful to him in that languishing condition that he almost never left my side; I broke into tears, as soon as he had withdrawn.

"Tourmeil, who could no longer control himself or view Monsieur de Briance as anything but an odious rival, absolutely insisted on fighting a duel with him. My brothers, seeing that their efforts to prevent him from doing so were useless, undertook to deliver a letter that he wrote to me, in which he asked to see me one more time; I agreed to that. They were so moved by our conversation and so touched by our grief that they deemed it fitting to separate us from each other. They were preparing to lead Tourmeil away when the apprehension that I felt over the fact that he was about to ruin himself made me grab him by the arm to stop him; I pointed out to him that his intention to fight against Monsieur de Briance would be no less fatal to me than to himself, since that duel would create a scandal capable of harming my reputation, and that he would not be able to remain with us peacefully or even think about seeing me again for the rest of his life, whatever advantage he might gain over his enemy. Those words calmed his fury and made so strong an impression on his mind that he declared, upon leaving me, that his obedience and his submissiveness to my orders would convince me more than ever of his fidelity and of his passion. After we had shed tears, my brothers led him away, and I remained in a state of affliction that cannot be understood by someone who has not felt it.

"After leaving my presence, Tourmeil sent word to Monsieur de Briance in a letter that the rich heiress whom he had spoken to him about did not suit him and that he wanted to travel for a few years before thinking of settling down.

"At first, Monsieur de Briance was deeply affected by Tourmeil's departure, but the certain amount of attention that he had noticed Tourmeil display toward me soon consoled him for his absence; and in the impatience he was feeling to wed me, he gave himself no rest until the day of our marriage. I was adorned, I let people dress me as they wished, I was led to the church with the same meekness and brought back to my father's house, where I spent the day receiving the compliments of all the persons of distinction who were in the town at that time.

"The next day, Monsieur de Briance took me to his house; nothing could be added to the sumptuousness of his house or to that of his retinue; he gave me jewels of very great value and showered me with all the presents that give a young person pleasure, but that was not capable of touching my heart; I had lost the only treasure that I truly cared about. Meanwhile, I lived with so much obligingness for Monsieur de Briance that he was very content with his lot, and his love for me seemed to increase every day.

"Tourmeil, having clearly felt that it would be impossible for him to calmly endure so fatal a blow, had gone to Paris to stay with one of his uncles who was his guardian and who was tenderly fond of him. He had led [his uncle] to believe that, having fought a duel over a rather slight altercation, it was necessary for him to leave France until an accommodation could be reached for this affair; the uncle, who had learned through Monsieur de Briance about the fight involving his nephew and my brother, easily believed that this second adventure was real, and he promptly gave him money. As soon as Tourmeil had received the sum, he set off for Lyon in order to get passage for Venice. However, he did so only after writing to my brothers and bidding farewell to me, assuring me of his immortal passion and wishing me a peace of mind that I have never enjoyed since his departure.

"My brothers hesitated a long time over whether they would show me this last mark of Tourmeil's love. But finally the chevalier brought me that fatal letter, I read it a thousand times, it renewed all my grief, and I became so cruelly distressed that the chevalier regretted having given it to me; in it I learned that Tourmeil instructed the chevalier not to send him a reply, because he would change his name upon embarking with the troops that the Venetians were sending into Morea, where he was going to seek an end to a life made so miserable on account of his unfortunate love, and that he was sacrificing his life for me with no regret.[75]

"I hid my grief with great care. The feeble state I was in was worsened by the violence that I was constantly doing to my feelings; after the doctors had ordered me to get fresh air in the countryside, Monsieur de Briance brought me to one of his estates, the solitude of which seemed to me more suited to my sadness than the frequent visits from people in high society; content with our marriage, he came by almost every day to hunt and to provide me, through his eager attentiveness, with the pleasures that he thought might be agreeable to me. My brothers, who were on the verge of going to Paris in order to begin serving in the army, came to see me at the start of spring.[76]

"They had been in that large and famous city for about six months, when my father, having become seriously overheated while hunting a deer, came down with pleurisy,[77] which in seven days' time stole from us a heart that was very dedicated to his children and the kindest one there ever was. Monsieur de Briance felt this loss as keenly as I did. This misfortune caused us to return to Rennes; my brothers also went there; and having shared the most desirable inheritance in the province with Monsieur de Briance, who gave them marks of his affection through an unexampled act of selflessness, they returned to Paris, whose pleasures had

---

75. Morea was the name the Venetians gave to the Peloponnesian peninsula in southern Greece, which they captured during the early years of the Morean War (1684–1699); in this conflict, Venice joined the Holy League against the Ottoman Empire. The Venetians ran Morea as an autonomous kingdom and occupied it until 1715, when it was recaptured by the Ottomans. Since Tourmeil would presumably have volunteered to fight for France if his own country were at war at this moment in the story, we must assume that his departure takes place during the final years of the Morean War and shortly after the conclusion of the War of the League of Augsburg (1688–1697), in which France had been a major participant. And since Tourmeil does not return to France until around 1702 (Madame de Briance's marriage lasts two years, and she has been widowed for three years when the novel begins), he apparently remains in Morea following the end of the war to assist the Venetian occupying forces.

76. This presumably refers to the beginning of the next major war involving France: the War of the Spanish Succession (1701–1714).

77. An inflammation of the lining of the lungs.

made them lose their taste for those of other cities. After that, having received authorization to lead two regiments that they bought,[78] they remained in the army all year long and arrived in this region only last year, when the honor that they had of seeing the two of you made them so impatient to return.

"It had been nearly two years since I had wed Monsieur de Briance when he was attacked by a violent fever that put him in danger as of the third day. I found myself sincerely distressed; he noticed that. And the last day of his illness, having asked me to send everyone else out of the room, he said to me as he reached out his hand to me, 'Madam, I would die with the regret of having caused your unhappiness if I had not always had good reason to believe that your virtue had made you overcome the fondness that you had for Tourmeil; his departure, which preceded our marriage by a few days, made me realize the grief that he felt over it, but I believed that it was nothing but the rapture of a young man, which time would calm. It is only fair that I make amends for this wrong. I am declaring him my heir,[79] and if he returns, as I hope he will, I beg you, madam, to receive him as a spouse worthy of you; I wish with all my heart that he will fill my place.'[80] I remained so astonished and so touched by this speech that I did not have the strength to answer it. My tears increased, Monsieur de Briance suffered a sudden weakness, I called for assistance, and he died while displaying until the last moment perfect lucidity and the courage of a hero. His death disconcerted me, I renounced all social activity, and I departed from Rennes, where we were at that time, in order to go live in seclusion in the countryside, where I have always remained since that time. And without the entreaties of my brothers, and their interests, which are very dear to me, I would not have abandoned the state of solitude in which I have always lived since the death of Monsieur de Briance and in which I am held back by the cruel anxiety that I feel over Tourmeil's absence. I will admit to you that I have made great effort to gain information about him, but since he changed his name upon embarking in the Venetian forces, it has been impossible for me to find out what has become of him."

Kernosy and Saint-Urbain told Madame de Briance that she ought not to lose all hope, that she was overly clever in devising ways to cause herself distress,

---

78. Although military leadership was reserved for members of the aristocracy, they were still obliged to purchase their commissions. They also had to pay up front for all expenses such as recruiting, equipping, and paying their soldiers, and they could only hope to be reimbursed by the royal treasury once the war was over.

79. Tourmeil would not inherit Monsieur de Briance's fortune directly, but rather only if he married Madame de Briance. During the early modern period in France, widows inherited not only the family estate but also the right to live autonomously, choosing a new husband only if they so wished.

80. In giving his wife his blessing to marry Tourmeil, Monsieur de Briance reverses the behavior of Monsieur de Clèves in the famous scene from *The Princess of Cleves* (1678), who on his deathbed expresses his fear and his grief over the possibility that his wife might remarry. In Lafayette's novel, this conversation contributes to the princess's decision not to remarry.

and that Tourmeil through his good sense might have escaped from the dangers that his despair had made him go so far to seek. These two charming sisters, after doing everything in their power to maintain her in that frame of mind, finished their conversation by thanking the marquise for the narration that she had been kind enough to share with them, and they retired to bed.

The next day, the actors, having taken leave of the company, departed much to everyone's regret, to go at once to Rennes according to the order that, they said, they had received from people whom they could not fail to obey. Several hours after their departure, a man with a nice enough appearance was seen entering the courtyard of the castle on horseback, followed by two valets; the viscountess, once she was informed of his arrival, went to receive him very graciously. She led him into her private study, where they remained in conference for more than two hours. The Baron de Tadillac, astonished by this long meeting, told us in jest in regard to the unknown man that he would have believed him to be a rival had he not remarked, while seeing him pass by, that he was no longer suited to the viscountess's taste, since she had no interest in outmoded suitors.

Finally, the viscountess came back to rejoin the company, and Fatville, upon entering the room for dinner, ran to embrace the unknown man, who as of that time was no longer unknown, because Fatville called him his uncle. She told her nieces not to get involved in games once they had withdrawn from the dining room, because she had to speak to them in private. This kindly aunt, having made both of them go into her private study, after making a long and tedious speech to prove to them that both had infinite obligations to her, informed Mademoiselle de Saint-Urbain that, as a consequence of those alleged obligations, she had just signed the articles for a marriage, very advantageous for her, with Fatville's elder brother, who was very rich, who was a bit less impolite than he was, and who had acquired a more sociable temperament by spending time with men of good breeding, whom he had encountered in the army during his several years of military service.

A stroke of lightning would not have stunned Mademoiselle de Saint-Urbain as greatly as this piece of news, so little expected and so opposed to her wishes; she did not hide the grief that she felt over it; Mademoiselle de Kernosy appeared as distressed as her sister; all of that served merely to bring down upon them a long speech from the viscountess about the blind obedience that well-brought-up girls owe to their parents, which Saint-Urbain had no desire to profit from. Finally, the aunt, believing that a diversion from tears was required, left her nieces in the study and came to inform the company of the news of Saint-Urbain's marriage. Fortunately, the Chevalier de Livry was not present; his agitation would have revealed the interest he took in the matter.

The Count de Livry left the room at once in order to inform his brother about this news and to take measures with him that would be capable of averting the misfortune with which he was threatened. On the other hand, the Marquise de Briance, having her brother's interests to take care of, and knowing from experience how greatly devastated a person could feel when on the verge of losing one's beloved, went to find Saint-Urbain, who burst into tears. The marquise pointed out to her that this marriage that had just been proposed was very far from being concluded, that countless pretexts could be found to delay it, and even to break it off, and that after all, since the viscountess was not her mother, she could, in an extreme case, refuse to obey and not sacrifice herself to her aunt's whims.

Kernosy approved this advice; Saint-Urbain, always disposed to entertaining a pleasing hope, thought she could glimpse the prospect of not being totally unhappy and found it suitable to skillfully play along for time. She dried her tears, resolving, according to her sister's opinion, supported by Madame de Briance, to receive Fatville's uncle with an apparent civility, in order not to alarm the viscountess, who, seeing her come back in a calm mood, did not doubt for a moment that it was the result of her moralizing, and she applauded herself more than once for having had the cleverness to persuade her niece. Fatville's uncle appeared at that moment and made his ceremonial introduction to Saint-Urbain, who answered him in few words, and Fatville added to the subject at hand all the worthless things that he had ever heard people say on similar occasions. Madame de Salgue,[81] having noticed that this marriage was not to Saint-Urbain's taste, spoke to her about it only in order to pity her. The baroness, persuaded that the chevalier had no further hopes of wedding Saint-Urbain and that after such an event she could more easily gain this suitor for herself through her charms, shrewdly concealed the joy that she felt over it in her innermost heart and took care not to display before Saint-Urbain any feelings other than those that her female friends were showing.

The chevalier, who had just returned with his brother, had great difficulty restraining himself, in order to hide the distress that he felt to see Saint-Urbain in a kind of indifference with regard to this cruel news and to learn the confirmation of it from the mouth of the viscountess herself, who informed the company at that very moment that Fatville's brother was scheduled to arrive toward evening. At that point, swept away by love and despair, without giving himself the time to examine anything, he ran to the stables to take a horse. And in order to get far away from the castle with greater haste, he pushed it at breakneck speed along the road to Rennes, upon which his odious rival was supposed to arrive.

The sun was starting to set when the sound of some horses drew the chevalier out of his daydream; he perceived in the distance a man on horseback

---

81. In Part Two the name is spelled "Salgues," as opposed to "Salgue," an inconsistency that is unlikely to have been due to the novelist. It is probable that different compositors worked in the print shop for the two volumes and that the discrepancy went unnoticed. We have chosen to standardize the spelling of the countess's name.

wrapped in a large red cloak, followed by three people, also on horseback. And not doubting that it was his rival, he rushed, sword in hand, to attack the man who seemed to be the master. "Let's see," he said, approaching him with a tone of voice that anger made unrecognizable, "whether you are worthier than I am of the treasure that you are seeking to take away from me."

This man, who was preoccupied with a grief just as pressing as that of the chevalier, at once threw off his cloak and drew his sword; they were fighting with equal advantage when the men of the unknown man's retinue prepared to separate them, but he ordered them to withdraw. The sound of that voice suspended the anger with which the chevalier was agitated. At once he made his horse move several paces back, and, lowering the point of his sword, he cried out, "What! I have just attacked the life of a person whom I would defend a thousand times at the expense of my own." The unknown man, who was Tourmeil, surprised to hear the voice of the Chevalier de Livry, which he could clearly discern, remained totally motionless and did not know what to think of such an adventure. Finally, these two friends, having recovered from their astonishment, and both of them feeling their hearts moved to tenderness, approached each other and embraced with all the joy that a true friendship can cause. The chevalier wanted to inform his friend in few words of the intention that had brought him to that place; Tourmeil kept interrupting him at every turn to speak to him about Madame de Briance. At that moment, curiosity was pushing both of them to ask questions of each other at the same time, and never was there a conversation less coherent or more touching; they forgot where they were going because of it.

A man on horseback, who was approaching at full gallop, stopped to ask them whether Kernosy Castle was still a great distance away from the place where they were, and he indicated to them that he was very eager to get there. The chevalier, curious to know the reason for that eagerness, replied to him that they were going there and that he could follow them; this man was the personal valet of Fatville's elder brother and a very talkative man. He was delighted to find matter for conversation. This pleasure, slowing his desire to continue his traveling, caused him to narrate at great length the story of an accident that had forced his master to stop in a village at two leagues' distance from Rennes, where he was being treated for an injury that had happened to his leg while falling off his horse; for that reason he had sent ahead this valet to bring the news to his brother, his uncle, and the viscountess.

Tourmeil, after hearing this narrative, said privately to the Chevalier de Livry that love was not favoring his rival's intentions and that this delay would give them the time to break off a marriage from which no appearance of a happy outcome could be seen. Following that, they continued their journey without speaking to each other; the chevalier was preoccupied by the current state of his destiny, and Tourmeil was feeling rapturous joy that kept increasing as he approached the place where Madame de Briance was. To be sure, the apprehension of not finding her feeling the same way as she had when he had left her caused him great anxiety; but nothing can outweigh, in a love-filled heart, the pleasure of seeing one's beloved again.

Upon arriving at the castle, Tourmeil asked the chevalier not to make his identity known to the company before he had learned in what manner Madame de Briance wanted him to interact with the viscountess. At that point, people were speaking only of the Chevalier de Livry. Everyone was uneasy over his absence. Kernosy, Saint-Urbain, and Madame de Briance, fearing that some misfortune had befallen him, begged the Count de Livry and the Baron de Tadillac to go out to look for him on the road to Rennes; but since the night was already somewhat advanced when they mounted their horses, they went astray, and after wandering uselessly in many roundabout directions, they returned to the castle only at the moment of the chevalier's arrival; he was entering his room with Tourmeil. The chevalier would have preferred to have them go upstairs secretly. That could not be done. He gave orders that a fire should be lit at once, that his friend should be furnished with all the necessary refreshments, and that he be allowed to rest while waiting until [the chevalier] himself was able to keep him company. Next he came out to introduce the personal valet of Fatville's brother, who made his formal greeting to the viscountess on behalf of his master and informed her of the news of his injury. The presence of the chevalier reassured all the charming ladies who took an interest in him. Only the Fatville family and the viscountess seemed to be attentive solely to the valet's speech. After several questions that they put to him in private concerning his master's fall, the two men resolved to depart the next day, in order to have him transported to Rennes.

Meanwhile Saint-Urbain and the marquise criticized the chevalier over his abrupt departure. But the shame over having made that useless trip prevented him from revealing to them its true motive. He only told them, in a whisper: "I will inform you this evening of the reason that made me go off on horseback with such great haste, and I am sure that Madame de Briance will be grateful to me for it."

The viscountess, having rejoined the company, asked the chevalier where he was coming from; the baron, who saw that this question was embarrassing the chevalier, as well as the Count de Livry who also had just arrived, answered her, "It's a little secret, madam, that concerns me, and of which I will have the honor of giving you an account in the coming days." In that manner he got them out of their predicament.

That very evening, Fatville and his uncle, before going off to their apartments, took leave of the company for several days. After each person had retired to bed, Kernosy and Saint-Urbain went into the marquise's room, where they were supposed to hold a meeting over the means to break off the marriage that the accident that had happened to Fatville's brother had delayed. The marquise's prudence made them hopeful that the result of the assembly would not be fruitless, and the influence that the baron had over the mind of the viscountess seemed to assure them that everything would work out according to their wishes.

The Count and the Chevalier de Livry were already there, in a state of joy that these two charming sisters did not find suitable to the present state of affairs that was in question. "What favorable hope," said Saint-Urbain as she entered, "can be inspiring the joy that I see all over your faces? Will we be permitted to join in?" Madame de Briance took the floor and answered them: "The unexpected good luck that Heaven is sending me today proves that one can expect everything from Fortune. Tourmeil has returned, and he returns with the same feelings that he had when he departed. When the chevalier was on the road to Rennes this evening, he encountered a man whom [Tourmeil] had sent to find out whether his presence would be agreeable to me." Kernosy and Saint-Urbain took such an interest in all things regarding Madame de Briance that they forgot for a moment their own interests and spoke of nothing other than Tourmeil; the intensity that they gave to the joy with which their hearts were penetrated, and their manner of congratulating her, indicated perfectly what pleasure this agreeable news was causing them to feel in the depths of their souls. Then the chevalier, seeing everyone enlivened with the same idea, said, "I clearly see that people won't be upset if I bring in the man whom Tourmeil sent to me." He left after saying in a few words to Saint-Urbain that the viscountess's project had sent him into despair, and he came back into the room at once with Tourmeil, whose unkempt appearance, similar to that of a man who is arriving after a long voyage, did not fail to charm all the people who did not yet know him, on account of his good looks. Madame de Briance, struck by the sight of a man so cherished and so unexpected, uttered a loud cry, remaining motionless in her chair. Tourmeil, surprised to see her in that state, falls to his knees at her feet and kisses her hands, without having the strength to utter a word.[82] By then, there was no one in the assembly who was not informed of her passion; the chevalier had told all of them about it before entering. Kernosy and Saint-Urbain did not believe him to be a person sent on behalf of Tourmeil. They recognized at once, by his majestic bearing, that it was [Tourmeil] himself.

The Count de Livry, in great joy to recover the best of his friends, ran to embrace him. And clearly judging that Madame de Briance and her suitor were still too preoccupied by their happiness to be able to speak of anything else, he proposed to the two charming sisters and to the chevalier to go into a nearby private study, where they, together with the Baron de Tadillac, who had just arrived, took definitive measures to get the viscountess to resolve to marry him. The chevalier calmly gave his advice on that subject, now that his mind was at ease with respect to Saint-Urbain, who had promised him that she would never obey her aunt if she proposed a marriage to her that ran contrary to the choice of

---

82. The original French switches into the present tense here to indicate a passage of heightened emotion; the scene constitutes the novel's climax.

her heart. The count was no less satisfied with the conversation that he had with Mademoiselle de Kernosy. And the baron committed to making every possible effort with the viscountess in order to break off the marriage that she had proposed with Fatville's brother and to obtain for all of them the fulfillment of their wishes. As a reward for his good will, the two charming sisters, seeing him impatient to learn where Tourmeil was, told him that he would find him in Madame de Briance's apartment. At once he went there to pay him a visit; his formal introduction was not of great length, but his heart was on his lips. Next he went with them to rejoin the company, which showed new signs of the joy that each person felt inwardly. They informed the new arrivals of the results of the assembly and of the awkward position they were in to find a trustworthy man who would have the cleverness to pretend that he was a messenger, and to tell the baron, while giving him a letter from his legal guardian, to make an answer that same day, because he was obliged to return in haste. Tourmeil offered them a nobleman in his retinue, capable of succeeding in whatever mission might be involved, and informed them of the place where he had left that man together with his other servants; the baron went there the next day in the early morning in order to instruct the man about everything he would have to do.

Meanwhile, the marquise, who did not yet want to make Tourmeil's identity known to the viscountess or to divulge his return without having removed all the obstacles that might have been able to suspend the execution of the late Monsieur de Briance's will, according to which Tourmeil was made full heir to the estate, asked the baron, whose brilliance let him rise above all sorts of difficulties, to imagine a means to have Tourmeil remain unknown for several days in the castle. "It's as good as done," he told her, "if you find it acceptable for Monsieur de Tourmeil to play [the role of] the leader in the troupe of our regional actors." "What is the likelihood that that could be pulled off?" rejoined Saint-Urbain. "We would then be required to have them here." The baron, having replied that the actors had not gone very far, put off for the following day the task of informing them of his plan, and Tourmeil promised that he would perform a role, rather badly, in order to better deceive the viscountess and to persuade her that he was truly an actor from a regional troupe.[83] Their conversation finished with that exchange. Since the night was already well advanced, each person retired to bed; the Chevalier de Livry took into his apartment the Count de Tourmeil, who was too preoccupied to fully give himself over to sleep; the pleasure of being near Madame de Briance and of finding her faithful filled his mind in such a manner that he lost the night's rest over it; and the marquise, agitated with the enchanting excitement that is inspired by the sweetness of seeing again the person one loves, did not spend the night with any more tranquility.

---

83. An allusion to the poorly performed play described earlier in the Story of Madame de Briance.

The baron went first thing in the morning to inform Tourmeil and the chevalier that, in order to satisfy the lottery note that ordered him to regale all the ladies with a party, he had held back the actors and the musicians, who were awaiting his orders in a village at three leagues' distance from the castle; that he had pretended that they had departed only in order to surprise the viscountess by their return, because the only things she found to her taste were those of an extraordinary nature. And in order for Tourmeil to be exempted from performing any role, the baron requested him to assume the rank of leader of the company.

"That is not all," he continued, looking at the Chevalier de Livry. "Let us give thought to the conclusion of our adventures. Please assist me, both of you, in arranging the arrival here of our supposed messenger, who will bring me a letter from my guardian, which I have told you about. I am going to write a draft of it; in it he will propose to me an advantageous marriage and will give me a direct order to depart with all possible dispatch. I will complain of the harshness of Fortune; I will communicate my letter to the viscountess, and this is precisely what will force her into a decision." "But if she consents to having you depart," rejoined the chevalier, "what will we do?" "Of course, I would have to go away," rejoined the baron. "I clearly see that you do not have much faith in my charms; I will find new expedients, if there is a need for that. Meanwhile, let's risk doing what I have resolved; I hope that the Count de Tourmeil will have the goodness to make a very legible copy of the draft that I will give him shortly. The viscountess does not know his handwriting; since he is here as a prisoner, he will have the time to do it successfully, and even to add to this letter, the outcome of which causes you so much fear, whatever he will judge the most appropriate to make it look very urgent."

It was at this juncture that the chevalier informed Tourmeil of the different interests that were bringing all of them together in the castle, and he gave him to understand that the jealousy that he [Tourmeil] had conceived against the baron was founded only upon some implausible reports that he had been given in Rennes about the passion of his alleged rival for Madame de Briance. Tourmeil, touched by the chevalier's speech, which was full of affection, admitted to him that he had let himself be surprised too easily, that he had believed that he was fighting against the baron when he saw himself attacked in a wood along the road to Rennes; but that the favorable reception from the marquise had entirely disabused him of his credulity, and he begged him urgently not to speak to anyone about this admission.

The baron came at that moment to rejoin them, and he read the letter, whose prodigious inventiveness brought them much pleasure. He then placed it in Tourmeil's hands so that, once Tourmeil had transcribed it, he could entrust it to that nobleman who was supposed to pass as a messenger. Finally, not wishing to let the time that he had set aside to give a party for the ladies slip by uselessly, he said to the chevalier that, having conceived of a plan to add a kind of opera to the theatrical entertainment, he could appeal to no one better than [the chevalier], since he had a great talent for composing verses, to write several sung dialogues comprising only one or two scenes; he was expecting this libretto without delay, in order to have it set to music by the most proficient among the musicians who were in his entourage. The chevalier replied that the anxieties with which his mind was agitated prevented him from undertaking that work but that Tourmeil would succeed at it better than anyone else. "If it is up to the most contented person," Tourmeil rejoined, "to write the verses in question, I could quite justly get the preference, but for any other reason the preference should be given to you." The baron, impatient upon hearing these compliments, replied to them at once, "I clearly see that this will turn into an exchange of compliments; I intend to stage an entertainment for the fulfillment of my task of giving a party, and if you annoy me I will propose that you also write the music for it." Finally, once the chevalier and Tourmeil had agreed that they would give the baron the verses that he desired, he went away, with his mind at ease, to pay court to the viscountess, who had just gotten up. Madame de Briance came to her brother's room, where she had the pleasure of seeing Tourmeil, and, not being able to get out of paying a call on the viscountess, she went to the latter's apartment a bit before the midday meal, accompanied by the chevalier, who offered to lend her his hand, after being informed by his valet that people had been careful to execute the orders that he had given first thing that morning, so that nothing of necessity should be lacking for Tourmeil during the day, and that he should be punctually served at dinner time.[84] Rules of decorum did not permit people to leave the company as soon as they had gotten up from the dinner table; each person remained out of courtesy to the viscountess, and the conversation, having lasted for quite a long time, gave Tourmeil enough free time to compose that dialogue in verse that he had promised the baron and that he presented to him that evening fully finished.

The chevalier, seeing the company fully engrossed in the conversation, escaped in order to return to his room, where he found Tourmeil, who was busy finishing those two scenes that the baron had asked for. He told him upon entering, "I have just abandoned everybody in order to join you, and I have no doubt that Madame de Briance has the clear intention of following me, for she is no less susceptible than I am to the pleasure of seeing you." Tourmeil wanted to make a courteous response to that speech, but the chevalier interrupted him, saying, "It is not to bring compliments upon myself that I am expressing to you the genuine feelings of my heart. Finish what you have started so well, so that you will be able to inform me at leisure of what happened to you since the fatal day when we had

---

84. In her edition, Marie-Madeleine de Lubert inserted here a fairy tale of her own composition, "Etoilette." Madame de Briance reads it to the company in order to prolong the conversation and give the chevalier an excuse to leave the room and rejoin Tourmeil so that they can work together on composing the opera libretto. We have placed this fairy tale in the appendix.

the regret of losing you; keep your word to me, I beg you." Tourmeil replied to him that his verses would soon be finished, that he would fulfill his promise, and even that he would tell him in confidence certain circumstances that one can reveal only to a perfect friend. He made haste to finish and began narrating the story that follows.

The Story of the Count de Tourmeil

Departure of the Count de Tourmeil for Venice. His embarkation and passage to Morea with the army of the Venetians. His adventures during the campaigns that he participated in while there. His return to Rennes. That which occurred during his sojourn in Kernosy Castle.[85]

"I left in despair, which had been inspired in me by the loss of the sweet hopes of my happiness, which I believed to be certain, and I made the trip from Rennes to Paris without even knowing who I was; I was beside myself; the thought that Mademoiselle de Livry was going to become the wife of Monsieur de Briance sent me into despair. This cruel idea, persistent in tormenting me, was constantly presenting itself to my mind in all of the most fatal forms possible; indeed, I would often shed tears, and I did not have the courage to stop them.

"Once arrived in Paris, I went to stay with one of my uncles, and I told him in few words the story that you have learned. I don't know how he let himself be persuaded; my mind was so confused that I said almost nothing to him that was plausible. His affection for me was, I believe, what brought him to give credence to my words. He gave me some money and promised to arrange for me to draw more money in Venice. Finally, after writing to you and to Madame de Briance, I departed from Paris, guided by my anxieties alone, which were preventing me from stopping at any place in the world; without being rushed, I made extraordinary haste.

"My uncle had written to Venice so that I might be given the money that he had promised me; it was a considerable sum; and, believing that he was sending me a pleasing piece of news, he informed me of the marriage of Monsieur de Briance to Mademoiselle de Livry. The certainty of my rival's happiness threw me into a mortal decline; I was ill for nearly a month, and I was just starting to be able to get out of bed when I learned that the troops of the Republic were going to be embarking soon. A nobleman who had been in my father's entourage and

---

85. This synopsis heading, not used with other embedded narratives, was presumably added by the first editor and not by the author, who is more likely to have used the same type of brief heading as in other places, such as the "History of the Count de Tourmeil." Later editors introduce this story with a brief heading.

who had been attached to me since my earliest childhood, seeing that I was not in a condition to put together the necessary horses and servants, offered, in order to relieve me of the anxiety that I felt over not being ready soon enough, to do this service for me; he provided me with magnificent equipment. As soon as he had finished, I, without waiting for my strength to be entirely restored, went to present myself to the general at the very moment when he was giving his orders for the embarkation of the troops. I told him that I was a Spaniard, that my name was Don Fernand, that, having had a quarrel followed by a duel, I had gone away in order to give time for my matter to be settled. The ease with which I spoke the Spanish language helped to deceive him. He received me with a kindness that touched me; he even offered to give me a position among his forces, for which I thanked him, and I served in the quality of a volunteer.

"The army sprang into action almost as soon as we had landed on shore; there were several occasions on which I gave signs of how little attachment I then had for my life. My despair was interpreted as valor, and it drew to me the esteem and the affection of our generals. Fortune, which was reserving for me the reward for the torments that she was making me suffer, preserved my life, the ending of which I regarded as the only good thing I could aspire to.

"One day, I had gone to take a stroll in the area surrounding the camp, followed only by the nobleman of whom I have spoken to you, who was then acting as my squire and whom I had informed of my misfortunes. I was lamenting over them while walking across a beautiful prairie when we heard a tumultuous noise mixed with [the sound of] women screaming. A short time later, we saw some soldiers appear, who were leading two female prisoners. We ran over to them in order to save those two unfortunate women from a fate even more cruel than their captivity.[86] These soldiers, to whom, fortunately, I was known, withdrew at my approach with a great amount of respect; and the sum of money that I gave them succeeded in persuading them to yield to me their slaves, who were utterly shaken from the agitation into which their misfortune had cast them. The sumptuousness of their clothing led me to believe that they were persons who were owed respect, and several words in Italian that they uttered rather confusedly while turning their gaze in the direction from which they had been brought led me to understand that they still did not believe themselves to be safe. I tried to reassure them; I offered them everything in my power, and I asked them where they wanted to be taken. After several hastily uttered statements of thanks, the woman who had spoken to me first said, 'Save us. Save us from a cruel man who believes that the slavery in which he holds us must extend even to our hearts.'[87] I admit to you that if I had been in a position to fall in love, I would doubtless have done so with one

---

86. Tourmeil implies that the soldiers were intending to rape these women.

87. In the Mediterranean, individuals could be enslaved through war, conquest, piracy, or frontier raiding. Although the women at first appear to be prisoners of war, we will later learn that they have

of these beautiful slaves, whose beauty, youth, and grief were so touching that my unresponsiveness on this occasion is doubtless the greatest proof of my passion that I have ever given to Madame de Briance."

"And yet," said the chevalier, smiling, "this is one of those circumstances that you have not revealed to her." "That is true," rejoined Tourmeil, "but doesn't it suffice that I was faithful? Why seek to take credit for simply having done my duty?

"I led my beautiful slave women into our camp, from which we were not far," continued Tourmeil. "Having yielded my tent to them and ordered my squire to have them served as well as the place we were in could permit, I went to the general's quarters. Once I was back in one of my tents, I started writing letters. My squire, who was always seeking to pull me out of the melancholy state that I was in, then said to me, 'How is it possible that you are not asking me for news of your beautiful slave women? Don't you want to go see them?' 'I will see them tomorrow,' I answered him. 'My own misfortunes preoccupy me so greatly that no one should be astonished if I am less sensitive to those of others.'

"'Are you,' he replied to me, 'in the same frame of mind in regard to these beautiful persons as Alexander was for his female prisoners?'[88] 'You wish to flatter me through your grandiose comparisons,' I answered him. 'But I assure you that I have no fear, as Alexander did, of falling in love with my female prisoners; I will expose myself to the power of their charms. Let's go see them.' He followed me and I found these two beautiful captives, lying down in a casual manner on a bed in their tent. The one whose beauty was the more perfect seemed the more distressed; I tried to console them with the assurance that they would be freed and that I would facilitate their return to whatever place they wished to be taken.

"'You are too generous, Don Fernand,' said the woman who appeared to be several years older; they had made inquiries to learn my name. 'You are too generous in restoring freedom to your slaves. If some reward more worthy of you than our perfect gratitude were capable of giving pleasure to a man such as you seem to be, we would offer you a ransom, which would doubtless touch a soul less noble than yours.

"'We are Greeks, born in Argostoli, capital of Cephalonia.[89] We were brought up on that island; our parents hold an important rank there, thanks to their wealth

---

been enslaved by corsairs (Barbery pirates). Corsairs were primarily Muslim and are estimated to have enslaved as many as 1.2 million Europeans between 1500–1800.

88. Alexander the Great was praised for his magnanimity and self-control when he refused to take sexual advantage of his female captives, most notably the wife and daughters of the Persian king, Darius. He later married Statira, one of King Darius's daughters.

89. Argostoli was, and still is, the capital of Cephalonia, the largest of the Ionian Islands to the west of Greece.

and their high birth; my sister's name is Fatime,[90] and my name is Praxile.[91] We lost my mother when we were still in our childhood, and we were destined by my father to wed two of our closest relatives. The festivities that preceded that unfortunate wedding celebration cost us our precious liberty. Several days preceding the one that had been chosen for our nuptials, we went for an excursion on the sea in a little rowboat that was quite ornate but had no defenses. Soliman, an elderly corsair who roamed those waters, concealed himself from our sight by means of a boulder, with the intention of surprising us more easily as soon as our boat had put out to sea. Then, having abducted us without encountering almost any resistance, he set sail in haste, leaving behind in the rowboat the small number of people who had accompanied us.

"'I will spare you the details of our grief, generous Don Fernand; it is easy to imagine it, if, however, one's imagination can go as far as the heart on such an occasion. We were served with much attentiveness and with more respect than we had expected from this barbarian. Soliman brought us to this country, and it was only after our arrival that he appeared infatuated with Fatime; that passion increased our grief. Finally, after three months of slavery, always agitated by our misfortunes and by the deadly fear that Soliman, weary of Fatime's rejections, would be led to commit some violent action, for he threatened her with that quite often, we won over one of our guards with the jewels that had remained in our possession, and he arranged for our escape last night, gave us horses, and he himself ran away from the wrath of Soliman. When we encountered your soldiers who made us prisoners again, we were going into the closest city to ask for asylum from Soliman's cruelty; but Heaven, after showering us with misfortunes, seems to have become weary of being hostile to us, since, through the encounter with Don Fernand, we have found a protector so noble-hearted that we hope to see our beloved fatherland again.'

"'Yes, madam,' I answered her, touched by the story that she had just related, 'you will see your fatherland again. I promise that to you and I will keep my word.' She gave me her sincere thanks and heaped complimentary words on me. Meanwhile the beautiful Fatime had not stopped shedding tears. Her beautiful

---

90. Fatima (ca. 609–632) was the prophet Mohammed's favorite daughter. The choice of this name thus accentuates the slave's beauty and chastity.

91. Praxilla was a Greek poetess who lived during the sixth or fifth century BCE. During Murat's time she was known for having invented a fluid and rapid poetic meter called the "praxilian" and for having composed hymns, dithyrambs, and skolia (drinking songs). Seventeenth-century French female authors had great admiration for the Greek poetesses of antiquity and often evoked their names as a form of homage. The famous novelist Madeleine de Scudéry (1607–1710), for example, wrote under the pseudonym Sappho, a Greek poetess who lived during the seventh and sixth centuries BCE. According to Murat's friend and fellow novelist Marie-Jeanne Lhéritier de Villandon, Murat's Parnassian nickname was Praxille (Lhéritier de Villandon, "Lettre à Mademoiselle d'Alerac," *Le Mercure Galant* [May 1696], 109).

eyes, whose languishing glances were sometimes turned in my direction, would doubtless have set any heart but mine on fire."

"Those beautiful eyes," said the chevalier, "were cut out of the story that you related to my sister." "The more beautiful Fatime is," rejoined Tourmeil, "the more the sacrifice is worthy of Madame de Briance.

"Praxile," he continued, "astonished to see Fatime display so keen a grief at a time when the hope of freedom should have consoled her, said to her, 'How is this, sister? You are distressed more keenly when Heaven is favorable to us than when it appeared to abandon us.' 'It is not without good reason,' I rejoined. 'The beautiful Fatime pines over the absence of the fortunate lover who is to be her husband.' 'Ah, Don Fernand,' she said to me, lifting up her eyes, 'do not add to my misfortunes by doing me such injustice.' She blushed after uttering these few words, and Praxile told me that the indifference that had always reigned in Fatime's heart caused her to take as an offense the mere suspicion that she might feel a passion. I left them after reiterating all the offers of service that I had made to them. In the following days, the reports of my adventure and of their beauty, having been spread throughout the camp, led the most high-ranking men in our army to ask me to see them. The first time that I brought them there, one of our generals, who was among my intimate friends, became smitten with a violent passion for the beautiful Greek woman.[92] Having noticed it, she begged me very urgently not to bring him into their tent again. This request was awkward for me; I tried to invent some pretext in order to lead my friend again to the feet of the beautiful Fatime; all my expedients were useless. The beautiful Greek women pretended to be ill and consistently refused entry into their tent to all the men who presented themselves. I alone had the privilege of seeing them whenever I called on them. Fatime seemed plunged into a profound sadness; she sighed, and, if I dare say this, she would sometimes look at me tenderly. My squire, who was always seeking to make me forget the passion that I had for Madame de Briance, pointed out to me every one of the actions of that beautiful person.

"One day, the two sisters, having entered my tent when I wasn't there, found writing-tablets that I had left behind; Fatime opened them to a spot that was filled with verses in French written in my hand, and since she couldn't understand them, she asked my squire for an explanation of them, and he, not foreseeing the consequences of that, explained them in Italian. It is necessary for the continuation of my tale that I recite them to you.

> Yield, feeble reason, yield to my grief and pain.
> I'll dwell on it always; your advice is vain.
> What good thing could ease my bad luck without peer?
>   I've lost the fair one I adore.

---

92. Fatime.

Of my faithful ardor, memory too dear,
> Alas, you please me as of yore,
> Though making my grief more severe.
No, to banish you from my soul I can't claim to do.
Redouble my love, increase my pain and smart.
To you, rather than reason, I give my heart;
You'll defend it better from any love that's new."

"This poem seems good to me," said the chevalier. "One has good reason to believe that pain inspires more beautiful things than joy." "With the exception that," rejoined Tourmeil, "I would prefer to be the most worthless poet in the world for my whole life than to think henceforth of complaining over my misfortunes. But let's come back to my tale.

"My squire noticed that Fatime had blushed during the explanation of this poem, and that very evening, while passing near their tent, he heard the two beautiful Greek women conversing about me. He rushed at once to tell me that I should come to learn a secret upon which the peace of my heart might depend.

"I thought that I was going to learn something concerning Madame de Briance; that thought made me go out with him; he led me in a great hurry to the very spot where he had heard them speaking together, and, pricking up his ears, he had me approach while whispering to me, 'Listen.' It was Fatime speaking. She was saying to her sister, 'Yes, Praxile, I found myself less to be pitied when I was in Soliman's power; death could free me from his unjust treatment; I would at least have had the sweetness to die calmly, and the sight of Don Fernand has forever robbed me of that calmness on which I have always based my happiness and my self-esteem.' 'I don't know what to tell you,' rejoined Praxile, 'to console you over a calamity that an angry Heaven is adding to our misfortunes. You have resisted with all your power this involuntary fondness that you feel for Don Fernand; he is unaware of your feelings. You have done your duty; all that remains for you is to flee in haste from a place where it seems to me that your honor is no longer secure.'

"'My honor,' rejoined the beautiful Fatime proudly, 'is secure in whatever place I might find myself, but here my heart cannot resist, and it is the sight of the dangerous Don Fernand that I wish to flee; the poem that his squire read to us told me conclusively what his sadness had already made me suspect. He is in love, and his love, however unhappy it appears to me, preoccupies him no less than a passion that would make him happy for life. Unfortunate Fatime,' she cried, sighing. 'What god is making you feel his wrath, by inspiring in you such tender feelings, which you must hide?'

"After hearing these last words, I moved away and I said to my squire, 'What relation does this conversation have with the peace of mind that you gave me hope for just now?' 'What?' he answered me, totally astonished. 'Can't the passion that the charming Fatime has for you make you forget . . .' 'No,' I replied to him, interrupting him. 'No, never will anything erase from my heart the tender and unhappy love that I have for Madame de Briance. What I have just learned only adds to my misfortunes the knowledge that I am an ingrate.'

"I then continued my path toward my tent, and every time I had an occasion to see these two beautiful Greek women, I never said anything to Fatime that could lead her to figure out that I had heard what she had said to her sister. One day I even insisted on speaking to her about the merit of my friend, who was burning for her with a passion as tender as it was unfortunate, but Fatime, looking at me with an air that inspired respect, said to me, 'Don Fernand, since you have restored my liberty to me, stop treating me like a slave.'

"Finally, after a month of staying in our camp, the beautiful Greek women begged me to make good on the promise that I had given them and to have them brought to the port of Xanthus, from which, they had learned, every year at about that time some merchant vessels would leave to set sail for Greece.

"'Until this day,' said Praxile, 'when we believed we had to leave in order to see our fatherland again, we have preferred, O generous Don Fernand, to be near you than in any other place in the world, and nothing must cause us a keener sorrow than to be unable to indicate to you, as we are obliged to do, our intense gratitude.' The beautiful Fatime added few words to this speech of thanks from her sister, busying herself eagerly with preparing everything for their departure. The one sister appeared devastated; the other could not prevent herself from letting the joy that she felt within her heart burst forth. I admit to you that in a happier state I would perhaps have been less faithful. But, accustomed as I was to thinking only of my misfortunes, my heart was not susceptible to anything else.

"I therefore had a vehicle prepared for the beautiful Greek women. Two female slaves, whom I had given them to serve them, were destined to follow them in their journey, and I left with them a man in my retinue named Des Fontaines, whom I knew to be loyal, to accompany them until they reached the point of embarkation.

"Meanwhile, my friend was grieving and was urgently begging me to retain them for some time longer, in the hope that he could touch Fatime's heart, but I resisted all his entreaties. Finally, once the day planned for the departure of the beautiful Greek women had arrived, I went first thing in the morning to their tent. I found them about to get into their carriage; my squire was accompanying Praxile; I presented my hand to Fatime, whom I led to the vehicle without saying a single word to her. She placed herself next to her sister, and I mounted my horse in order to escort them myself for a distance of several leagues from the camp.

"When we had arrived at the place where I was to leave them, I had the vehicle stop in order to say farewell to them. They got off under a cluster of trees not far removed from the road. That was the fatal moment when Fatime's constancy abandoned her. She was unable to restrain some tears that flowed from her beautiful eyes, by which I was truly touched. I approached her, and she, seeing me totally disconcerted, said to me while looking at me tenderly, 'What, Don Fernand! So you do feel moved by our departure?' 'No one can leave the beautiful Fatime,' I told her, 'without feeling intense pain. And would to Heaven,' I added, sighing, 'that my heart had been at liberty to form amorous desires worthy of her.'

"'Ah, Don Fernand,' she rejoined as she abruptly withdrew, 'let me depart. What an idea you have just added to all the misfortunes of my life!' She went back as fast as she could to her vehicle; Praxile, who had been passing the time speaking to my squire, followed her at once. Having said a few more words to them, I let them depart, and I took the road back to our camp.

"It was at that point that I felt my heart beaten down with the keenest jolts of human weakness; I can't hide from you, chevalier, that the tears, the beauty, and the tenderness of Fatime made me wish that I could cure myself of a passion that, due to my frequent thinking about it, was causing unbearable fits of emotion in me. In private, I was leading the saddest and most listless existence in the world; I appeared altogether different in the eyes of the men with whom I had the honor to associate, and yet I let no occasion escape, however dangerous it was, without exposing myself to the obvious danger of losing my life.

"Several weeks elapsed without my having learned any news of Des Fontaines, to whom I had entrusted the task of accompanying the beautiful Greek women. My order was to escort them only as far as their point of embarkation; but this man had always had a desire to travel: this led him to depart along with them without my consent. Finally, I received a letter that he had written to me before setting off to sea. He asked my forgiveness and sent me word that Praxile appeared perfectly content to return to her country but that Fatime was in a dejected state that made them fear that the weariness of sea travel would expose her to life-threatening danger, although the trip was short.

"Des Fontaines arrived two months after his departure to rejoin me in the army. 'Well,' I said to him, 'did our beautiful Greek women arrive safely to their homeland?' 'They arrived there safely,' he answered me, 'but the beautiful Fatime did not enjoy that pleasure for long; she died several days after seeing her family.' How extremely upset I felt at that news! You can't conceive it, chevalier. I can't conceive it myself. My man, having observed that, stopped short, and I said to him, carried away with emotion, 'So tell me, please, what misfortune ended Fatime's life.'

"'Our trip had been uneventful,' he went on; 'we embarked with a joy that was troubled only by Fatime's poor health. The father of these beautiful persons, having been informed of their arrival, came to receive them at the port, accompanied by two young men, sumptuously dressed and of very pleasing appearance, who displayed a joy as perfect as his. Praxile embraced her father with a satisfaction that cannot be expressed, and Fatime, at the sight of him, appeared to forget her listlessness. They introduced me to their father; I was showered with presents and treated just as Don Fernand himself would have been.

"'A few days after our arrival, they made all the preparations for the nuptials of these two Greek women, who were supposed to wed the two young men whom I had seen coming to receive them as they got off the ship; but this festivity was disturbed by a violent fever that attacked the beautiful Fatime. She languished for several days. Finally, she expired, displaying infinite courage and a thousand regrets for life.

"'Never has grief appeared in as many different forms as it did then. The father of this beautiful girl, her sister, the suitor who was destined to be her husband, all of them were in a state of despair, and I was just as grieved as they. After satisfying the strong desire I had to see that beautiful country, I indicated to Praxile the intention that I had of leaving in order to rejoin you; she entrusted me with this box and ordered me to present it to you on her behalf.'

"Des Fontaines gave me the box; I found in it two letters, one from Praxile, and the other from the father of these beautiful Greek women. They were filled with signs of their gratitude toward me and of their grief over the loss of Fatime. I next opened another packet that was in the same box; it contained the portraits of these two charming Greek ladies, adorned with diamonds of enormous value. I sighed at the sight of the portrait of the unfortunate Fatime, and I entrusted the captain of a ship that was scheduled to depart to go to Argostoli with every rare object I could find to send to Praxile and to her father, along with a letter to indicate to them how much I shared their justified grief. I learned through the return of that captain, who brought me a reply from Praxile, that she had married that relative who had been destined for her and that she would have been very happy if the loss of the beautiful Fatime had not clouded her joy.

"This distressing loss redoubled my sorrow; I reproached myself for having contributed through my hard-heartedness to the misfortune of Fatime, and when the occasions to distinguish myself became less frequent in the army, or when there was any kind of break in the fighting, my anxieties would return in full force, overwhelming my mind. Sometimes it was Madame de Briance who occupied it; at other times, it was Fatime's death. Finally, being unable to live with peace of mind in Morea any longer, I returned to Venice at the start of the winter with several volunteers from my group of friends, who were going off to spend the carnival season there.[93]

"As soon as I had arrived in that city, my squire went to the office of the banker from whom I had received money in the past; there he found several letters for me, which that man had kept, not knowing how to forward them to me,

---

93. The carnival season in Venice culminated with a festival during the ten days leading up to Ash Wednesday, the first day of the Christian celebration of Lent, and is still world famous for its bright colors, elaborate costumes, and masks.

for I had not informed him that I was embarking with the troops of the Republic. I opened my letters, and the first being, by chance, the one that had arrived last, I found in it the only piece of news that could persuade me to come back to my country, which was that of the death of Monsieur de Briance. My uncle sent me word of it, and even of the provisions of his will, which were in my favor. I missed him as the best of my friends; his death erased from my memory all the misfortunes that he had caused me.

"The burning desire that I had to see Madame de Briance again led me to depart at once; I wrote to my uncle that in a short time I would go to Paris to find him, but at that moment I did not wish to make any stops. I finally arrived in Rennes, and it is there that I learned that you and the Count de Livry were staying with Madame de Briance. That news would have given me an extreme joy, had I not learned almost at the same time that the Baron de Tadillac was there with you, that he had stayed there for several days incognito, that afterward he had gone to Rennes to seek out a troupe of actors, and that, finally, all of you were together in Kernosy Castle.

"At that time, I had no doubt that Tadillac was in love with Madame de Briance. I accused her of an infidelity that I had so little deserved; I also complained about your forgetting me; but, I said to myself, after having reflected on this, 'They don't know what has become of me; Madame de Briance perhaps believes that I am no longer alive. Let's go,' I continued a moment later; 'let's go shower her with reproaches and see whether this new rival is worthier than I of a treasure that has cost me so dearly.'

"I departed from Rennes; I left almost all of my servants in a town that is several leagues from here. I had my mind and my heart so filled with my sorrows and my jealousy that at first I failed to recognize your voice, and I took you for the rival whom I was coming to seek. The few words that you said to me upon approaching me further helped to deceive me. I praised Fortune for the occasion that she presented me with to fight my rival; it took nothing less than the joy of finding a friend such as you again to suspend my anger."

"I am obliged to you," the chevalier then said, "for the kindness that you have done me by telling me what I was so eager to learn. The narrative that you have just given of your adventures convinces me of your good behavior. But I feel sorry for the beautiful Fatime. It is indeed on account of your prudence that you have not spoken to my sister about her. In her place, I would have had dreadful suspicions about your fidelity." "I gave her Fatime's portrait yesterday," Tourmeil rejoined, "without speaking to her of the passion felt by this beautiful Greek woman. I told her only that I had received it from a merchant in Cephalonia; and I gave myself great pleasure in sacrificing this portrait to Madame de Briance, without offending the memory of Fatime."

The chevalier found this behavior by Tourmeil quite sensible. Not wanting to leave him alone, he remained in conversation with him for the rest of the day;

then he returned to the company of the ladies, who were delighted by the fact that Fatville and his uncle, by departing first thing in the morning, had freed them from two men from the provinces who were quite fatiguing. Madame de Briance noticed [her brother] and had a definite suspicion that her suitor had remained alone. She came up with a pretext that gave the whole company an occasion to retire sooner than usual. The selected persons proceeded, as was their custom, to her apartment; Tourmeil, having also gone there, had the pleasure of learning from the mouth of his beloved that her feelings for him remained the same as they had been when he departed.

The following day, since the weather was fine, the Livry gentlemen and the baron, upon getting up from the table, proposed going out for an excursion. The viscountess, always obliging when it came to entertainments in which Tadillac had some role, went down into the garden without wasting any time; and she had the ladies enter her carriage, so that they would have the pleasure of making the trip into the woods without getting tired, for the paths leading there were quite spacious; and the baron got up on the coachman's seat, preferring that occupation to that of conversing with her. Meanwhile, the viscountess found this gallant act quite worthy of esteem and admired at great length the good grace of this new Phaethon, who did not have a fate as cruel as that of the first one;[94] for he led the horses and the chariot successfully right up to the place that he had intended. First he led them away from the castle, then he turned so many times into various side pathways that he would have had great trouble going back to the castle if he had had that intention. The second carriage, which was being led by the Chevalier de Livry, followed the path of the first one, which was traveling in front. And night fell while the baron, pretending to be looking for the right road, kept getting further and further from it. The viscountess's personal servants were paid to not reveal the real path.

The viscountess began to get frightened. The other ladies, seeing themselves well accompanied and in a region that was familiar, had no anxiety. The baron and the chevalier kept going forward. Finally, they noticed a lot of lights. At once all were of the opinion that they should venture into that place in order to seek a guide who could, with the help of a torch, lead the carriages back to Kernosy Castle without going astray. The baron had stopped while awaiting the decision on that proposal; the jumbled sound of the words that the various people were

---

94. In classical mythology, Phaethon, son of the sun god Helios and the nymph Clymene, needing to give a public proof of his divine birth, insisted on being allowed to drive the chariot of the sun, normally driven by his father. Unable to control the horses, he flew too high and scorched the heavens, then flew too low and caused major damage to the earth. Finally, Zeus intervened and killed him with a thunderbolt. The comparison is humorous in that it reveals both the learning and the pretentiousness of the viscountess, as no real analogy can be made between the carriage in question and the supernatural chariot of the sun. Phaethon was also the eponymous hero of an opera by Lully and Quinault (1683).

uttering at the same time was preventing him, he said, from knowing the opinion of the viscountess. She imposed silence in order to tell him that it was necessary to advance without delay toward that light that appeared from the distance. He obeyed at once and continued his path until he emerged onto a very beautiful driveway, from which people had a full view of a country home, square in shape, whose windows, which were filled with bright lights that had been placed symmetrically, created an effect that was as pleasing as it was surprising.

When they were within earshot of that country home, they heard the sound of some instruments being tuned, and the voices of several people who seemed to be immersed in whatever function each one had been entrusted with. The viscountess deliberated for quite a long while as to whether she should make her identity known. And Mademoiselle de Saint-Urbain, seeing that she was having difficulty reaching a decision, said to her, "Why not? This adventure does not appear to be dangerous; I hope that we will get out of it without a mishap." "I am going to make the experiment," said the baron, getting down from the seat he was on. Once the two carriages had stopped, the door was opened without waiting for him to knock. When they got into the courtyard, four men dressed as savages[95] came with torches in their hands to receive the viscountess, and, having noticed her at the head of a group of ladies who had already set foot on the ground, two of the men walked in front of her while the other two placed themselves at the sides of the group that was following, and all four led the company as far as the entryway of a large hall adorned with a large number of chandeliers, whose light brought a new daylight to replace the one that had just finished. Two savages, who were waiting in that hall, having brought armchairs close to a large fireplace, withdrew after making deep bows.

About a quarter of an hour had gone by since people had entered when a young child appeared, dressed in Roman garb, who greeted the viscountess and asked her whether she would find it agreeable for the Lord of the Shining House to come and make her an offer of service. The viscountess, charmed with this proposal, asked the supposed dwarf[96] to assure the lord of that house that she

---

95. When used as a noun, the term "savage" generally referred to the non-Christian inhabitants of continents recently discovered by Europeans, and particularly (within the French context) to the native peoples of North and South America. Here, however, it is not clear whether the "savages" in question represent an actual group of people, or whether the term is simply applied to convey that the men are dressed as exotic creatures from a fantastical realm. Positive portrayals of native people from the New World, known as "noble savages," were prevalent in a variety of literary genres during the eighteenth century, including comedy (Delisle de la Drevetière's *Arlequin sauvage [Harlequin the Savage]*), tragedy (Voltaire's *Alzire*), opera (Rameau and Fuzelier's *Les Indes galantes [The Amorous Indies]*), short story (Voltaire's *L'ingénu [The Sincere Huron]*), and novel (Graffigny's *Lettres d'une Péruvienne [Letters from a Peruvian Woman]*), to cite some of the best-known examples.

96. Dwarfs, common in multiple folklore traditions, were usually limited to minor roles in medieval romances. In the *Amadís*, most dwarfs are treacherous and cruel, but one of them, Ardian, is loyal and honorable and becomes a companion of the title character (book 1, chapter 19). The fact that Tadillac

would be extremely pleased to see him. Once the child had left, the baron said that he was jealous of this unknown prince who seemed to be disputing with him the honor of the viscountess's favor. Then the Lord of the Shining House appeared, preceded by four men dressed in Roman garb, who were carrying torches before him. He was wearing a scarlet robe in Armenian style lined with sable, a magnificent scarf over it, and on his head, he had a kind of small helmet, covered with white feathers and flame-colored, while gracefully holding in his hand a little golden cane. It was Tourmeil, who, in order to please the baron, was playing a role in this little festivity, and, being obliged to appear in a bizarre costume before Madame de Briance, had not wanted to look too slovenly. The baroness was the only person who was allowed to remain ignorant of the truth of this adventure, so that the others would have the pleasure of seeing her astonishment. She was charmed by the lord of the Shining House; she even forgot for some time the fondness that had always been noticed in her for the Chevalier de Livry.

"Madam, Fortune has led you to my realm," said the Lord of the Shining House to the viscountess. "I have already thanked her for that, and I would have flattered myself with the belief that this great day was to be, as a famous enchanter[97] predicted to me, the one on which I would achieve supreme happiness through the arrival of a lady who is made charming on account of her fine qualities, and whose pleasant disposition makes one value her personality more than the great wealth she possesses. I take great care not to raise my thoughts so far up as to you, madam. I know," he continued, pointing to the baron, "that Destiny has reserved you for this faithful knight. He is worthy of you, through his love and through his merits; I will not disturb a union that is to be so fine."

The bombastic language that the viscountess was using in the reply that she made to this kind speech would have made it too long, and perhaps tedious, if the savages had not come to interrupt the course of her words by bringing in a table that was set with a very elegant meal.

The lord of the house did the honors of his residence. People sat down at the table; he seated himself next to Madame de Briance and, by speaking to her in a familiar manner, he upset the baroness, who could not bear it that the Lord

---

allows the part to be played by a little boy and to have him dressed in a Roman costume reminds the reader that this entertainment has been planned on very short notice and that the costumes are limited to those in the possession of the local acting troupe.

97. Enchanters were common in medieval romances. In the *Amadís*, one of them (Arcalaus) functions as a primary enemy of the title character; however, others are more benevolent and assist or reward supremely gifted heroes. Apolidon, a prince with magical learning, conquers the Firm Island from a giant and converts it into a palatial residence. When he is required to leave it, he constructs two enchanted places, an arch and a chamber, to ensure that no one may rule that island after him without demonstrating perfection in both feats of arms and fidelity in love. The hero successfully passes these tests and gains rulership of the island (book 2, chapters 1–2). The baron's idea of creating the Shining House was probably inspired by this episode in the *Amadís*.

of the Shining House, whoever he might be, appeared more touched by someone else's charms than by hers. The viscountess congratulated Madame de Briance on her conquest and said to the Lord of the Shining House that it would no doubt be through that beautiful woman that the enchanter's prediction was going to be fulfilled. He replied to her with a serious air that he was beginning to think the same thing.

Oboists played during the meal; the savages served as waiters. As soon as the meal was finished, the Lord of the Shining House led the company into a hall that was separated by a small vestibule from the one where they had just had supper; he again gave his hand to Madame de Briance because, he said, he did not wish to oppose the orders of Destiny by exposing himself too closely to the charms of the viscountess.

She was the first to sit down in an armchair that was prepared for her, facing a small stage that was properly set up; the ladies placed themselves in the second row, and once the gentlemen had seated themselves in the third row, the actors appeared after the overture had ended. They performed *The Bourgeois Nobleman* with all its embellishments[98] and drew the applause that they deserved. "These are our actors from Rennes," said the viscountess, having recognized them. "That is true," replied the Lord of the Shining House. "I knew that they had had the honor of pleasing you, madam, and with a stroke of my wand I transported them here, in order to entertain you."

The viscountess understood through this response that everything that was happening was a gallant invention by the baron. And for fear that he might be convinced that she had been deceived at first, she said, raising her voice, "Whoever the lord of this house might be, I am greatly obliged to him for having performed for me all these pleasing enchantments, which assuredly have cost him more trouble and more planning than he wants to make us believe."

The baroness, having also recognized the actors, correctly judged that it was Tadillac who was giving this entertainment. But the Lord of the Shining House was still puzzling her: he had so much wit and such a polite air that she could not take him for a regional actor or for a man from the provinces.

This nobleman, accomplished in every way, who was occasioning the jealousy that was thus creeping among the ladies, stood up as soon as the actors had finished, made a deep bow to the viscountess, and started the ball with her. Fearing that the Livry gentlemen, the baron, and Tourmeil would tire themselves out with dancing, the ladies each took, in their turn, the hand of the actors who

---

98. Molière's comedy *Le Bourgeois gentilhomme* (*The Bourgeois Nobleman*, 1670) was originally a comedy-ballet, a type of hybrid work that included extensive passages of singing and dancing, with music composed by Lully. However, after Lully won a royal monopoly for his opera company, he imposed severe restrictions on the use of instrumentalists, singers, and dancers by troupes focusing on spoken drama. As he gradually succeeded in getting those restrictions enforced, the Parisian troupes kept many of Molière's hybrid plays in their repertoire but most often with little or no singing and dancing.

distinguished themselves in that activity. The gentlemen did the same thing with respect to the actresses. By this means the company became more numerous, the ball lasted longer, and the pleasure from it was no less agreeable.

They had already been engaged in this entertainment for two hours when they suddenly saw four savages enter, each one holding two torches. At once the Lord of the House presented his hand to the viscountess and led her into the hall where they had had supper. The baron took Madame de Briance; the Livry gentlemen offered their hands to the two charming sisters. The actors and actresses followed in the same order; finally, the entire company, having entered that hall, found refreshments that the exertion of dancing had not made unwelcome. Some people took hot chocolate, others coffee, still others liqueurs, of which there were several kinds. Finally, they found enough food to satisfy each individual's taste, for confections, both dry and liquid, were not lacking.

Once that was done, they returned to the hall for dancing. But how great was the astonishment of the company when they found the stage illuminated once again, with a stage set that represented a wood so realistically that they could almost have believed that they had become lost in one, as had been the case while coming from Kernosy Castle to the Shining House. The overture was performed. As soon as it was finished, the performers sang the following text, which Tourmeil had composed, in which he had not forgotten Madame de Briance, knowing full well that she would be present at this mini-opera, which contained only two scenes, as the Baron de Tadillac had wished.

If one finds faulty versification in certain places and inelegant terms in others, one must attribute these defects solely to my memory; I[99] heard this play recited only once; I may perhaps have substituted some words, just as they came to me, in order not to give the work in a seriously incomplete form.

(Enter Philemon and Tirsis)[100]

PHILEMON
When Cupid in this peaceful place
Wants to assemble all the sweetest pleasures,
Why, Tirsis, are you troubling it
By sighing and by cares which are all useless?

---

99. This unexpected first-person intrusion by the narrator was presumably intended to suggest to the reader that this is a "true" story and that the person recording it is one of the characters (that was explicitly the case in Murat's preceding novel, *A Trip to the Country*).

100. In classical mythology, Philemon and his wife, Baucis, were poor but kindhearted peasants who gave hospitality to two strangers. Those strangers, who were the gods Zeus and Hermes in disguise, rewarded them by turning their house into a shrine, allowing them to serve there and letting them die of old age together. Tirsis (from the Greek name Thyrsis) was a standard name for shepherds in pastoral poetry. In Virgil (Eclogue 7), Thyrsis is a participant in a song contest.

TIRSIS

In this isolated wood I seek in vain
A gentle rest to restore my peace of mind.
Alas! Can there be any tranquility for me?
Pitiless Cupid has decreed that I must love.
I've fled to free myself from his barbaric laws,
But he has made my shepherdess so lovely
That once he has displayed her to our gaze,
One can avoid her just by going far away.

PHILEMON

To aid a tender swain who's true beyond compare,
Cupid, let all your arrows fly,
And pierce the heart of this lady fair,
Since on her face all charms you multiply.
To aid a tender swain who's true beyond compare,
Cupid, let all your arrows fly,

TIRSIS

And pierce the heart of this lady fair.

PHILEMON

To aid a tender swain who's true beyond compare,

TIRSIS AND PHILEMON

Cupid, let all your arrows fly.

TIRSIS

The ungrateful one comes to this wood.

PHILEMON (*withdrawing*)

I've no wish to disturb your secret words of love.

(*Enter Silvia*)

SILVIA

I come to seek in this remote location
A spot to bewail the suffering caused by love;
I'll find no calm there for my sad anxiety.
Ah, I find you here! How fortunate is my fate!

TIRSIS

Oh stop running away from an unlucky lover.

Why are you letting loose your anger, so unjust,
    Against an ardor that's so perfect?
    Whatever god may work against me,
Cupid, the tender Cupid, vouches for my heart.[101]

Eternal love to your charming self I swear;
I will burn always with a flame so fair,
And if I dared betray oaths so tender as this,
    May the most formidable deity,
The god who works to send true lovers bliss,
    Never be favorable to me.

SILVIA

I want to believe your oaths at last;
They have disarmed my anger with you.
A shepherdess who's young and vain
Was boasting that she caused your cares and sufferings,[102]
    But at each moment my love reassures me
    That I deserve a heart that's true.
    I want to believe your oaths at last;
    They have disarmed my anger with you.

TIRSIS AND SILVIA

Our lively passion let's increase,
Let's banish what's sad and alarming,
And may all Cupid has that's charming
Within our hearts reign without cease.

SILVIA

I admit, 'twas vainly that I thought to break my chain;
    It is my destiny to sigh for you.
I no longer fight the fondness sweeping me along.
Far from still complaining of the excess of my grief,
I always will complain of the most unjust anger
That caused me to prefer the furies of my hatred

---

101. The blank spaces in published opera libretti of the period typically signaled the switch from recitative to a more melodic passage (aria or arioso).

102. This extremely scaled-down plot complication, resolved in a matter of just a few lines, may have been inspired by the Quinault-Lully opera *Amadis*, in which the heroine Oriane, believing an inaccurate report that Amadis had fallen in love with Briolanie, a queen to whom he had promised assistance, has rejected him. She is eventually persuaded that his love for her remains unalterable, and there is a happy ending.

To the pleasures of a love so charming and so sweet.
I admit, 'twas vainly that I thought to break my chain;
It is my destiny to sigh for you.

TIRSIS
Nightingales in this peaceful wood,
If it is possible, forget your tenderest loves;
To sing of the fair lass for whom I first felt passion,
Use every sunny day.
Learn carefully the songs that I am going to teach you;
They alone will always suit my mind;
Never will my heart, faithful and tender,
Tell you to sing about new objects of my love.
Learn carefully the songs that I am going to teach you.

You, Cupid, who alone cause my life's happiness,
Make the gods jealous of a man so fortunate;
For their glorious fate I feel no enviousness;
Being loved by Silvia, yes,
Is a far sweeter fate.

TIRSIS AND SILVIA
Our lively passion let's increase,
Let's banish what's sad and alarming,
And may all Cupid has that's charming
Within our hearts reign without cease.[103]

The author of these words and the man who had set them to music had good reason to be content with the applause of the company. The audience left that hall in order to go into the adjacent hall, where they conversed for a very long time, waxing enthusiastic over the beauties of this mini-opera. Daylight was beginning to appear, and the Lord of the Shining House, who had not stopped doing the honors in his residence and in whom the fatigue of having stayed up all night had generated an appetite in the morning, clearly judged that the whole assembly had to be feeling the same need. He gave orders for the tables to be set, and although the meal was as elaborate as the one at supper, the pleasures of eating were not what occupied people's thoughts the most; they each seemed delighted to be

---

103. Short court entertainments such as mini-operas typically ended with an extended passage of choral celebration and dancing. Tadillac does not feature one here because he has too few actors available. Moreover, those who are proficient dancers have already participated in the ball preceding this performance.

sitting near the person of whom they were fond. The Livry gentlemen were next to the young Kernosy ladies; the baron was paying court to the viscountess; the Count de Tourmeil, indifferent to all the delicious foods that were in front of him, thought only of satiating himself with the pleasing conversation that he was having with Madame de Briance. On the other side [of the table], Madame de Salgue was congratulating herself, for she saw that Tadillac was paying formal respects only to the viscountess. The baroness, who alone was devoured by jealousy, could not bear the idea that a person other than herself could have managed to win the heart of the Lord of the House by her charms. The company was so overwhelmed with joy that they might imperceptibly have reached the noon hour while still at table, if the servants of the viscountess had not come to inform them that the carriages were ready. By then it was broad daylight, which, having dispelled all the enchantments of the previous night, gave them the means to recognize that the house they were in belonged to a nobleman, one of their neighbors, who some three or four years earlier had had built there a large country home in the modern style.[104]

That nobleman never came there except in the summer months. His absence provided an easy opportunity for Tadillac to win over the caretaker and to make him consent, in return for a suitable reward, to allow him to hold the celebration of this party there, and the ingenuity of it was so pleasing to the ladies that they showered him with a thousand praises for it. From that time on, the viscountess was unable to live without him; she was enchanted with his obliging manners; and the Lord of the Shining House, despite all of his favorable qualities, had not altered the passion that this lady was feeling for Tadillac. There is no reason to be astonished at this; the Lord of the Shining House had left her in her state of error on purpose, and she sincerely believed him to be the leader of the troupe of actors.

They did not arrive at Kernosy Castle until after noon; the viscountess's servants were not concerned about her absence; Saint-Urbain had taken care to inform them that the group would not be coming back until morning. They said to the baron, as he entered, that a messenger, arriving post-haste, had come to deliver a letter to him in person and appeared very eager to speak to him. The baron acted as though this news had greatly surprised him, because he was being spoken to in the presence of the viscountess, who took an interest in what was being said to him; she ordered him to come to inform her of the news that this messenger was bringing him, once she woke up. She was going to get several hours of sleep, in order to recover from the fatigue caused by the preceding night. Before entering her room, she advised him to go get some rest as well and to alert

---

104. The "modern style" was developed by Alexandre Jean-Baptiste Le Blond (1679–1719) and Jean I Berain (1640–1711) during the final decades of the seventeenth century. This style, which promoted a carved, curved, and lighter ornamental interior, would eventually become the standard aesthetic of the French Enlightenment, an aesthetic known as the "rococo."

his servants that they should not fail to send up this messenger when he came to request it. The ladies, following the viscountess's example, went to bed. The Livry gentlemen and the Count de Tourmeil, who had arrived with the actors, whose leader he appeared to be, spent the rest of the day entertaining one another. The Baron de Tadillac was unable to be part of that company, for the supposed messenger came back precisely at the moment when they entered their apartment; the servants had him go upstairs in accordance with the order they had received about that, and Tadillac retained the man for a long time, doing so on purpose to prevent anyone from suspecting that man's impersonation.

The baron went to see the viscountess as soon as she had awakened. His gloomy demeanor made her tremble. She insisted on learning the cause of the dejection that appeared on his face, and in reply she heard only deep sighs. Finally, the baron told her that he was indeed unhappy that he was being torn away from her. "But why?" rejoined the viscountess, utterly astonished. "Just see, madam, if you please, the letter that I have received," said the baron. It was the one that Tourmeil had written. Having read it, she attempted to console him with a speech that indeed came from the heart. "Your uncle is very insistent," she said. "I see that he is offering you a wealthy match, and that he intends for you to go, without wasting a minute, to keep the promise that he has made on your behalf; but you could find elsewhere a fortune just as considerable. I . . ." As she was about to continue, Madame de Sugarde entered; the baron was obliged to withdraw and was not present that evening at the play.

The viscountess spent her time there reflecting on Tadillac's absence. Finally, fearing that he would make the decision to obey his guardian, she went off alone to lie down on a small day bed that was in her private study; her state of worry had made her dispirited, and her mind came to be at ease only after the arrival of the baron, whom she had had summoned. "You are going to learn," she said to him, as soon as he had entered, "the degree to which I am moved by true merit.

"I cannot bear for a man such as you to seek elsewhere a fortune that it is in my power to make just as agreeable as the one that is being presented by your uncle. I am declaring to you that I consent to marry you, and that henceforth nothing will able to separate us if you love me as much as I have led myself to believe . . ." The baron interrupted her by throwing himself at her feet and told her a great number of flattering things, which the viscountess took to indicate the excess of his passion. Saint-Urbain came at that very moment to inform them that supper had been served; they left the viscountess's study together; the baron took her arm to go downstairs, and he entered the hall, still holding on to her, with a gaiety that was auspicious for the two charming sisters and for their suitors.

The evening gathering was not long; they each went their separate ways after leaving the table, because the entertainment of the preceding night was making it vitally essential to take rest. The baron, after paying his respects to the viscountess, whom he had just led to her apartment, went over to Madame de Briance's room, where he knew that the Count de Tourmeil, the Livry gentlemen, and the young Kernosy ladies were. He gave an account of the good outcome of his letter. They congratulated him on it; and he received their compliments with such good grace that people clearly saw that his mind was happy. It was not without good reason; he knew that by marrying the viscountess, as he had always ardently wished, he was assuring through that marriage his fortune and his happiness.

"Your wishes are fulfilled," the chevalier said to him. "But what will become of us at present? There is still nothing to flatter our hopes." "You are quite hasty," the baron replied to him. "I have hardly had a moment to thank the viscountess. Tomorrow I will work on behalf of all of you; I hope that the Count de Livry will be content, and that Mademoiselle de Saint-Urbain will never become the wife of Monsieur Fatville. I even dare to flatter myself that if there is an occasion to introduce Monsieur de Tourmeil to the viscountess, she will be delighted to learn of his passion for Madame de Briance and that she will make use of all her influence to advance their marriage."

The next day, the baron, who very sincerely wished to contribute to the happiness of his two cousins, went first thing in the morning to pay a visit to the viscountess, in order to be able to converse with her in private. He proposed to her the alliance with the Livry gentlemen for her two nieces. The aunt accepted the proposal to give Kernosy to the Count de Livry; "but," she said to the baron, "since I am granting you a part of what you are asking of me, do me the pleasure of speaking to Saint-Urbain and get her to agree to obey me. I have reasons that oblige me to absolutely insist on her marriage with Monsieur de Fatville. If I could get out of it, I would do it in order to please you. So, go announce to her that the Fatville gentlemen and their uncle will arrive here today."

The commission that the baron had just received, contrary to his expectations, put him in an awkward position; he did not believe it was advisable to reveal to the chevalier the truth of the matter or to send Saint-Urbain into despair by informing her of her aunt's intention. He told her only that the Fatville gentlemen were due to arrive that evening. That charming person, extremely upset to hear such terrible news, pretended to have taken ill and went off to take to her bed, in order not to be obliged to appear in public. Madame de Briance kept her company, and Kernosy did not abandon her. But the viscountess absolutely insisted that she come out to do the honors of the house.

Fatville the counselor and his uncle arrived toward evening; a little later, Fatville's older brother arrived on a litter,[105] because he had not yet sufficiently recovered from his fall to the point of being able to ride a horse; he entered the hall used for the plays, where people were then assembled. The viscountess received

---

105. A portable bed serving the function of a stretcher.

him in a pleasing manner and told him that as soon as the play was over,[106] she would present him to her niece, who had taken ill. The Chevalier de Livry felt a wave of anger at the sight of his rival, which his prudence would not have been able to restrain him from expressing, if it had not been fortified by that of his brother and by the advice that Tourmeil had given him.

After the play, the viscountess led Fatville and his company into Saint-Urbain's room. This unexpected visit greatly embarrassed the niece. But, great as her embarrassment was, the same feeling that was noticed on the face of Fatville's older brother was even greater; he was unable to utter two words in succession and did not stop looking at Tourmeil, whom he found in the room. Madame de Briance, who was then alongside him, said to the viscountess, while bowing to her, that she had summoned him in order to teach her several selections from their mini-opera. That speech increased the older Fatville's suspicion; he again stared at him; Tourmeil, not wanting to be recognized, left at once; but the man from the provinces appeared no calmer for that.

Unable to understand what was the cause of this agitation of mind that reigned on both sides, the viscountess led away the Fatville gentlemen and left Saint-Urbain at liberty with Madame de Briance. After the others had departed, they pondered over the strong emotions that had appeared on the face of the man from the provinces at the sight of Tourmeil, and not finding any plausible reason for it, they concluded that he added to his many other faults that of being jealous for no reason.

Meanwhile the chevalier was in despair; he did not find Saint-Urbain sufficiently resolved to disobey her aunt. "Ah, my brother," he said to Tourmeil, for he often called him by that name, "how unhappy I am! How I envy your destiny! You are tenderly loved, and nothing stands in the way of your hopes." "You are also loved," Tourmeil replied, "and when one is loved, one offends Cupid by complaining with so much violence. You can't really be in love if you hope for nothing: for hope is inseparable from love, and at the very moment that a person believed himself to be in love without the flattering assistance of hope, he would die of grief, if hope were not hidden in the depths of the heart that believes it has lost it."

Tourmeil tried in vain to console the chevalier; it took a lot of effort to persuade him to return to the viscountess's room. He finally went there and, upon entering, looked at his rival with a terrifying jealousy, which he would not have able to control if he had not sensed his friend by his side, who refused to abandon him on that occasion. Tourmeil, less preoccupied than the chevalier, examined the man from the provinces with more attention than he had done in Saint-Urbain's room, and after hearing him speak several times, he said with astonishment to the chevalier, "That's him. Yes, that is indeed him." The chevalier asked him for an

---

106. This time the novelist does not supply the name of the play performed, presumably because she could not think of another popular work with a thematic relation to her plot.

explanation of those words. "Let's leave the room," replied Tourmeil, lowering his voice. "I am going to give you cause for hope."

The viscountess then proposed to the Fatville gentlemen to sign, after supper, the articles that she had drawn up with their uncle. Kernosy, who was grieved by this proposal, left the room in order to alert her sister of their aunt's plan.

Meanwhile, Tourmeil, having informed the chevalier of the secret that was to contribute to his happiness, sent word to the baron that he should come and meet with him. The viscountess, who was noticing the great agitation among the entire company, fearing that Saint-Urbain, who showed little inclination to follow her wishes, might think of escaping from her in order to go to a convent or to the home of one of her relatives, secretly gave orders to have the doors of the castle locked; but the keys were brought to her with less discretion. An absentminded valet gave them to her in front of the Fatville gentlemen.

The presence of Tourmeil and of the Chevalier de Livry, the murmuring that was spreading throughout the castle, the sight of the keys that had just been brought—all of that seemed to announce to the elder Fatville the impossibility of his marriage. The apprehension of some misfortune disturbed his mind to such a degree that, throwing himself suddenly at the feet of the viscountess, he said to her, "Ah, madam, do you want to ruin me? I have been recognized; I cannot doubt that. Monsieur de Tourmeil and the Chevalier de Livry are here. Make my peace with them; I accept whatever conditions they will want to impose on me." "Whatever is at issue here?" said the viscountess, surprised by the words and the actions of the man from the provinces. "What quarrel do you have with the Chevalier de Livry, and where did you see here this Count de Tourmeil of whom you are speaking to me?" "Ah, nephew," cried Fatville's uncle, "you are going to ruin yourself on account of your fright. The viscountess was totally unaware of the unfortunate affair that has happened to you." "Yes," said the chevalier, coming back to the room, "madam did not know it, but I was coming to inform her of it.

"Fatville, whom you see here, madam," he continued, noticing that people were listening to him attentively, "is complicit in that assassination attempt in Rennes that followed the quarrel that I had had with a provincial nobleman. I was wounded, and Monsieur de Tourmeil, the dearest of my friends, came close to losing his life by heroically defending mine. It was from the very hand of this coward that Tourmeil received a blow with a sword from behind. We had not learned his name because the one assassin who was captured did not know it himself; he only said in his deposition that the man who had wounded Tourmeil was a friend of the provincial nobleman with whom I had had the quarrel."

Fatville's uncle, who was quite intelligent, judging well by the confusion in which he saw his nephew that he was not in a condition to respond, stated to the Chevalier de Livry all the reasons that a man of honor can give to defend a bad cause and to try to bring an amicable conclusion to the business. "So that," said Fatville the counselor, "that is undoubtedly what the accursed sprites had come to predict to us." That foolish remark would not have gone unnoticed, and people would not have failed to be amused by it, if they had not been so preoccupied by other matters.

The viscountess, who prided herself on her greatness of soul, appeared outraged by Fatville's malicious action, and yet, out of consideration for his uncle, she begged the chevalier to forgive that unfortunate gentleman. The chevalier, who was genuinely magnanimous, willingly granted the viscountess everything that she was asking from him. She was touched by that. "But," rejoined the frightened Fatville, "I will not be able to enjoy the forgiveness that the Chevalier de Livry agrees to grant me if Monsieur de Tourmeil is not as magnanimous as he is." The chevalier, who clearly saw that there was no way to conceal the Count de Tourmeil from the viscountess any longer, asked her to accompany him to her private study; the baron followed them there; they informed her in a few words about the various considerations that had obliged Tourmeil to disguise his real rank for several days. The viscountess approved of this secrecy because of the novelistic qualities she found in this adventure. The baron, seeing her in good humor, said to her, "Madam, there is no likelihood that you would have given Mademoiselle de Saint-Urbain to Fatville without having urgent reasons to force you into it. I strongly commend the chevalier for pardoning that treacherous man since you have asked him to do so, but, madam, you should make better use of the pardon that Tourmeil will doubtlessly also grant him at your request."

The viscountess thought that the Baron de Tadillac was right. She saw herself as being obligated to show some form of gratitude to the chevalier, who had just granted forgiveness to Fatville so readily upon her request; and since, in her novel, heroines who devoted little care to their financial interests were not admitted, her resolution was, following Tadillac's opinion, to profit from this occasion in regard to the twenty thousand pounds that she owed to Monsieur de Fatville. After all, Fatville was all too fortunate to extricate himself so cheaply from the business at hand; he had given his promise to the viscountess that he would cancel this debt before marrying her niece, [but] his uncle would even have offered just as large a sum in order to arrange his reconciliation with Monsieur de Tourmeil and the Chevalier de Livry.

Once this resolution was adopted, the chevalier left the room and the baron remained alone with the viscountess, not wanting to let cool the good will that he saw her display toward the Chevalier de Livry. He proposed, with no further ado, that she should give Mademoiselle de Saint-Urbain to the chevalier, who had an abundance of wealth and merit, was of high birth, and was already related to her, now that she had granted Mademoiselle de Kernosy to his brother. "I am finally seeing the light," the viscountess then said. "Here, your two cousins are both in love; but since I find the same advantages in them as I had found in giving my niece to Fatville, and since, what is more, I can easily judge that you approve this match, I accept it with pleasure."

The baron was charmed by the viscountess's consent; he begged her to ensure, that very evening, the happiness of so many lovely people and his own, by permitting him to declare the good fortune that she was reserving for him. The viscountess, who was moved by the baron's speech, summoned Madame de Briance and the Livry gentlemen in order to inform them that she had accepted the proposal that the baron had made to her on their behalf. Never has a more perfect joy succeeded a more dreadful sadness so quickly.

The fortunate lovers ran to announce their happiness to the Kernosy ladies. Madame de Briance was delighted to see her brothers even more perfectly united to her through this alliance. And the Fatville men were satisfied by the generosity of their enemies. Madame de Salgue, exempt from jealousy and touched by the love and the charms of the baron, was the first to show the viscountess the joy that she felt for her marriage. The Baroness de Sugarde was the only discontented person; there was no more hope with the Chevalier de Livry. This reflection could cause her nothing but grief, but the time was not appropriate to let her feelings show.

That night, it was impossible for the god of slumber[107] to reign even for one moment over a group so devoted to joy. The agreeable agitation that being fortunate in love brings to people's hearts causes just as much turmoil for them as the cruelest sadness. Everyone, instead of going to bed, vigorously applied themselves to the task of concluding the business with Fatville before the night was over. Tourmeil forgave him on conditions that were advantageous for the viscountess. But in regard to himself, he experienced only the pleasure of granting a magnanimous pardon to his enemy, as the Chevalier de Livry had done.

As soon as it was daylight, the Fatville men departed from the castle, and all the lovers, satisfied with their lot, thought of nothing other than choosing the date for their wedding. It was pushed back only by three days; even then they found the time too long to suit their impatience. The lavishness that presided over that event was far surpassed by the amount of joy and love involved. The Count de Livry wed Mademoiselle de Kernosy; the chevalier, Mademoiselle de Saint-Urbain; the baron, the viscountess.

Tourmeil became happy by marrying Madame de Briance only several months after his friends, since family reasons delayed their marriage. He sighed and complained grievously at being the only unhappy person on a day destined for the happiness of the others. "You are not reflecting on your good fortune," the baron told him on the day following their nuptials. "You say that you are the most unfortunate of all lovers, but I am sure that today you are the most in love." Tourmeil took very little relish in this type of consolation; but Cupid only delayed

---

107. Hypnos (Somnus, in Latin) was the Greco-Roman god of sleep. However, in many ancient texts, including those of Hesiod, Homer, and Ovid, Sleep functions more as a personification than as a god. He would be familiar to Murat's readers as a character in various machine plays and operas, sometimes accompanied or replaced by his son Morpheus, the god of dreams.

his bliss in order to make it even more perfect. He wed Madame de Briance and was truly happy with her. It even seems that their marriage made their love still more ardent and tender.

They spent several additional months all together at Kernosy Castle. After that time, Tourmeil and the Livry gentlemen led away their beautiful wives. And the baron would perhaps have become bored to remain alone with his own wife, if the presence in the neighborhood of the charming Madame de Salgue had not compensated him for it.

THE END

Bearskin

by Marie-Madeleine de Lubert

Figure 2. "Noble-Thorn and the Fairy Azerole," engraving by Clément-Pierre Marillier (1740–1808). Clément-Pierre Marillier, [*Recueil. Oeuvre de Marillier: Illustrations pour les* Voyages imaginaires]. [Paris: 1786], p. 68. Bibliothèque Nationale de France, Réserve EF-79-4.

Inscription: "*Prens courage, ma fille, j'ai éprouvé ta patience assez longtems, la récompense viendra*" ("Take courage, my daughter, I have tested your patience long enough, the reward will come").

Bearskin

[While in the original edition the characters go directly to the apartment of Madame de Briance to hear the continuation of her story after Saint-Urbain has finished, in the 1753 edition they stay up to hear a fairy tale first.]

"You will make of it what you want," said the viscountess. "If you had mixed in some fairy magic, you would have amused me even more; for I confess to you that these sorts of stories appeal to me very much."[1] "If I had known your taste, Madam," replied Saint-Urbain, "I would have served you according to your liking." "It is not yet late enough," said the Count de Livry, "to withhold from the viscountess this satisfaction; and if she will allow me, in a moment I will tell her a fairy tale." The viscountess seemed thrilled; all of the ladies demonstrated the same enthusiasm: and Fatville asked if it was going to be a true story, because otherwise he would go off to bed; people assured him that he could go off to bed with total confidence. As soon as he had left, the viscountess called for silence and the Count de Livry began as follows.

Bearskin
A Tale

"Once upon a time there was a king and a queen who only had one daughter; she was the only one that they had been able to keep out of a number of other children they had had. The princess's beauty and charming personal qualities compensated them for the painful loss of so many young princes. She was called Noble-Thorn.[2] The endless amount of effort that had been put into her education succeeded marvelously, and at the age of twelve she was as knowledgeable as her teachers. Her intelligence and her uncommon beauty caused her to be sought after by all the eligible kings and princes that there were at that time.

---

1. In attributing to the viscountess a passion for fairy tales, which is not found in Murat's original version, Lubert was presumably inspired by d'Aulnoy's novel *Don Gabriel Ponce de Leon*. In the latter novel, Juana, the character who corresponds to the viscountess, not only enjoys reading such tales and hearing others recite them, but is also capable of reciting them herself. Juana praises the fairy tale genre at great length, insisting on its literary merit and appeal to people of good taste, as well as to its value as entertainment. Lubert will include a brief praise of the genre following the recitation of the second fairy tale, "Etoilette."

2. Noble-Épine ("aubépine" in modern French) was a nickname for "hawthorn," a genus of several hundred different variations of shrubs and small trees of the *Crataegus* species, native to Europe. The hawthorn was sometimes used in Renaissance poetry to suggest the beauty of unspoiled Nature. The name may suggest a harmony between humans and nature that is broken by evil forces (in this case, ogres), thus preparing the reader for the upcoming metamorphosis.

"The king and the queen, who adored her, feared losing her, and they were not in a hurry to accord her to the eager marriage proposals of the princes, her suitors. Noble-Thorn, content with her fate, herself dreaded a marriage that would take her away from the king and the queen, whom she loved tenderly.

"The news of Noble-Thorn's beauty traveled all the way to the court of a king of the ogres whose name was Rhinoceros. This ruler, powerful in lands and in riches, had no doubt that the princess would be given to him as soon as he asked for her hand; and he dispatched his ambassadors to see the king, the father of Noble-Thorn: they arrived at this court, and they asked for an audience under the pretext of renewing an ancient alliance treaty that at one time had existed between the two crowns. At first people found it amusing to see such unusual beings; the young princess herself laughed out loud: however, the king ordered that they be received with great splendor.

"On the day of the audience, all the members of the court made an effort to dress superbly; but their joy soon turned to sadness when it was found out that King Rhinoceros was asking for Noble-Thorn's hand in marriage.

"The king, who was listening attentively to the ambassador, remained so shocked by the proposition that he was unable to speak. The ambassador, fearing a refusal, hastened to take back the floor, assuring the king that if he did not betroth his daughter to Rhinoceros, [Rhinoceros] himself would come with an army of a hundred million ogres who would ravage his kingdom and devour the entire royal family.

"The king, who was familiar with the ogres' protocols, having no doubt that the ambassador's threat would soon be followed up with action, asked for a few days to prepare his daughter to receive the honor that Rhinoceros was paying her and abruptly broke off the audience.

"This good father, mortally distressed by the fact that he did not dare refuse [to give] his daughter's hand, retired to his private study and had her summoned. The princess flew there, and when she had learned the sad fate to which she was destined, she let out distressing cries, and throwing herself at the feet of her father the king, she begged him to order her death instead of such nuptials.

"The king took her in his arms, cried with her, and told her about the threat that the ambassador had made. 'You will die, my daughter,' he added, 'we will all die, and you will have the terror of watching us all be devoured by the cruel Rhinoceros.'

"The princess, as frightened by this image as by her dreadful marriage, consented to giving her hand and was very willing to sacrifice herself in order to save the king, the queen, and the entire kingdom.[3] She even went on to assure

---

3. This plot development evokes the story of "Beauty and the Beast" (Aarne-Thompson tale type 425C "Tales of Enchanted Husbands"), which was first published by Gabrielle-Suzanne Barbot de Villeneuve in 1740. A second version of this same tale, abridged and rewritten, would appear in 1756,

her mother the queen of this; the queen was in an appalling state. Noble-Thorn, resolved to do anything for such cherished people, consoled her mother with all of the most truthful-sounding things she could imagine; and with a steadfastness that made her even more admirable, she saw the preparations for her marriage, and walked to the altar where the ambassador was waiting for her, with a modesty that wrested screams and sobs from everyone.[4]

"She left with the same show of firmness and brought along with her only a young person for whom she cared a great deal and who was very attached to her: her name was Coriande.[5]

"As there were many leagues between this kingdom and that of the ogres, the princess had the time to open her heart to Coriande and to let her see the extremity of her pain. Coriande, touched by the princess's misfortune, took part in her pain, being unable to give her any other consolation, and swore to her that she would never forsake her. Noble-Thorn, sensitive to the rare and tender friendship this girl was showing her, felt less anguished now that her pain was shared.

"Coriande had not dared tell the princess that she had gone to see the fairy Azerole,[6] godmother of the princess Noble-Thorn, to inform her of the terrible fate that was awaiting her, and that she had found the fairy quite enraged over the fact that no one had consulted her about this matter; and that she had even said to Coriande that she would never intervene in Noble-Thorn's affairs.

"Coriande did not find it appropriate to add to her mistress's sorrow by telling her this, but her mind was occupied by it, and she was secretly lamenting the fate of the princess abandoned in this way by her godmother. The length and the weariness of the voyage had not diminished Noble-Thorn's beauty at all: upon seeing her, the ogre was so surprised by it that he let out a cry that made the island where he had established his residence tremble.

---

shortly after Lubert's reedition of *The Sprites*, in Jeanne-Marie Leprince de Beaumont's collection *Magasin des enfants* (*Storehouse for Children*). Leprince de Beaumont's tale is the version most commonly retold today.

4. It was a common practice among royal families during the early modern period in Europe to have international, arranged marriages officiated by proxy, as is the case here.

5. Coriande: The name is a derivative of "coriander," a spice produced from the round, tan-colored seeds of the coriander plant, which was used to treat digestive problems including upset stomach, loss of appetite, nausea, and hernia during the eighteenth century. This name also hints at a primordial harmony between humans and nature.

6. Azerole: a fruit similar to a quince produced by the medlar shrub or *Crataegus azarolus*, a species of the hawthorn family. The fruits ripened during the winter after other ripe fruits were no longer available and were believed to have medicinal properties. Lubert appears to have chosen this name in honor of *La Princesse Azerolle ou l'excès de la constance* (*Princess Azerolle or Excessive Constancy*), published in 1745 in an anonymous collection of five fairy tales, which was in fact written by her friend, Françoise de Graffigny. In the earlier tale, Azerolle is the name of the heroine, not the fairy. A different work by Graffigny (*Letters from a Peruvian Woman*) is also mentioned later in this fairy tale.

"The princess fainted from fright into the arms of Coriande, and Rhinoceros, who on that day had taken on the form of the animal whose name he bore,[7] put her on his back along with Coriande and ran to his palace, where he locked them both in.

"Then he regained his natural form, which was no less atrocious, and hastened to Noble-Thorn's rescue. When the princess opened her eyes and saw herself in the hairy arms of this monster, she was no longer able to restrain her screams and her tears. The ogre, who did not think that anyone could find him unattractive, asked Coriande what was wrong with her, as if she could be thinking that a screaming girl like this would be pleasing to him! Coriande, frightened by the ogre's rage, answered that it was nothing and that the princess was subject to vapors.[8]

"Noble-Thorn had closed her eyes to spare herself the terror of seeing her hideous husband, and the ogre, who thought she was still in a faint, felt a pang of humanity. He left, and commanded Coriande to take care of her: Coriande assured him that all [Noble-Thorn] needed was rest.

"The ogre left the princess and went off to hunt bears (this was his favorite pastime);[9] he was counting on catching two or three for Noble-Thorn's evening meal.

"As soon as he had left, the princess, sobbing, threw her arms around Coriande's neck, begging her to help her. Moved by her mistress's pain, this poor girl wracked her brain and, seeing several bearskins that the ogre had collected in order to dress in during the winter, for he was very stingy, she advised the princess to hide herself in one of them. Noble-Thorn consented to that after Coriande had reassured her that she should not be distressed over leaving Coriande alone to be exposed to the ogre's rage.[10]

Then Coriande chose the most beautiful of those skins and began to sew the princess inside of it; but—a miracle!—barely had the skin touched Noble-Thorn when it attached itself to the princess on its own, and with that she appeared the most beautiful bear in the world.

---

7. In French fairy tales, ogres often had the ability to change shapes, as in the tale of "Puss-in-Boots."

8. According to humoral medicine, fits of hysteria could be brought on by vapors or other invisible substances in the air.

9. Bear-hunting is also the favorite pastime of Adolphe, the hero of "L'Ile de la Félicité" ["The Island of Happiness"], the first literary fairy tale of the French tradition. The tale was published in 1690 as an interpolated narrative in Marie-Catherine d'Aulnoy's novel *Histoire d'Hypolite, comte de Duglas* (*The Story of Hypolitus, Earl of Douglas*).

10. Another example of Lubert's self-conscious borrowing of motifs from other fairy-tale writers. In incorporating Aarne-Thompson tale type 510B "Unnatural Love," Lubert evokes similar tales by Charles Perrault ("Peau d'âne" ["Donkey Skin"], 1694) and Giambattista Basile ("L'orsa" ["The She-Bear"], 1634–1636). Basile and Perrault were the two most well-known, male fairy-tale writers of the seventeenth century.

Coriande attributed this unexpected aid to the fairy Azerole; she related that to the princess, who herself agreed with it, for during the course of her metamorphosis she had retained the ability to speak and all of her mental faculties.

Coriande opened the doors and let out the beautiful bear, who was impatient to leave; and Coriande did not doubt that the fairy would guide her, since she had brought about the metamorphosis. As soon as her beautiful mistress disappeared from view, she abandoned herself to regret; but about an hour later she heard the ogre return and pretended to be sound asleep.

"'Where is that Noble-Thorn!' cried Rhinoceros in a thundering voice. Coriande pretended to be waking up and, rubbing her eyes, acted as if she did not know where the princess had gone.

"'How could she have left?' said the ogre. 'That is impossible, for I [alone] have the key to my door.' 'Sure, sure,' said Coriande, pretending to believe that the ogre had made away with her, 'it is you who have eaten her, and you will be well punished for that; this is the daughter of a great king, she was the most beautiful person in the world, she was not created in order to marry an ogre, you will see what will happen to you because of this.' The ogre, quite stunned by this accusation, and by the screams that accompanied Coriande's reproaches, swore that he had not eaten the princess and flew into such a rage that Coriande's fake sorrow changed into a fright that was quite real; for the ogre threatened to eat *her* if she would not be quiet. She grew silent indeed and pretended to look for the princess, which calmed Rhinoceros's fury somewhat. He even looked with her for eight days, but Azerole had put everything to right. Invisibly, she had guided the beautiful bear; and this unfortunate princess had found an abandoned boat on the shore, which she boarded. But one can well judge that without the help of the fairy she would have perished a thousand times; for the princess, having entered the boat, felt it moving away from the shore.

"Frightened by the present danger in spite of her misfortune, and not seeing any remedy for it, she lay down and went to sleep. When she awoke, she found herself at the edge of a meadow so beautiful and so well enameled with flowers that she was overjoyed by the sight of it. The bear, who felt the boat come to a stop, jumped out into the meadow [and] thanked the gods and the fairies for having led her unharmed to such a beautiful country.

"After having fulfilled this duty, her first task was to look for something to live off of, for she was very hungry. She made her way across the meadow and entered a beautiful forest, inside of which there was a hollow rock carved in the shape of a cave, and right beside it a pretty fountain whose water flowed all the way to the meadow, and large oak trees laden with acorns. The bear, who was not yet accustomed to this kind of food, at first despised it, but with hunger becoming more pressing, she tried to eat some of them, and she found them very good; then having quenched her thirst at the fountain, she resolved to retire inside the cave during the daytime in order to avoid any unpleasant encounters and to come out only at night. Another reason also contributed to this decision: in drinking from the fountain, she had seen her reflection in its crystal water. Her horrid bear face had frightened her, and she very nearly regretted the loss of her own, even though it had caused her to become Rhinoceros's spouse. This thought consoled her, however, and made her consider her situation and her ugliness with more peace of mind. As she was very intelligent and rational, she understood that ugliness is not such a great misfortune when beauty can only cause sorrows. The bear moralized in this way in her cave; she drew true wisdom from this and began to be content with her fate.

"This country was governed by a young king whose mother was still alive; no one was so handsome, so charming, and so filled with fine qualities as this prince. He was adored by his subjects, respected by his neighbors, and very feared by his enemies; just, clement, magnanimous, moderate in his victories, powerful in the face of adversity, he had every virtue possible, and people complained only about his indifference to beautiful women; but he was afraid of himself, because he knew he had a very sensitive soul, and he had retained from his mother, the queen, the notion that a king must know how to reign over himself before reigning over others. His face was as perfect as his soul, therefore, all of the women at his court were burning with the desire to set his heart aflame: his name was Zelindor,[11] and his country was called the Kingdom of Happiness.

"If the beautiful bear had known the name of this kingdom, she would not have been shocked to find herself so contented with her state of affairs; for one of the privileges of this cherished land was that of being happy there.

"Zelindor, young and gallant, held or attended parties every day; he often went hunting, because this image of war pleased his magnanimous soul.

"The bear had already been living in this country for three months when Zelindor came to hunt in her forest.

"The bear, contrary to her custom, had left her cave during the day in order to take a walk along the edge of the sea. She was returning slowly to her home, breathing in the perfumed air of the flowers that dotted the meadow, when she saw the hunting party before her. She forgot the danger a bear courts on such an occasion and stepped aside to watch it pass.

"Everyone who was accompanying the king recoiled in fright at the sight of this terrible beast. The courageous and young king was the only one to advance, sword in hand, to stab her. The bear, seeing him approach, humbled herself at his feet and lowered her head, waiting for the blow. Zelindor, touched by this

---

11. A reference to the main character of the one-act opera-ballet *Zélindor, roi des Sylphes* (Zelindor, King of the Sylphs), composed by François Rebel (1701–1775) to a libretto by François-Augustin Paradis de Moncrif (1687–1770). It was created at Versailles in 1745 and was revived in March 1753, comprising the last significant success of Madame de Pompadour's troupe, the Théâtre des Petits Cabinets.

action, gently touched the bear with the iron of his sword without causing her any harm;[12] she then arose and went on to flatter him with what she believed to be the most pleasant expressions, to kiss the hand of the king, and to lick it. The king, even more surprised by the beast's caresses, forbade those who had come closer to shoot her, and he himself took off a beautiful scarf that he had been wearing over one shoulder, and that girded his belt, and tied it around the neck of the bear, who allowed him to do it.[13] In this way he himself led her back to his palace and commanded that she be placed in a small flower garden at the back of his private study.[14] The beautiful bear understood very well everything that was being said, but she could no longer pronounce a single word, and this discovery cost her some tears. As soon as she was in the garden, the young king came to see her, and he fed her out of his own hand. Her heart, which had not changed as her face had, was moved as she looked upon the beauty of the young king. 'What a difference,' she said to herself, 'between the dreadful Rhinoceros and this handsome prince!' But returning her thoughts to herself, she quickly added: 'How horrible my face is! What use is it for me to find him so handsome?' Driven to despair, the bear shed even more tears at that moment than she had shed when she had realized that she was mute.

"She left what the king had brought her and went to lie down on a beautiful bed of grass that bordered a magnificent ornamental pond in this garden. Zelindor, who saw that she was sad, came to her side and told her some very tender things. The poor bear felt her despair increase twofold and fell over backward, nearly dead. The king, touched by her state, took some water in his hand and poured it on his bear's muzzle and helped her as best he could. The bear opened her eyes, which she had bathed in tears, and with her two front paws, taking the hands of the king, she shook them respectfully, seeming to thank him.

"'But how charming you are,' said the young Zelindor; 'how is it, my good little bear, that you seem to understand me?' The bear made a small sign with her head, indicating yes. The king, transported with joy to find that she had reason, embraced her; the bear modestly prevented him from doing so and drew back. 'What!' said the king, 'you flee my caresses, my little bear? Well, what do you want, then? Do you not like me?' The bear, at these words, in order to conceal her

---

12. This action foreshadows the characters' wedding day. However, in that scene the king will touch the bear with his scepter instead of his sword. Lubert may have intended a parallel with the scene in the biblical book of Esther, where the king's touching the queen with his scepter likewise saves her life.

13. The scarf also reappears in the wedding scene, as the king's male relatives use it to lead the bear to the altar. The scarf thus functions as a visible sign of the affective bond between the lovers.

14. In Basile's tale "The She-Bear," the prince who encounters the princess disguised as a bear while walking in the woods likewise brings the bear home himself and orders his servants to place her in a garden by the side of the royal palace. In Basile's version of the tale, however, the prince ends the bear's enchantment that same night with a passionate kiss, having been seduced by the way in which she cooks for him, feeds him, and serves him.

emotions, prostrated herself on the grass at Zelindor's feet, and rising immediately thereafter, she picked a branch from one of the orange trees that adorned the edge of the pond and presented it to the king.

"This king, more charmed than ever by his bear, ordered that she be well taken care of, [and] gave her a beautiful rocky cave, surrounded by statues, and that contained a bed of grass for retiring upon at night. He came to see her at every possible moment; he talked about her to everyone; he was crazy about her.

"The bear would have sad thoughts when she was alone: the handsome Zelindor had touched her heart; but how could she ever be pleasing to him with this horrible face! She would neither sleep nor eat, and she spent her days scratching the most beautiful verses in the world on the trees of the garden: jealousy had combined itself with love; she was in a fatal state of melancholy, except when the king came to see her. Another worry came to her; perhaps the king was married; she had almost been so to Rhinoceros, whom she found to be even more dreadful since she had seen the charming Zelindor.

"One evening, by the light of the moon, retracing all of her misfortunes at the edge of the ornamental pond where she would often come, because the young king always took walks there, she cried so many tears that the water became clouded by them; a fat carp who was not sleeping appeared at the surface: 'Beautiful little bear,' she said to the princess, 'do not be so distressed, the fairy Azerole is protecting you, and she will make you as fortunate as you are beautiful.' Then, jumping lightly onto the lawn, the carp appeared as a beautiful lady, tall and majestic, magnificently dressed. The bear threw herself at her feet. 'Take courage, my daughter,' said the fairy Azerole; 'I have tested your patience long enough, the reward will come. You are not married to the ogre Rhinoceros, and you will marry the handsome Zelindor. Keep this secret a little longer, every night you will leave your bearskin; but you will need to put it back on as soon as morning comes.' With that the fairy disappeared, and the stroke of midnight[15] having sounded, the bearskin left the princess. How many blessings did she send from her heart to her good fairy godmother, what happiness, what joy she felt! She spent the night picking flowers, she used them to make garlands and crowns, which she attached to the door of her love's private study.

"The time that had been prescribed to her without a limit being put on it made her impatient; but in order not to make it any longer through fault of her own, whatever toll it took on her, she took back her bearskin at daybreak. She wrote charming things, sometimes about her jealousy, sometimes about her tender sentiments; her heart furnished her thoughts with novel inspirations and with turns of phrase that delighted the prince, for he would read them.

---

15. Allusion to Perrault's earlier adaptation of Aarne-Thompson tale type 510A, "Supernatural Helpers," "Cendrillon ou la petite pantoufle de verre" (Cinderella or the little glass slipper), written in 1695 and published in 1697.

"He had allowed people to come to see the bear; these crowds displeased her. When one is preoccupied by a great passion, only solitude is pleasant. She wrote this to the young king; the verses that expressed this opinion were so tender and so refined that he was charmed by them and had his garden closed; no one could enter it but him.

"For his part, the young king was reflecting on the intelligence he found in the bear, not daring to admit to himself that an overwhelming fondness was attracting him to her; he rejected this thought, not wanting to see himself as capable of anything more than humanity and compassion. However, he no longer liked to go hunting, he did not find entertainment anywhere, and took pleasure only in seeing his bear. He conversed with her on a hundred subjects, and she scribbled in the sand or on the writing tablets he would give her, opinions, advice, maxims full of wisdom.

"'But you are not a bear,' he was saying to her one day. 'In the name of the gods, tell me who you are; will you refuse me this confession still longer? You love me, I do not doubt that, my very happiness depends on believing it; but save my honor by preventing me from reciprocating the love of a bear. Confess to me who you are, I beg you to with this same love that you know so well.' This moment was urgent, the bear had trouble resisting; but the fear of losing her lover made her decide to anger him instead. She responded only by jumping and frolicking, which made Zelindor sigh bitterly. He returned to his court outraged with himself for finding himself capable of such a ridiculous passion.

"Zelindor, in despair for having imagined that the bear could be a person of reason, resolved to wrest himself from this monstrous passion; and ordering that the bear be well taken care of, he resolved to go on a trip: he insisted on leaving without seeing her and, taking along with him only two of his closest men, mounted his horse and set off away from his palace. He had scarcely entered the forest where he had met the bear when, recalling the memory of that adventure, he commanded his men to go a little farther off and to leave him alone.

"These young courtiers were very attached to him, and they were distressed to see how, for some time, his mood had become so altered; they obeyed him and moved some ways away. The young king got off his horse, and lying down at the foot of a tree, he lamented the singularity of his fate and fell into a deep state of reverie, out of which he was drawn by the very tree against which he was resting, which trembled violently and opened to reveal a lady of rare beauty, so brilliantly covered in jewels, that the king was dazzled by her.

"The king quickly rose and bowed deeply to the fairy (for he had no doubt that she was one). 'Let time run its course, Zelindor,' she said. 'Do you believe that a king whom we protect could ever be unhappy? Return to your palace, run to save from despair the one whom too much sensitivity has caused you to abandon.' The fairy disappeared after these words: the king, fortified by an oracle that his heart did not want to doubt, quickly got back on his horse and returned to his apartment as fast as he could.

"He entered the garden immediately, and not seeing the beautiful bear, he ran to find her in her cave.[16]

"The unfortunate princess had learned about the king's departure from those who were taking care of her, who were discussing it among themselves. She had not seen him for three days; this news overwhelmed her, she fell into a faint on her bed of grass, and it was in this fatal state that the king found her. He could not have approached her more eagerly! What agony to see her almost dead! She was as cold as ice; her heart was barely beating. The king let out piercing cries and bathed her with his tears, calling her by the most tender names.

"The sound of his voice penetrated her soul and held it back just as it was about to take flight: she opened her eyes and extended her paws to embrace her lover, thinking that she was about to die. But the tenderness of the king, and the forgiveness that he asked of her, brought her back to life: he begged her to forget his curiosity and swore to her that he adored her. This confession overjoyed the poor bear. They spent a delightful day together, and although the king alone spoke, the bear did not fail to listen to him and to respond to him in her customary way.

"She showed the young king what she had written about his absence; he was enchanted by it. Indeed, never has anyone ever seen such a well-executed combination of intelligence and spontaneity, of reason and emotions: in fact, what she had written resembled the famous *Letters of a Peruvian Woman*,[17] a masterpiece of feeling that the public will always admire.

"Zelindor only stopped reading in order to throw himself at the feet of his tender beloved and to kiss her on her paws.

"Without realizing it, the hours drifted by; lovers have never been good at measuring time, which seems endless in times of absence and too fast in times of pleasure. Midnight struck, the bearskin fell and left uncovered the exquisite Noble-Thorn. She was wearing a sumptuous gown, and her beautiful hair needed no adornment. 'What a miracle!' cried the king. 'How is that? Was it you whom I was fleeing, and whom I was afraid to love?' The embarrassed princess did not respond, her modesty made her appear even more beautiful; she was also afraid that the fairy Azerole would reprimand her for having forgotten herself to the point of revealing her secret to her lover. She was still in this troubled state when the fairy appeared. 'Fortunate lovers!' she cried, 'from tomorrow on you will enjoy

---

16. A second allusion to Villeneuve's 1740 fairy tale "Beauty and the Beast." However, in this instance, the gender roles are reversed.

17. Allusion to the aforementioned 1747 epistolary novel by Françoise de Graffigny, which tells the story of a young Incan princess named Zilia who is abducted by the Spanish during their conquest of the Inca Empire. In the novel, Zilia writes a series of letters to her fiancé, Aza, recounting the story of her capture, subsequent rescue by French sailors, and eventual introduction into French society.

the fruits of your sorrows, you have endured enough torment: You, my daughter,' she said to the princess, 'give your hand to your lover as a reward for his affection. And you, handsome Zelindor, go to your court to make all the necessary preparations to marry this princess; be afraid no longer that after your union there will be any metamorphosis: but Noble-Thorn must remain under this law for another twenty-four hours. Go, and let her sleep, she needs rest, I will take care of making her worthy of you.'

"The young king went off, leaving the fairy and the princess together. He was transported by such great joy that instead of going to bed, he had the entire palace awakened, assembled the council, and said that he wanted to get married the next day, that it was necessary to prepare his throne and to have the entire castle lit up, especially the great hall. He also ordered all the ladies to dress magnificently. From there, he went to the queen his mother to invite her to his wedding.

"The queen, who had just learned that her son had woken everyone up, seeing him excessively excited and speaking with a cheerfulness that he had not had for a long time, feared that he might have had some sort of accident. What he was saying, however, was so legitimate, so logical and of such good sense, that if it had not been for the precipitous marriage, she would have found him the way that she had always seen him. She only asked him which person he would choose. 'You will be charmed by her, madam,' the young king replied to her. 'I can tell you no more.'

"Zelindor spent the whole night having an apartment furnished for his exquisite princess; this care, which filled him with thoughts of her, seemed to him to be the most agreeable; never was anything so elegant and so well ordered.

"The ladies of the palace, awakened by this news and not hearing anyone name the person whom the king was marrying, all flattered themselves individually to be the object of his choice; as such they neglected nothing regarding their appearance. They believed they could not spend enough time on it, even though it was not necessary to appear in the great hall until the following evening: the hearts of more than one of them had been touched by the young king.

"Once the hour came, the palace was superbly lit up, and the queen and the ladies went to the great hall, which was gleaming with so many lights that they would have put to shame even the sunniest of days. The young Zelindor, even more charming and adorned with all that art could provide to enhance his noble figure, finally appeared; and letting his gaze wander over this crowd of beauties: 'In truth, my ladies,' he said to them, 'I would feel deep regret over not having chosen from among you a beauty worthy of the throne, if the woman who is going to appear did not just justify me.' After these words, having sat down on his throne, he commanded that people go to find his bear.

"Everyone looked at each other, not understanding what the king could be intending to do with it. People were whispering: 'Is the king going to marry it?'

"The bear appeared, she was led by two princes of the blood,[18] who were each holding the end of the king's scarf, which she had around her neck. At her approach, the young king descended from his throne, and gently touching the bear's head with the end of his scepter, he said to her, 'Appear, beautiful princess. Come and erase with your charms the offense I am giving to so many beauties.'

"He had barely pronounced these words when the bearskin fell, and the admirable Noble-Thorn appeared in all her radiance, eclipsing all those who up to that point had claimed to be beautiful.

"The fairy Azerole revealed herself at that moment: she had dressed the princess herself, so one can imagine that no detail had been overlooked in her finery. Zelindor threw himself at the feet of Noble-Thorn, who tenderly raised him up and gave him her beautiful hand.

"The wedding was celebrated with royal magnificence; and the two spouses, charmed by one another, lived in such a state of union and tenderness that it should cause to die of shame the crude and vulgar people who believe that marriage is the tombstone of love.

"In less than two years, Zelindor and the queen Noble-Thorn had two sons as charming as they themselves.

"Since everything that had happened to Noble-Thorn, Rhinoceros had not stopped searching for her and tormenting the poor Coriande, whom he accused of having aided the princess's escape. When he returned, quite weary from all his running, he beat her and left her for dead, but Coriande was so attached to her mistress that she preferred to suffer all the ogre's fury than to learn that the monster had found her.

"However, he did so much research that he finally discovered that the princess was in the Kingdom of Happiness and that she had married its ruler. This news sent him into such a great rage that he would have devoured Coriande if he hadn't thought that bringing about her death so quickly would give her too much pleasure. He informed her that he knew where Noble-Thorn was, and he swore with the most atrocious blasphemies that he was going to take revenge on her: he took Coriande, and attaching her to the blades of a windmill, he told her that she would turn like that until he returned, that he would eat her along with her mistress, after having roasted them over an open fire.

"He did not know that the good fairy Azerole was also protecting Coriande: knowing her attachment for Noble-Thorn, she played a trick on the eyes of the ogre, who, thinking that he was beating Coriande, was actually only beating a bag of oatmeal, the same one that he attached to the windmill.[19]

---

18. *Princes du sang*: those who are legitimately descended from the male line of the sovereign; in this case, either the king's younger brothers, uncles, nephews, or first cousins.

19. Allusion to d'Aulnoy's "Gracieuse et Percinet" (Graciosa and Percinet, 1697). In this tale, however, the hero Percinet, who has fairylike gifts, protects the heroine Gracieuse from being beaten with rods

"Finally, he left with seven-league boots[20] and soon arrived at the Kingdom of Happiness: he learned of the good fortune the queen was enjoying: he thought he would go mad with fury because of it. He contained himself, however, and having taken up lodging in one of the suburbs of the capital, he disguised himself as a merchant selling distaffs,[21] this being the only means by which he could enter the palace, where the queen could have recognized him; he therefore took it into his head to make his rounds in the surrounding streets and to cry out at the top of his lungs: *Golden distaffs and silver spindles for sale!*

"The wet nurses and the governesses of the little princes were at the windows, and as they found this merchandise very pleasing, they had the merchant brought up to their chamber. If they were surprised by his frightening face, they wanted the distaffs even more, and bargained for them. 'I am more curious than I am in a hurry to have the money,' he said to them. 'Although I know that my spindles and distaffs are worth as much as entire kingdoms, I will give you all six if you agree to let me spend one night only in the little princes' bedchamber: I have ambition, and I will be very highly regarded in my country if I can brag about having had this honor. See if you want to, at this price my spindles and my distaffs will be yours.'

"Shocked by the merchant's stupidity, driven by the desire to have his treasures at such a cheap price, and for that matter not seeing any harm in it, the wet nurses and the governesses granted his request and told him to come back in the evening, that he would have a good bed in the bedchamber of the little princes. He appeared charmed, left his distaffs, came back that evening, and went to bed just as he had requested.

"As soon as he was certain that the nannies were sleeping soundly, he got up quietly, entered the bedchamber of the queen, which he knew was close to that of her children, took from the sheath that was hanging from the princess's headboard a knife that she always wore attached to her belt, mercilessly slit the two young princes' throats with it, then came back quietly to replace the knife in its sheath, and escaped as quickly as possible.

"As soon as the wet nurses and the governesses woke up, they were shocked not to find the distaff merchant; they imagined that he had told them that he was in a hurry to return to his country and that without a doubt he had left at daybreak; but what was their anguish and their shock when, approaching the cradles

---

at the order of her wicked stepmother by putting a spell on the eyes of her stepmother's attendants. They think they are beating the heroine with rods but instead they are using feathers.

20. Seven-league boots are a common element of European folklore; wearing seven-league boots allowed a person to cover seven leagues per step (roughly twenty-four miles), which resulted in great speed.

21. A tool used in spinning, designed to keep unspun fibers untangled until they can be spun into yarn or thread.

of the young princes, they saw these beautiful children with their throats slit and bathed in their own blood! They let out dreadful cries, everyone in the palace came running, the king and the queen came there themselves. What a sight for them to behold! The despair of the king, the mortal sorrow of the queen, the distressing cries of the entire court made this fatal moment even more horrific. People did not know whom to accuse of such a monstrous crime: the governesses and the wet nurses took care not to reveal their fatal secret, and it was necessary to carry off the queen, who had fainted in her husband's arms.

"People searched in vain for the perpetrator of this tragic affair; all that the king announced was useless, and the most excessive rewards had as little an effect; Rhinoceros alone knew his secret and was quite certain that it would not be revealed.

"The ogre had hidden himself in another neighborhood of the city, and having taken off his merchant outfit, he donned that of astrologer. He waited peacefully until the curiosity and the suffering of the king would lead him to his home, which in fact occurred. People had said so many times in front of the king that there was an extraordinary man who could reveal the past and the future with such clarity, they cited so many examples of this that Zelindor wanted to try out this famous soothsayer: he went there in person and asked him about the horrible massacre of his children.

"The astrologer, thrilled with himself for being able to commit a horrible wickedness, gravely told the young king that the guilty woman was in his own palace: [the king] shuddered at these words. The fake astrologer continued and assured him that if he had all of the women who were living there summoned, and if he looked himself at the knives that he found hanging from their belts, he would discover the murderess without fail, as the knife would still be bloody.

"The astonished king followed this monster's advice as soon as he got back to his palace and found no trace of that which he was seeking. So, he returned to the astrologer the next day and told him that his searches had been in vain. 'You did not search well,' this vile being replied, pretending to be enraged that someone was appearing to doubt his knowledge. 'How is that!' replied the king, 'you want me to search my mother the queen and the queen my wife?' 'Without a doubt,' replied the dreadful Rhinoceros, 'I advise that you not fail to do so.'

"Zelindor had no faith in the astrologer's words and returned home very sad. The queen his wife came to him with open arms; he grew pale as he approached this princess, as soon as he saw the sheath at her side, he took it, he opened it, and he pulled out the knife still stained with blood. 'Ah, perfidious creature!' he cried; at these words he fainted into the arms of his retinue. The queen, totally frightened, asked what this was about, and what was wrong with the king her husband; people informed her. 'What horror! What a lie!' cried the innocent Noble-Thorn. 'Me! How could I have slit the throats of my dear children!' She could say no more and let herself fall down as if dead on a sofa. The king, who saw her in this sorrowful state as he opened his eyes, turned them away from her immediately, and ordered that she be led to the tower, which was done immediately, and she was left with only two women to serve her. Her trial was informed by these deceiving appearances, and she was condemned to be burned alive.

"This poor princess, barely emerging from her faint, seeing herself in a dreadful place, and her two maidservants dissolved in tears, asked them if it was possible that the king her husband could really suspect her of massacring his sons. She was told yes, and in addition that her condemnation had already been pronounced. 'Oh, heaven!' cried this unfortunate queen, 'of what am I guilty to merit such torture? How can it be! Zelindor accuses me and condemns me to death without even hearing me out? I have lost his affection; I have nothing more to do but die.'

"The king, himself pierced by a mortal blow, could not resolve himself to see Noble-Thorn die, however guilty he believed her to be; and seeing that the stake had already been erected and that people were already getting ready to tie the queen to it, he had the doors to the palace opened and went down to the public square at the very moment when the innocent queen was leaving her tower with a countenance that was as self-assured as it was modest. 'Stop!' he cried out: his voice was so weak and so quaking that people barely heard it, and the queen climbed up on the stake.

"The barbaric Rhinoceros, disguised for the third time, was in the square amid the rest of the people in order to feast his cruel eyes upon the execution of the unfortunate Noble-Thorn. He was riling up the crowd with his speeches and was recounting in horrible detail how the queen had slit the throats of her children.

"All of a sudden, a miracle![22] A thick cloud emerged from the east and came to descend upon the stake, which it drenched with a rain of water and orange flowers. Then it opened and revealed, upon a chariot of rubies, the beautiful fairy Azerole, with the father and the mother of the young queen, the two little princes seated at their feet upon magnificent tiles, and the faithful Coriande holding their harnesses.[23]

"'Naïve and yet excusable King,' said the fairy, 'behold what your excessive affection for your children was going to expose you to. Noble-Thorn was going

---

22. The sudden appearance of the fairy on this chariot is an example of the plot device known as a deus ex machina; it was frequently used in early-modern machine plays and operas in which an unexpected power or event intervenes in order to rescue favorable characters from a hopeless situation. Objections to the use of these kinds of supernatural interventions to resolve plot complications dated from the time of Aristotle (*Poetics*, 1454a-b), and Murat herself had criticized this technique in her 1699 novel, *A Trip to the Country*. In that novel, her female narrator explicitly eliminates fairies from the novel's only "fairy tale" for that very reason.

23. During the eighteenth century, it was customary to make harnesses (*lisières*) for young children out of hemmed cloth or ribbon in order to guide them as they walked.

to perish and to leave you inconsolable forever. This is the one who should be punished,' she added, touching the dreadful Rhinoceros with her golden wand. 'He is the one who thought he had gotten away with this crime, and who wickedly accused the queen of it.'

"The ogre remained immobilized by the subtle power of the wand. The fairy placed the beautiful Noble-Thorn on her chariot and recounted her entire story. The charmed crowd, which always changes its opinions in accordance with the different impressions it receives, did not wait until the fairy had finished speaking; it seized Rhinoceros and threw him onto the stake, which, because it was already aflame, consumed the wicked ogre in a moment. Zelindor, all in tears, begged the fairy to obtain his forgiveness from the beautiful queen. Noble-Thorn threw herself into the arms of her husband and embraced him tenderly. Such a touching scene made everyone cry out: 'Long live King Zelindor and Queen Noble-Thorn!'

"The two spouses begged the fairy to enter their palace with the King and the Queen whom she was transporting. This illustrious group was received with unparalleled ovations: the trumpets and the drums did not cease to sound and to beat for eight days. The young Noble-Thorn presented her husband to the King and Queen, her mother and father, who thanked him for loving their daughter so much. The fairy blessed them with all sorts of good fortune and they lived happily ever after for many, many years.'"

When the Count de Livry had finished speaking, everyone praised his memory; the viscountess went even further than the others and praised his obligingness. "I assure you, madam," he said to her, "that I quite reproach myself for the length of this story; but I was scarcely remembering it, and I think I have added some things to it that were not in the original." The viscountess responded that apparently the original was not so fine and that she was partial to his manner of telling [it]. People talked for a little longer about the characters of this tale; and as it was time to let the viscountess go to bed, people wished her good night and each went to bed quite contented with what they had just heard.

Étoilette

by Marie-Madeleine de Lubert

Étoilette

Since Tourmeil had promised to work on the verses that the baron had requested of him, people stayed for a longer time with the viscountess. Madame de Briance, in order to spare the effort of conversation, said that she had a fairy tale to tell: the viscountess, who had already shown her preference for these kinds of works, was delighted that Madame de Briance wanted to lend herself to this type of amusement: she even pressed her not to postpone this enjoyment. Madame de Briance, who was informed by the Chevalier de Livry that Tourmeil had one already written, and that was in his strongbox, told [the chevalier] to go and get it. The chevalier brought it immediately; and seeing that everyone was ready to listen to Madame de Briance, he left to keep Tourmeil company. The marquise, obliged to deprive herself of the pleasure of seeing her beloved, was at least able to give herself the pleasure of keeping her thoughts on him by reading his work. She began as follows:

Etoilette[1]
A Tale

"A king and a queen, masters of a very beautiful realm, reigned over subjects who were virtuous and very valiant. They were greatly fortunate that this last quality was found in their subjects, for they were obliged to carry on a continual war against a king who, for rather plausible reasons, claimed tribute over his neighbor. This king was named King Warlike, a name that fit him perfectly. He would come every year at the head of an army to ask King Peaceful to put into effect certain very ancient treaties, made under duress. Peaceful would always refuse to submit to them, not only because they were onerous but also because he had never committed to them.

---

1. The plot is largely adapted from an anonymous thirteenth-century chantefable, *Aucassin et Nicolette* (*Aucassin and Nicolette*) written in an alternation of verse and prose. Lubert chose to rename all the main characters: the rulers Bougar and Garin become Guerrier (Warlike) and Pacifique (Peaceful), while Aucassin and Nicolette become Ismir and Etoilette. The last of these names, meaning "little star," was likely inspired by Aucassin's song to the night sky in section 25, beginning "Etoilette, je te vois" ("Little star, I see you"). Lubert also changed the setting from southern France (the cities of Valence and Beaucaire) to an unnamed fantasy realm and promoted the rulers from counts to kings. A modern French translation of the chantefable by Lubert's friend Jean-Baptiste de La Curne de Sainte-Palaye had appeared in the February 1752 edition of the *Mercure galant*. On Lubert's rewriting of this tale, see further, Blandine Gonssollin, "Deux réécritures polychromes de Marie-Madeleine de Lubert," *Féeries: Études sur le conte merveilleux, XVIIe–XIVe siècle* 17 (2021), https://doi.org/10.4000/feeries.3679.

"Peaceful had a son who was very good-looking, young, full of intelligence and valor, charming—in short, perfect, if he had not experienced love. But just as he was moving out of childhood, this fatal passion took such a hold over his heart and made itself so totally master of it that his reputation was eclipsed by it. Filled to the brim with thoughts of his love, he let his father's realm be ravaged with impunity; insensitive to the ruining of his country and to the grumblings of the people, he was preoccupied only with his beloved.

"Peaceful was justly annoyed by this conduct from the prince; he was threatened with finding himself besieged in his own capital and abandoned by his own subjects, who in their despair might decide to recognize the authority of King Warlike in order to preserve their lives and their possessions, which were so poorly defended by their legitimate sovereign; he resolved to speak seriously about the matter to his son.

"When Ismir (that was the name of the young prince)[2] had arrived at the king's waking ceremony,[3] the good old man said to him, 'My dear son, you have seen how much valor my people have employed to defend your heritage as long as you were not old enough to share their danger in battle. They were hoping that you would not fail to live up to the family from whom you are descended and that one day perhaps you would surpass the glory of your ancestors; however, now that you are in a position to assist in their efforts and to avenge our wrongs, how does it happen, my son, that you scoff at becoming the leader of my armies? Don't you know that a prince must set an example? The whole universe has its eyes on you; you owe an accounting of your actions to posterity. What opinion do you want them to have of your virtues? I have grown old performing these tasks; I have maintained the glory of this kingdom. Now, weakened by old age, almost deprived of my sight, I can no longer help my unfortunate people to repel the violence of an aggressor who unjustly wages war against us; counsel and experience are the only resources that I can still offer them. I had counted on your fighting ability; will you deceive my hopes, my dear son? Will you let me go down into the grave with the grief of seeing the crown that awaits you snatched away from you? No, you will not make me blush. Be worthy of me and of the illustrious blood that flows in your veins. Hurry off to the defense of faithful subjects who must soon receive their laws from you.'

"'Father,' replied the prince with a calm demeanor, 'it isn't lack of courage that makes me view with indifference the danger with which your realm is threatened. Nor would it be the hope of ruling that would make me take up its defense;

---

2. The name is a derivative of the Muslim name "Izmir." In choosing this name for her hero, Lubert again gives a nod to her source text, *Aucassin and Nicolette*, as "Aucassin" is similarly derived from a Muslim name (al-Kassim or al-Ghassan), even though in both cases the heroes are Christians.

3. *Lever*: A formal ceremony where the king was attended by leading nobles while getting out of bed and then getting dressed. It was instituted in France by King Louis XIV.

and I would see the moment that would crown me through legitimate succession only with a violent grief. None of those motives can touch my heart. But you are making me unhappy by refusing me permission to marry the beautiful Etoilette; that is the only treasure I yearn for; my mother is treating her like a vile slave, because the secret of her birth has not been revealed to you. My pleas have not been able to move her nor to erase that odious title that I implored you not to taint her with. Grant her to me according to my wishes, and I will become a hero.'

"'What,' replied the old king with great emotion, 'a slave girl seems preferable to you over the safety of the state, over the respect that you owe to your father! What am I saying? Over the respect that you owe to yourself! You would dishonor your life through so shameful a match? And when the daughters of the greatest kings ardently desire to see you choose among them, a slave, a girl without social status, without parents, captured in a city abandoned through the terror of our arms, preserved only through the compassion of my general, and whom the queen, your mother, took care of out of pity, you want me, unworthy son, to give you in marriage to that wretched creature? You want her to become my daughter-in-law, and you want me, in order to satisfy your insane desires, to cover myself with shame, to make a slave girl sit on my throne? Don't presume that, and if you still have any proper feelings, blush over the weakness of such a proposition.'

"'That slave girl whom you so greatly despise, father,' replied Ismir, somewhat agitated, 'is greater in her captive state than the highest-ranking princesses; her virtue, her courage, her sensitivity, all make her worthy of the most august throne. Why should I become the husband of a princess infatuated with her rank, capricious, and having no real affection for me? It is true, Etoilette has no parents or high-ranking connections that we know of, but aren't you a sufficiently great king to take the place of all that for her? I have no need of vain titles; love alone can make me happy. Her good behavior and beauty have formed my attachment; Etoilette's virtue has made it deathless, and I would rather abandon the crown than renounce...'

"'That is enough, my son,' interrupted King Peaceful; 'tomorrow you will learn my wishes.' The prince bowed respectfully to the king, his father, and withdrew, very uneasy about the consequences of this conversation.

"The king went at once to the queen's apartment and recounted to her, in the bitterness of his heart, what had just transpired between him and his son. This noble lady, naturally proud and quick tempered, easily obtained from the king, her husband, that he should let her do as she wished and assured him that he would soon be avenged. This king was so outraged against his son that he gave the queen limitless power to compel the prince to obedience, without even informing himself of the means that she would employ to do so.[4]

---

4. In *Aucassin and Nicolette*, the mother, who is neither powerful nor violent, plays only a minor role, merely supporting the father's arguments. It is the viscount, Nicolette's adoptive father, who, when

"Etoilette was the first to feel the effects of the queen's fury; she was arrested, and cruel soldiers put her in chains. 'Why are you chaining me?' she asked them with a gentle sweetness and a tone of voice capable of moving rocks to pity. 'If it is by the order of the king or the queen, just tell me that, and I will obey; but people are mistaken if they think that, through such harsh treatment, they can compel me to give up the charming Ismir; I may well never marry him, but I will always love him.' These barbarous men, without deigning to answer her, carried her away with violence and took her to the keep of an old tower, where ordinarily only people accused of the most serious crimes were locked up; having thrown her into that dreadful prison, they locked its doors with care and withdrew in secret.

"The beautiful and unfortunate Etoilette recognized the queen in these traits so characteristic of her vengeance. Her soul was not at all shaken by these cruelties; but it was a great sorrow for her to no longer see the man for whom she would have sacrificed her life; to preoccupy herself with him was for her a type of relief, and no demonstration of anger against her persecutors escaped her lips. Tightly bound and lying on the bare earth, she remained that way until evening. Then an elderly slave woman brought her something to eat and untied her without saying a word. Etoilette thanked her affectionately, without speaking ill of anyone, and the slave withdrew. A hard and small pallet was the only piece of furniture that was available to Etoilette to rest her delicate body, which was so bruised by the shackles with which she had been chained. She threw herself upon it, shedding tears that were wrested from her by the memory of her tender beloved, and spent the cruelest of nights; but she was suffering for her beloved, and that thought alone inspired her to continue suffering.

"She was brought food at normal hours; she didn't touch it. A beautiful cat, as white as snow, who hopped across the rooftops every evening, would enter through the window of that wretched keep and would eat Etoilette's supper. It would lie down at night, stretching out near the beautiful captive, and would warm her; this was no insignificant service, for at that time the weather was dreadfully cold. The hours, which seemed like instants in Ismir's presence, had then become like long years.

"Meanwhile a rumor spread that the beautiful Etoilette was lost. No one was unaware of this fact, nor of the prince's love for this charming slave girl, nor of the repugnance that the king and queen had for it. Thus, people were easily persuaded either that Etoilette had fled or that the queen had had her put to death. People did not dare speak of this to the prince; he did not even suspect what had happened, because since his conversation with the king, he had not dared to go into the presence of his mother, whose violent character he knew well. However, it was only in the queen's apartments that he used to see Etoilette; she was so prudent that she would not have received him elsewhere, and he preferred to deprive himself of

---

ordered by the ruler to send the girl away, hides her in the tower of the castle that he owns in the countryside; he does not mistreat her, as in Lubert's version.

the pleasure of seeing her for a few days rather than expose this charming girl to feeling the effects of the anger that the queen would presumably have toward him. He also feared that Etoilette, using the power she had over his heart, would herself force him to consent to the desires of the king, his father, and he would have suffered death rather than give her up and leave her under the tyrannical power of the queen. As it was not possible for him to be unaware of the disappearance of his dear Etoilette for long, the prince's intimate confidant finally risked announcing to him this unpleasant news.

"Who could express Ismir's grief and distress? He formed a hundred resolutions and settled only on the one to kill himself; his confidant was able to turn him away from that only by representing to him that if Etoilette was still alive, as there was reason to believe, the king and the queen would condemn to death that innocent beauty, whom they would regard as the sole cause of the prince's death; that therefore it was necessary for him to preserve himself for her sake and to hope for all good results from time. The unhappy Ismir yielded to this wise advice; but he resolved to lock himself in his private study and to leave it only after the beautiful Etoilette had been restored to him.

"King Peaceful, having learned of his son's excessive grief and of his fatal resolution, received word at the same time that King Warlike, having gained various advantages and overcome all the defensive barriers, was about to appear at the gates of the capital. He ran to Ismir's apartment. This distressed father said to him, 'To what shame, my son, will you be given over on account of a mad love? You abandon your homeland, your father, and your crown in a cowardly fashion. See, Ismir, see the extreme circumstances to which I have been reduced. Feast your eyes on my cruel grief and on my despair; enjoy the pleasure of seeing me, in my old age, tainted with shame, along with the illustrious blood of your ancestors. King Warlike, at the head of a formidable army, is already at the foot of our walls and is threatening to scale them. My troops, leaderless and ready to abandon us, are going to give you the dreadful spectacle of seeing me handed over as a prey to the fury of an irate enemy. If the interest and the preservation of your father cannot touch you, if you have resolved to let me perish, then let me die; I consent; but, in the name of the gods, save our unfortunate and faithful people, and save yourself, my dear son!'

"He stopped after those words, grief having stifled his voice, and he fell upon a chair while tearing out his white hair.

"Ismir, shaken to the depths of his soul by this speech and by the cruel situation in which he found his father, took the hands of this sad old man, grasped them tenderly in his own, and cried out, falling at his feet: 'My father, please forgive me! Live on, if you want me to live; add on to that, as the ultimate favor, that Etoilette will be restored to me after I have vanquished your enemies; I am going off to fight them; keep your crown; Etoilette alone will constitute my bliss; just tell me that she is still alive.'

"The old king, delighted to find his son still worthy of him, embraced him while shedding tears of joy; he assured him, by the most sacred oaths, that there had been no attempt on Etoilette's life and that he would see her upon his return. Persuaded by those oaths, already enjoying in his hopes the happiness of seeing his dear Etoilette, the tender Ismir kissed the king's hands, which he bathed with his tears. Attendants brought him a magnificent suit of armor, totally resplendent with gold, rubies, and diamonds; his father himself insisted on arming him and gave him a spirited steed. Ismir, more handsome than the sunlight, impatient to fight, once again clasped the knees of the king, his father; and filled with joy and eagerness, he proudly mounted the horse, went straight to the gates of the city, which he ordered to be opened for himself at once, and rushed toward the enemy.

"The joy of seeing Etoilette again soon threw him into a gentle daydream that nearly proved fatal to him; he forgot all of a sudden that he was in the presence of enemies, and he regained awareness only when he was completely surrounded by them and in the greatest danger of losing his life or his liberty.

"The advance guard, who had seen such a good-looking horseman advance, took him at first for one of the principal officers of King Peaceful, whom this ruler was perhaps sending to make some proposals; but having noticed that he kept on advancing, without deigning to reply to the questions that were put to him, they surrounded him. Ismir then emerged from his deep daydream and recognized the danger to which he had so imprudently exposed himself. But, far from being afraid, quickly drawing his sword, he swooped like an eagle upon the men who happened to be closest to him; he struck down twelve of them in an instant and had them make way for him. The others, angered and eager to avenge their companions, then attacked him from all sides; but the terrifying Ismir soon made them repent their rashness, and cutting the arms off some of them, slashing through [the torsos] of the others, and making heads fly off, he unhorsed, killed, or put everyone to flight. Meanwhile, his troops, whom the amazing speed of his war horse had prevented from joining up with him, finally arrived, and they profited so well from the terror that the incomparable Ismir had spread throughout the enemy army, and from the disorder that had taken over there, that, courageously charging the [enemy] troops, who were astonished by an attack so sudden and so unforeseen, they made everyone yield. In vain did King Warlike make the greatest efforts to rally his fleeing troops; Ismir noticed him, and there took place between them a terrifying battle, in which each one put on full display his valor and his strength; King Warlike, finally vanquished, saw himself in the power of his enemy, and the rest of his army scattered.

"Thus ended that glorious day. Ismir returned to his camp, where joy reigned all night, and he sent messengers to King Peaceful with news of his victory. He treated his illustrious prisoner with generosity, had him served just like himself, and at daybreak, having set him on a horse with rich trappings, he brought him to the king, his father.

"Peaceful received him with inconceivable effusions of joy and ordered festivals that were to last several days.

"Ismir, still preoccupied with his love, was waiting for the reward that had been promised him; his father did not speak to him about it, and he did not dare to remind him of it that day; but the very next morning he went to ask him for Etoilette.

"'What are you daring to say, Ismir?' replied the king with a firm and peremptory tone. 'Do not hope that an unworthy obligingness will ever make me consent to a thing that would tarnish the glory with which you have just covered yourself. Choose a princess worthy of you; don't speak to me any more about something that has already angered me so many times; you would force me to adopt a violent course of action.'

"Thus are promises fulfilled once the fear of danger has dissipated. However resolute Ismir was naturally, he trembled at these crushing words, not for himself but for Etoilette's life. He did not answer a word, and, concealing his anger, he left, went to find the captive king, and, approaching him with extreme agitation, he made him tremble with fright. 'Have no fear, sire,' he said to him with a trembling and faltering voice; 'I have come to restore your freedom; I can do that; I am your conqueror; therefore, receive it from my hand; but on one condition, which is that as soon as you have arrived in your country, you will promptly reassemble your army and come to seize this realm, from which candor and good faith have been banished; I myself will aid you in the conquest of it.'

"King Warlike, astonished by so strange a proposal, stared at Ismir, whose facial expression had totally changed; and after pondering for a moment, he replied, 'Prince, freedom is of such great value that I would accept it with intense gratitude, even if you did not add a present as considerable as the one that you would like to give me; but, however precious it is, I will never accept it if I must betray my moral principles and despoil my liberator of a treasure that I would preserve for him at the expense of my own life; no, I will not tarnish my reputation that way.'

"O virtue, how powerful is your example! Ismir, recalling all his own virtue, and touched by so magnanimous a refusal, burst into tears; then he recounted to the king his sorrows and the reasons that gave him the right to complain about his father. King Warlike listened to him attentively, pitied him, consoled him, and promised him asylum in his own country, if he needed it.

"Ismir, still resolved to restore liberty to his prisoner, came himself at the start of night to open the doors of his prison, accompanied him on horseback as far as the boundaries of the city, and came back to the palace in secret.[5]

---

5. Lubert has substantially modified her source in this passage. In *Aucassin and Nicolette*, the hero, after taking the captured enemy ruler to his father's court, makes him promise never to wage war with

"King Peaceful, having learned of his enemy's escape the very next day, had no doubt that his son was the perpetrator of it. The queen, even more angry, forced her husband to have Ismir arrested at once, and he was locked up in the lower level of a tower at the far end of the gardens, where numerous guards were stationed. He did not become upset at this and considered himself only too happy to be alone and to be able to think about his love without interruption.

"Meanwhile, the young Etoilette, still a prisoner, felt the loss of her freedom only because she could no longer see her beloved. The public celebrations, the report of which reached her, had made her suspect that he had won the victory, and her elderly jailer had confirmed that to her, which consoled her a bit for what she was suffering, being separated from Ismir. One night, when she was at the window of the keep, as there was bright moonlight, in one of those moments where the silence of all nature seems to give more power to people's ideas, the overheated imagination of Etoilette retraced for her all her misfortunes in such vivid colors that her eyes, accustomed to tears, shed them with even greater abundance, and her cheeks and her bosom were totally covered in them. Her cat, her sole and faithful companion, had sat down on the window next to her and attentively looked at the unhappy Etoilette, who did not notice; in turn, this charming cat started sighing, and with her paw she gently wiped away the tears of her mistress.[6] Etoilette could not stop herself from caressing her. 'Alas, my dear Blanchette,'[7] she said to the cat, 'you alone in the universe sympathize with my woes; Ismir himself, preoccupied with his glory, perhaps thinks of me no longer.' 'I seek to relieve your woes, beautiful Etoilette,' replied the cat, 'and to start, I inform you that your beloved is not ungrateful, and that he is suffering as much as you in the tower where his father has had him locked up.' Many people will doubtless be surprised that Etoilette did not faint to hear a cat speak; but, besides the fact that the cat was saying very interesting things, since she was speaking to her of her beloved, it is because Etoilette had greatly adorned her mind by the reading of fairy tales, which the people of refined intellect in that country made their chief

---

his country again and sets him free. The father then imprisons Aucassin, not for an act of treason but rather for continuing to insist on marriage to Nicolette.

6. From this point on, the tale diverges significantly from *Aucassin and Nicolette*, especially in the addition of multiple supernatural elements. The cat, who is a fairy godmother in disguise, is, of course, an invention of Lubert. In the medieval work, Nicolette escapes on her own initiative from the tower on the viscount's property: she makes a ladder out of blankets and towels and uses it to climb down to the garden below.

7. An enchanted white angora cat with magical powers also figures in d'Aulnoy's fairy tale "La chatte blanche" (The white cat, 1698); in the latter tale, the cat is not the fairy protectress but rather the heroine. Turkish angoras had been popular at the court of Louis XIV and remained fashionable among members of the aristocracy throughout the French Enlightenment. For example, in Isabelle de Charrière's novel *Lettres de Mistriss Henley publiées par son amie* (*Letters of Mistriss Henley Published by Her Friend*, 1784), the behavior of the heroine's white angora cat contributes to the friction in her marriage.

study. However, she was a bit surprised; we mustn't conceal the truth; but, far from being frightened, she took the cat into her arms and went to sit down on her little pallet to hear in more comfort what the cat still had to say to her. 'What, my little Blanchette, you take an interest in my sorrows?' said Etoilette, while giving a thousand kisses to that pretty animal. 'Yes, charming Etoilette,' replied the cat, 'and you will soon see for yourself.' Then, jumping to the ground, she suddenly became a tall and beautiful lady, dressed in ermine, with strings of diamonds shaped into garlands over her dress and with a ravishingly beautiful head of hair.[8]

"As soon as Etoilette saw this sudden metamorphosis, she threw herself at the fairy's feet. 'Stand up, beautiful Etoilette,' the fairy said to her while embracing her, 'I am Herminette, and I customarily live in this tower, in order to help the unfortunate people who are locked up in it, sometimes as unjustly as you are. But since I presided over your birth, and since you are the daughter of the powerful king of Fortunate Arabia,[9] I have taken more particular care of you; not being able to overcome the destiny that is pursuing you, at least I have wanted to console you, on account of the goodness of your heart, which I recognized through the care that you have taken of me, under the shape that I had borrowed. I judged you worthy of my help and of my favors, and you are going to see the effects of them.'

"Etoilette was so ecstatic over what she was hearing, and so delighted to learn that her birth made her of equal status with her beloved, that she did not think of interrupting the fairy Herminette. But as the fairy had informed her that Ismir was in prison, she dared to ask her the reason why and whether she would not deign to protect him also. The fairy satisfied her curiosity over the prince's detention and added that she could not yet do anything for him. 'But, my dear child,' she added, 'in this very instant I am going to give you the means to see him and to console him. While waiting, take this little box that I am giving you and remember to open it only in your very greatest danger. I will always protect you, so long as you don't reveal this secret to your beloved. I am going to get you out of the tower; that is all I can do for you at this time.'

"With those words, the fairy struck the walls of the keep with her wand; the stones gently tumbled, and, rearranging themselves in a wondrous manner, they formed at once a wide and convenient staircase, by means of which Etoilette descended after the fairy had again embraced her and had made her promise that

---

8. The fairy's clothing and physical appearance evoke those of other fairies from medieval French literature. For example, the fairy companion of Lanval in Marie de France's eponymous narrative poem, dating from around 1170, also wears ermine and garlands of jewels.

9. The Romans gave the name Felix Arabia to an area now comprising Yemen and southwestern Saudi Arabia, differing from the rest of the Arabian lands by its good climate and fertility. In the medieval text, Nicolette has known all along that she is the daughter of the King of Carthage, but she does not divulge this information until, near the end of the story, she arrives back in Carthage, having been taken there by Saracen pirates, and is recognized by her father. Unable to bear separation from her beloved, she disguises herself and escapes, ultimately reaching Aucassin in his home city in France.

she would not tell her beloved who had freed her. Etoilette, delighted, swiftly descended this miraculous staircase and found herself in an immense prairie that faced one side of the tower; then, turning around, she saw with peculiar astonishment that the stones that had formed the staircase, picking themselves back up, resumed their original place, just as if skilled workers had supervised the work. She continued on and went straight to the tower where the prince was locked up. That tower, placed in one corner of the gardens, was surrounded by guards, except on the side bordered by the prairie, because there was just a single window, very narrow and covered with bars; a sentinel was on duty night and day on the tower's platform.

"Etoilette shuddered as she approached Ismir's prison and, favored by cloud cover, she approached the little window without being seen. As the moon emerged, it provided her then with enough light to make out her dear Ismir; he was lying on a mat of reeds, pale, disfigured, almost motionless. But one cannot deceive the eyes of a lover.

"'Ismir! My dear Ismir!' she cried out to him softly, 'here is your Etoilette whom love is returning to you. Approach, dear prince; come to assure her that you still love her. If only it were possible for me to come all the way to you!' This cherished voice, which passed through Ismir's heart, deeply moved all his senses; he got up, tottering, and found enough strength to approach the window, where the charming Etoilette was stretching out her arms to him. 'Sovereign of my life, delight of my soul!' cried out the loving prince while kissing Etoilette's hands a thousand times. 'Is it really you that I am seeing?' He did not have the strength to say any more; joy and grief weighed him down to such a degree that he nearly fainted; and if the beautiful princess had not held on to him, he would have fallen. The tears that he shed in abundance, and with which he showered Etoilette's hands, comforted him slightly.

"His beloved was hardly in better shape; finally, after a rather long silence that was more eloquent than the best ordered speeches, they began to converse about their shared misfortune; they asked each other a hundred questions, repeated the same things a thousand times, and mutually swore their eternal passion to one another.

"At that moment, Etoilette did not tell her beloved how she had escaped from the tower in which the queen had had her locked up; but she did have the pleasure of informing him that she had been born a princess. Ismir had never been concerned that Etoilette might lack that title; he was so little surprised by the news that he did not even inquire how she had come to learn of it.

"He spoke only of the means to rejoin her soon; and not doubting that the king would set him free as soon as he learned of Etoilette's escape, he advised her to go far away as quickly as possible from that deadly place, imploring her to hide her beauty as much as might be possible, vowing that his death would be inevitable if he came to learn that another man loved her and was fortunate enough to please her. 'My heart belongs to you forever, dear prince,' Etoilette tenderly replied. 'Be persuaded of my constancy; I would choose death rather than be unfaithful to you.'

"The prince, reassured, begged Etoilette to let him know as soon as possible the place of refuge she would choose by sending the letter to his confidant Mirtis, a young nobleman who was entirely devoted to him; he indicated to her the hamlet that was at the edge of the prairie as a place where she could wait for him for a few days. They were thus making their arrangements when a large white male cat, passing close to Etoilette, cried out to her as it ran, 'Run away, my daughter; the king's armed guards are looking for you in order to kill you.'[10] Fear seized these two lovers: Etoilette, in a state of surprise, saw no way to avoid the troops except to wrap herself up in her cloak and to hide in a very thick shrubbery that had grown at the foot of the tower.

"She was just in time, for Peaceful, having indeed been alerted that Etoilette was no longer in the keep, had at once sent out armed guards and musketeers on horseback to pursue her; his plan was to have her burned alive; but these troops, who passed so close to Etoilette, did not notice her and hurried further on in all directions. As soon as they had moved away, the poor princess, trembling with fear, went back to the window where Ismir was almost dead, so greatly did he fear for her. Etoilette cut off a tress of her beautiful blonde hair and gave it to the prince as a token of her love; then, as fright gave her wings, she hastened toward the hamlet with such a light step that the grass barely bent under her feet; her feet were bare, and her legs, which resembled columns of ivory, eclipsed the whiteness of the lilies and daisies.

"Meanwhile, the princess was so upset that she got lost; and at the break of dawn, finding herself at the entrance of a vast forest, she plunged ahead. After an hour of walking, she arrived at a beautiful green area, watered by a rustic fountain, shaded by oak trees as ancient as time and prodigiously tall; overcome with exhaustion, Etoilette sat down in that spot.

"There, recalling all her misfortunes, comparing the very short time in which she had enjoyed the happiness of seeing her beloved again with the immensity of the time that she might spend without rejoining him, she shed so many tears that the ground was drenched with them. Sleep, whose sweetness she no longer knew, came to close her eyes, and she fell deeply asleep.

"Now, that forest was the one that for many centuries had been inhabited by the yellow centaurs; it was the refuge that they had chosen after the unfortunate

---

10. In the medieval text, in which Nicolette likewise goes to the tower where her beloved is imprisoned and speaks to him through the window, it is the watchman of the tower who takes pity on the lovers and warns Nicolette to escape before the soldiers arrive.

conflict that they had against the Lapiths, at the wedding of Pirithous.[11] Some of them, who were engaged in hunting, passed by chance near Etoilette. The novelty of such a person and her ravishing beauty caused them to stop, and many others soon joined them. The princess, upon opening her eyes, was seized with an extreme fright at finding herself alone in a wood amid a company of such beings; but when she saw the centaurs marvel at her and say to one another that she was doubtless a fairy or some deity, her fear was at once dispelled.

"'Since humans are conspiring to kill me,' she said to herself, 'and since the only man whom I could ask for assistance is not in a position to give me any, let's see what happens; this species of creature is perhaps less barbaric; besides, any effort I might make to escape would be in vain, and I am in a position where I must ask for their protection.' After these brief reflections, the princess modestly lifted her eyes up to the centaurs and said to them, 'My friends, you see before you an unfortunate girl who is fleeing the fury of a powerful king; grant me asylum among you. I have nothing to offer you but gratitude and my friendship, if you wish to receive it.'

"The centaurs, who were not versed in polite language but were frank and sincere, answered her that they would be delighted if she consented to remain with them and that they would protect her with pleasure.

"Then one of them told her to get on his back; the others helped her; and this company, moving away, led Etoilette into a vast cave where there dwelled several female centaurs, whom they entrusted to take care of her.

"The female centaurs received Etoilette with great joy and were eager to serve her. Every day they would arrange for her some new entertainments such as hunting, fishing, and jousts that were held among the strongest male centaurs. Etoilette awarded the prizes; these consisted of a flower or a crown of oak leaves; they received them from her hand with more satisfaction than if she had given them a kingdom.

"They loved her, they respected her and were sincerely distressed by the fact that she was always sad and solitary; one day, they asked her the reason for this profound sadness. Etoilette had too much confidence in them to refuse to give them an account of her misfortunes; they were touched by them, and the princess, profiting from their sympathetic mindset, said to them in addition, 'Since you

---

11. In Greek mythology, when the hero Pirithous, a Lapith, married Hippodamia, he invited a group of centaurs, to whom he was related. But the centaurs, not used to wine, got drunk, disrupted the festivities, and abducted some of the women. A battle ensued between the two groups, in which Pirithous, joined by his best friend Theseus, was victorious. However, this conflict led to a permanent feud between the Lapiths and the centaurs, during the course of which each group invaded the territory of the other, sometimes succeeding in expelling them and forcing them to move elsewhere. In the medieval text, there is no supernatural element here: Nicolette, going through the forest, comes across a group of shepherds and asks them to give her message to Aucassin; then she finds an isolated spot and builds herself a hut.

have so much good will toward me, one of you must go to the court and invite Ismir to come to 'hunt a white doe with silver feet' who has taken refuge in this forest; he will understand at once what that means.' She was unable to continue and shed a torrent of tears. The centaurs, who were unmannerly but good-hearted and sensitive, vowed not only to undertake her errand but also to ravage the kingdom of her persecutor and even to put him to death, if she wished it. 'God forbid,' cried the princess, 'that I should demand from your friendship such a vengeance; Ismir's father will always be respected by Etoilette, and I would defend his life at the expense of my own.'

"The centaurs, whose hearts were naturally simple and just, found in so noble a feeling new reasons to respect Etoilette. One of them was chosen to go to the court of King Peaceful; his intelligence and his good sense gave hope to Etoilette that he would succeed in his mission.

"Meanwhile, helped by the centaurs, she made for herself a little dwelling, to which she would often retire in order to shed tears over the memory of her beloved. The forest was so thick and so filled with centaurs that no one dared approach it. According to an old belief that had spread throughout the land, the centaurs devoured humans; in this way, widespread fear provided individual safety for the princess; there, she lived in a state of profound peace that was disturbed only by her anxiety over her love.

"The centaur who had been sent as a deputy soon arrived in the capital; he learned that Ismir, after being released from the tower, had fallen into a melancholy so dreadful that the doctors were in despair of being able to cure him, that the king, very distressed over his son's condition, was inventing new entertainments every day in order to dispel his sadness, but that the prince took no part in them, that he did not wish to see anyone and kept himself almost always shut in.

"The centaur easily guessed the cause of Ismir's illness; and since he did not want to risk revealing his secret, he decided to go boldly into the king's gardens, hoping to attract Ismir there. The sight of so extraordinary a creature did not fail to cause a great stir at court and to throw everyone into a state of fear. The centaur would walk around solemnly and would greet the people who appeared at the windows. At first there had been talk of killing him; but besides the fact that it wasn't easy to do, people feared that the other centaurs would come to avenge him; thus, that project was abandoned.

"He would appear every day at the same hours, would feed on fruits, and would sleep on a grassy area at the far end of the gardens.

"Several people from the court, more courageous than the others, risked approaching him and even took strolls with him, and that boldness was taken as a very lofty effort of fearlessness because ever since the centaur had taken over the gardens, no one had risked appearing there. After that, people began to approach him even more closely; they dared to offer him milk and fruits; he ate and drank, graciously thanking the individuals who presented him with those things. This familiarity seemed charming; people came running in droves, and the company became so numerous that the centaur was sometimes exhausted by it. They spoke to him, they asked him lots of questions; and since his answers were rather ambiguous, people did not fail to say that he was marvelously clever; those who understood him less praised him more; fools retained some of his statements; even greater fools wrote them down; that is the origin of so many books that people only pretend to understand and of that way of expressing oneself that has since acquired the name of 'persiflage'—a word that no academy has ever succeeded in defining. This silliness amused the good centaur, but eventually he got annoyed with having become so fashionable and with not seeing Ismir. His reputation became established, just as it has happened to many people, precisely by the factors that should have caused him to lose it; he alone was astonished by that; he did not yet know that there have been centuries of insanity when fools set the tone, just as there are centuries when reason and good sense preside; when the good qualities of the latter become dormant, society lapses into childishness. People spoke so much of the amazing centaur, people repeated so often what he had said, that eventually the news came to the ears of the solitary Ismir. At first he did not pay much attention to it; but, pestered by the small number of people whom he permitted to see him, he went down one morning into the gardens. The crowd that was surrounding the centaur moved aside a bit out of respect, and people cried out, 'Make way, make way for the prince!' The centaur, even without all those cries, would have recognized Ismir, so vivid was the description that Etoilette had given of him. If the prince found the yellow centaur wondrous among his species, the centaur was no less in amazement over the grace and majestic air of Ismir.

"'My lord,' the centaur said to him, bowing, 'I have for a long time desired to be one of your friends, and I have come to beg you to grant me a favor.' The prince signaled that people should move further away and responded with kindness to the centaur, who, in order not to reveal Etoilette's secret too openly, proposed to Ismir to come to their forest to hunt the white doe with silver feet.

"The prince, through the power of that passion that gives such flashes of insight to the mind, immediately interpreted the metaphor and was astonished that his charming Etoilette had not been devoured by the centaurs, among whom he understood that she had taken refuge. He stared at the handsome centaur in order to see all the way into his soul; and finding him calm and assured, he promised to go the very next day, right at dawn, to hunt in the yellow forest, if the centaur was willing to lead him there.

"'That is my intention, sir,' replied the centaur. 'But come alone, and leave the concern of guarding you to our inhabitants; you will discover that you have no better friends.'

"Ismir made countless friendly remarks to the centaur; he spent the rest of the day with him, informing himself of the manners, laws, and customs of the centaur race. Ismir, charmed with the envoy, refused to leave his side, had supper with him and spent the night with him in the grassy area. The centaur, delighted with these marks of confidence and seeing himself alone with Ismir, finally revealed to him the full secret of his mission and spoke to him at great length of Etoilette. Ismir nearly died of joy and did not know how to express his gratitude to the centaur. He did not sleep at all that night; dawn was too slow in coming for his taste; and as soon as it did appear, he awakened the kindly centaur, who was still sound asleep, for he was not in love.

"The prince had magnificent armor brought for himself and the centaur, and after he got on his back, they went away at once. On the way, Ismir promised that as soon as his father had forgiven his marriage to Etoilette, he would send a delegation to cement a lasting peace with the land of the centaurs and to have a thousand of them as his guard; the conversation often revolved around the princess, and soon they arrived within view of the yellow forest, the approach to which caused Ismir to feel a violent agitation; they penetrated that thick forest with incredible difficulties, without the prince's wanting to rest, and at last they arrived at Etoilette's little dwelling. She was inside, and as soon as these tender lovers perceived one another, they rushed toward each other, embraced tightly, and gave themselves over to all the pleasure of seeing themselves reunited. Their tenderness touched both the male and the female centaurs, to the point that tears came to their eyes. Etoilette, noticing that Ismir had been injured from the sharp spines of the hedges that blocked the entry to the forest, forced him to lie down on a bed of grass within her little hut, gave him something to eat, and with her white and delicate hands she applied to his wounds some herbs, the medicinal properties of which she had learned from the female centaurs. She could not stand to have anyone else take part in these tender acts of care. Soon Ismir was cured; love often cures people who are even sicker. The prince felt happy with his beloved among the kindly centaurs; Etoilette, however, did not want to receive his promise of marriage and give him her own, except with the consent of those who had given her life;[12] apart from that, their happiness was perfect.

Ismir, seeing the princess resolute in that intention, proposed to her that they take a ship; Etoilette agreed to that, persuaded that the fairy would direct their course. They announced their departure to the centaurs, who were truly grieved over it, and they led Ismir and Etoilette to the sea. At their departure, they left behind in that wild place a memory of their charms and of their virtues that tradition still preserves there. They did not remain on the shore for long, and soon they perceived the most beautiful ship in the world anchored nearby; they approached and observed with extreme surprise that it was made of cedar wood and rose wood, the ropes were made of garlands of flowers, and the sails out of

---

12. Etoilette wants permission from her biological parents, King Fortunate of Arabia and his wife.

gold gauze, upon which were embroidered depictions of large cats; a hundred white angora cats served as sailors.[13]

"Etoilette easily understood that this miraculous ship was a new kindness from the fairy Herminette; she invited the young prince to enter, and they set off accompanied by the meowing of the cats, who made desperate sounding noises as a sign of rejoicing.

"The two young lovers had no reason to regret their trust; the vessel was filled not only with all things necessary to support life but also with rich and elegant garments, of all colors and for all seasons. The ship, having put out to sea, sailed with a very favorable wind, and the white cats maneuvered wondrously. In periods of calm, they gave splendid concerts upon excellent instruments, and the princess, in order to amuse herself, learned from them how to play the guitar.

"Ismir, delighted to see the princess without witnesses and at all hours, never stopped talking to her about his love; she always believed she was hearing him for the first time, and in turn she would profess her eternal tenderness to him; night alone would separate them, and they had so much impatience to see each other again the next day, it was as if they had undergone the rigors of a long absence.

"It was very difficult to keep a secret while being so greatly in love. Ismir was always finding that Etoilette was concealing some circumstances in the story of her imprisonment. He complained of it so tenderly and pressed her so hard that Etoilette was unable to prevent herself from admitting that Herminette had revealed to her the secret of her birth, and she ultimately divulged to him what the fairy had so strongly urged her to keep hidden.[14] She commended herself for having let her beloved in on this secret; but she soon bore the punishment for it: the sea became violent, and the sky became covered with thick clouds, from which there came horrifying flashes of lightning and a dreadful thunder.

"Etoilette clearly perceived that this was an act of vengeance from the fairy; she tried hard to appease her and begged her to strike only herself, since she alone was guilty; and not deigning to make use of the box that Herminette had given her, which would have saved her from so great a danger but perhaps would not have preserved her beloved, she rushed to throw herself into his arms, in order to have at least the pleasure of dying with him. In vain did Ismir urge her to open the box. 'Given that it can save only me,' she replied, 'I find it useless.' Hardly had

---

13. In d'Aulnoy's tale, the court of the white cat likewise consists primarily of small cats who are endowed with a variety of talents, including the ability to play the guitar and other instruments.

14. Since Etoilette had already revealed the secret of her noble birth to Ismir upon her liberation from the tower, the transgression that she commits here is not the revelation of that information but rather the revelation of the fairy's interventions, which had allowed her to learn this identity. Insistence on anonymity is another common trope of medieval French fairy literature. The hero of Marie de France's "Lanval," for example, is punished in similar fashion to Etoilette for revealing the existence of his fairy protectress.

she finished saying these words when a thunderbolt fell upon the ship with a horrifying din and plunged it into the abyss of the sea. The two lovers, locked in a tight embrace and bobbing up and down in the waters, were pushed around by the waves. A big wave separated them; the darkness of night and the strong motion of the waves prevented them from coming back together, and they were thrown separately into different countries.

"Ismir had fainted from grief, and as he was floating on the sea, some fishermen noticed him; they jumped into the water and brought him to their dwelling.

"The country where this prince had washed up was called the Isle of Rest; not the slightest sound was heard there; people always spoke softly, and they walked only on tiptoes.[15] There were never quarrels, rarely wars; and when it was absolutely necessary to wage a war, only the ladies fought, doing so from a distance by throwing lady apples.[16] The men did not get involved; they would sleep until noon, spin, make ribbons, take the children for walks, put on makeup and beauty patches. These men took such delicate care of Ismir that he soon opened his eyes. When he saw himself surrounded and not perceiving Étoilette, he uttered cries that frightened the fishermen; they stopped their ears and signaled to him to speak softly. He therefore began to recount to them, in an undertone, the reason for his despair, and these kind men wept copiously; but their wives, who returned after a hunt and who saw their husbands in tears, ordered them to leave. Ismir informed them of the cause of this feeling of pity, and they consoled him with a courage that verged somewhat on harshness. Ismir spent the night in the hut, and the next day he gave many precious stones to the women in charge, in gratitude for the care that had been taken of him; they set no value on those things and gave them to their husbands. The prince departed, and after traversing a vast prairie, he arrived at a city that was made entirely of rock crystal and shining like the sun; he entered it, in hopes of finding his dear Étoilette there, and passed through several neighborhoods without encountering hardly anyone. He reached a stately palace made of the most beautiful crystal in the world and entered the courtyard in order to rest there. There, seated on a bench, he gazed upon this stately building; he walked all around it several times, quite astonished to find no door.

"The people of that country did not trouble themselves about doors; those things made too much noise; and when someone came to their house, they would throw down silken ladders, by means of which people would enter through the windows; people left the same way. They had no staircases either; other people

---

15. The Isle of Rest episode is a greatly expanded version of the sojourn in the land of Torelore in *Aucassin and Nicolette*, where standard gender roles are similarly reversed. Lubert's additions include such fantasy elements as the rock crystal buildings and the lack of doors and windows; the most intriguing omission is the custom of having men, rather than women, bear children. In the medieval text, Aucassin and Nicolette remain together in Torelore; they will be separated only later, after the land is invaded by Saracens, who capture the young people and put them in different ships.

16. *Pomme d'api*: a small, flat-shaped apple of French variety.

would have too easy a time coming to see them, and they did not like visits that were painful, annoying, and always useless. This palace was the dwelling of the king of the country; his ministers, engaged in the important task of teaching the young princesses to walk, having noticed Ismir, judged, based on his magnificent clothing, that he was some foreign ambassador, quickly placed the princesses back in their cradles, let down a big sack made of blue velvet, suspended by silken ropes, and signaled to the prince to place himself in it. Ismir understood their sign and saw himself hoisted all of a sudden into a rich apartment.

"He advanced toward a four-poster bed, whose curtains were of very rich material and enhanced by purple and gold cords; twenty pans filled with the most exquisite perfumes were burning around the bed, where the monarch, fully stretched out, was attentively listening to his chancellor, who was reading to him the tale of Bluebeard.[17]

"Ismir, astonished to see a man of admirable plumpness, enhanced by garments of the brightest and reddest colors, with a crown on his head, could not doubt that this was the king. 'Sire,' he said to him after bowing to him in a quite knightly fashion, 'might you not be ill?' 'No, my son,' he answered quite softly, 'I feel very well; but I am resting a bit while my wife is at the war.' 'Why, fie on you!' Ismir briskly replied. 'Don't you feel ashamed to behave that way? You let your wife go off to the war, and you are resting? Truly, that is unforgivable.' 'My son,' replied the king, 'those are our laws and our customs from time immemorial; if you want, my chancellor will read them to you, because, for my part, I have not wanted to tire myself by learning them.' Ismir, carried away by a noble anger at the sight of so much cowardice, took a strong spear, the only one to be found in the whole land and which had never yet been used, gave a hundred blows with it to that effeminate king, harshly shook off his blankets, and threw them out the window.

"He was about to give the same treatment to the chancellor and the ministers, but they started weeping along with their dear master and begged Ismir to calm his anger. Since he was naturally good-hearted, he easily came back to pity and said, however, to the king, 'Sire, if you don't promise me to abolish your ridiculous customs and to go to war yourself like other kings, I will tear down your beautiful crystal palace. Moreover, I wish to accompany you, but let it be right away; otherwise, I will beat you black and blue, along with your chancellor and all your brutish ministers.'

"You can easily imagine how scared they were. The poor king vowed, sobbing, to do everything that Ismir wanted, for he feared a new round of blows from the terrifying spear, which the prince was swinging in a totally martial fashion.

---

17. Allusion to "Barbe-Bleue" ("Bluebeard"), from Charles Perrault's *Histoires ou contes du temps passé* (*Tales or Stories from Times Past*, 1697). In having her characters share her own love of fairy tales, Lubert employs a literary strategy that was common among the fairy-tale writers of the first French vogue (1690–1715), who often alluded to one another's tales in order to generate publicity for the genre and for the literary circles associated with it.

"The king had some of the queen's armor brought to him, placed himself in the sack with Ismir, to whom they gave the finest horse in the stables; the king mounted another horse, and they departed at top speed for the army. The queen, at the head of a huge squadron of ladies, was valiantly defending the passage over a small river, on the other side of which the enemies were arrayed for battle. The lady apples were flying from both sides, and the people who received the slightest bruise withdrew from the fight.

"Ismir looked for a moment on this fine combat, while bursting out laughing. 'Sire,' he said to the king of the Isle of Rest, 'do you want me to rid you of all those people?' 'Most willingly, my dear friend,' he replied. At once Ismir gives free rein to his horse, moves through the queen's squadron, and like a torrent that comes down from a mountain, passes the river and arrives on the other shore.[18]

"The enemies, who were not expecting such great rashness and who at first had believed that Ismir was a lady, as he was so young and so good-looking, were quite undeceived when they saw him with the spear in his fist, striking, killing, knocking down, and overturning everything. The queen became very scared, for Ismir's horse had so animated all the others that they too crossed the river, despite the efforts of the riders. The king, perceiving that Ismir was going about it for real and was killing without granting quarter,[19] ran up to him, and taking the rein of his horse, he said to him, 'But, in all honesty, you can't be serious. Stop now! Are people to be killed this way without mercy? Wouldn't it be great if you also taught them to kill, so that they could come and do the same thing to us! We only wanted to make them flee, and behold, there is no one left except the people whom you have killed or wounded.'

"Ismir shrugged his shoulders; he did stop, however, seeing that everyone had fled; and while still conversing, he brought the king, the queen, and the army back to the crystal palace.

"This prince, who had just acquired so much glory, did not become more arrogant as a result; while reviewing the troops, he carefully examined all the ladies of the army, hoping that Etoilette would be among them. The sorrow of having made that search so uselessly made him sigh bitterly, and he became sad despite all the comments from the king, who was the most immoderate chatterbox in his whole kingdom, with his low voice.

"Instead of reentering the palace, Ismir resolved to seek Etoilette in all lands and on all the seas, and he wanted to take leave of the king and the queen; the king insisted that he would not allow him to part company with them so soon and urged him so strongly that he placed himself again in the ridiculous sack and was again hoisted up into the apartments.

18. The shift to the present tense here accentuates the shift in Ismir's personality, in that he finally enlists in combat of his own free will.

19. *tuer sans quartier*: to continue to kill one's vanquished opponents without showing mercy or concession.

"Prince Ismir, who yielded to these bothersome requests only with reluctance, got into a bad mood and asked the king why he had the notion of not having any staircases in his house. 'My predecessors never had any,' he replied. Ismir brusquely rejoined, 'That's a fine reason to keep a custom that is so silly and so inconvenient.' The king, over whom the prince had acquired great influence, promised to have one constructed, if Ismir was willing to trace out the design of one. Ismir, touched by such deference, believed he had a duty not to leave such docile people in a state of ignorance, and he consented all the more willingly to stay a year with them, since he was hoping to learn there, rather than elsewhere, some news of his dear Etoilette. He found a certain sweetness in not being in the places where his love had arisen and where it had grown so great.

"During his sojourn in the Isle of Rest, a miraculous change took place in the customs of these effeminate inhabitants; he accustomed their ears to noise, gave them some knowledge of architecture, of sculpture, and of the useful arts; he even undertook to train them for war and succeeded in instilling discipline in them and in making them do the military drills and maneuvers quite well. But he was unable to give them firmness of soul, valor, and boldness. After three different armies had descended upon the coasts all of a sudden, Ismir, delighted at encountering so fine an occasion to put his lessons into practice, assembled the various corps of troops and wanted to lead them toward the enemy; but these mere shadows of soldiers were unable to withstand the sight of [their opponents], and their terror was such that Ismir found himself abandoned at once. He performed miracles of valor in order to save at least the king. This unfortunate ruler and Ismir were captured and the city was sacked. While the enemies were finishing the process of destroying it and pillaging its riches, they had Ismir carried into one of their boats. This prince, who had lost nearly all his blood, had fainted; he remained for a long time in that condition; and when he opened his eyes, he was very astonished to find himself alone and to see the boat sailing on its own. He found himself as strong as before and felt no wound, and the miraculous boat caused him to arrive in two days' time in a port that he recognized at once: it was the port of the capital of his kingdom.[20]

"Several people who were walking around there in a state of deep mourning recognized Ismir at once, helped him to get out of the boat, and, shedding tears, prostrated themselves at his feet and began to cry out: 'Long live the king!'

"These acclamations made the prince shudder, and he soon learned that the king, his father, and the queen, his mother, had died, nearly at the same time, from grief over having lost him.

"Ismir, worn out by lack of food and fatigue, put his own needs aside in order to indulge his sorrows; his innards were shaken; he wept bitterly over his

---

20. In the medieval text, the trip does not feature supernatural intervention: following a storm at sea, the Saracen ship bearing Aucassin wanders aimlessly and by chance ends up in the hero's native city.

father and his mother and insisted on being led right away to their tomb. It was only after satisfying the demands of piety that he put on royal attire and that he received the homage of the nobles and the respects of the common people.

"Etoilette was not the last thing on his mind; and the very next day he also sent a distinguished delegation to the yellow forest to inform the centaurs of his accession and to request a thousand of them for his guard.

"They received these marks of friendship and of memory with much gratitude, and they sent off the individuals whom the king requested; they had as their commander one of the most esteemed individuals in the forest, who brought to the new king a pigeon and a dove; the pigeon had the talent of finding lost things. As soon as Ismir was informed of that, he ordered it to go and look for Etoilette; and believing that he could not take enough measures to be assured of success, he also ordered the head admiral to set out to sea with a fleet of a thousand ships.

"The dove never left the king's side and ordinarily remained perched on his shoulder; the centaur commander assured the prince that in time it would serve to have Etoilette recognized.

"After several days had passed, Ismir's subjects, who saw that he was constantly immersed in sadness, solitary, and often shutting himself in with the captain of the guards, resolved to propose to him that he give them a queen, in order to ensure the succession to the throne for his family. The most esteemed individuals came to meet with him and implored him, on behalf of his people, to accede to their wishes, so that they might have princes from his lineage. At that proposal, Ismir felt anguish in his heart, and the tender love that he preserved there for Etoilette made his tears flow. He replied, 'I do not want to refuse my subjects the reward that they await as a result of their loyalty to me; but I beg you, my friends, to leave me the time to carry out some additional searches for the beautiful Etoilette, whom, as you know, I loved so tenderly. My love for her has done nothing but increase; she was worthy of it; and even if she were not the daughter of the powerful king of Fortunate Arabia, her good qualities alone make her worthy of the throne. If, in one year, I am given the certainty that she no longer lives, you yourselves will choose for me a princess to your liking; before that time, do not speak to me about it if you do not want to distress me, which is something I do not believe you would want.'

"The deputies, having humbly prostrated themselves on the ground, replied that nothing was more reasonable than what the king was proposing. New ships were equipped and sent off to sea with incredible speed, in order to go again in search of Etoilette in all the parts of the world. As soon as they arrived in some port or at the smallest beach, people would cry out, 'Whoever gives us news of the beautiful princess Etoilette will be rewarded with a fine province; our king will give it to that person, plus one hundred thousand gold pieces and a fine horse.'

"This lavish promise excited everyone's ears; but Etoilette was not to be found. The admiral would have grown weary of so many useless voyages if he had loved Ismir less; but, unable to resolve to come back without having news of the princess, he kept on sailing. Meanwhile, let us see what had become of her.

"The waves had carried Etoilette onto the shore, quite close to a very beautiful city; she was rescued by the king of the country, who was then strolling along the seashore. This ruler was so moved by Etoilette's youth and charms that, through a generous compassion, he ordered that the beautiful stranger be carried into his palace and receive as much care as if she were his own daughter. He had had a daughter long ago, but she had been lost for a long time, and since he had no more hopes of seeing her again, he resolved to adopt the one whom fortune had led onto his coast.

So there she was, served, dressed like a princess, and adored by the whole court. The queen bestowed a thousand marks of affection upon her, and the king's son did even more than the queen. Etoilette received their affectionate treatment with all the gratitude imaginable, but she was constantly shedding tears; the festivals, hunting parties, tournaments, and everything that the king could imagine to entertain her did not diminish her grief.

The queen, who truly loved this beautiful girl, begged her one day to tell her the cause of her sadness; the crown prince was the only other person present at that conversation. Etoilette raised no objections to telling them of her misfortunes; she only kept back the information that Herminette so strongly urged her to keep secret. Experience teaches people better than all lessons do; she feared being punished a second time by the fairy. Etoilette depicted her love for Ismir in such sincere terms that she touched both the kindly queen and the young prince; but when she informed them that she was the daughter of the king of Fortunate Arabia and that she had been captured during the sack of the city, the queen fell upon her neck, took her in her arms, and called her a thousand times her dear daughter. The young prince, delighted to be reunited with so lovely a sister, went at once to let his father know of such a fortunate discovery. While the queen and the princess were giving themselves over to joy and pouring out their hearts, the good king arrived. Etoilette wanted to throw herself at his feet, but he took her tenderly into his arms, and from that point on there was nothing but embraces, questions, explanations, confused words, and expressions of infinitely touching things.

The joy became widespread and was communicated to the whole court; cannons were fired; violins played; people ate pigeons, sugared almonds, and jam; and people drank the most exquisite wines until they got out of breath. Rockets, firecrackers, puppet shows, and people cheering made a tremendous amount of noise. Everyone wanted to see the princess at the same time, and each person brought presents, jewels, diamonds, fabrics, little dogs, sheep, monkeys, and parrots. Etoilette received everything with an air of kindness and gratitude that delighted everyone, and nobody returned home without having drunk coffee with milk or redcurrant juice.

The tumult finally died down, and the princess began to think about her dear Ismir again; the uncertainty surrounding his fate poisoned all her pleasures; she sighed, she found relief through tears, and she complained of not being able to share with this prince the happiness that had come to her.

To crown her suffering, the king, her father, gave her hand in marriage to the powerful Emperor of the Deserts, in order to solidify and make more lasting the peace that he had just concluded with that dangerous neighbor.

"The princess nearly died of grief over such distressing news; she threw herself at the feet of the king, her father, and explained to him that, having pledged her troth to Prince Ismir, she could absolutely not belong to another. The king treated her as if she were delusional, and despite her tears and her arguments, he ordered her to make herself ready to receive the Emperor of the Deserts as her husband; she went a hundred times to throw herself into the arms of the queen and to implore her aid. This kindly mother shared her grief and tried to console her, but she could not imagine any remedy; it was necessary to obey.

"The princess became so violently upset over this that she refused all nourishment; she didn't sleep at all. The preparations for her marriage continued to advance, and the fatal moment was approaching. One night, when she was feeling even more dejected than usual, she remembered the little box from the fairy Herminette, and since the present danger seemed more substantial to her than the ones that she had encountered at sea, she resolved to make use of it this time and opened it. A dark haze emerged from it and enveloped Etoilette; a quarter of an hour later, once the cloud had dissipated, she found herself on a ship made of mother-of-pearl, in a room adorned with mirrors and with tapestries of silver brocade; she perceived, by the ship's movement, that she was at sea. A beautiful rock crystal chandelier lit up her room; the princess, once she had somewhat recovered from her amazement, got up from the sofa on which she was sitting, and finding herself facing a large mirror, she saw with a fright that she had become an Ethiopian,[21] dressed in Moorish fashion with silver and rose-colored gauze, with a guitar on a shoulder strap, held up by a cord made of white and rose-colored diamonds, and with belt and heavy shoes trimmed the same way.[22]

21. The source of this episode, which is not found in the medieval tale, is likely Jean de La Fontaine's short novel *Les Amours de Psyché et de Cupidon* (*The Loves of Cupid and Psyche*, 1669). In this text, when Psyche yields to curiosity and opens the box sent by Proserpina, a vapor emerges and she is transformed into an Ethiopian. She retains her beauty, according to the narrator and everyone who beholds her, though she thinks that the change in skin color has destroyed it.

22. In the medieval tale, the heroine's escape and her return to the hero's land happen purely through her own determination and resourcefulness. Nicolette, faced with a forced marriage, escapes from her father's palace at night, carrying her viol (an instrument she has learned to play during her stay in Carthage), uses an herb to dye her face black, acquires male attire, and takes passage on a ship, posing

"This luxury did not console her for the loss of the most beautiful complexion in the world.[23] 'Barbarous Herminette!' she cried out in distress, 'if you have preserved my beloved, will he want to still love me under this dreadful color?[24] Take away my life if you are condemning me to seeing him change his feelings.'

"She did not stop with that and rushed onto the deck, resolved to bury herself in the waves. As she was climbing over, a powerful hand restrained her; she turned around and saw the fairy. 'Weak Etoilette,' Herminette said to her, 'the loss of your beauty makes you seek death, as though that good quality were the only one that could make you happy.' 'Alas,' replied the distressed princess while shedding a torrent of tears, 'I cherished it only for Ismir, and Ismir won't love me anymore.' Sobs drowned her voice. 'But if the Fates,' rejoined the fairy, 'had linked your lover's life to the loss of your beauty, what would you choose: that he should die and you get your face back, or that he should live and you remain an Ethiopian?' 'That he should live,' rejoined Etoilette quickly, 'but that I should die, if I were to stop being pleasing to him.' 'You will both live,' replied the charming Herminette while embracing the princess, 'and you will live happily and contentedly. So much constancy and a love so perfect deserve to have my protection.' She disappeared as she finished these words, and Etoilette no longer worried over her color. The little ship sailed uneventfully and finally entered the port of Ismir's kingdom.

"The beautiful Ethiopian woman, after jumping lightly onto land and twirling her guitar, on which she played divinely, went through the city and turned her steps toward the king's palace.

"Ismir at that very moment was descending its staircase in order to take a stroll along the seashore, as he did every day, and to look for the arrival of his admiral, from whom he had had no word.

---

as a jongleur. It is in this garb that she arrives in Aucassin's city; she entertains him and his courtiers with a song describing their love. Washing her face suffices to restore her original complexion. Needless to say, Lubert added all the supernatural elements, including the luxurious magical ship that sails by itself, the pigeon and dove with special powers, and the box that grants a wish.

23. Negative connotations associated with a dark complexion had a long tradition in France, dating from at least the Middle Ages. In French medieval texts, for example, peasants associated with pagan beliefs and practices were often described as "dark" or "tawny." Medieval religious paintings and sculptures also often depicted the devil with dark skin. By the twelfth century, the physiognomy of these figures became more specifically African, with white skin representing Christian superiority (Guillaume Aubert, "'The Blood of France': Race and Purity of Blood in the French Atlantic World," 461–462, note 44).

24. The racist implications of this statement, which are striking to the modern reader, would likely have been less apparent to Lubert's contemporaries, as essentialist notions of racial difference were less developed in France than they were in Spain and England during this same time period. This nuance is apparent in the fairy tale to the extent that Etoilette retains her beauty, grace, and eloquence despite her change in skin color, enabling the king to identify her as "a person of importance," even though she must return to her original appearance before their love affair can continue.

"Etoilette recognized the prince immediately and, seeing him with the crown on his head and a cloak of black gauze, had no doubt that he had become king. She was astonished only to see him with a dove on his shoulder; she trembled as she advanced and yet produced a speech of greeting that was very polite and very refined. The young king, delighted with the intelligence and the grace of the Ethiopian woman, was convinced, based on the elegance of her attire, that she was an important person. One must tell all: a secret premonition that only true lovers know inspired curiosity in him; thus, he eagerly approached her and asked her what brought her to his court.

Etoilette, filled with such great joy at seeing her beloved, nearly died of grief at not being recognized by him; but joy prevailed, and especially the confidence that she felt based on the fairy's promises. Without replying to the king, she tuned her guitar and sang these words; it is clear that she made them up on the spot.

> From a far-off land my way I wend,
> To your sorrows for to put an end.
> Etoilette, the fair and true,
> Maintains her perfect love for you;
> A king from her region she spurns,
> Who offers her his heart that yearns.
> But this king, handsome, so they say,
> Will never to her seem such a prize
> As Ismir, with blond hair and dark eyes.
> And she would rather let them slay
> The damsel gracious, fair and trim
> Than see her break her faith with him.
> And that's the message of my lay.

"Ismir, delighted with the song, said to the Ethiopian woman, 'Lovely dark creature, so you know my dear Etoilette, since you assure me that she still lives?' Hardly had he finished those words when the pigeon arrived, flying swiftly, and came to set himself upon the princess's head; the dove beat its wings; the fairy Herminette also arrived all of a sudden, and, touching the Ethiopian woman with her golden wand, she spared her the trouble of replying, for she then became once again the faithful, the divine, and the ravishing Etoilette. Ismir thought he would die of joy and amazement; he threw himself at the feet of his beloved, who raised him at once in order to set him at the feet of the fairy: 'Love each other always this way, my children,' she said as she embraced them. 'I have come expressly to crown such a fine passion.' Ismir was beside himself; Etoilette was no longer thinking clearly; the only feeling that she could distinguish in such a jumble of thoughts was the gratitude that she wanted to express to the fairy. The king gave his hand to them and led them to his apartment. There, their surprise became even greater, for they found present the king, the queen, and the prince of Fortunate Arabia, whom Herminette had had transported there in an instant through those powerful enchantments to which all of nature must submit.[25] The family members, with the greatest willingness in the world, granted the beautiful Etoilette to the loyal Ismir; the wedding was delayed only until the day that followed this joyful day. Ismir, having finally become the husband of Etoilette, was just as happy as a husband as he had been faithful as a lover, and they always lived in the midst of pleasures and of the most perfect contentment."

Having finished her reading, Madame de Briance received the compliments of the entire company. "In truth, madam," said the viscountess, "I do not remember having spent so agreeable a day in my whole life, and the tale that you have just been obliging enough to read to us is a charming work. I cannot conceive why people who have the talent for imagining in this way do not amuse themselves by composing these kinds of stories all the time." The Marquise de Briance replied to the polite comments of the viscountess with other similar comments, and they each recalled what they had found most noteworthy in this little work.

---

25. This reunion with the heroine's family, possible thanks to the fairy's magic powers, does not happen in the medieval tale.

Bibliography

Primary Sources

Principal Works by the Countess de Murat

1697 *Mémoires de Madame la comtesse de M****. Paris: Claude Barbin.
1698 *Contes de fées, dédiés à la Princesse Douairiere de Conty*. Paris: Claude Barbin.
1698 *Nouveaux contes de fées*. Paris: Claude Barbin.
1699 *Histoires sublimes et allégoriques*. Paris: F. et P. Delaulne.
1699 *Voyage de campagne par Madame la Comtesse de M****. Paris: Veuve de Claude Barbin.
April 14, 1708–June 8, 1709 - *Le Journal pour Mademoiselle de Menou*. Paris: Bibliothèque de l'Arsenal. Ms. 3471.
1710 *Les Lutins du château de Kernosy, nouvelle historique: Par Madame la comtesse de M****. Paris: J. Le Febvre.

Other Works by the Countess de Murat

1695 A sonnet. *Recueil de pièces curieuses et nouvelles* . . . 3, no. 1: 61–62. The Hague: A. Moetjens.
1703 *Zatide, histoire arabe*. [Also attributed to Eustache Le Noble.] Paris: Pierre Ribou.
1714 "L'esprit folet, ou le Sylphe amoureux." In *Avantures choisies, contenant L'Amour innocent persécuté; L'esprit folet, ou le Sylphe amoureux; Le Coeur volant, ou L'Amant étourdi. Et La Belle Avanturière*. Paris: P. Prault.
1715 An elegie, an epistle, and an eclogue. *Nouveaux choix de pièces de poésie*. La Haye: H. Van Bulderen. 1:220–222; 2:157–161, 161–164.
1755 A chanson and an epistle. *Choix de chansons*. Paris. 45–46.
1865 A chanson and a sonnet. *Recueil de Maurepas*. Leyden. 2:225–26; 5:56.

Works Misattributed to the Countess de Murat

1671 *Le Comte de Dunois*. Paris: Claude Barbin.
1695 *La Comtesse de Chateaubriand ou les Effets de la jalousie*. Paris: Théodore Guillain.

Principal Later Editions of Les Lutins du château de Kernosy

Les Lutins du château de Kernosy, nouvelle historique : Par Mad. la comtesse de Murat. Nouvelle édition. Revûë, corrigée et augmentée de deux contes. Leyden: np, 1753.

Le Séjour des amans ou les Lutins du château de Kernosy. Leyden: np, 1773.

Murat, Henriette-Julie de Castelnau, comtesse de. "Les Lutins du château de Kernosy." In *Voyages imaginaires, songes, visions et romans cabalistiques.* Vol. 35. Amsterdam, Paris: Garnier Frères, 1788.

Modern Editions and Translations of Other Works by the Countess de Murat (in Order of Most Recent)

"Happy Pain" and "Little Eel." In *Miracles of Love: French Fairy Tales by Women.* Edited by Nora Martin Peterson. Translated by Jordan Stump. New York: Modern Language Association, 2022.

"L'heureuse peine" and "Anguillette." In *Prodiges d'amour: Contes de fées au féminin.* Edited by Nora Martin Peterson. New York: Modern Language Association, 2022.

Madame de Murat: Journal pour Mademoiselle de Menou. Edited by Geneviève Clermidy-Patard. Paris: Classiques Garnier, 2016.

Henriette-Julie de Castelnau, comtesse de Murat: Voyage de campagne. Edited by Allison Stedman with Perry Gethner. Rennes: Presses Universitaires de Rennes, 2014.

"The Savage, A Story." Edited and translated by Allison Stedman. In *Marvelous Transformations: An Anthology of Fairy Tales and Contemporary Critical Perspectives*, edited by Christine A. Jones and Jennifer Schacker, 201–218. Toronto: Broadview Press, 2013.

"To the Modern Fairies." From *Sublime and Allegorical Histories.* Edited and translated by Sophie Raynard and Ruth B. Bottigheimer. In *Fairy Tales Reframed: Early Forwards, Afterwords, and Critical Words*, 203–205. Albany: State University of New York Press, 2012.

A Trip to the Country. Edited and translated by Perry Gethner and Allison Stedman. Detroit: Wayne State University Press, 2011.

"Little Eel" and "Wasted Effort." In *Enchanted Eloquence: Fairy Tales by Seventeenth-Century French Women Writers*, Edited and translated by Lewis C. Seifert and Domna C. Stanton, 231–279. Toronto: Iter and the Centre for Reformation and Renaissance Studies, 2010.

Les fées entrent en scène. Edited by Nathalie Rizzoni. Paris: Honoré Champion, 2007.

"'Une Fée Moderne': An Unpublished Fairy Tale by la Comtesse de Murat." Edited by Ellen Welch. *Eighteenth Century Fiction* 18, no. 4 (Summer 2006): 499–510.

Madame de Murat: Contes. Edited by Geneviève Clermidy-Patard. Bibliothèque des Génies et des Fées. Vol. 3. Paris: H. Champion, 2006.

"Perrault's Preface to Griselda and Murat's 'To Modern Fairies.'" Edited by Holly Tucker. *Marvels and Tales: Journal of Fairy-Tale Studies* 19, no. 1 (2005): 125–130.

"Le Prince des Feuilles." In *Le Cabinet des Fées*, edited by E. Lemirre, 555–569. Arles: Piquier, 2000.

"The Palace of Revenge." In *Beauties, Beasts and Enchantment*, edited by Jack Zipes, 129–144. London: Penguin Books, 1991.

Scrittori di fiabe alla corte del Re Sole: Tra scienza e teatro. Edited by Barbara Piqué. Rome, Bulzoni, 1981.

Les Nouveaux Contes des Fées. In *Nouveau Cabinet des Fées*, edited by Jacques Barchilon, vol. 2, 201–432. Geneva: Slatkine Reprints, 1978.

Secondary Sources

Argenson, René d'. *Rapports inédits du lieutenant de police René d'Argenson (1697–1715) publiés d'après les manuscrits conservés à la Bibliothèque Nationale.* Edited by Paul Cottin. Paris, 1891.

Aubert, Guillaume. "'The Blood of France': Race and Purity of Blood in the French Atlantic World." *The William and Mary Quarterly* 61, no. 3 (July 2004): 439–478.

Blasutto, Fabio, David de la Croix, and Mara Vitale. "Scholars and Literati at the Academy of the Ricovrati (1599–1800)." *Repertorium Eruditorum Totius Europae* - RETE (2021) 3:51–63. https://doi.org/10.14428/rete.v3i0/Ricoverati.

Bloom, Rori. *Making the Marvelous: Marie-Catherine d'Aulnoy, Henriette-Julie de Murat, and the Literary Representation of the Decorative Arts.* Lincoln, NB: University of Nebraska Press, 2022.

Boulay de la Merthe, Alfred. *Les Prisonniers du roi à Loches sous Louis XIV.* Tours: J. Allard, 1911.

Brocklebank, Lisa. "Rebellious Voices: The Unofficial Discourse of Cross-Dressing in d'Aulnoy, Murat and Perrault." *Children's Literature Association Quarterly* 25, no. 3 (Fall 2000): 127–136.

Cherbuliez, Juliette. *The Place of Exile: Leisure Literature and the Limits of Absolutism.* Lewisburg, PA: Bucknell University Press, 2005.

Clermidy-Patard, Geneviève. "Henriette-Julie de Castelnau, comtesse de Murat." *Dictionnaire des femmes de l'Ancienne France.* Paris: SIEFAR, 2007. http://siefar.org/dictionnaire/fr/Henriette-Julie_de_Castelnau.

———. "Henriette-Julie de Castelnau, Countess de Murat, 1668?–1716." In *The Teller's Tale: Lives of the Classic Fairy Tale Writers*, edited by Sophie Raynard, 81–87. Albany, NY: State University of New York Press, 2012.

———. *Madame de Murat et la "défense des dames": Un discours au féminin à la fin du règne de Louis XIV*. Paris: Classiques Garnier, 2012.

———. "Madame de Murat et les fées modernes." *Romanic Review* 99, no. 3–4 (May–November 2008): 271–280.

———. "Madame de Murat: La Vogue du conte littéraire." In *Madame de Murat: Contes*, 9–51. Paris: Champion, 2006.

Coulet, Henri. *Le Roman jusqu'à la Révolution*. Paris: Armand Colin, 1967.

Cromer, Sylvie. *Édition du Journal pour Mademoiselle de Menou, d'après le Manuscrit 3471 de la Bibliothèque de l'Arsenal: Ouvrages de Mme la Comtesse de Murat*. Sorbonne: Thèse de 3ᵉ cycle, 1984.

———. "Le Sauvage: Histoire Sublime et allégorique de Madame de Murat." *Merveilles et contes* 1, no. 1 (May 1987): 2–18.

DeJean, Joan. *Tender Geographies: Women and the Origins of the Novel in France*. New York: Columbia University Press, 1991.

Denis, Delphine. *Le Parnasse galant: Institution d'une catégorie littéraire au XVIIᵉ siècle*. Paris: Champion, 2001.

DiScanno, Teresa. "Les Contes de Mme de Murat ou la préciosité dans la féerie." In *Studi di Letteratura Francese : A ricordo di Franco Petralia*, 33–40. Rome: Signorelli, 1968.

Du Bosc, Jacques. *L'Honnête Femme: The Respectable Woman in Society*. Edited and translated by Sharon Diane Nell and Aurora Wolfgang. Toronto: Iter and the Centre for Reformation and Renaissance Studies, 2014.

Duggan, Anne E. *Salonnières, Furies, and Fairies: The Politics of Gender and Cultural Change in Absolutist France*. 2nd edition. Newark: University of Delaware Press, 2021.

———. "The Ticquet Affair as Recounted in Madame Dunoyer's *Lettres Historiques et Galantes*: The Defiant *Galante Femme*." *Papers on French Seventeenth Century Literature* 24, no. 46 (1997): 259–276.

Engerand, Roland. *Les Rendez-vous de Loches*. Tours, 1946.

Félibien, André, sieur des Avaux et de Javercy. *Relation de la fête de Versailles du dix-huit juillet mille six cent soixante-huit; Les Divertissements de Versailles donnés par le Roi à toute sa cour au retour de la conquête de la Franche-Compté en l'année mille six cent soixante-quatorze*. Dédale: Maisonneuve et Larose, 1994.

Félix-Faure-Goyau, Lucie. *La Vie et la mort des fées, essai d'histoire littéraire*. Paris: Perrin, 1910.

Froloff, Natalie. "Preface." *Contes de Perrault*. Paris: Gallimard, 1999.

Genieys-Kirk, Séverine. "Narrating the Self in Mme de Murat's *Mémoires de Madame la comtesse de M*** avant sa retraite*." In *Narrating the Self in Early*

Modern Europe, edited by Bruno Tribout and Ruth Wheelan, 161–176. Oxford: Peter Lang, 2007.

Gethner, Perry. "Murat, Durand and the Novel of Leisure." In *Creation, Re-creation and Entertainment: Early Modernity and Postmodernity*, edited by Benjamin Balak and Charlotte Trinquet du Lys, 25–36. Tübingen: Gunter Narr, 2019.

Gonssollin, Blandine. "Deux réécritures polychromes de Marie-Madeleine de Lubert." *Féeries: Études sur le conte merveilleux, XVIIe–XIVe siècle* 17 (2021). https://doi.org/10.4000/feeries.3679.

———. Review of Contes, by Mademoiselle de Lubert, edited by Aurélie Zygel-Basso. *Féeries: Études sur le conte merveilleux, XVIIe–XIVe siècle* 4 (2007): 256–259. https://doi.org/10.4000/feeries.473.

Guitton, Édouard. "Madame de Murat ou la fausse ingénue." *Études creusoises* 3 (1987): 203–206.

Jones, Christine A. *Mother Goose Refigured: A Critical Translation of Charles Perrault's Fairy Tales*. Detroit, MI: Wayne State University Press, 2016.

Jones Day, Shirley. *The Search for Lyonesse: Women's Fiction in France (1670–1703)*. New York: Peter Lang, 1999.

Lafayette, Marie-Madeleine Pioche de la Vergne, comtesse de. *La Princesse de Clèves*. 1678. Paris: Flammarion, 1996.

Lemeunier, Frédéric. *La Buzardière et ses seigneurs*. Le Mans: Éditions de la Province du Maine, 1967.

Lenglet Du Fresnoy, Nicolas. *De l'usage des romans, où l'on fait voir leur utilité et leurs différents caractères*. Amsterdam: Vve Poilras, 1734.

Levot, Prosper. *Biographie Bretonne*. Vannes: Cauderan, 1852–1857.

Lhéritier de Villandon, Marie-Jeanne. *Oeuvres meslées*. Paris: Jean Guignard, 1695.

Le loisir lettré à l'âge classique. Edited by Marc Fumaroli, Philippe-Joseph Salazar, and Emmanuel Bury. Geneva: Droz, 1996.

Lundlie, Marshall. "Deux précurseurs de Carmontelle: La Comtesse de Murat et Madame Durand." *Revue d'Histoire Littéraire de la France* 69 (1969): 1017–1020.

Mademoiselle de Lubert, *Contes*. Edited by Aurélie Zygel-Basso. Bibliothèque des Génies et des Fées. Vol. 14. Paris: Honoré Champion, 2005.

Marchal, Roger. *Madame de Lambert et son milieu*. Oxford: Voltaire Foundation, 1991.

Michaud, Louis-Gabriel. *Biographie universelle ancienne et moderne, nouvelle édition*. Vol. 29. Paris: C. Delagrave, 1856.

Miorcec de Kerdanet, Daniel Louis Olivier. *Notices chronologiques sur les théologiens, juris-consultes, philosophes, artistes, littérateurs... de la Bretagne*. Brest: Michel, 1818.

Norman, Buford. *Touched by the Graces: The Libretti of Philippe Quinault in the Context of French Classicism*. Birmingham, AL: Summa, 2001.

Perrault, Charles. *La Marquise de Salusses, ou la patience de Griselidis*. Paris: J.B. Coignard, 1695.

Pilon, Edmond. *Bonnes fées d'antan*. Paris: E. Sansot, 1909.

Raynard, Sophie, ed. "Henriette Julie de Murat, *Sublime and Allegorical Histories (1699)*." *Fairy Tales Reframed: Early Forwards, Afterwords, and Critical Words*. Edited by Ruth B. Bottigheimer. Albany, NY: State University of New York Press, 2012. 199–205.

———, ed. *La Seconde Préciosité: Floraison des conteuses de 1690 à 1756*. Tübingen: G. Narr, 2002.

———, ed. *The Teller's Tale: Lives of the Classic Fairy Tale Writers*. Albany, NY: State University of New York Press, 2012.

Rivara, Annie. "Deux conceptions de la temporalité et de l'histoire, Le *Voyage de Campagne* de Mme de Murat (1699) et les *Mémoires de d'Artagnan* par Courtilz de Sandras (1700)." In *L'année 1700*, edited by Aurélia Gaillard, 91–109. Tübingen: Gunter Narr, 2004.

———. "Le Voyage de campagne comme machine à produire et à détruire des contes d'esprits." In *Le Conte merveilleux au XVIIIe siècle: Une poétique expérimentale*, edited by Régine Jomand-Baudry and Jean-François Perrin, 353–369. Paris: Kimé, 2002.

Rizzoni, Natalie, and Julie Boch, eds. *L'âge d'or du conte de fées: De la comédie à la critique (1690–1709)*. Bibliothèque des Génies et des Fées, vol. 5. Paris: Honoré Champion, 2007.

Robert, Raymonde. *Le Conte de fées littéraire en France de la fin du XVIIe à la fin du XVIIIe siècle*. Paris: Honoré Champion, 2002.

Robinson, David Michael. "The Abominable Madame de Murat." *Journal of Homosexuality* 41, no. 3–4 (2001): 53–67.

Sanders, Scott M. "Singing through the Pain: Murat Riffing on Montaigne." *Eighteenth-Century Fiction* 35, no. 4 (October 2023): 445–462.

Ségalen, Auguste-Pierre. "Madame de Murat et le Limousin." In *Le Limousin au XVIIe siècle*, 77–94. Limoges: Trames, 1979.

Seifert, Lewis C. *Fairy Tales, Sexuality and Gender in France (1690–1715): Nostalgic Utopias*. Cambridge: Cambridge University Press, 1996.

Seifert, Lewis C., and Domna C. Stanton, eds. *Enchanted Eloquence: Fairy Tales by Seventeenth-Century French Women Writers*. Toronto: Iter and the Centre for Reformation and Renaissance Studies, 2010.

Sermain, Jean-Paul. *Métafictions : La réflexivité dans la littérature d'imagination (1670–1730)*. Paris: Honoré Champion, 2002.

Sévigné, Marie de Rabutin-Chantal, marquise de. *Correspondance*. Edited by René Duchêne. 3 vols. Paris: Gallimard, 1972–1978.

Showalter, English, Jr. *The Evolution of the French Novel (1641–1782)*. Princeton, NJ: Princeton University Press, 1972.

Stedman, Allison. "Lafayette Rewrites History, Murat Rewrites Lafayette: The Novel and the Transfiguration of the Social Sphere in Old-Regime France." *Cahiers du dix-septième: An Interdisciplinary Journal* 14 (2012): 1–21.

———. "Proleptic Nostalgia: Longing for the Middle Ages in the Late Seventeenth-Century French Fairy Tale." *Romanic Review* 99, no. 3-4 (May–November 2008): 363–380.

———. *Rococo Fiction in France, 1600–1715: Seditious Frivolity*. Lewisburg, PA: Bucknell University Press, 2013.

———. "Le rôle de la poésie dans la société mondaine de la fin du XVIIe siècle." In *Le poète et le joueur de quilles: Enquête sur la construction de la poésie (XIVe-XXIe siècles)*, edited by Olivier Gallet, Adeline Lionetto, Stéphane Loubère, Laure Michel, and Thierry Roger, 169–178. Mont-Saint-Aignan, France: Presses Universitaires de Rouen et du Havre (PURH), 2023.

Storer, Mary Elizabeth. *Un Épisode Littéraire de la fin du XVIIe siècle: La Mode des contes de fées (1685–1700)*. Paris: Honoré Champion, 1928.

Verdier, Gabrielle. "Figures de la conteuse dans les contes de fées féminins." *Dix-septième siècle* 180 (July–September 1993): 481–499.

Viala, Alain. *La France galante*. Paris: PUF, 2008.

Villiers, Abbé Pierre de. *Entretiens sur les contes de fées, et sur quelques autres ouvrages du Temps : Pour servir de préservatif contre le mauvais goût*. Paris: Jacques Collombat, 1699.

Welch, Marcelle Maitre. "Manipulation du discours féerique dans les Contes de fées de Mme de Murat." *Cahiers du Dix-Septième: An Interdiscplinary Journal* 5, no. 1 (Spring 1991): 21–29.

———. "Rébellion et Résignation dans les contes de fées de Mme d'Aulnoy et Mme de Murat." *Cahiers du Dix-Septième: An Interdisciplinary Journal* 3, no. 2 (Fall 1989): 131–142. *Le XVIIe siècle, Dictionnaire des Lettres françaises*. Edited by Georges Grente. Paris: Fayard, 1996.

Index

Accademia dei Riccovrati (Academy of the Sheltered), 4n8
Alcibiades, 45
Alexander the Great, 38n10, 75nn60–61, 101n88. *See also* Athenaeus; Chares
Amadis de Gaula, 110n96, 111n97
Argenson, René d', 13–14n47
Argenton, countess d', 14n48
Aristotle, 141n22
Athenaeus, 18n54, 75nn60–61, 78nn60–65, 79n66. *See also* Alexander the Great; Chares
Aucassin et Nicolette, 145–152nn1–6, 153n9, 156n11, 161n15, 164n20, 168n22
Aulnoy, Countess d' (Marie-Catherine Le Jumel de Barneville): Accademia dei Riccovrati, 4n8; "La Chatte Blanche," 152n7, 160n13; *Don Gabriel Ponce de Leon*, 14, 23, 28n67, 127n1; "Gracieuse et Percinet," 138n19; *Histoire d'Hypolite* ("L'Ile de la Félicité"), 7n20, 130n9; inventor of the fairy tale, 6n17, 7n20, 8, 10, 27, 130n9; literary circle, 1; *Nouveau gentilhomme bourgeois*, 22; *Voyage d'Espagne*, 12
Auneuil, Countess d' (Louise de Bossigny), 27n66

Basile, Giambattista, 130n10, 133n14
Bédacier, Catherine Durand. *See* Durand, Catherine
Berain, Jean I, 117n104. *See also* rococo
Bernard, Catherine, 4n8

Bloom, Rori, 12, 30
Boursault, Edme, 15n50. *See also* epistolary novel
bouts-rimés, 4–5n12, 72–74n57, 85n73
Brueys, David-Augustin, 57n44. *See also* comedy

Caesar, Julius, 38n10
Campistron, Jean Galbert de, 26. *See also* Lully, Jean-Baptiste; opera
carnival (ficitional): Kernosy Castle and, 38, 39n15, 40n18; Paris and, 34n3; Rennes and, 67, 82; Venice and, 107n93
Catholicism. *See* religion
Caumont de La Force, Charlotte-Rose, 3, 4n8
Cervantes, Miguel de, 20
Champmeslé, Charles Chevillet de, 55n42, 76n55. *See also* comedy
Chares, 75n60. *See also* Alexander the Great; Athenaeus
Charrière, Isabelle de, 152n7
chivalric operas, 26. *See also* opera
chivalric romances, 16, 20, 38n9, 45n23. See also *Amadis de Gaula*; Herberay des Essarts, Nicolas; Montalvo, Garci Rodriguez de; romance novels
chivalry: as female fantasy, 23n60, 24n62, 26, 38n9, 45n23; as male code of conduct, 1–2, 16–18, 20, 24n62; in relation to gallantry, 21
Colbert, Jean-Baptiste, 46n25
comedy, 21–22, 24–25, 38n11, 110n95; performed in the novel, 39n16, 49n29, 52n36, 55n42,

179

57n44, 58n45, 71n55, 112n98.
See also Brueys, David-Augustin;
Champsmeslé, Charles Chevillet
de; Dancourt, Florent; Delisle
de la Drevetière, Louis-François;
Dufresny, Charles Rivière;
Hautroche (Noël Le Breton);
Molière (Jean-Baptiste Poquelin);
Palaprat, Jean de; Regnard,
Jean-François
conte de fées. See fairy tale
Conti, Princess de. See Marie-Anne
de Bourbon, Princess de Conti
Corneille, Pierre, 25, 52n36, 57n44
courante, 40n19, 62

Dampierre, Mlle, 3, 14
Dancourt, Florent, 25n45
Darius (king of Persia), 101n88
Darmancourt, Pierre Perrault, 8n25
Delisle de la Drèvetière, Louis-
François, 110n95
Deshoulières, Antoinette, 1, 24n62, 54n41
Desmarest, Henry, 26
Destouches, André Cardinal, 26
Donneau de Visé, Jean, 15
Du Bosc, Jacques, 23n60
Du Fresnoy, Nicolas Lenglet, 26, 27n63
Dufresny, Charles Rivière, 25
Durand, Catherine, 14–15n51, 16

education: for male aristocrats, 74n59, 86; for women, 1, 22n57, 59n46, 127. See also Fénelon, François de Salignac de La Motte; Perrault, Charles
elegy, 50n32
Enlightenment, 16, 18, 28, 30, 74n59, 117n104, 152n7

entertainment: court and, 25–26, 29n67, 35n4; fairy tales and, 6–8, 17; ghost stories and, 17; leisure novels and, 13, 15; *Mercure galant* and, 15; in the novel, 18–19n54, 24, 26, 44, 46, 98, 109, 111n98. See also comedy; gallantry; opera; tragedy
Epernon, Duchess d', 85n73
epistolary novel, 15n50, 136n17. See also Graffigny, Françoise d'Issembourg d'Happoncourt de; Guilleragues, Gabriel-Joseph de
exile 2, 5, 13–14n47, 15n51, 17

fairy tale: debates over, 7–10; as a feminist genre, 1, 17; Italian origins of, 11–12n36; in the *Journal pour Mademoiselle de Menou*, 5, 13; mirrors in, 61n47; as a modern genre, 10; Murat and the development of, 6–7, 30; Murat's rejection of, 2, 12–13, 17–18n54, 28, 30; as a novelistic genre, 7–8; as a pedagogical genre, 7–8, 10; rewritings of, 22; as salon entertainment, 6. See also Aulnoy, Countess d' (Marie-Catherine Le Jumel de Barneville); Auneuil, Countess d' (Louise de Bossigny); Basile, Giambattista; *Histoires sublimes et allégorique*; Leprince de Beaumont, Jeanne-Marie; Lhéritier de Villandon, Marie-Jeanne; Lubert, Marie-Madeleine de; Perrault, Charles; Straparola, Giovanni Francesco; Villiers, Abbé Pierre de; *Voyage de campagne*
Fatima, 102n90
female solidarity, 1, 2, 7
Fénelon, François de Salignac de La Motte, 59n46

Fiorilli, Tiberio, 41n20
Fuzelier, Louis, 110n95

gallantry: appearance and, 43; behavior and, 51, 63, 67, 82–84, 109, 132; entertainment and, 18–19, 36, 46, 50nn31–33, 71n56, 83–84, 98, 109–117n98; violations of, 38n10, 46, 48
gender reversal, 62n50, 136n16, 161n15
Genest, Claude, 20, 71n55
ghost stories, 30; in the novel, 16, 55–56; in the *Voyage de campagne*, 13, 17–18, 54n41. *See also* Kernosy Castle: haunted reputation of; sprites
Gomberville, Marin Le Roy de, 16n52
Graffigny, Françoise d'Issembourg d'Happoncourt de, 110n95, 129n6, 136n19
Guilleragues, Gabriel-Joseph de, 15n50

Hauteroche (Noël Le Breton), 19, 39n16
Herberay des Essarts, Nicolas, 23, 38n9
Hesiod, 123n107
Histoires sublimes et allégoriques, 6n17; 9–12
Homer, 123n107
homosexuality, 13–14

idylle, 25–26
imagination, 43, 63, 77, 102, 152; versus reason in d'Aulnoy, 22; versus reason in Cervantes, 20; versus reason in Molière, 22; versus reason in Murat, 20–24

Journal pour Mademoiselle de Menou, 5, 13

Kernosy Castle (fictional): alternative to Versailles, 14, 17–20, 52n34; architecture of, 16–17, 32–33, 53; genealogy of, 39n12; haunted reputation of, 16, 18, 33; location of, 33n2; name origin of, 33n1

La Calprenède, Gautier de, 16n52
Lafayette, Countess de (Marie-Madeleine Pioche de la Vergne), 62n48, 90n80
La Fontaine, Jean de, 55n42, 71n55, 167n21
La Gruyère (inventor), 46n25
Lambert, Marquise de (Anne-Thérèse de Marguenat de Courcelles), 5
La Motte, Antoine Houdart de, 26
La Suze, Henriette de, 1
La Tour d'Auvergne, Marie, 3n5
Le Blond, Alexandre Jean-Baptiste, 117n104. *See also* rococo
Le Camus, Charlotte de Melsons, 4n8
leisure novel, 2–3, 14–20, 22–23, 29–30; fairy tales and, 12; female solidarity in, 5; *Journal pour Mademoiselle de Menou* as, 13; *Voyage de campagne* as, 85n73
Leprince de Beaumont, Jeanne-Marie, 27n65, 129n3
Lhériter de Villandon, Marie-Jeanne, 4–9, 11, 59n46, 84n73, 102n91
Louis XIV: court of, 10, 14, 17, 24, 54n34, 146n3, 152n7; family of, 3, 8, 10, 14n48, 84n73; as patron of the arts, 23, 33n1, 40n17; regime of, 2. *See also* war
lovesickness. *See* psychosomatic illnesses

Lubert, Marie-Madeleine de: d'Aulnoy and, 28n67, 127n1; d'Auneuil and, 27n65; Basile and, 130n10; Bible and, 133n12; fairy tales and, 27–30, 79n66, 98n84; Graffigny and, 129n6, 136n17; Murat and, 27–30; novelistic rewritings by, 27–29n65, 79n66, 98n84, 129n3; Perrault and, 130n10, 162n17. See also *Aucassin et Nicolette*
Lully, Jean-Baptiste, 23–24, 26, 40n17, 52n38, 53n39, 109n94, 111n98, 115n102

machine plays, 17, 123n107, 141n22
madrigal, 50n31, 51, 71–72
Maintenon, Marquise de (Françoise d'Aubigné), 5
Maria Theresa of Austria (queen of France), 3
Marie-Anne de Bourbon, Princess de Conti, 10n30
Marie de France, 153n8, 160n14
marriage: arranged, 17, 21, 129n4; in d'Aulnoy, 22, 23; in "Bearskin," 128–129, 133n12, 137–138; commemorations of, 25; critique of, 1–2, 17, 21, 78n64, 147n7; in "Etoilette," 147, 159, 167; forced, 1–2, 167n22; in Molière, 22, 38n11; Murat's own, 3, 5; in the novel, 22–23, 59, 77, 86–98, 119–124; in *Voyage de campagne*, 13
Mémoires, 5–6
memoir novels, 5–6, 9, 17
Menou, Mlle de, 4–5, 12–14n47, 30
Mercure galant, 2n1, 15, 24n62, 102n91, 145n1
minuet, 40n19, 54

Mohammed, 102n90. See also religion
Molière (Jean-Baptiste Poquelin), 19, 21–22, 25, 38n11, 49n29, 52n36, 112n98
Moncrif, François-Augustin Paradis de, 132n11
Montalvo, Garci Rodriguez de, 23n9
Morvan de Bellegarde, Jean-Baptiste, 27
Murat, César de, 3
Murat, Countess de (Henriette-Julie de Castelnau): children and, 3; early life of, 2–3; editorial choices of, 33n1, 62nn49–50, 75n61, 78nn64–65, 84nn72–73, 113n99, 141n22; exile and, 2, 13–14, 17; fairy tales and, 6–13; leisure novel and, 14–23; literary prizes and, 4n8; marriage and, 3; *Mémoires* and, 5; Parnassian nickname, 102n9; poetry and, 3–5n7; relationship to d'Aulnoy, 1, 4n8, 6n17, 8, 10, 12, 14, 22–23; relationship to Deshoulières, 1, 54n41; relationship to Lhéritier, 4n8, 5n12, 6–11, 59–60n46, 84n73, 102n91; scandal and, 13–14; sexual orientation and, 13–14. See also education; fairy tale; female solidarity; *Histoires sublimes et allégoriques*; *Journal pour Mademoiselle de Menou*; leisure novel; salons; *Voyage de campagne*
Murat, Nicolas de, 3
mythology, 6, 24, 59n46, 109n94, 113n99, 156n11

Nantiat, Mme de, 13

opera: 19–20, 23–26, 34n3; performed in "Bearskin," 132n11,

143n22; performed in the novel, 40n17, 52n38, 53n39, 84, 97, 98n84, 109n94, 110n95, 112n98, 113, 115nn101–102, 116n103, 120, 123n107. *See also* Campistron, Jean Galbert de; Desmarest, Henry; Destouches, André Cardinal; Fuzelier, Louis; La Motte, Antoine Houdart de; Lully, Jean-Baptiste; Moncrif, François-Augustin Paradis de; Quinault, Philippe; Racine, Jean; Rameau, Jean-Philippe; Rebel, François
Orléans, Elisabeth-Charlotte d', 8n25
Orléans, Duke d' (Philippe III) [Regent], 48
Ovid, 123n107

Palaprat, Jean de, 57n44
Paris: high society of, 3; literary circles of, 1, 17; Murat and, 3, 11, 13; in the novel, 34, 37–38, 42–44, 47–48, 59, 81–82, 89, 99, 108; theatres of, 25; versus provinces, 9, 15, 21. *See also* carnival
Pascal, Françoise, 1
pastorale héroïque, 26
pedagogical literature, 7, 8, 10. *See also* fairy tale; Fénelon, François de Salignac de La Motte; Perrault, Charles
Perrault, Charles, 7–12nn21–22, 27n65, 28, 130n10, 134n15, 162n17
Peterson, Nora Martin, 29
piracy, 100n87, 153n9
Pompadour, Marquise de (Antoinette Poisson), 132n11
Praxilla, 102n91
La Princesse de Clèves, 62n48, 62n50, 90n80

psychosomatic illnesses: cures for, 159; lovesickness, 87, 99, 107

Quarrel of Ancients and Moderns, 11n34
Quinault, Philippe, 23–24, 52n38, 109n94

racial bias: American Indians and, 112n95; North Africans and, 167–169nn21–24. *See also* slavery
Racine, Jean, 20, 25–26, 49n29, 55n42, 58n45
Rameau, Jean-Philippe, 110n95
rape, 100n86
Razilly, Marie de, 4
Rebel, François, 132n11
Regnard, Jean-François, 25
religion: Catholicism and, 34n3, 36n5, 107n93; Islam and, 101n87, 102n90, 146n2
Rennes, 25, 30; in the novel, 44, 47, 59–60, 62, 67, 74, 82–84, 89–99, 108, 112, 121
rococo, 117n104
romance novels, 15–16. *See also* Gomberville, Marin Le Roy de; La Calprenède, Gautier de; Scudéry, Georges de; Scudéry, Madeleine de; Urfé, Honoré d'

Sainctonge, Louise-Geneviève Gillot de, 26
Saint-Aignan, Duke de (François de Beauvilliers), 24n62
Saint-Evremond, Charles de, 5
salons, 1–6, 8, 10, 17, 19, 21, 24n61, 28, 38n8, 58, 71nn56–57. *See also* Aulnoy, Countess d' (Marie-Catherine Le Jumel de Barneville); Lambert, Marquise de (Anne-Thérèse de Marguenat

de Courcelles); Lhéritier de Villandon, Marie-Jeanne
saraband, 64
Schacker, Jennifer, 29
Scudéry, Georges de, 16n52. *See also* romance novels
Scudéry, Madeleine de, 16n52, 21n56, 23n60, 102n90. *See also* romance novels
Seifert, Lewis, 27, 29
Sévigné, Marquise de (Marie de Rabutin-Chantal), 3
Siemens, Melanie R., 12
slavery: in "Etoilette," 147–148; Mediterranean, 100nn87–102; in the novel, 100–102, 105
Socrates, 45n24
Sorel, Charles, 16
sprites: impersonation of, 34–35, 53–56
Stanton, Domna C., 27, 29
Stedman, Allison, 30
Straparola, Giovanni Francesco, 11n36
Subligny, Adrien de, 21n56. *See also* Scudéry, Madeleine de

tragedy, 19, 25, 110n95; performed in the novel, 49n29, 52n36, 54n42, 57n44, 58n45, 71n55. *See also* Corneille, Pierre; Genest, Claude; Racine, Jean
A Trip to the Country. See *Voyage de campagne*
Tucker, Holly, 12

Urfé, Honoré d', 16n52

verisimilitude, 8, 79n66
Villedieu, Madame de (Marie-Catherine Desjardins), 1, 15n50, 23n60
Villeneuve, Gabrielle-Suzanne Barbot de, 128n3, 136n16
Villiers, Abbé Pierre de, 5, 9–12
Virgil, 113n99
Voltaire (François-Marie Arouet), 74n59, 110n95
Voyage de campagne (*A Trip to the Country*), 6, 12–14, 16–17, 28–30, 54n41, 85n73, 113n99, 141n22

war: in "Bearskin," 132; in "Etoilette," 145–146, 150, 151n5, 161–162, 164; expenses associated with, 90n78; Franco-Dutch, 3n2; League of Augsburg, 89n75; Morean, 89n75, 99, 107; in the novel, 20, 42, 60, 89–100; Spanish Succession, 42n21, 89n76. *See also* slavery

The Other Voice in Early Modern Europe:
The Toronto Series

Series Titles

MADRE MARÍA ROSA
Journey of Five Capuchin Nuns
Edited and translated by Sarah E. Owens
Volume 1, 2009

GIOVAN BATTISTA ANDREINI
Love in the Mirror: *A Bilingual Edition*
Edited and translated by Jon R. Snyder
Volume 2, 2009

RAYMOND DE SABANAC AND SIMONE ZANACCHI
Two Women of the Great Schism: The Revelations *of Constance de Rabastens by Raymond de Sabanac and* Life of the Blessed Ursulina of Parma *by Simone Zanacchi*
Edited and translated by Renate Blumenfeld-Kosinski and Bruce L. Venarde
Volume 3, 2010

OLIVA SABUCO DE NANTES BARRERA
The True Medicine
Edited and translated by Gianna Pomata
Volume 4, 2010

LOUISE-GENEVIÈVE GILLOT DE SAINCTONGE
Dramatizing Dido, Circe, and Griselda
Edited and translated by Janet Levarie Smarr
Volume 5, 2010

PERNETTE DU GUILLET
Complete Poems: A Bilingual Edition
Edited with introduction and notes by Karen Simroth James
Poems translated by Marta Rijn Finch
Volume 6, 2010

ANTONIA PULCI
Saints' Lives and Bible Stories for the Stage: A Bilingual Edition
Edited by Elissa B. Weaver
Translated by James Wyatt Cook
Volume 7, 2010

VALERIA MIANI
Celinda, A Tragedy: *A Bilingual Edition*
Edited with an introduction by Valeria Finucci
Translated by Julia Kisacky
Annotated by Valeria Finucci and Julia Kisacky
Volume 8, 2010

Enchanted Eloquence: Fairy Tales by Seventeenth-Century French Women Writers
Edited and translated by Lewis C. Seifert and Domna C. Stanton
Volume 9, 2010

GOTTFRIED WILHELM LEIBNIZ,
SOPHIE, ELECTRESS OF HANOVER
AND QUEEN SOPHIE CHARLOTTE OF
PRUSSIA
Leibniz and the Two Sophies: The Philosophical Correspondence
Edited and translated by Lloyd Strickland
Volume 10, 2011

In Dialogue with the Other Voice in Sixteenth-Century Italy: Literary and Social Contexts for Women's Writing
Edited by Julie D. Campbell and Maria Galli Stampino
Volume 11, 2011

SISTER GIUSTINA NICCOLINI
The Chronicle of Le Murate
Edited and translated by Saundra Weddle
Volume 12, 2011

LIUBOV KRICHEVSKAYA
No Good without Reward: Selected Writings: A Bilingual Edition
Edited and translated by Brian James Baer
Volume 13, 2011

ELIZABETH COOKE HOBY RUSSELL
The Writings of an English Sappho
Edited by Patricia Phillippy
With translations from Greek and Latin by Jaime Goodrich
Volume 14, 2011

LUCREZIA MARINELLA
Exhortations to Women and to Others If They Please
Edited and translated by Laura Benedetti
Volume 15, 2012

MARGHERITA DATINI
Letters to Francesco Datini
Translated by Carolyn James and Antonio Pagliaro
Volume 16, 2012

DELARIVIER MANLEY AND MARY PIX
English Women Staging Islam, 1696–1707
Edited and introduced by Bernadette Andrea
Volume 17, 2012

CECILIA DEL NACIMIENTO
Journeys of a Mystic Soul in Poetry and Prose
Introduction and prose translations by Kevin Donnelly
Poetry translations by Sandra Sider
Volume 18, 2012

LADY MARGARET DOUGLAS AND OTHERS
The Devonshire Manuscript: A Women's Book of Courtly Poetry
Edited and introduced by Elizabeth Heale
Volume 19, 2012

ARCANGELA TARABOTTI
Letters Familiar and Formal
Edited and translated by Meredith K. Ray and Lynn Lara Westwater
Volume 20, 2012

PERE TORRELLAS AND JUAN DE FLORES
Three Spanish Querelle *Texts:* Grisel and Mirabella, The Slander against Women, *and* The Defense of Ladies against Slanderers: *A Bilingual Edition and Study*
Edited and translated by Emily C. Francomano
Volume 21, 2013

BARBARA TORELLI BENEDETTI
Partenia, a Pastoral Play: *A Bilingual Edition*
Edited and translated by Lisa Sampson and Barbara Burgess-Van Aken
Volume 22, 2013

François Rousset, Jean Liebault, Jacques Guillemeau, Jacques Duval and Louis de Serres
Pregnancy and Birth in Early Modern France: Treatises by Caring Physicians and Surgeons (1581–1625)
Edited and translated by Valerie Worth-Stylianou
Volume 23, 2013

Mary Astell
The Christian Religion, as Professed by a Daughter of the Church of England
Edited by Jacqueline Broad
Volume 24, 2013

Sophia of Hanover
Memoirs (1630–1680)
Edited and translated by Sean Ward
Volume 25, 2013

Katherine Austen
Book M: A London Widow's Life Writings
Edited by Pamela S. Hammons
Volume 26, 2013

Anne Killigrew
"My Rare Wit Killing Sin": Poems of a Restoration Courtier
Edited by Margaret J. M. Ezell
Volume 27, 2013

Tullia d'Aragona and Others
The Poems and Letters of Tullia d'Aragona and Others: A Bilingual Edition
Edited and translated by Julia L. Hairston
Volume 28, 2014

Luisa de Carvajal y Mendoza
The Life and Writings of Luisa de Carvajal y Mendoza
Edited and translated by Anne J. Cruz
Volume 29, 2014

Russian Women Poets of the Eighteenth and Early Nineteenth Centuries: A Bilingual Edition
Edited and translated by Amanda Ewington
Volume 30, 2014

Jacques Du Bosc
L'Honnête Femme: The Respectable Woman in Society and the New Collection of Letters and Responses by Contemporary Women
Edited and translated by Sharon Diane Nell and Aurora Wolfgang
Volume 31, 2014

Lady Hester Pulter
Poems, Emblems, and The Unfortunate Florinda
Edited by Alice Eardley
Volume 32, 2014

Jeanne Flore
Tales and Trials of Love, Concerning Venus's Punishment of Those Who Scorn True Love and Denounce Cupid's Sovereignity: A Bilingual Edition and Study
Edited and translated by Kelly Digby Peebles
Poems translated by Marta Rijn Finch
Volume 33, 2014

Veronica Gambara
Complete Poems: A Bilingual Edition
Critical introduction by Molly M. Martin
Edited and translated by Molly M. Martin and Paola Ugolini
Volume 34, 2014

Catherine de Médicis and Others
Portraits of the Queen Mother: Polemics, Panegyrics, Letters
Translation and study by Leah L. Chang and Katherine Kong
Volume 35, 2014

Françoise Pascal, Marie-
Catherine Desjardins, Antoinette
Deshoulières, and Catherine
Durand
Challenges to Traditional Authority: Plays by French Women Authors, 1650–1700
Edited and translated by Perry Gethner
Volume 36, 2015

Franciszka Urszula Radziwiłłowa
Selected Drama and Verse
Edited by Patrick John Corness and Barbara Judkowiak
Translated by Patrick John Corness
Translation Editor Aldona Zwierzyńska-Coldicott
Introduction by Barbara Judkowiak
Volume 37, 2015

Diodata Malvasia
Writings on the Sisters of San Luca and Their Miraculous Madonna
Edited and translated by Danielle Callegari and Shannon McHugh
Volume 38, 2015

Margaret Van Noort
Spiritual Writings of Sister Margaret of the Mother of God (1635–1643)
Edited by Cordula van Wyhe
Translated by Susan M. Smith
Volume 39, 2015

Giovan Francesco Straparola
The Pleasant Nights
Edited and translated by Suzanne Magnanini
Volume 40, 2015

Angélique de Saint-Jean Arnauld d'Andilly
Writings of Resistance
Edited and translated by John J. Conley, S.J.
Volume 41, 2015

Francesco Barbaro
The Wealth of Wives: A Fifteenth-Century Marriage Manual
Edited and translated by Margaret L. King
Volume 42, 2015

Jeanne d'Albret
Letters from the Queen of Navarre with an Ample Declaration
Edited and translated by Kathleen M. Llewellyn, Emily E. Thompson, and Colette H. Winn
Volume 43, 2016

Bathsua Makin and Mary More with a reply to More by Robert Whitehall
Educating English Daughters: Late Seventeenth-Century Debates
Edited by Frances Teague and Margaret J. M. Ezell
Associate Editor Jessica Walker
Volume 44, 2016

Anna Stanisławska
Orphan Girl: A Transaction, or an Account of the Entire Life of an Orphan Girl by way of Plaintful Threnodies in the Year 1685: The Aesop Episode
Verse translation, introduction, and commentary by Barry Keane
Volume 45, 2016

Alessandra Macinghi Strozzi
Letters to Her Sons, 1447–1470
Edited and translated by Judith Bryce
Volume 46, 2016

Mother Juana de la Cruz
Mother Juana de la Cruz, 1481–1534: Visionary Sermons
Edited by Jessica A. Boon and Ronald E. Surtz
Introductory material and notes by Jessica A. Boon
Translated by Ronald E. Surtz and Nora Weinerth
Volume 47, 2016

Claudine-Alexandrine Guérin de Tencin
Memoirs of the Count of Comminge and The Misfortunes of Love
Edited and translated by Jonathan Walsh
Foreword by Michel Delon
Volume 48, 2016

Feliciana Enríquez de Guzmán, Ana Caro Mallén, and Sor Marcela de San Félix
Women Playwrights of Early Modern Spain
Edited by Nieves Romero-Díaz and Lisa Vollendorf
Translated and annotated by Harley Erdman
Volume 49, 2016

Anna Trapnel
Anna Trapnel's Report and Plea; or, A Narrative of Her Journey from London into Cornwall
Edited by Hilary Hinds
Volume 50, 2016

María Vela y Cueto
Autobiography and Letters of a Spanish Nun
Edited by Susan Diane Laningham
Translated by Jane Tar
Volume 51, 2016

Christine de Pizan
The Book of the Mutability of Fortune
Edited and translated by Geri L. Smith
Volume 52, 2017

Marguerite d'Auge, Renée Burlamacchi, and Jeanne du Laurens
Sin and Salvation in Early Modern France: Three Women's Stories
Edited, and with an introduction by Colette H. Winn
Translated by Nicholas Van Handel and Colette H. Winn
Volume 53, 2017

Isabella d'Este
Selected Letters
Edited and translated by Deanna Shemek
Volume 54, 2017

Ippolita Maria Sforza
Duchess and Hostage in Renaissance Naples: Letters and Orations
Edited and translated by Diana Robin and Lynn Lara Westwater
Volume 55, 2017

Louise Bourgeois
Midwife to the Queen of France: Diverse Observations
Translated by Stephanie O'Hara
Edited by Alison Klairmont Lingo
Volume 56, 2017

Christine de Pizan
Othea's Letter to Hector
Edited and translated by Renate Blumenfeld-Kosinski and Earl Jeffrey Richards
Volume 57, 2017

Marie-Geneviève-Charlotte Thiroux d'Arconville
Selected Philosophical, Scientific, and Autobiographical Writings
Edited and translated by Julie Candler Hayes
Volume 58, 2018

Lady Mary Wroth
Pamphilia to Amphilanthus *in Manuscript and Print*
Edited by Ilona Bell
Texts by Steven W. May and Ilona Bell
Volume 59, 2017

Witness, Warning, and Prophecy: Quaker Women's Writing, 1655–1700
Edited by Teresa Feroli and Margaret Olofson Thickstun
Volume 60, 2018

Symphorien Champier
The Ship of Virtuous Ladies
Edited and translated by Todd W. Reeser
Volume 61, 2018

Isabella Andreini
Mirtilla, A Pastoral: *A Bilingual Edition*
Edited by Valeria Finucci
Translated by Julia Kisacky
Volume 62, 2018

Margherita Costa
The Buffoons, A Ridiculous Comedy: *A Bilingual Edition*
Edited and translated by Sara E. Díaz and Jessica Goethals
Volume 63, 2018

Margaret Cavendish, Duchess of Newcastle
Poems and Fancies *with* The Animal Parliament
Edited by Brandie R. Siegfried
Volume 64, 2018

Margaret Fell
Women's Speaking Justified *and Other Pamphlets*
Edited by Jane Donawerth and Rebecca M. Lush
Volume 65, 2018

Mary Wroth, Jane Cavendish, and Elizabeth Brackley
Women's Household Drama:
Loves Victorie, A Pastorall, *and* The concealed Fansyes
Edited by Marta Straznicky and Sara Mueller
Volume 66, 2018

Eleonora Fonseca Pimentel
From Arcadia to Revolution: The Neapolitan Monitor *and Other Writings*
Edited and translated by Verina R. Jones
Volume 67, 2019

Charlotte Arbaleste Duplessis-Mornay, Anne de Chaufepié, and Anne Marguerite Petit Du Noyer
The Huguenot Experience of Persecution and Exile: Three Women's Stories
Edited by Colette H. Winn
Translated by Lauren King and Colette H. Winn
Volume 68, 2019

Anne Bradstreet
Poems and Meditations
Edited by Margaret Olofson Thickstun
Volume 69, 2019

Arcangela Tarabotti
Antisatire: *In Defense of Women, against Francesco Buoninsegni*
Edited and translated by Elissa B. Weaver
Volume 70, 2020

MARY FRANKLIN AND HANNAH
BURTON
She Being Dead Yet Speaketh: The Franklin Family Papers
Edited by Vera J. Camden
Volume 71, 2020

LUCREZIA MARINELLA
Love Enamored and Driven Mad
Edited and translated by Janet E. Gomez and Maria Galli Stampino
Volume 72, 2020

ARCANGELA TARABOTTI
Convent Paradise
Edited and translated by Meredith K. Ray and Lynn Lara Westwater
Volume 73, 2020

GABRIELLE-SUZANNE BARBOT DE VILLENEUVE
Beauty and the Beast: The Original Story
Edited and translated by Aurora Wolfgang
Volume 74, 2020

FLAMINIO SCALA
The Fake Husband, A Comedy
Edited and translated by Rosalind Kerr
Volume 75, 2020

ANNE VAUGHAN LOCK
Selected Poetry, Prose, and Translations, with Contextual Materials
Edited by Susan M. Felch
Volume 76, 2021

CAMILLA ERCULIANI
Letters on Natural Philosophy: The Scientific Correspondence of a Sixteenth-Century Pharmacist, with Related Texts
Edited by Eleonora Carinci
Translated by Hannah Marcus
Foreword by Paula Findlen
Volume 77, 2021

REGINA SALOMEA PILSZTYNOWA
My Life's Travels and Adventures: An Eighteenth-Century Oculist in the Ottoman Empire and the European Hinterland
Edited and translated by Władysław Roczniak
Volume 78, 2021

CHRISTINE DE PIZAN
The God of Love's Letter and The Tale of the Rose: A Bilingual Edition
Edited and translated by Thelma S. Fenster and Christine Reno
With Jean Gerson, "A Poem on Man and Woman." Translated from the Latin by Thomas O'Donnell
Foreword by Jocelyn Wogan-Browne
Volume 79, 2021

MARIE GIGAULT DE BELLEFONDS, MARQUISE DE VILLARS
Letters from Spain: A Seventeenth-Century French Noblewoman at the Spanish Royal Court
Edited and translated by Nathalie Hester
Volume 80, 2021

ANNA MARIA VAN SCHURMAN
Letters and Poems to and from Her Mentor and Other Members of Her Circle
Edited and translated by Anne R. Larsen and Steve Maiullo
Volume 81, 2021

VITTORIA COLONNA
Poems of Widowhood: A Bilingual Edition of the 1538 Rime
Translation and introduction by Ramie Targoff
Edited by Ramie Targoff and Troy Tower
Volume 82, 2021

VALERIA MIANI
Amorous Hope, A Pastoral Play: *A Bilingual Edition*
Edited and translated by Alexandra Coller
Volume 83, 2020

MADELEINE DE SCUDÉRY
Lucrece and Brutus: Glory in the Land of Tender
Edited and translated by Sharon Diane Nell
Volume 84, 2021

ANNA STANISŁAWSKA
One Body with Two Souls Entwined: An Epic Tale of Married Love in Seventeenth-Century Poland
Orphan Girl: The Oleśnicki Episode
Verse translation, introduction, and commentary by Barry Keane
Volume 85, 2021

CHRISTINE DE PIZAN
Book of the Body Politic
Edited and translated by Angus J. Kennedy
Volume 86, 2021

ANNE, LADY HALKETT
A True Account of My Life and Selected Meditations
Edited by Suzanne Trill
Volume 87, 2022

VITTORIA COLONNA
Selected Letters, 1523–1546: A Bilingual Edition
Edited and annotated by Veronica Copello
Translated by Abigail Brundin
Introduction by Abigail Brundin and Veronica Copello
Volume 88, 2022

MICHELE SAVONAROLA
A Mother's Manual for the Women of Ferrara: A Fifteenth-Century Guide to Pregnancy and Pediatrics
Edited, with introduction and notes, by Gabriella Zuccolin
Translated by Martin Marafioti
Volume 89, 2022

MARIA SALVIATI DE' MEDICI
Selected Letters, 1514–1543
Edited and translated by Natalie R. Tomas
Volume 90, 2022

ISABELLA ANDREINI
Lovers' Debates for the Stage: A Bilingual Edition
Edited and translated by Pamela Allen Brown, Julie D. Campbell, and Eric Nicholson
Volume 91, 2022

MARIE GUYART DE L'INCARNATION, ANNE-MARIE FIQUET DU BOCCAGE, AND HENRIETTE-LUCIE DILLON DE LA TOUR DU PIN
Far from Home in Early Modern France: Three Women's Stories
Edited and with an introduction by Colette H. Winn
Translated by Lauren King, Elizabeth Hagstrom, and Colette H. Winn
Volume 92, 2022

MARIE-CATHERINE LE JUMEL DE BARNEVILLE, BARONNE D'AULNOY
Travels into Spain
Edited and translated by Gabrielle M. Verdier
Volume 93, 2022

Pierre de Vaux and Sister Perrine de Baume
Two Lives of Saint Colette. *With a Selection of Letters by, to, and about Colette*
Edited and translated by Renate Blumenfeld-Kosinski
Volume 94, 2022

Dorothy Calthorpe
News from the Midell Regions *and* Calthorpe's Chapel
Edited by Julie A. Eckerle
Volume 95, 2022

Elizabeth Poole
The Prophetess and the Patriarch: The Visions of an Anti-Regicide in Seventeenth-Century England
Edited by Katharine Gillespie
Volume 96, 2024

Mary Carleton and Others
The Carleton Bigamy Trial
Edited by Megan Matchinske
Volume 97, 2023

Marie Baudoin
The Art of Childbirth: A Seventeenth-Century Midwife's Epistolary Treatise to Doctor Vallant A Bilingual Edition
Edited and translated by Cathy McClive
Volume 98, 2022

Marguerite Buffet
New Observations on the French Language, *with* Praises of Illustrious Learned Women
Edited and translated by Lynn S. Meskill
Volume 99, 2023

Isabella Andreini
Letters
Edited and translated by Paola De Santo and Caterina Mongiat Farina
Volume 100, 2023

Mary Carey
A Mother's Spiritual Dialogue, Meditations, and Elegies
Edited by Pamela S. Hammons
Volume 101, 2023

Isabella Whitney
Poems by a Sixteenth-Century Gentlewoman, Maid, and Servant
Edited by Shannon Miller
Volume 102, 2024

Camilla Battista da Varano
The Spiritual Life *and Other Writings*
Edited and translated by William V. Hudon
Volume 103, 2023

E. Polwhele
The Faithful Virgins
Edited by Ann Hollinshead Hurley
Volume 104, 2023